The Other Side of Wonderful

Caroline Grace-Cassidy

Published 2013
by Poolbeg Press Ltd
123 Grange Hill, Baldoyle
Dublin 13, Ireland
E-mail: poolbeg@poolbeg.com
www.poolbeg.com

1

A catalogue record for this book is available from the British Library.

ISBN 978-1-84223-544-7

Printed and bound by CPI Group (UK) Ltd, Croydon, CR0 4YY

www.poolbeg.com

About the Author

Caroline Grace-Cassidy was born in Dublin. She lives in Knocklyon with her husband Kevin and two daughters Grace and Maggie.

Caroline works extensively as a writer, television and film actress and as a regular panellist for *Midday* on TV3.

First and foremost she is a very proud mammy.

Her debut novel, *When Love Takes Over*, was also published by Poolbeg.

Also by Caroline Grace-Cassidy

When Love Takes Over

Published by Poolbeg

Acknowledgements

Acknowledgements – such a long word and it mocks you *"Don't forget anyone now!"* as it sniggers behind its many vowels. So I'll start at the top and work my way down . . . no, that'll mean the people at the bottom will feel they are less important than the people at the top . . . okay, so I'll start with the people who see me every day with no make-up, still love me and more importantly still recognise me!

For my husband Kevin Cassidy whose support is completely and utterly unwavering. Without his hand on the small of my back pushing me back up the stairs to write, no book would ever be finished. Kevin, thank you for your understanding and patience and for how incredible you are with our girls. Thank you for 'keeping it all together' when I'm writing and most importantly thank you for always refilling my wineglass to the very top. On behalf of your three girls: we love you.

For Grace and Maggie Cassidy, my wonderful daughters, you both bring us so much joy every single day. Even when you both reach that screaming high-pitch octave that only little girls can reach! Mammy and Daddy are your greatest fans. Love, adore and worship you both.

I am indebted to my parents Robert and Noeleen Grace for all they have done and continue to do for us all. They are the most amazing, supportive, hip, loving, funny and loyal unit. Also Samantha my sister and Keith my brother, horse-rider and rock-and-roll-star siblings and truly fantastic friends! I love you all and am so lucky to have the four of you in my life. Thank you for being so supportive and for always being there for myself and Kevin and the girls. Rock solid fam'bly.

Paula Campbell, one of the Top 10 most influential women in

Ireland, don't you know! Super mammy and friend. Thank you. The feeling of seeing my book on a bookshelf for the very first time was magical.

To Sarah, Ailbhe, David and all at Poolbeg, thank you so much for all your hard work. You are always wonderful to deal with.

Gaye Shortland, I'm sure you have a third eye you whip out at night. Thanks again for a brilliant edit and your words of encouragement for my writing.

My heartfelt thanks to Tara, Amy and Honour for taking such fantastic care of Maggie, and to Miss Dore and The Learning Curve for teaching and taking care of Grace.

For Louise Murphy Bates, who in fairness paid for my pints of Budweiser for many years and sometimes still does. Bul & Bud always pal.

For Elaine Crowley, I love working on *Midday* with you and all the girls . . . thanks for making me laugh every single time I'm with you.

Thanks to all my girlfriends without whom . . . I'd be sober way more often! Marina Rafter, Amy Conroy, Susan Loughnane, Alison Canavan, Jenny Barrett, Tara Durkin O'Brien, Lisa Carey, Maia Dunphy, Lucy Kennedy, Amy Joyce Hastings, Samantha Doyle, Nicola Pawley, Ciara O'Connor, Nicola Charles, Aveen Fitzgerald, Claire Guest, Maeve Callan, Caroline Cassidy, Angela Cassidy, Sorcha Furlong, Sarah Flood, Jenn McGuirk, Elaine Hearty.

And to all the wonderful Irish authors – especially Ciara Geraghty for motivating me to write in the first place with your ridiculous talent.

Special thanks to three incredibly inspiring Irish women: Victoria Smurfit, Miriam O'Callaghan and Caroline Downey.

Margaret Kilroy – not a day passes that I don't think about you.

This was, at times, a difficult book to write and a very emotional journey. Huge thanks to all who helped me with the research and facts for the book. Rathfarnham Garda Station, Women's Aid, The Sims Clinic, National Flight Centre, and especially to Tara who told me her story and talked to me so openly and honestly at length.

My most heartfelt thanks of all are to you wonderful readers. I hope you enjoy *The Other Side of Wonderful*. Thank you so much to all of you who bought *When Love Takes Over* and for sending me your emails and comments. Without readers I can't write stories and I love writing stories! It's always amazing to hear from you all so please do continue to email, tweet, and facebook me through my website, www.carolinegracecassidy.com.

Love, Caroline. x

For my parents, Robert & Noeleen Grace

Thank you both for everything . . .

Chapter 1

Cara Byrne eased her foot lightly off the accelerator and the car pulled up slowly outside the hotel as morning was slowly stretching itself awake. It was an ungodly hour to begin her day but she'd better get used to it. This dark morning was the start of her brand-new life and her new career, as the hospitality manager at the Moritz Hotel, in the quaint old village of Knocknoly. She stared out the frosted car window before rubbing the condensation clear with the palm of her cold thin bluish hand. Her eyes devoured the building. The architecture of the hotel was uniquely beautiful, reminding her of a fairytale castle she had loved in her favourite torn storybook as a little girl. It was a perfect building, one of a kind, stonewashed white all over, with bay windows on the lower level and magnificent oriel windows on the upper levels. It looked to her like a perfect parcel, with the enormous wooden mahogany door a brown sticker to seal it together. A little spot of Irish paradise. The hotel sat in the middle of acres and acres of unspoiled green fields and was a truly breathtaking sight as the early morning stirred. The sky was bleeding shades of greys and blues, waiting for the sun to combine the two colours together.

She flicked off the engine and the lights on her trusty silver Ford Fiesta. She really had to get the heater fixed. She really had to do a lot of things. All in good time, she answered herself in her head. That was another thing she had to stop doing – talking to herself – because most of the time she did it out 'crazy lady' loud. The November morning was bitterly cold but crisp. The type of hour and air that made you really feel alive. It hit you full-on, like opening one of those huge freezers in the supermarket except you couldn't slam it shut again.

She looked at the hotel again. There were people silhouetted in some of the windows already. Upstairs and downstairs. Setting up for breakfast and for the hotel's day ahead.

As she watched them Cara took a deep breath. This was *the* job she had always wanted. She had gone back to college and studied hotel management at the Dublin Institute of Technology while continuing to waitress at The Law Top at nights and weekends. This job had really always been her ambition but life had side-tracked her before she'd had time to blink. Sometimes it took life to kick your arse bloody hard to make you realise what you really wanted from it.

Cara slid on the light-switch above the rear-view mirror and checked her face. She smiled widely at her reflection and then unsmiled as the crow's-feet jumped out at her. She rubbed at them gently then flicked the light off. Bloody face cream advertising all lied. There should be a law against it.

Starting over at thirty-five would certainly be a challenge.

She had tied her long, wild loose red curls up in a bun and added jet-black mascara to her green eyes and a dab of BB tinted moisturiser. BB tinted moisturisers were all in and, while she hadn't a clue what they did, she bought into the hype anyway. Cara bought into the hype of everything unfortunately – she was that kind of girl. If someone said something worked then she believed them. "It really works – honestly, I can't live without it," the counter assistants with their perfect skin would tell her every time and every time she fell for it. Nothing was ever what it seemed though. She laughed inwardly at that thought. How bloody true! She had always been too innocent. A sucker. That was the problem: she hadn't been able to see through the bullshit and the fancy packaging.

Cara's skin was dotted with light-brown freckles and she

loved them. There was no point in piling on the make-up today or she would have to do the same for the next however many years she worked here. 'Start as you mean to go on,' was her new motto. Cara just wanted to be herself again.

She smoothed down her crisp white shirt as she sat in the driver's seat and was confident that the charcoal-black Stella McCartney suit she had spent a small fortune on would take her through the next few years – all she'd need were some different-coloured shirts and vest tops in summer. "Dry clean on your day off," Zoe Doyle, her course tutor, had said as she'd strongly advised her on the costly purchase. She took Zoe's advice. She had learned that skill only too harshly. She had finally learned to listen to people who knew what they were talking about.

Her mother Esther had bought her a sleek brown-leather Wilsons dual-pocket briefcase that would carry her laptop when she actually bought one of her own. She'd always wanted a sleek briefcase. Esther must have saved hard to afford this, or had a secret windfall at the bingo. In her old job as a waitress at The Law Top Cara used to watch the career women – the solicitors, the barristers and the judges – come and go with their all-important briefcases. She had felt so stylish but professional last night as she had posed in front of the mirror with hers. She was ready. She knew she was more like Melanie Griffiths than Sigourney Weaver in *Working Girl*, but she was working her way up. She was proud of herself. The briefcase somehow made it official. Cara Byrne was a businesswoman. She wouldn't look back. She couldn't look back.

She had better get in there and meet the manager. She hadn't met Mr Jonathan Redmond yet as she hadn't been interviewed here but at the sister hotel, the Zatlend in Cork, where the heads of the conglomerate and managers Amy and Graham Haswell had met with her.

Five more minutes, she decided, and slid the light on again. She picked up her notes. It was Steve, her dear friend and barman at The Law Top, who had seen the job advertised and passed the ad on to her. "Saw this and thought of you," he'd said as he slid the paper cutting across the bar to her, wiping as he went. He had circled the advert in bright red pen. She never in her wildest dreams thought she'd get the job. In fact, the night before the interview she had decided she wouldn't go. It was her mother who had talked her round over a large Toblerone and a pot of hot Barry's tea.

She licked her thin index finger and thumb and flicked through her notes for the thousandth time. The Moritz Hotel had been built in the eighteenth century and was a residence and stately home to the Harte clan. It had been passed down through the generations until the youngest of the sons, Emerson Harte, had sold his birthright to a moneylender in order to pay off gambling debts. How tragic, Cara thought once again as she flipped over the page. It had been falling into ruins until a famous Polish film director spotted it in the early seventies and used it as a location for his film *Thin Ice*. The filmmaker fell in love with the place and bought it. When he passed away it was sold to the American conglomerate that restored the old place to its original splendour.

The Moritz was now considered one of the more exclusive hotels in Ireland without being too posh or too stuffy. It was comfortable, it embraced you. It was immaculate, with great friendly staff, and an award-winning chef from Marseille, Delphine Coudray. It oozed a beautiful relaxed atmosphere. It was everything a hotel should be. Cara had visited for lunch before going to Cork for her interview and felt relaxed and pampered as soon as she entered the building. It wasn't huge by any means. It now had twenty-two bedrooms, four of them luxury suites, with a stunning bridal suite, and in the last few years they'd had the Haven Spa built onto the side, along with a small fitness centre and swimming pool. Down a long winding cobbled pathway opposite a wonderful courtyard there was the Breena Stable Yard, where guests could avail of complimentary horse-riding around the magnificent five-acre grounds and even down into the local village of Knocknoly. Cara had ridden only once as a child, on a donkey in Blackpool on the North Pier. The donkey had been called Buckles, she remembered now. She was looking forward to taking horse-riding up properly when she was a bit more settled into the job. She loved the idea of the freedom she associated with it. Ahh, freedom!

Cara rolled down the car window and let the freezing morning air fill her lungs. Someday she'd have a car that boasted electric windows and heated seats. She laughed as she pictured Esther's face as her bum got hotter and hotter.

The scent of freshly ground coffee mixed with the cold fresh air was wonderful. She would eat something soon – she knew she still had to put on over a stone. "Build yourself up, love, won't you?" her mother had told her as she left for Knocknoly. Esther had stood in the glass porch of Cara's Auntie Ann's house, and waved her goodbye and good luck.

Cara's life had been very tough over the last year and a half but that was all behind her now. She was a free woman, retrained, with an exciting new start. "Close that closet!" She whispered the mantra to herself, clicked the fingers on her left hand and smiled.

She had rented a beautiful small stone cottage in the village, just over the bridge from the Moritz. Mr Peters, the elderly owner, had more or less told her she could redecorate any way she pleased and she fully intended to do so. To be honest it must have been a few years since the cottage had seen any TLC. 'Musty' was the word that sprang to mind. But it was her very first place of her own and she planned to make it all hers. In fact, if this job turned out the way she was hoping it would, she might just try and buy the place one day.

She turned off the overhead light, rolled up the window, got out of the car and locked it. She zipped down and removed her grey hoody and opened the boot to remove her suit jacket and briefcase. She inhaled deeply before exhaling very slowly and watched her warm breath escape on the cold air.

"Welcome to your bright new future, Miss Cara Byrne," she whispered to herself as she began to walk and the stony gravel crunched noisily under her feet.

Chapter 2

Sandra Darragh pinned her shiny gold name-badge onto her black blazer and, squeezing her eyes shut tight, she lashed the L'Oréal Elnet hairspray onto her tidy bun. Her poker-straight shoulder-length black hair had still been damp from the swim as she rolled it into the knot but she was rushed for time. She took her short yellow comb from her bag and brushed down her straight thick blunt fringe. It was almost as far as her eyes — she needed a trim. She loved the early-morning swims in the Haven Spa's pool before it was opened to the guests. Jonathan Redmond had told her she was welcome to use it anytime she liked. The swim was also doing wonders for her figure she'd noticed as she dried off this morning. It was toning her up in all the right places. It woke her up and got her ready for the day's duties on the busy reception desk.

As the head receptionist and first point of contact with the guests, she tried to set a good example. Her uniform was kept pristine and she was always immaculately presented in a black blazer, a crisp white shirt, a yellow-and-red tie, a tight knee-length black skirt, barely black tights and black kitten-heeled shoes. She liked how she looked in the uniform. She wore quite a lot of make-up to work but liked to look as though she'd made an effort. She was a bit old-school, she supposed, and four years on Aer Lingus as a number-one stewardess before she married

Neil Darragh had whipped grooming into her. She checked her blood-red nail polish.

She looked together. As if her life was in any way together! She half smirked at her reflection and her wonderfully pretty face lit up as her gleaming white teeth sparkled. Her skin was so brown people always remarked on the whiteness of her teeth. She had never had them bleached – it was just that the white stood out against her naturally dark skin colour. Her big brown eyes were always lined in soft brown kohl pencil, making them seem even darker and wider. Her life was so busy right now with all the extra hours she had taken on. Dealing with the guests, functions, the administration for the front desk and overseeing all reservations was hard enough, but now she had the added pressure of a failing marriage to worry about too.

Well, she had always had to worry about Neil Darragh, she supposed. Worry was all she had seemed to do for the two and a half years since their wedding and she was well and truly fed up with worry. That's why she treasured the swim so much. It gave her some headspace under the clear cool blue water, the early-morning chlorine unblocking her head. She could forget every worry for those precious minutes and enjoy the nothingness of the moment. As her arms powered through the water she threw each worry away.

The Irish recession had hit them extremely badly. In fact it had punched them so hard in the face it was proving impossible to get back up. Neil had been out of work for over ten months now and it was a hard slog. He was slipping back to his old ways and she knew the warning signs only too well: the monosyllabic answers when his head was somewhere else; leaving the room when she came in; constantly checking his appearance in the hall mirror; the new hair products; washing and ironing his own clothes; the brand-new aftershave hidden behind logbooks and documents in the glove compartment of his van; all sorts of appointments and meeting with suppliers and builders in Dublin; the faraway look in his eyes. The unease of a man with a secret. "I'm thinking of taking up squash" or "Sorry, love, but this is dragging on – I think I'll have to stay over." *Ding! Ding!*

Ding! He'd done it once before. The affair, that is. With Kelley, a girl from the US who was an au pair in Knocknoly last summer – a twenty-something LA blonde who, to be quite honest, had done nothing wrong. He had told her they'd been separated for six months. Sandra felt like she was privy to every moment of the affair as she had eventually read almost every text message between them.

* * *

Everyone had warned Sandra about Neil Darragh. He was a player. When she used to return home for her weekends off work he would flirt madly with her – she, however, never took him too seriously. She knew him to see as he was a local too but they had never mixed in the same circles growing up. Neil was the owner at the time of a small business during the building boom – Darragh Electrics. He employed three local Knocknoly lads and was making quite a lot of money back then. He would praise her to the hilt every time he saw her. Throwing compliments at her like confetti. Everyone knew that Neil Darragh fancied the pants off Sandra Loughnane. He would look at her all night, catching her eye at every opportunity but as soon as new blood entered Hines, their local bar, his attention was gone. She used to laugh and even slag him. "Women are nuts if they believe any of your crap, Neil Darragh! I wouldn't touch you with a bargepole! God help the woman who falls for your pathetic one-liners." She always secretly thought he was attractive though and, although she tried hard not to be, she was flattered by his attention – what woman wouldn't? She liked his devil-may-care attitude and lust for life. "If you'd have me, Sandra Loughnane, I would wear blinkers. I'd never leave the house again – or, as Twink says, I'd zip up my mickey!" She had laughed and flicked her hair and walked away from him, knowing full well he was checking out her ass. He said it was her I-don't-care-what-you-say-you'll-never-get-me attitude and the fact she never gave in to his advances that made him fall head over heels in love with her. Made him never give up. She was a challenge, he'd told her. She had started to really fancy him madly too. It very slowly crept up on her without her realising. She looked forward to the weekends she had off and got butterflies in her tummy as she pushed open the door of Hines to see him on his regular high-backed stool up at the bar, his soft black leather jacket hanging off the back of it. He always winked madly at her and it made her laugh it was so naff. She had loved his wild curly light-brown hair and the fact he was tall and strong. Neil had muscle in all the right places from good old-fashioned hard work rather than gym-bought muscles – and he was her type. She had been enjoying working at Aer Lingus and had loved the fact she was seeing the world, but there was something nagging in her head. The age issue was hanging over her. The dreaded age issue. So, slowly but surely she had given in to Neil's charms, but on what she hoped were her terms.

Neil, rather sheepishly for a change, had stopped her one evening on the Knocknoly Bridge. She was heading to the Moritz for a drink with Louise, an older friend of hers who was the owner of Louise's Loft, a tidy two-storey coffee shop in the village. He had quite awkwardly yet very politely asked her to be his guest at his brother Tom's wedding in Clontarf in Dublin and she had agreed. She had gone up to Dublin the next day and bought a beautiful fitted full-length off-the-shoulder red satin dress in Coast. When the day came she pulled out all the stops. She had her make-up done by Tara at the Haven's beauty salon and had her long black hair GHD-curled, sweeping her fringe to the side. Sipping a glass of champers she had slipped into the red dress and black stilettos.

He had gawped as he picked her up in his dad's car and had treated her like a princess all day long. The wedding itself wasn't really her cup of tea. It was overly fancy and a little too posh for her liking. 'Stuffy' was the word she would use to describe it. But they'd had the most amazing time together and at the very end of the night, as the DJ played Elvis Costello's version of "She", Sandra had goose-bumps all over and reached up on her tippy toes and kissed him for the first time. She hadn't really been expecting to do that and it was electric. She could hear him groan through their open mouths. He grabbed her close and she ran her hands through his curly hair. That was that. She went home with him the next night and never left: they were officially a couple.

He'd said he was happier than Tom Cruise that time he leapt up and down on Oprah's settee and that John Wayne would be spitting hay. She didn't understand the John Wayne reference but let it go – she'd never really liked Western movies so the joke was lost on her.

"About time you got serious with someone!" her married friends at Aer Lingus had said when she filled them in. She had been fielding the questions of her advancing age and her reproductive timing for a while now. She had turned thirty and had suddenly felt the hands on the clock were moving way faster than they had in her twenties. The music from *Countdown*, as the hand on the clock raced to 'time up' for the contestants, frequently played in her head. It was hard not to watch the clock with everyone reminding her all the time. If she heard the words "You'd want to get a move on!" from one more person she would scream. She was moving as bloody fast as she possibly could. "Well, if you only want one or two you might be okay but not if you want a proper family. Sure you have no idea if you'll get pregnant straight away, that's the problem," was the usual age-related reproductive discussion in the galley when she used to say she was in no rush to tie the knot. Everyone was obsessed with age.

She honestly was just content and happy at that time to be with Neil and move into a new area of her life. They both wanted children – she had asked him that at Tom's wedding. "Sure I do," he had answered open-mouthed as his lips came down heavy on hers again while they danced. Well, she was happy to be on the right track, where she was supposed to be at that stage and, although she didn't verbalise it, really it was all a bit of a relief. She had wanted to find her true love. Apart from Neil being a great guy, she admitted rather coyly to herself that he had also ticked her three boxes: she wanted a marriage; she wanted children; she wanted to buy a house and raise her family in her beloved Knocknoly. It wasn't as if a woman could find this in her twenties any more anyway – find a guy who was willing to settle down in his twenties and she'd show you that face cream really stopped wrinkles. It just didn't exist. Men were not ready to settle down until their late thirties as far as she could see. It was all right for them: they could reproduce into their seventies. She had been out with lots of guys but none of the short-lived romances had ever seemed like they could last forever. She was looking for something special but somehow deep down she'd known she wanted to marry a local lad.

Although she'd ditched her pill and moved into Neil's place straight after the wedding she hadn't slept with him for six weeks. They were intimate in other ways but he was half crazy with desire to make love to her and that was her plan. She loved that she was making him wait as it was something Neil Darragh wasn't used to and she hoped she could tame him. Nevertheless, no one had been more surprised than Sandra when, just six short months after they first slept together, he dropped to one knee the night of her thirty-first birthday and proposed, albeit fairly drunkenly. In fact there was an audible gasp around the entire pub. Dermot Murray had dropped his pint glass and it shattered all over the floor. In fairness to Neil he had bought the ring and everything so he was prepared. She had been over the moon and the sense of relief that washed over her was completely unexpected.

Neil really didn't want a big do so they married quietly in a registry office in Dublin on Grand Canal Street seven months later and had a big party back in Hines. It suited Sandra perfectly. It had been a lovely day if a little underwhelming but now she was Mrs Darragh and she could concentrate her energies on building her family in Knocknoly. They had been casually trying for a baby before the wedding and now she felt it was time to get serious about it. She hadn't quite decided what to do about her job just yet.

Neil had settled into married life really well and maybe, just maybe, if the baby had come along as planned they might still be okay? But it hadn't and they had been through so much in such a short space of time. In fact, Sandra couldn't remember the girl she was back then – she'd lost her. That fun-loving, life-loving, flirty, carefree side of her had been deeply buried and Sandra didn't think she could ever dig her back up.

They began the 'serious' trying for a baby straight after the wedding. When nothing happened she still wasn't overly concerned and put it down to her job. Lots of girls had erratic periods because of the flying and she assumed it was to do with this. As the first year of marriage passed in the blink of an eye and her periods were still very irregular she decided to leave the job. It was so hard to use the ovulation sticks when her dates were all over the place. It was reducing the probability of becoming pregnant if she couldn't monitor when she was ovulating.

"That's a bit drastic, isn't it?" Neil had said as he picked her up one evening at Arrivals at Terminal 2 of Dublin Airport and she told him she was handing in her notice.

She had just done two trips over and back to Rome and she was wiped out. She was becoming too old for the job, she realised. Her back ached, her ankles were swollen like balloons and her skin was dehydrated.

"We want a family, don't we? I'm not getting any younger, Neil!" she crossly answered him as she slammed shut the door of his red works van. "We don't have a lot of time."

"Well, yeah, I suppose we do want a family but it's not the be-all and end-all, is it?" He indicated and airport security signalled him out. Neil raised his hand in thanks.

She had glared at him. "What does that mean exactly?"

He was staring straight ahead out the van window as the rain began to fall. He flicked on the wipers as he leaned in closer to the windscreen. "I'm just saying, Sandra, there's more to life than having kids, that's all." He shifted gears and shrugged his shoulders as he turned up the volume on his favourite radio station, Sunshine 106.8, and whistled along, his fingers drumming gently on the steering wheel.

She sat back and closed her eyes, her blue resignation form folded neatly in her bag on her lap. There wasn't more to life, as far as she was concerned. Time was against her. She wanted children. That was the plan. That's the way life was supposed to go.

* * *

The phone rang at reception and Sandra jumped but the answer machine kicked in and she heard her own voice say: "*Thank you for calling the Moritz Hotel. We are sorry there is no one available to take your call at the moment. Please leave a message with your name and contact number and a member of staff will return your call as soon as possible.*" She hated the sound of her own voice. Did she really sound like that?

She'd attend to the messages as soon as she'd checked all the emails.

"Fuck you, Neil!" she mouthed now as she shook her head fiercely. Her fringe bounced and then fell immediately back into place. She knew he was up to something – she could feel it in her bones. Instinct. She didn't know what to do. Her parents were of no help and she had no brothers or sisters to confide in. There wasn't anyone she could call a real friend in Knocknoly any more, except Louise. All her old friends had left the village. Moved on. But Louise was older and more like a mother figure. Sandra loved Louise dearly and had confided in her lots in the past but she didn't want to drain their friendship. Louise had heard it all before. To be honest she didn't want any pity again. Sandra had had it up to her neck in pity. Pity could go shitty.

She had started to hunt for Neil's mobile phone again when he was asleep and she hated herself for it. But she could never find it and when he was awake he never ever left it out of his hand, or if he did it was always powered off. It was also password-protected now – it hadn't been before. It had been how she had found out about Kelley. That dread text message on that dread mobile phone. She had grabbed it off the glass table in Neil's bungalow to check the time and as she did a text message beeped in. She clicked on it and opened it. It was the last thing she'd expected to see. In fact, she sometimes *almost* smiled at the irony of it all: she had been so sure he was planning a surprise birthday party for her and she wanted to suss it out. Boy, was she wrong!

It read: **I have heard from someone I trust in the village that you are not separated. I feel physically sick. I won't see you again. K**

Sandra scrolled up to the previous messages, her heart fluttering.

Meet me at back of stables – usual place usual time. Why aren't you answering my calls? N

Up again.

Last night was incredible. Hope the horses don't tell Dermot! I'm really falling for that Irish charm . . . and torso ;) LOL. Kxxx

And: **Wow! I still can't walk properly. Can't wait to see you again, you sexy little yank. I have it so bad for you. N**

There were dozens of them, thanks to the new iPhone all saved and sitting there for Sandra to read like a bad Jilly Cooper copy. Why she had been so surprised was anyone's guess, but she had been. She had thrown up on the floor. Shocked to her very core. She couldn't believe he could do this to her, to them. They had just been through so much together with the IVF. He had begun the affair the night they found out there was no pregnancy. How had she not copped? 'The wives are always the last to know' was a famous saying but she'd always thought those wives must be thick as planks.

He had been a workaholic, no doubt about it, so he was rarely at home. He used to leave the house at six o'clock in the morning and return at eight o'clock at night and then back out for a few pints in Hines after his dinner. Sandra knew he was always on the flirt but was sure that was as far as it went and she really saw no harm in it. It wasn't until she would join him later for a drink on occasions and other women in the bar would say to her "How do you put up with him?" or "If he was my husband I'd give him what for!", as they laughed and blushed with delight at his obvious flirting with them, that it had begun to bother her. It had built up in her as the instances went by, bothering her more and more. She had told Neil on the walk home from the pub one evening how she felt but he just laughed and assured her it was only a bit of gas and she was the only woman for him. He had pulled her in close and she had snuggled into the shoulder of his black leather jacket on Knocknoly Bridge. Secure. She honestly trusted him. That walk home seemed to her a lifetime ago now too.

They really were struggling to pay the outrageous mortgage on their Knocknoly new build right now. They had bought it at a stupid time and for a stupid price and she blamed herself completely. She had been sucked in by Cherry Hill with its modern detached four-bedroomed redbricks that professionals from Dublin were buying to commute to busy Dublin-based jobs. Knocknoly was a small village but with the M50 nearby now the commute to Dublin took only just over an hour. Anyway, she had really wanted Neil to buy it and they had, despite indications of a recession looming. It was now a ghost estate. It was so unlike her – she just wasn't one of those types of women who wanted fancy bricks and mortar but suddenly the house had become a must-have. She knew why really. After her first unsuccessful round of IVF and Neil's affair with Kelley she wanted change. Distance. To start over again. She forgave the affair because he had filled her with such lies, saying that he had been traumatised over the fact they couldn't have kids and that the IVF had been so hard on his masculinity. He said he needed to prove to himself that he was still a man. And he had cried and cried. He swore it meant nothing and it would never, ever happen again. He was on his knees begging her. He loved her. He said it had happened straight after they got the negative result from the doctor over the phone. They had gone to the pub on his request and there she was. Sandra had seen her there too. Kelley. She remembered her only too well. She was all big hair and smiles and happiness. Wildly fertile no doubt. Not a care in the world. He told Sandra he'd just wanted to be happy and had started to talk to Kelley to forget his troubles. He said he didn't know why he told her he was separated but he had. They had begun a short but fierce love affair.

At the time Sandra was reading *The Secret*. She was forced to make a choice. Did she want to believe that she was in the wrong place in her life? That she had no control over her circumstances, both with Neil's affair and the fact she couldn't get pregnant? Did she want to end the marriage and start all over again? Or did she want to believe in the Law of Attraction? The Law of Attraction said that like attracts like, so when you think a thought you are attracting like thoughts to you. Sandra wanted to have her marriage and her baby so she chose to believe in the Law of Attraction. She had to trust the Universe that she was in the right place. She also didn't want to let any more hurt into her life so she chose to forgive and more importantly to try and forget and move on. Her vows had meant something to her even in that small registry office. Grudges were a waste of time and only brought ill health. Sandra believed in giving second chances. So she was telling the Universe that she needed a bigger house to hold all her babies. That's what Cherry Hill had been about. It gave her hope that if she decorated a nursery in this house surely they would be blessed with a baby to fill it?

If the baby came along, Neil would be happy. The baby.

Sandra hung her polka-dot swimsuit on the small low radiator, trying to recapture the calm she had felt during her swim. But the door of her mind was open wide and negative thoughts kept pouring through one by one.

They had spent over ten thousand euro they didn't have on IVF and that was with the Drugs Payment Card. It had only succeeded in driving them further apart. She squeezed her eyes tight. Apart from the IVF costs, right now the house was worth a fraction of what they had paid for it, so financially they were ruined. They had sold Neil's beautiful character-filled self-built bungalow and moved. The estate had twenty houses in all and only eleven had ever sold before the blast of the downturn hit them. The estate was now forbidding and unfinished and Sandra absolutely hated it. She had pictured the house complete with that nursery and swings in the garden and not like it stood today. It felt just like her. Barren. But with the belief that nothing more could come into her experiences unless she summoned it through persistent thoughts, she forgave Neil. With full intentions of giving her marriage a second chance they had moved in just as she was about to start the second round of IVF. A whole new beginning. The longing for this baby had quickly turned into a physical pain. Trips into Dublin to meet old friends for lunch were no more as there were just too many prams and mothers. She openly stared at pregnant women in the street and she seemed to see them everywhere. The most annoying part for her wasn't so much seeing all these babies but the faces on some of the mothers. Unhappy faces. She knew darn well that having kids was tough and that everyone's circumstances as a parent were different, but she just knew she'd be the happiest mother alive if God sent her this child. It wasn't fair. How come everyone else seemed to get pregnant at the drop of a hat? Funnily enough, when she first began trying to fall pregnant she'd had a life too. Having a baby hadn't occupied her every waking thought. She just presumed it would happen. When nothing did after a year it slowly became the way it was now. It crept up on her. It became her life. She'd never expected to feel like this. She had started to shun the women in Knocknoly whom she knew were pregnant or who already had kids. A lot of them met in Louise's Loft on a Friday morning for coffee and cake and she always drove to work on those mornings so she didn't have to walk past the shop. It wasn't that she wasn't happy for others – it was just all too painful. She felt left out. She felt lonely and – she hated herself for this – jealous. So bloody jealous. It was even more strange to her because growing up she had never really been all that maternal – in fact the cabin crew used to draw straws to decide who would be unlucky enough to have to work sections of the aircraft carrying the most children – but as she grew older she had really looked forward to starting a family. Neil had said, amongst other nasty things, that she had become scarily obsessed and he was probably right. She had been obsessed. Completely obsessed. Demented. She had asked Jonathan to give her more hours at the hotel in the first instance so she could save money on the side for the second IVF and he had been fantastic to her. But suddenly her 'IVF job' that she had enjoyed immensely had become a highly pressurised full-time breadwinning role when Neil's work ran dry.

She took out her Strawberry Red Revlon lipstick and applied it expertly without the need of a mirror. She heard the big mahogany door of the hotel open with that familiar double creak and quickly snapped the lid back on her lipstick and made her way from the back office to the reception desk.

"Good morning, how can I help you?" she asked the stunning redhead who stood in front of her, as she slipped in behind her shining wooden reception desk.

"Oh, good morning! I'm Cara Byrne, your new hospitality manager. I'm here to meet with Mr Jonathan Redmond."

She was so quietly spoken that Sandra had to lean in to hear her.

Cara extended her thin hand and Sandra shook it warmly.

The newcomer's eyes darted in her head and she seemed very anxious, nervous even, but it was her skin that Sandra couldn't take her eyes off. It was translucent through a scattering of freckles.

"Oh yes, of course, welcome! I'm Sandra Darragh, head receptionist, great to have you here. Let me just buzz up to Jonathan for you. Why don't you take a seat?" Sandra lifted the receiver from the phone and held it over her shoulder. "Can I ask Tiff to bring you a coffee or a tea first?"

Cara laughed and shook her head. "No thanks, I'm good. I've had about three cups of coffee already." She took a seat on the long red-and-gold low-slung couch that was opposite reception. The morning's newspapers were already laid out on a tall glass table beside her and a vase filled with fresh wild purple flowers was giving out the most gorgeous scent around the small reception area. She picked up a newspaper and flicked through it, not really reading the usual doom and gloom. Sandra had a great front-of-house manner and an aura about her that made you feel like you'd really love to befriend her and get to know everything about her, Cara thought. She was on the phone to Jonathan now, relaying other information first, and judging by her easy tone with her boss the two obviously had a really comfortable working relationship. Cara glanced up at the massive glistening chandelier that hung above the reception. It was magnificent. The hotel was lovely and warm without being overpowering. She looked across through the glass double-doors off the reception area to the intimate dining room that was now set for breakfast. Starched white linen tablecloths and silver cutlery sparkled back at her. A long table set out with juices of every colour in large jugs suddenly made her mouth feel dry. The large open windows looked out onto the breaking morning and Cara's eyes were drawn to the open fields, mountains and sea in the far distance that peeped back in at her. A white horse walked by, led by a tall man in a green husky jacket and a well-worn tweed cap. Next door was the bar area and it was in dark mahogany wood with black leather couches and high-backed stools. An open fire was being cleaned out and fresh turf lay beside it waiting to be lit.

The lift pinged and the gold doors opened slowly into reception. An elderly couple got out and smiled at Sandra.

"Morning, Ronan and Phyllis!" Sandra waved at them and smiled broadly. "Ronan, your racing paper is here as requested. Phyl, do you want me to book Tara in the Haven for that foot massage this morning? I really think it would help you."

The older couple fussed around the desk as Sandra expertly took care of them and Cara lost herself in the lives of others.

* * *

Jonathan Redmond hung up the phone, stood up and stretched his arms over his head. At six foot three inches he often got cramped sitting at his desk. He went to his filing cabinet and pulled out the file on Cara Byrne. He was sure she was the perfect person for this job. Over the last few years the Moritz had become a very popular venue for small intimate weddings and private functions and they needed someone on this full time. He glanced over her CV and read through her experience again. Although she had no hotel experience, her on-the-ground experience meant more to them. She knew how to deal with people. Her years as a waitress combined with her recent college training made her ideal in his eyes. There was no point in having the education if you couldn't deal with people and this industry was all about people. Pleasing people. Understanding people. Taking good care of people. There was no point in working in the trade if you weren't a people person. Jonathan opened his desk drawer and pulled out his electric razor. Snapping the button to on, he quickly shaved. Then he left the office.

Shutting the door securely behind him, he headed down towards the reception. As he walked he ran his expert index finger over the gold picture frames that adorned the walls of the hotel corridor, to check for dust. He was strict as a manager but also fair and kept a small but professional and tight team around him. Having grown up in Knocknoly himself he knew most of the older staff well. In fact his very first job had been as a dish-washer in this very hotel. Over the last few years in Ireland hotel staff had been mainly Eastern European but most had since left to return home and grateful Irish workers were now employed once more. Jonathan had returned only a year and a half ago after years in London. He had managed a top hotel, The Kingston in Knightsbridge, for ten years but was now happy to be back. He had closed the door behind him as the London hotel went into receivership. His thirties had been spent there and he knew it was time to go home. New decade, old life. He had never married. He occasionally wished he had met Miss Right but he was very set in his ways and, with the hours he kept, he just couldn't seem to hold down a relationship. In London he had lived in at The Kingston so he was never really off duty. Hotel life was all he really knew.

Jonathan loved his job. The Moritz had always been a part of his life and was very close to his heart. He had moved into his parents' old home – they had long since passed and the house had been willed to him but he had rented it for years. His two brothers were in their late fifties and had moved to Australia and he heard from them infrequently. His mother had been forty-five when he was born. Not so very rare in this day and age but considered very unusual in those days. He was always the kid with the *old* parents. Sometimes he wished for her sake that he had married when she was alive, as she worried so about him but she was at peace now and he had his own life to lead. He had been on various dates but never, ever with members of staff: that was a hard and fast rule. Gail, a therapist in The Haven had asked him out on a date after months of them sort of flirting and, as tempted as he was, he'd had to turn her down. She left the following week, apparently saying she was mortified and couldn't work with him any more after that, which really upset him as she had been a fantastic girl. Tara, the salon manager, had been furious with him.

He just couldn't mix business with pleasure. It never worked. Dermot Murray, the stable manager, had no such rules. Jonathan laughed quietly. Dermot was a tonic and a breath of fresh air around the place. What you saw was what you got. Dermot lived his life the way he wanted to live it and Jonathan really admired him for that. The two had been friends since they were boys.

He pressed the lift button and the circular green light lit up around it, then he rubbed it with his jacket sleeve and stared at himself in the clean gold reflection of the lift doors. He was wearing a dark navy Tom Ford suit, dark navy shirt and a red-and-yellow tie. The red-and-yellow tie was worn by all employees and he liked to be seen as a regular member of staff. He wasn't asking Cara to wear the tie though as he wanted her to appear more casual. His shoes glistened with fresh polish. That was another of his rules: shoes polished every night. His dark brown eyes took in every inch of the mirrored lift for marks now as he stepped in. He had dark circles under his eyes, he noted – as he hadn't been sleeping too well lately.

The hotel was doing okay, all things considered. They were keeping their heads above water. The recent renovations had been really necessary, he knew, but they hadn't come cheap and they couldn't afford to let any finances slide. That was the reason he was employing Cara Byrne. They needed to keep the functions coming in and keep offering superb value for money. Recession or no recession, he was confident that people still needed a break and that couples still tied the knot. He was happy to deliver value for money and demanded the best service from his staff. It had always been his ambition to own the Moritz. Someday. He closed his eyes for a few seconds as the lift powered down and the doors opened onto reception.

"Cara?" He stood towering above her as she sat on the couch, apparently engrossed in the elderly couple chatting to Sandra. He extended his hand.

"Hi – yes!" She jumped up a little too quickly and shook his hand.

"It's great to meet you at last. Can we chat in the office?" He pointed to the small room behind Sandra's reception desk.

She followed him quickly, briefcase tucked tightly under her arm.

Chapter 3

The cottage was in darkness when Cara got home, just as she had left it that morning. Knocknoly was literally over the bridge from the hotel so she could easily walk to and from work. But she didn't feel that confident just yet. November seemed to be constantly dark and she couldn't wait for spring to get here. She closed the door quickly and latched the thick safety chains and double bolt she'd had fitted that morning while she was at work. She flicked on the lamp and the room was softly illuminated. The landline rang out shrill and loud and she jumped.

She grabbed for the receiver.

"Oh, where have you been, love?" Esther Byrne was talking way too loudly as usual. Cara held the phone away from her ear as she flopped on the wicker chair and kicked off her black heels. "I'm fine, Mother! Relax, will you?"

"Well, why aren't you answering your mobile thingy then?"

Her mother still worried about her at thirty-five years old. She supposed she had given her the very best of reasons to worry.

"I've had a really busy day, Mam, and you know I have to turn my phone on silent while I am in work – at least in the beginning – and I have literally walked through the door this second."

No response came from the other end and Cara heard the tiny sounds that told her Esther was peeling the blue-and-gold paper off an éclair and popping the sweet into her mouth. Her mother had always kept a bowl of éclairs on the phone table on a white doily. Esther was addicted to éclairs. "I don't have a problem!" she would insist. "It's under control." The bags and bags of éclairs under the kitchen sink would not agree. Empty éclair wrappers turned up in the most unexpected places.

"Did you bring éclairs to Auntie Ann's house, Mam? You are still in Ann's, right?" Cara clutched the phone tightly to her ear.

"I am, and, no, I didn't bring them to Ann's – she kindly bought me a few bags for while I am staying here. Jesus, I'm not an addict! I wouldn't bring them to someone else's house! So go on, will you, tell me everything! How was it then? What's everyone like?"

Esther's sucky tones were paused as Cara filled her in on every detail. Her mother had been so encouraging and the main reason Cara had gone back to college. Cara hated herself for what she had put Esther through but she was learning not to look back. It was all about moving forward.

"Hmmm, he sounds a bit sexy, ya' wha'?" Esther said at the description of Jonathan and Cara laughed.

"You know what, Mam, do not go there. He is my boss and, yeah, he isn't too hard on the eye but a man is the last thing on this earth I want. Go easy on the éclairs, will you? Seriously, you won't have a tooth left in your head!"

Cara turned her head and quickly scanned the front room, the windows and doors. She pinched the bridge of her nose.

"Sorry, love," her mam said, speaking lower. "Listen, I need to get ready for bingo and let Victoria out for her wee-wees. I still don't know this bus timetable so I haven't a clue where I am. I miss my own place and my own bus." Esther's voice was sad.

"I know, Mam, I know you do. I'll talk to you tomorrow. Win big, okay?"

"Are you okay there then? Did you sort all the security stuff out?"

"Yes – now go, you bingo fiend!" Cara laughed and hung up.

She flicked on the TV and let some evening soap show fill the house with noise. She padded into the kitchen and opened the fridge. She had bought a few essentials on her way down last night. Her appetite still wasn't back by any means but she was feeling like she could pick at something. She removed two eggs from the box and whisked them into a bowl as she heated oil in the pan. She grated some cheddar cheese into the eggs, added salt and pepper and even sliced in a few baby tomatoes. She poured the mixture into her hot pan and it hissed as a woman screamed out on the TV in the background. She froze. Suddenly she couldn't stomach the smell. She turned off the gas and emptied the mixture into the bin before pouring herself a large glass of white wine. She turned off the TV and headed into her bedroom.

* * *

"I'm home!" Sandra called out as she banged the large red hall door on the chilly dark night.

She made her way down the long hall towards the warmth of the kitchen. The kitchen was the only room in the house that kept any heat in it. She untangled her bright orange woolly scarf as she wondered if Neil was home at all. The van was in the driveway but he sometimes used his Vespa. If so, what sort of mood would he be in? Was she imagining the worst? Was she being unfair to him? Her eyes narrowed and she dropped the scarf onto the crook of her arm. The kitchen was dark and she flicked on the lights. The table lay bare and there was no sign or smell of her pre-made lasagne heating. It was also freezing in there so no one had been in the kitchen all day. She double-checked that she had remembered to leave the lasagne out this morning and sure enough she had. It sat lonely in its shiny coat of tinfoil on the chrome counter.

She blew her fringe high into the air. Where was Neil? Her heart began to race as she dug deep into her coat pocket and pulled out her mobile. She threw her scarf onto the tall silver stool and it slid to the floor. She clicked into favourites and clicked on 'Darling Hunny'. The line connected. It rang out. She hung up. She dialled again. It rang out and she hung up. She wouldn't ring again. She needed to step away from the mania that was about to take over her life again, the web of lies and deceit.

Her phone buzzed and she pounced on it.

"Yes?" It was Neil and it sounded like he was in a breeze.

"Where are you?" she asked.

"I'm on a beach in Lanzarote sippin' a fuckin' Piña Colada – what do you mean where am I? I'm on the bike. I had to pull over to answer you. I'm just pulling into the driveway." He hung up.

Minutes later he slammed the front door behind him, went straight up the stairs and then banged the bedroom door behind him. She stood still as her ears worked overtime. Then she could hear the awful surround sound from the HD television blasting through the walls upstairs. So loud. She tentatively made her way up, pulling her weary body by the long banister as she went.

There he lay in the dark room watching the opening credits of *Reservoir Dogs*. Again.

She blocked her ears and stood in front of the TV. "Will you lower that down, Neil?" she shouted at him. "What are you doing? Why didn't you put the dinner on? Where have you been?" She could feel the vibrations from the noise through the bedroom floor.

He pressed pause and she flicked on the light. He lifted his right hand and with his thumb bashing against his four closed fingers he mimicked her nagging: "*Blah, blah, blah, blah, blah, blah, blah, blah*! Give it a rest, would you, please?" His eyes were dark.

"What are you doing, Neil?" she asked again.

"What?" he responded. "Turn out the light, will you!" His voice was raised now.

She stared at him in disbelief. "Come down. We need to talk. It's only six o'clock in the evening."

"No, I'm watching this, Sandra. I want to relax. I want to be left alone." He un-paused the TV and the sound of John Travolta's husky voice filled the room.

She stood for a moment at a loss for words, then bashed the

light off and closed the bedroom door hard behind her. She hated confrontation. She would heat up the lasagne and throw a few microwave chips on, then call him to come down when it was ready. This was worrying the life out of her. She laid out cutlery for two and mixed him up a bowl of his favourite sauce – a mixture of mayo and tomato ketchup with a splash of balsamic vinegar. 'Maychupic' they called it. Then she sat down with a strong cup of coffee while she waited for the dinner to heat through. She no longer drank decaf. She wanted alcohol but it was only six o'clock. She opened the fridge and fished out a mint Kit Kat as she waited. She unwrapped it slowly, snapped it in half and dipped one cold finger into her hot coffee. She watched the chocolate melt and carefully timed her retrieval before it was melted too far.

What was going on? Her life had gone so quickly from being happy and carefree to this horrible existence. Did Neil want out? Should she ring his brother Tom in Dublin and see if he would talk to him? As much as she disliked Tom, he was married too and maybe he could help? Talk some sense into Neil? Her husband looked like he hated her, like she was an annoying insect he just couldn't swat away and suddenly she felt incredibly angry with him. She felt like shaking him and shouting, "What the hell is going on? Look what I have gone through for us already!" but what good would that do? He'd only deny everything and tell her she was paranoid and maybe she was. She'd been through so much physically and mentally with the IVF that her head wasn't in the best place and she knew that.

She had been on her feet all day and she was exhausted. She'd had a couple of difficult guests and had skipped lunch to sort out an overflowing tray of reservations and cancellations. The credit-card machine had been acting up and she was worried that some transactions might have gone through twice. The photocopier had jammed for the third time this week and she'd had a row with the company who had supposedly fixed it.

She sipped the strong coffee and dipped her second stick in and again watched the chocolate melt. Her marriage was in an awful place but she didn't have the first clue how to try and fix it. They hadn't had sex in months now and the communication was almost at a standstill. She was tired all the time and when her head hit the pillow every night she was gone. Sex would never be the same again anyway, she thought as she licked her chocolaty fingers. It had become a chore to them both and she honestly couldn't remember the last time they'd had sex for fun. Sex was practical. Sex was the means to an end. The thought of donning some sexy Gossard gear and going into that room to seduce her husband just wasn't on the cards. He would throw this fact in her face soon enough and she knew that.

Neil had a high sex drive and when Neil wanted sex he usually got it. It was another reason she was so suspicious: he had shown no interest over the last sixteen weeks. He always asked, she never did – that was the way they had sex. He was always the instigator. The way he looked at her these days was hardly through the eyes of a man filled with desire for his wife. Sure isn't he getting it somewhere else, she hissed in her head. Also, if she was really honest she just wasn't physically attracted to Neil in any way lately either. She wasn't the most highly sexed woman in the world, she admitted to herself a little guiltily as she swirled her coffee cup. But she did her best. She had fancied him madly in the beginning, she really had. In the early days, after that six-week wait, they hadn't been able to keep their hands off each other. The chemistry had been incredible and she knew deep down it was the reason Neil had proposed so fast. He thought it would be like that forever. He wished. She wished.

The microwave pinged her back to reality. She stood up wearily as she dumped her coffee cup in the stainless-steel sink. She opened the oven and the smell of the lasagne hit her. She stood in front of it, letting the hot air heat her legs. She was starving but had no appetite. She had no idea how it had all come to this. She was still a young woman, only thirty-five, and she hadn't envisioned this as her life. How had it all gone so wrong? It seemed to have happened in the blink of an eye. She rinsed the cup and as she dried it she glanced out her window at the empty shell of a house across the road with concrete slabs strewn all over the garden and building tools deserted in the big empty windows. Graffiti adorned every grey wall.

When she left Aer Lingus eventually she had taken a part-time job on reception at the Moritz Hotel in the village. She had done summer work in the hotel growing up so she was very familiar with all the sides to hotel work. Jonathan Redmond was back in the village and he had taken over as the manager. The job was more so she had something to do while she timed sex to the day every month and waited to become a stay-at-home mammy. Although she had really enjoyed the air-stewarding she'd always known it was a short-term career, so when her body had started to grumble she knew her flying time was up. It was always in her mind that at this stage of her life she would be a stay-at-home mother anyhow. It was the way it was supposed to be. It was what she wanted. Then the need to become pregnant had taken over her life. She was on the internet every day researching it. She read every magazine article on becoming pregnant and obeyed every law. She stopped drinking alcohol, stopped the occasional ciggy, took her folic acid, cut out caffeine, cut out sugar, cut out dairy, tried relaxation therapy, squeezed fresh lemon juice in her water every day, stopped wearing tight jeans and leggings, cut out anything that wasn't one-hundred-per-cent healthy and she walked loads. Neil was fed up with her asking him to cut out the pints, eat better, wear looser boxer shorts and so on, but he tried his best. She was constantly on pregnancy websites like EU MOM and Rollercoaster and had even made some virtual friends in the Trying-To-Conceive clubs. She was a wannabe-mammy.

Now, however, her job was full-time and it was keeping them out of the courts.

She went back upstairs and pulled on her tracksuit and runners, carefully putting her work uniform onto its silver steel hanger and leaving it hanging under the open bathroom window as she did every night to freshen it up. Michael Madsen was shouting out of the bedroom now. Neil should be thanking her for working so hard for them but he never had. She went back to the kitchen and ladled the lasagne onto two white Paul

Costello plates and put Neil's into the microwave. She hadn't the energy for him.

"Dinner's in the micro!" she called up the stairs to him. Then she stamped her foot down on the pedal of the bin and dumped her plate straight in. Right now Sandra Darragh really hated her life.

Chapter 4

Cara sipped on her chilled white wine, popped a vitamin supplement into her mouth and threw her head back to swallow. She had stopped taking Valium – she didn't want to depend on them any more. She stretched out her long lean legs under the goose-feather duvet and reflected on the day. It had been a whirlwind of an introduction. She had been whisked around every room in the hotel, introduced to every member of staff and had taken notes until she could no longer physically hold the pen. She smiled and rubbed the dent that was still in her finger.

She took a longer drink and glanced around the cosy bedroom. At least the heating had been re-plumbed recently and it worked really well, heating the small house in under an hour and giving piping hot water. The bare brick bedroom walls really needed a bit of work. She would buy some paints and a dressing table and some shelves. Bits and pieces. The bedroom door was wide open and she could see right into the single living room, the small kitchenette and the bathroom. Spacious wasn't a word to describe the cottage. It had been the main reason she had taken it. No hidden nooks or crannies. There was one long window across the living room that looked out onto Mr Peter's big open field that was home to a dozen or so cows. She would name them all some evening. They were putting her right off a good steak, she knew that much. In the distance she could actually see the twinkling lights of the hotel over the bridge. The cottage seemed really remote yet it was still near so many people.

Suddenly her heart started to race, she felt incredibly dizzy and her palms began to sweat. She immediately sat up in the bed, leaned over and put her head between her legs. Not again, she thought, please no! She knew what to do. "It's only a panic attack, it's only a panic attack," she repeated over and over again. She grabbed for her bag on the floor and pulled out the brown-paper bag which she placed over her mouth. She got out of the bed, slumping to the floor until her breathing came back to normal.

"On the floor again, Cara." She felt the cold stone of the bedroom wall on the back of her head as she dropped the bag. "When will you ever get off the floor?" She lay back on the rough old green carpet, closed her eyes and waited for playback.

* * *

"Hey, you look like you need a drink? Take one for yourself and could you please pop it on our bill?"

The pristine black-and-white pilot's uniform was too much for Cara to stop staring at. She closed her mouth. Shit! She must have been staring in an open-mouthed trance. "No, thank you, honestly, I'm fine. I can't drink while I'm working. I'm so sorry – what did you say again? Will you be having bar food or from the A La Carte menu, sir?" She picked up the worn Guinness beer mats and replaced them with fresh ones she kept in the pocket of her apron. He was too gorgeous to be true. And he was in uniform. Hat in hand. And he wasn't wearing a wedding ring. Esther would have her draped over his shoulder if she could see him. Cara wished she hadn't devoured the entire box of Celebrations with Esther last night while watching reruns of *Holby City*. She sucked in.

"Can I have a look at the bar menu, please, and order two still Ballygowans from you when you're ready?" He twirled his hat in his hands and then laid it on the empty chair beside him.

She thought she had seen him in here before but she'd never

served him. Cara pushed a strand of loose red hair back into its ponytail and smiled at him. "Coming right up and I will drop the menus down to you in a second." She headed for the kitchen, pushed the swinging doors with her back and wiped her hands on her red chequered apron.

"Wow! Wow! Wubbzy!" She leaned on the stainless-steel kitchen countertop and grinned at Maeve the chef. "Maeve, there's a pilot on table seven. He is TDF!"

"What's this?" Maeve shouted at Hanja. "Is this two crab cakes for table one or one crab cake for table two?"

"Is one crab cake for table two!" Hanja the Hungarian waitress daggered right back at Maeve. "Can't you no read Enegalish, Chef?" She tied her chequered apron tighter around her back now and stuck her chin out in defiance.

"Oh ho, Missy, I can read English all right!"

Cara smiled and stuck a hand up to stop Maeve mid-rant. "Did you hear me, Maeve?"

The older woman adjusted her black-and-white bandana and waved a silver carving knife in Cara's direction.

"He's what? Deaf? Get him to point out his order on the menu then – I haven't the bleedin' time for this!" Maeve licked her lips. "Aoife, table four to go! What are ya' standin' there for like a goon? Go! It's gettin' cold!"

Aoife grabbed her tray and backed out of the kitchen.

"No, Maeve, he's TDF – To Die For!" Cara pretended to swoon and Maeve whooshed her out of the hot kitchen with a dish cloth.

Cara poured two still Ballygowans and added lemon and crushed ice from behind the bar. The pilot had been joined by a man in a dark suit now and the two looked very deep in conversation, with papers scattered all over the table.

As she placed the drinks down, the pilot quickly looked up and smiled at her.

"So your new court date will be the twenty-fifth," she heard his companion say as she sashayed away.

Court date, hey? For being too damn sexy to the human race, she imagined. She couldn't get the image of Debra Winger and

Richard Gere out of her mind now with her and the pilot in their shoes walking out of the bar. She whistled the theme tune to *An Officer and a Gentleman* quietly to herself. It was one of her and Esther's favourite movies of all time.

The Law Top bar area began to fill up as hungry workers made their way in – some regulars, some new faces. That was the best thing about working near the Four Courts on the Quays in Dublin: the mixture of people she got to meet each day. It really was a world within a world.

"Pinta Carlsberg there when yer ready, Cara, love!" Young Seán Hackett stood before her.

"Ah Seán, you're not up again, are you? What on earth have you done now?" She hurried in behind the bar to help Steve.

"Ah now, g'wan, don't be like that! I done nothin'. I was atta weddin' in Wexford and wanted to leg it early cos it was totally shite, like."

He pulled himself up onto the bar stool as Cara drew his pint.

"So?" she glanced up at him.

"So? How was I meanta ger home at ten o'clock for the Celtic highlights on RTÉ when the minibus wasn't leavin' till three in the bleedin' mornin'?" He twisted his little finger into the fist of his left hand, a habit of his.

Cara shook her head as she dragged the brown bar-tap down low to top up the head on the pint. She deposited the pint in front of him on a beer mat.

He lifted it to his lips and took the largest drink that almost left the pint half empty. "I had ta borrow a motor, didn't I?" He twisted his gold stud in his right ear now.

She shook her head. "Whose car, Seán?"

"How'd I know whose car? It didn't have a bleedin' name tag on it, Cara, now did it?" He grinned at her and despite herself she gave a little laugh.

"That's awful, Seán. You stole some guest's car to drive home to Dublin? You can't do that."

"I borried it, Cara. I only borried it. I was gonna leave it outside Store Street Station except the bleedin' thing had no back light and I got pulled over by the scum. That's the last time I borry a car from Wexford – bleedin' kip! Plus I'd just got a lovely delivery of Columbia grass and I was happily spliffin' away on the drive so I'm bin' done for dat too. Harassment." He drained the pint now. "Better go. I've no one representin' me, free legal aid me hole." He hopped off the stool.

"I'll see you in six months so, Seán." Cara wiped down the bar and threw the dirty cloth into the sink under the bar.

"Yeah, looks like it – and, Cara, try an' clean dem taps in the six months I'm gone down, will ya? Dem pints are rotten to the core."

The son of two heroin addicts, Seán Hackett really had little chance in life. He swaggered out of the bar, grey hoody pulled firmly up over his shaven head now.

She made her way back over to the pilot's table and removed her notebook and pen from her belt pouch. "Gentlemen, are you ready to order now?"

"What do you recommend today?" Mr Pilot asked her, his blue eyes absolutely piercing. It was the deepest colour blue she'd ever seen. She was locked into them.

His eyes were totally mesmerising. It was as though he was looking deep into her very soul. She pointed to the specials on the blackboard with her pen as she tried to find her voice. "Maeve the chef does a mean beef stew and, on a day like this, it's what I will be having later with a pile of crusty home-baked bread," she managed.

"Stew for me so – and how about you, Tristan?" He looked at the other man who nodded his approval and also ordered the stew.

Cara liked her job. She enjoyed being a waitress and tending the bar although most of the time she was also a cleaner and stocktaker. She had worked at The Law Top for eight months now and had worked in other bars and in Rosie's restaurant before that. She hadn't gone to college like she had wanted as her dad had died suddenly and that had left her and Esther alone. And totally broke. They needed money to live. She was happy in her work. She wanted to work with people and she was doing just that. A desk job wasn't her thing really. Just as well, she thought as she slapped the order docket on the wall and left the stifling heat of the kitchen. Problem was she worked such long hours she never got to socialise and therefore was as single as the Number One bus. She had a nice group of friends in work and they'd often sit down and open a bottle or two after the last customer had been pushed out and the door bolted. But it was usually feet up, smelly tights and swollen ankles on chairs and the male members of staff were privy to all the moans and groans – not exactly sexy. She was still only thirty-three and a half – she smiled at the adding on of the all-important half.

"Docket down! Two stews for seven!" Maeve shouted through the hatch as Cara pushed her pen behind her right ear and hopped back into work mode for the rest of the lunch rush.

Chapter 5

"I love it!" Jenny Brophy beamed as she looked around the new function room, twirling backwards as she went. It was for a Christmas wedding and Cara was so excited to start work on it. Her first real wedding. It didn't give her much time but she loved to work under pressure. That's why she'd loved the waitressing work so much. They had done mock-up weddings in college but this was planning for real with real people and food and flowers and music. For some the most important day of their lives.

"Do you want to wait another while and see if Max shows up?" Cara asked the bride-to-be, as her fiancé had been delayed.

"Ah no, I mean he said it's all up to me anyway so I think I'm happy to book it. He's booked up with tennis lessons all day and he's doing commentary on TV this evening for the Templeogue Tennis Tournament. I've always wanted to get married here, Cara, but didn't think the function room would be available at such short notice since it was being renovated."

"It's been closed for six weeks so we couldn't take any bookings just in case it ran over – so you're lucky," Cara informed the pretty, over-excited girl.

"As soon as Max uttered those words I knew I wanted to march him down the aisle fast. I'm not getting any younger and I want a big family."

Cara smiled at her and nodded even though she thought Jenny looked about fifteen.

The function room with its impossibly high ceiling was freshly painted and redecorated in warm creams and browns with heavy gold drapes and cream tie-backs. There was space for ten round tables on the newly sanded-down original wooden dance floor, each sitting eight comfortably. The long wedding table sat under the bay window with an incredible view of the sea behind. It was a warm romantic room, perfect for an intimate wedding, and soon Cara would be decorating it for Christmas. She'd do it now if she had her way but Jonathan didn't want Christmas pushed on the guests too early. "Some people hate Christmas, Cara," he'd said. "It's November so they don't expect to be surrounded in tinsel with Bing blaring out, or Michael Bublé – not just yet." She had nodded and backed down immediately.

"I'm so excited!" Jenny was snapping picture after picture of the room on her iPhone. "Okay, then, let's mark the diary, Bride-to-be!" Cara opened the large red book on December 3rd, the preferred date.

"Oh I'm so, so, so excited! Sorry!" Jenny was beaming from ear to ear.

"Don't be sorry! So the Brophy and Burrows wedding it is then." Cara marked the book and they shook hands. "Now I need to talk to you about the one-thousand-euro deposit and when the rest is due and all that yucky unromantic stuff – but how about over a warm drink in the bar?"

"Sounds great." Jenny snapped another few pictures and they left the room together. "Good morning, Jonathan." Cara smiled at the manager as he pointed to a black mark on the floor beside the reception desk that was being dutifully attended to by Big Bob the handyman.

"Morning, Cara, how's everything going for you today?" Jonathan smiled warmly at her. The past couple of weeks had been a bit of a blur.

"This is Miss Jenny Brophy – she has just booked her wedding with us for December the third," Cara said proudly with her hand on the small of the other woman's back. She knew that it was important for Jenny to trust her completely from the offset, otherwise the girl would be constantly worried and that would make Cara's job so much harder. The timeframe was so short Cara needed everything to run smoothly.

Jonathan smiled widely and shook her hand. "Fantastic. Cara will make it a day to remember, I have no doubt."

"Good for you, girl!" Bob smiled up from his bended knee as he rubbed at the mark with a white cloth.

Cara showed Jenny into the lounge and ordered two coffees and a selection of assorted biscuits.

"It's got something special, this place, hasn't it, Cara?" Jenny asked as the open turf and log fire crackled in the grate and they sank into the two soft leather seats in front of it.

"It's really beautiful. I'd love to get married here myself – maybe one day." The words had left Cara's mouth before her brain had even processed them.

"Oh, aren't you married?" Jenny looked slightly shocked.

"No," Cara said and shook a sugar sachet fiercely. "I'm divorced."

* * *

It was bitterly cold as Sandra took her lunch break beside the stables on one of the rustic picnic tables. She had to take a packed lunch to work with her now. Even with the staff discount she still couldn't afford Delphine's delicious homemade soup and homemade tomato bread which she used to devour in the bar area of the hotel. They really were penniless. She pulled the leather belt on her green Oasis coat tighter and pulled the collar up. She couldn't find her scarf this morning and she was really feeling the cold. She opened her lunchbox and took out a rather pathetic cheese-spread sandwich and a small yogurt.

"Lunch for a mouse?"

Dermot Murray approached her and she had to laugh. She loved Dermot – he was so full of life. He was slightly weather-beaten but still very attractive with long blond floppy hair and twinkling green eyes – early forties, she knew, although she didn't know his exact age. Hands like shovels. She had known Dermot almost all her life and she had often talked to him while growing up. She usually saw him in Hines of a Friday or Saturday night and she always went over to chat with him. Dermot never failed to have a smile and a word for Sandra. It had been ages since they had talked properly though.

He was dressed today in his usual husky jacket, hat, cream jodhpurs and black riding boots.

"Ah, you know how it is, Dermot – penny-pinching as usual!" She pushed up on the bench, gathering her black skirt under her, and made room for him.

"Really?" He took off his riding hat and rubbed at his floppy blond hair. "I thought you were one of the fancy yuppies now up in the new builds?" He flicked under his nose with his index finger and smiled a great big smile. His eyes crinkled. Perfectly straight teeth.

Sandra grinned back. "Well, I am, we are, but as I've no doubt you've heard around this village Neil's lost his business – he had to close Darragh Electrics – there are no jobs and the last few months have been . . . well . . ." She couldn't believe this was happening: she was welling up. She tried to swallow the tears but it made it worse as what happened next was an explosion of emotion that, judging by the look on Dermot's face, was enormous.

He grabbed her lunch box, shut it tightly and put his arm around her as he ushered her into the tack room of the stables. She sat under the racks of saddles and cried her heart out, the smell of saddle soap and hay filling her overworked nostrils. Dermot hugged her gently and said all sorts of comforting things she couldn't really hear through her sobs. Eventually she managed to pull herself together.

"I'm so sorry, Dermot, I am mortified. I don't know what on earth came over me." She blew her nose into the white soft tissue he handed her. "I don't know what came over me," she repeated and tried to stand up.

"Shush, Sandy, sit still for a while and let me put the kettle on, will you?"

She nodded and blew her nose again then leaned her head against the cold steel saddle-racks, inhaling the smell of leather and freshly laid shavings. What had she done? This was so embarrassing. She knew Dermot well enough to know he wouldn't spread it around the hotel but she needed to cop herself on.

Things at home were worse and she was finding the lack of time in her life totally draining. Neil was definitely up to something. She had called his brother Tom in his shop this morning just to say she was worried about the lack of work, but Tom told her he had enough problems of his own and to "tell the lazy fucker to get his big white arse out of bed and go work in McDonald's". So no help at all. As usual. She had taken to sleeping in the spare room. There was no wallpaper on the walls in there and no curtains on the windows but it didn't matter so much in November as it was dark at the time she got up and when she went to sleep. Neil never once asked her why she wasn't in his bed.

Dermot returned and handed her a chipped blue Royal Dublin Horse Show mug with the sweetest-tasting tea ever. She sipped it gratefully. "Thanks," she said, smiling at him.

He put his big hands around her still shaking ones, steadying the mug, and said, "Listen, I'm always here if you want to talk. I would do anything for you, but you already know that. However, we are under pressure now to get to the monthly staff meeting – you know what Big J's like for timekeeping."

"Oh shit, the meeting, I forgot!" For some reason she suddenly did want to tell him everything. She felt so comfortable around him, always had. She sipped the tea. "Take me for a drink after work, will you, Dermot?" she almost whispered.

"Sure, of course. I've a long hack out into Knocknoly woods and up the back mountain at four o'clock with six Australian guests but I'll be back by six. Say I meet you in Hines – that be okay or would you rather somewhere more private?"

"No, no, Hines is fine." She drank some more of the comforting sweet tea and then handed him the cup.

He held out his hand to her. She took it and he pulled her up gently. Then they made their way back into the hotel.

* * *

"Okay, great, that's everyone." Jonathan discreetly glanced at his Tag watch as Dermot and Sandra entered the room. Her red-rimmed eyes were not lost on him. "So the meeting today as always is to communicate with one another. If anyone has any business now's the time to share. Cara booked her first wedding today so *bualadh bos* for her!"

Everyone clapped. Cara blushed and looked around the table. There were seven people here and she tried to see if she could remember their names and job descriptions. There was Jonathan – manager of course. Sandra who didn't look herself today – head receptionist. Dermot – stable manager. Big Bob – handyman. Mike – bar manager. Tiffney – restaurant manager. Old Mrs Reilly – head of housekeeping. Yes. She was delighted with herself. She was getting to know everyone. She would ask surnames and try to get to know people individually as the days progressed.

Old Mrs Reilly, as she was known, was a total character. She was probably in her seventies although Jonathan had mentioned she always said she was sixty-four so no one knew her actual age. "She's been sixty-four for the last ten years, I think," he had told Cara, laughing. She managed her bedrooms to the highest standard and she had a couple of local girls working alongside her. She had her hand up now.

"Mr Redmond, I have asked Big Bob again and again this morning to please go up and change the light bulbs in sixteen and twenty-one. He still has not done this. I wonder if perhaps you could ask him as I feel he may be holding a grudge against me as I refused to go on a date with him. He wanted me to go up above to Dublin, to see the Pussycat Dollies at the O2 arena."

Everyone around the table laughed and the older woman buffed her slightly purple-tinted hair with her hand. She wore enormous silver dangly earrings and bright cerise-pink lipstick.

"I did not ask you on a date to the Pussycat Dolls!" Bob raised his voice and pushed his large brown glasses high onto the bridge of his red-veined nose. "'Twas you who asked me to go and me a good Catholic man, and I don't approve of filth like them girls, parading around in their undergarments – it's disgraceful if you ask me! I hear they don't even eat food – they eat pepper and water and maple syrup. I read the fancy magazines the guests leave lying around too, you know, Mrs Reilly." He removed the glasses now and rubbed them viciously with the end of his white shirt.

"Whatever you say, dear Bob!" Mrs Reilly winked at Cara. "Talk to the hand!" She clicked her fingers at him, raised her left hand and shook her head from side to side as he sat open-mouthed staring at her.

Cara stifled a giggle.

"In fact, you are correct, Bob," Mrs Reilly went on. "It was only when I saw yer nose buried in the article about them in that English magazine and you devouring the pictures with yer eyes – well, I just presumed you were a fan of the girls." She was smirking wildly now. "I happen to think they are terrific, fair play to them, that's what I say! If I'd had the opportunity to dress in me knickers and bra and parade around Knocknoly in the fifties, I surely would have. I was quite the fox, you know – in fact I stopped the traffic."

"There was no traffic here in the fifties!" Big Bob snapped back. "You daft old bat!"

"Thank you, Mrs Reilly, Mr Bedford." Jonathan smirked despite himself. "Bob, what about the bulbs?"

"Do them now, sir!" Big Bob answered and saluted, sliding his glasses back up his nose with his index finger.

"Well, if Brad and Angie are quite finished arguing," Jonathan laughed, "has anyone else anything work-related to discuss?"

Mike spoke now. "Just to check with you, Jonathan. I spoke with the lovely Nicola Pawley at Diageo and she said she'd give us those extra coolers for the bar if we display product for one year. That okay with you?"

"I'm okay with that as long as it's not advertising those Alcopop thingies. I hate how they look and I don't even like the message they send out – but if it's Guinness or brand beer then that's fine, Mike," Jonathan said.

Tiffney now raised her hand. She was Eastern European but Cara wasn't sure yet from where exactly. She was very quiet and a really hard worker. Cara guessed Tiffney probably wasn't her real name but maybe easier for working in Ireland.

"Yes, Tiff?" Jonathan pointed to her.

"Please, if I may, I need new covers for the bar and restaurant menus. The older ones are – what's the word? – grotty – and I feel guests deserve nice covers. I have looked in Eason on the net in Sandra's office and they do very nice ones for a good price. I will print out pictures and a price list and leave it in your office, yes?"

Cara watched the other girl talk. She could be anything between twenty-five and thirty-five. She had sad eyes, limp hair and was hunched over. Her body language spoke volumes to Cara who was an expert on body language.

"That's fine, Tiff – you just go ahead. I trust you so just send me up the invoice." Jonathan poured some water from the clear glass jug with sliced lemons on the table.

Mike coughed and looked at Tiff before saying, "If you want, Tiff, I could drive you to the Eason's on O'Connell Street up in Dublin and we could take a look round? Check the rotas when they come out on Friday and see if we have a slot where we are off together. Maybe grab a bite to eat while we are there? Show you some of the old country, ya know?"

"Thank you, no. I will stay here, Mike." Tiffney didn't raise her eyes from her notebook.

The young man just nodded and grabbed for the water jug.

"Okay, so December will be on top of us before we know it," Jonathan went on. "Cara is going to decorate the hotel, with Big Bob helping her. We now have a wedding to host as well as the Christmas programme so it's going to be full-on. Bookings for Christmas are flying in, Sandra says, so that is great. If any of you have any ideas on your sections, please speak to Cara. I haven't done the Christmas rota yet – I'm mulling that over still. The Christmas party will not be until the end of January, I'm afraid, as we will be just too busy. However, if we have a really good Christmas, I promise you a special treat. I'm always on your side so remember that, and we are all a team. There is a list in my office and on the staff bulletin board behind reception, of the different events we will be hosting. Cara will now be taking them over so liaise with her from now on. It's a busy time. We don't have a lot of staff because that's the way I like it – a smaller ship sails quicker – so you all need to pull together. Any questions?"

The table remained silent.

"Okay then, thank you all for your time, my door is always open and have a nice day." Jonathan lifted his green folder and banged it gently up and down on the table before pushing back his seat and leaving the room.

* * *

The hotel was busy today, Cara noted, as she made her way to the staff bulletin board which was in the small office behind reception. She needed to copy whatever was on it and to sit down and study it.

Cara was feeling confident and optimistic. It was a feeling she was beginning to remember well. She caught sight of her reflection in the large mirror in the lobby. She had teamed her Stella McCartney suit with a tight pale-blue shirt from Gap and had stuck one of the small purple flowers from the garden in her lapel. Her red hair was pulled back in a slick high ponytail and she looked fresh and business-like.

Sandra was already back at her post on reception and Cara smiled at her as she passed. There were no slackers in this job. Not like in The Law Top where she used to have to scream at the kitchen staff out the back to put out their cigarettes and come back in to work. All the time. She had begun to feel like a mother to some of them. There was no appointed bar manager for whatever reason so she had to pull her weight to get people to do their jobs. It drove her mad that she and Steve and Aoife and Maeve worked their butts off and the part-timers couldn't give a damn. The staff at the Moritz were there to work.

Cara nipped in behind reception. She couldn't put her finger on it but something wasn't quite the same with Sandra today. The two women had not really spoken much on a personal level – in fact not at all, Cara thought, as she opened the lid of the photocopier. They were both busy and just went about their work. Cara hadn't had a social drink with anyone since she had been here. She would like to make some friends but she was taking her life one day at a time and it suited her that way. She wasn't really up to socialising just yet. She took the colourful pins out of the bulletin board and took the relevant pages down. She placed one onto the glass surface of the photocopier and closed the cover. She hit the blue button on the machine and nothing happened. She lifted the lid again. She was going to buy some paint and brushes this evening on the way home and get started on her bedroom after she called Esther.

"Come on, work, you pig!" she muttered at the photocopier and pressed the button again and again.

"Are you okay in there?" Sandra was leaning against the door.

"I don't think this copier likes me. I feel like a nervous child every time I touch it, hoping it will work."

Sandra laughed and then sighed. "Amongst a whole pile of other shit it's becoming the bane of my life." She bent down and pulled out the plug and then plugged it in again. "There you go, Cara, try that! See? I'm a technical wizard!" She laughed as the machine purred into action, then her phone rang and she went back to answer it. This time it worked. Cara folded the pages neatly into her briefcase and then decided to photocopy some other material from the bulletin board while the blasted thing was working. She photocopied a list of every member of staff and their hours along with their mobile phone numbers. She copied a history of the hotel that was a newer version than the one she had. Then she copied the side of her face. She couldn't resist. She had an overwhelming urge to photocopy her arse. She smiled – her sense of humour must be returning! What other shit did Sandra have going on, she wondered as she listened to the other woman on the phone, giving expert driving directions down from Dublin.

Cara didn't miss Dublin, not yet. She missed being able to see her mam but nothing else really. Cara had always felt protective of her mam – Esther was just that type of person. She really liked this village of Knocknoly. It had everything she could need and it was so tranquil. She had explored it quite well lately and knew some of the locals to say a polite hello to now. She had made a friend in Louise, the owner of Louise's Loft, the small café on the edge of the village. A lot of the locals called her The Apple. Because of her amazing flaky apple pies, Cara had asked? Louise had grinned. "I think it's more because of my love for cider," she said, sniggering into her hand. Louise made all the produce herself and it really was remarkable. She sold the most amazing pastries and savouries like her beef-and-Guinness pies and her cheese-and-ham quiches – and of course her flaky apple pies. It was all simple, healthy, homemade cooking.

Cara loved the lack of traffic and the fresh air and she really loved the lack of McDonald's, Burger Kings, Centras and Spars. The originality of the village was very special. After the ruckus that had been her life she craved this quiet.

She really should buy some more of those wedding books on "Organising That Perfect Day", she thought. She fished in her briefcase for her diary to make some notes and let the copier work away.

Then she sat on the black-leather swivel office chair and closed her eyes as the warm pages purred through.

* * *

"There's a note left for you here, Cara," Steve said as she turned the tip jar upside down onto the table and the coins clattered around before falling still. Lunch had been manic busy and now her feet really hurt.

"For me?" She whipped the note from his hand as he stood over her. There was a number and underneath it said in red felt-tip pen: "*Please call your friendly pilot. He'd love to buy you that drink.*" She went bright red to match the writing as Steve ran through the bar à la Laura Ingalls from *Little House on the Prairie* with his arms extended and making aeroplane noises. Why he was doing that she had no idea.

"Bit of a pigtailed girl," he explained, "a chicken-shit if you ask me. Why didn't he just ask you out to your face?" Steve was miffed now.

He had never asked Cara out but she had always imagined he fancied her a little bit. On the other hand maybe he just liked her but she wasn't a romantic interest for him. She would never approach him first, that was for sure. Some days she thought they would make a good couple and other days she knew they wouldn't work.

Cara put her hands on her hips in mock protest.

"You read it, Steve Brady?"

"Well, he handed it to me and asked me to give it to you. You know the types we get in here – it could have been pornographic."

Cara sat down and kicked off her red FitFlop runners. The state of her! She had barely any make-up on, her hair was frizzy from the heat of the kitchen and lack of leave-in conditioner, she had been way overeating lately and she was knackered. Yet he wanted to go out with her. This had never happened to her before. Oh, she knew she was attractive but in an if-you-like-that-kind-of-look way and to be honest she didn't think she was most men's cup of tea. A busty blonde she was not. "You're a bit like Black Magic," her mother had always told her when she was growing up. "Some people will absolutely love you and others just won't get you at all. Or that Marmite stuff – no, I've never tried it, I just don't like the look of it – so there you go, you see what I mean?" The pilot obviously liked Black Magic.

"Are you gonna ring him before he flies away?" Steve whispered at her in a mock Southern American accent before flicking the copper coins into the jar and building a one-euro-coins tower.

"Mind your own business!" She stuck out her tongue playfully.

"He looks dodgy if you ask me," he sniffed.

"Well, I didn't ask you, did I now?" Bloody right she was going to ring him. How long should she wait? Esther would have a field day on this one.

She collected her tips, slipped her sore feet back into her runners and headed for her bus home. What should she say? 'Hi, it's Cara from the bar – you wanted me to call?' Or: 'It's Cara, the girl from the pub' – or should she say 'the woman'? Oh, what would she say? It had been so long since she was on a date. It was so long really since she had felt that a member of the opposite sex fancied her. If Steve had really fancied her he would have asked her out by now. It was like that old saying about actors working together on a set: they were so close all day they felt they should be together. It wore off. It never worked out in the real world. That's what Cara needed, someone in the real world, outside the four walls of the bar, to like her. She was excited and the adrenalin pumped through her veins as she slid her bus card into the machine and it beeped in recognition.

She sat at the back of the bus, the engine roaring noisily under her. Who knew where this might lead? She was more than aware of her biological clock.

He hadn't even left his name on the note, she now realised. That was unusual.

She practised what she would say all the way home.

* * *

Esther spat her éclair into her hand.

"Seriously, Mam, that's so gross!" Cara grimaced.

"A pilot!" she put the éclair back in her mouth and then spat it back out again. "Jesus! Ring him now before he changes his mind! He might have been dizzy from that altitude. He must be loaded if he's a pilot!" She popped the drippy brown toffee back in.

"Money, doesn't interest me in the slightest, Mam." Cara opened the microwave and looked at the baked ham, turnip and potatoes on the plate. Closing the door again, she pressed two minutes and it beeped into action.

"Well, it bloody well interests me, madam!" Esther sat at the small kitchen table and shook her head as she chewed rhythmically. "A pilot, if you don't mind. All she ever meets in that place are muggers and rapists – suddenly it's a pilot and she's acting as if it's no big deal!"

"It's not, Mam – it's only a drink!" Cara rubbed at her eyes she was so tired.

"Listen, if he likes you at all, he must fancy the pants off you. You are his type. You know what I always say about your type? Black Magic? Did you check for a wedding ring?"

Cara laughed at her this time and at the ping removed her dinner with the tea towel wrapped around her hand. "No ring," she admitted as she sat down.

Her mother poured her a strong cup of tea and replaced the ancient knitted brown tea cosy.

"No ring!" Esther swallowed hard. "Look, I'm off to bingo with Mrs McGurn – ring him while I'm gone, won't ya?"

"Yes, Mam. Now can I eat in peace?"

Her mother tied her grey scarf tight around her neck. "Now, that's a lovely bitta ham from FX Buckley's on Moore Street so eat it all up. Not that you ever leave a screed, mind you. And stay away from the éclairs – I've only five left and I have to ring your Auntie Ann when I get in later."

Cara waved her fork at her mother, her mouth full.

Esther removed her purse from the kitchen drawer, then another purse with coins from another drawer, then her big change purse from her bag, and stuffed them all in her Green Bingo Bag.

"See you later, love."

The door banged and Cara ate in comfortable silence. She never put the TV on as she listened to too much talk all day in work. She took the note out and looked at it again. She would call him after eight o'clock, she thought as she cut into her ham and smeared some mashed turnip on top. First a long soak in a hot bubbly bath. She ate her dinner slowly and then rooted in the fridge for some leftover carrot cake. As she munched it from her hand she made her way upstairs. Their little house was a two-up two-down. She pushed open the door of her bedroom and stood in front of her mirror, chewing. "Well, Cara, a pilot no less – a pilot fancies you." She laughed at her reflection and stepped out of her working clothes. She smelled of stew. She let her long red curls tumble around her shoulders and went in to run the bath. She didn't care that he was a pilot to be honest – all she cared about was that he was utterly drop-dead gorgeous. And he was available. She put her phone with the piece of paper tucked neatly under it on the edge of the bath, added bath salts and immersed herself into the warm bubbles.

"Wait. Don't call him yet," she said out loud as she ran her razor under her arms. Then she sat bolt upright, grabbed for her phone and punched the precious numbers in.

After four rings he picked up. "Hello?"

She closed her eyes tight. "Hi, em, this is, well, it's the girl from the bar, today . . ."

"Aah, Red – I'm delighted you called."

His voice was lower-toned than she remembered. She smiled and squashed some white bubbles between her finger and thumb. She wasn't normally the nervy type. "Well, actually, I don't usually do this," he said, "but, listen, I would have asked you out face to face but I was in a business meeting and the guy wouldn't leave my side. It didn't seem appropriate for us both to approach you so the note was all I could think of. So will you come for a drink with me then?"

"Yes," she laughed. "That would be lovely."

"Great, how about tonight?" he replied.

"Tonight?" she said, her voice raised.

"Well, I'm only in Dublin tonight. I fly out to Dubai tomorrow for two weeks."

Oh, what the heck, Cara thought as she tried to hush the obvious sounds of the bath water with the palms of her hands and sat up straighter.

"Sure, okay, why not? Where and when?" She bit her bottom lip hard.

"Say O'Donoghue's on Baggot Street, around nine?" he suggested.

"Great, well, I'll see you there – oh sorry, I don't even know your name!"

"My name is Alex Charles," he laughed. "Sorry, how rude of me – and you are?"

"Cara" she said, "Cara Byrne."

"See you later, Cara Byrne," he said slowly and hung up.

* * *

O'Donoghue's bar was heaving when Cara arrived and loud traditional Irish music rang out all around. She headed straight for the toilet to check her appearance one last time. She had let her long red hair loose after her bath and it curled around her petite face. She had worn tinted foundation, dark-grey eye shadow, dark-grey eyeliner, pink blusher and kept her lips nude. She wore a tight white vest shirt and a denim miniskirt, with thick black tights and black pumps, and had added some silver chains around her neck. She applied some rosy Vaseline on her lips now to liven up her lips a little and let out a deep breath.

"Are you in a queue, dear?" an American lady asked her.

"No, sorry, go ahead!" She smiled and pushed the door open as she squeezed past. Roomy was not a word to describe the toilets in O'Donoghue's.

She saw him at the bar as soon as she left the loo. He was tall and dark and totally breathtaking. He had dark stubble now and it suited him. Every woman was looking at him, she noted, as she held her head high and pushed her way through the crowd towards him. He was engrossed in the live music in the corner, tapping his fingers on his pint glass. She reached up on her tippy toes and poked him gently on the shoulder.

"Ah, Red, you made it! Don't you look beautiful?" His eyes caressed her body and she blushed. "So what will you have to drink, Cara Byrne?"

She loved how her name sounded on his lips and she ordered a gin and tonic. They made their way out to the beer garden when her drink arrived so he could smoke. It was well heated so she didn't mind. There was a spare barrel and two stools at the very back, away from the music, and she ran for it.

"Eager beaver!" he laughed. "As they say," he added, slightly awkwardly.

They both sat on the high stools. Cara was aware that a group of girls at a barrel beside them all stopped talking to gawp at him and now there were peals of laughter from them.

"So, pleased to meet you, Cara." He stuck out his hand and she took it. He held it for a moment too long.

"Pleased to meet you too, Alex," she returned.

Then he suddenly said, "So, great stew today by the way – good advice."

They smiled at one another.

"So, Cara Byrne, tell me all about you, tell me everything, I want to know it all." He grinned and she laughed as he opened a fresh packet of Marlboro Red. He removed the silver foil and wrapped the clear wrapping paper in it and sealed it tightly. He dropped it into the ashtray and lit a cigarette up slowly and confidently.

He was wearing a tight black T-shirt and light blue jeans with black Nike runners. He seemed so much younger than when he was in uniform. He had eyes like Ray Liotta, she realised. That was it! Before she knew it she said out loud, "Wow, you look really like the actor Ray Liotta!"

He blew smoke high into the air. "I get that all the time – and you, you look like Nicole Kidman, right?"

She laughed. She wouldn't say she got that all the time but it had been said once or twice and that was enough for her. "Ha, I wish that were true!" She sipped her G&T, waiting for his response.

"You are far more beautiful than Nicole Kidman but we could become a pair of look-a-likes and quit our day jobs."

She was thrilled at the word *we*. "So a pilot's life must be pretty exciting stuff?" she asked him, genuinely interested.

They struck up an easy conversation and he told her he had worked as a pilot for five years. "It was never a question of what career I would take really as my dad was a pilot. He had my name down for the Pilot Training Centre in Killowen in

Waterford since I was a boy." He picked up his pint and the beer mat stuck to it. They both laughed. He prised it off and dropped it onto the ground. "That's where I received my ATPL licence. The course took fifty-seven weeks to complete but Dad was always singing its praises." He stuck his chin down into his neck and squinted his eyes tight, pointing his baby finger in the air. "You know, son, I can't recommend the pilot college highly enough. I know from experience that airlines favour students who have trained in Europe and trained with one organisation." He stared into the distance now.

"Okay, yep, I get you!" Cara laughed.

"Yeah, that was the way it was. Then I went out to Florida and finished off my practicals. I do love it, though. It's such a buzz still, climbing into the air – the power is overwhelming at times. The adrenalin rush. I can't imagine I will ever tire of it."

They ordered another round from a lounge boy. Alex told her he was from Dalkey in Dublin, had one sister and went to boarding school in Kerry from the age of twelve. He was so easy to talk to and a fantastic listener. She found herself, after the fourth G&T, doing exactly what he'd asked the second they'd sat down – telling him all about herself. She told him about her beloved dad's passing at forty-nine of a heart attack, how she found him in the chair in their front room when she came down for her Rice Krispies that Friday morning in March, how she still lived with her mother and still couldn't face leaving her on her own. Didn't ever want to leave her on her own. Cara opened up to this stranger about how she felt responsible for Esther, about how Esther was still quite innocent and childlike yet a perfectly functioning adult and mother. She knew her dad would have wanted her to look after Esther as he had. He told her he understood as he was also really close to his own mother. She went on to tell him how she'd have loved to have gone to college but they needed the money. She'd always been really interested in working in hotel hospitality ever since her first family holiday years back when she was ten years old. They stayed at The Cliffs in Blackpool and she'd adored it. Her dad had been a bus driver and he had spent every penny as he earned it. He liked his pints, did her dad. He wasn't an alcoholic by any means – well, if he was he was the best advertisement for one she had ever known. He was always jolly, always laughing, and he always left the pub at nine o'clock on the dot every night to say goodnight to her and see his wife. On Friday nights he brought home fish and chips and sometimes a portion of curry sauce. He was so loving. A gentle soul, her mother fondly called him, but sometimes she called him "that bloody eejit" as he had left them penniless. He had spent some formative years going to school in Blackpool when his parents had sent him over to England to live with his wonderful auntie, Kathleen Fogg. His aunt had taken great care of him and looked after him as one of her own. "That's what family did for each other in those days," he had explained to her. On their holiday, the one and only in Blackpool, he showed her all the places he went, took her to the top of the Blackpool Tower and then to the Pleasure Beach. They went on the tram and walked the piers. Cara had thought she'd died and gone to heaven as she rode ride after ride in the Pleasure Beach and ate candy floss and got one of those huge red candy soothers that she hung around her neck on a red ribbon. It had lasted forever. It had been warm and sunny. The town seemed so full of cheer and goodwill it made her smile. It had been full of Irish families all enjoying themselves and they had mixed with many over the holiday. Simple pleasures. At the hotel every night the three of them sat in the bar at the same corner table and there were magic shows and dancers and singers. This was where Cara's love for the hotel industry was born.

"I love all this," she told her dad as she sucked her cherry Coke through her luminous green straw.

"Listen in school, love," he had said as he pulled hard on his Major cigarette. "Learn – take the opportunity education can give you – take it all in and go to college. One day you could become a part of this industry – wouldn't that be grand all the same?" She could still see that box now: green and white with his trusty gold Zippo lighter on top. Esther had his name engraved on it one Christmas. Every time someone struck a Zippo gas lighter it brought her straight back to Lar Byrne.

Esther was always on at him to quit. "They killed your own father!" she would chastise him but he would laugh. "It's my life, Esther, and I enjoy my fags – leave me in peace, would you?" But Cara would notice he'd always squeeze Esther's leg fondly as he spoke. Lar loved Esther, that much was true.

"Why am I telling you all this?" she asked Alex. She shook her head as she watched him light another cigarette.

"Because I want to know. Because I asked." He leaned towards her as Christy Moore's "Ride On" was sung out around them. "Because I think you are the most beautiful girl I have ever seen in my entire life. You took my breath away the moment I saw you." His eyes were heavy with desire. "Because I believe in fate and that's what this is, Cara Byrne. This is fate." He steadily placed his cigarette in the ceramic ashtray holder and leaned in and kissed her slowly on the lips and she felt dizzy. How had this happened? That morning when she set out for work she was slightly grumpy and just wanted an early night and to watch *The Kardashians*. Now this? Now she was sitting here with birds singing in her head and stars floating before her eyes. She felt beautiful. She was smitten. He was too good to be true. This didn't happen to girls like her. Did it?

* * *

"It's jammed again, has it?"

Cara jumped out of her skin as Sandra put her hand on her shoulder.

"Oh sorry, Cara, you were miles away. I didn't mean to startle you. I just heard that dreaded whirring noise – it's haunting me. Are you okay?" Sandra put her hand on Cara's shoulder.

Cara stood up. "Yeah, it has. Sorry, Sandra, I was miles away, yes – daydreaming again . . . listen, I have enough copies here now anyway, thanks."

She squeezed past Sandra and went out, leaving Sandra to clear up her mess.

Put your spillage in the bin yourself, Sandra thought as she looked at the clock. Someone hit the bell on reception. Sandra let out a slow breath – it was one of those days.

"Ah, Phyl, what can I do for you?" she asked the guest.

"Well, the thing is, Sandra, we have been talking in there and you know how much we love this hotel and we will be fifty-five years married in January and, well, we want to book a party!" Her eyes lit up.

"Hang on a minute, Phyl – excuse me." Sandra hurried to the foot of the stairs – Cara was halfway up. "Cara!"

"Yes?" Cara turned round.

"Mrs Delaney has a question about a party. Could you deal with it now or are you busy? I can ask her to come back later?"

"Sure, absolutely, now is perfect, Sandra." Cara made her way back down the deep-blue-and-white carpeted stairs.

She escorted the older woman back into the lounge. The piano that Jonathan had bought last week at an auction in Newry was now in use and a young man in a tuxedo tinkled quietly on the keys in the background.

"So what did you have in mind?" Cara removed her notebook and pen from her briefcase as they sat.

"Well, something big – like invite all our family and friends – he's not been too well, you know, love, he –"

"Good afternoon," Tiffney interrupted them, a silver tray balanced on her left hand with her orders pad and pen on top. "May I get you anything to drink, ladies?"

They ordered two teas and continued.

"The thing is," said Phyl, "I wouldn't be great on computers and emails and all that and he's useless. We can hardly use our mobile phones! So I'd need a bit of help, love. Our son Liam is in Australia and won't be back and our daughter Maia has crippling MS, so I can't ask her to help."

"I can do it." Cara took the other woman's hand. "Mrs Delaney, can I call you Phyllis?"

"Of course, love."

"Right – let me grab the red diary and look at available dates. Where is Mr Delaney?"

"Ah, he's lying down again – he has angina and he's not too well with it today. But call me Phyl, will ya?"

"Well, let him rest, Phyl – aren't we women better at these things anyway?" Cara proclaimed as Tiff arrived with the tea and a plate of assorted chocolate biscuits.

Phyl stuffed a chocolate shortbread in her mouth and nodded in agreement.

* * *

Hines was quiet as Sandra sat up at the bar.

"Hi ya, Charlie, a pint of Budweiser extra cold, please," she said as she twisted the stool around to face him.

"Haven't seen you in here in an age. How's Neiler?" Charlie flipped a beer mat over in his hand and dropped it in front of her.

"Fine, thanks." Sandra smiled at him. "We're busy, you know yourself."

"Make that two, will you, Charlie?" Dermot came up behind Sandra and sat up on a stool alongside her.

"Mind if we head into the snug?" she asked and he shook his head.

He paid and took the pints, one in each hand, and followed her in.

She sat as Dermot put the pints down and pulled the old sliding wooden door across. "Thanks for the pint and for today," she said, lifting her glass when he had slid in opposite her, and they clinked.

"No bother at all. You okay now, Sandy?"

She nodded. His eyes were so kind. Sometimes she thought that Dermot had the right idea: single, no kids, no mortgage and free as a bird. He lived in the hotel-owned cottage beyond the stables. She remembered talking to Dermot in Hines, just after she got serious with Neil, about how in love with him she was and about marriage. His eyes had clouded over and he had told her she was mad. He had actually walked away on her and left Hines early. Marriage was not for Dermot, she had guessed.

"Ah, things are just tough, really tough, but I'll be fine," she said. "I'm just being a bit overly sensitive at the minute." She reached up and tugged the bobbin from her tight bun and shook her black hair out. It fell perfectly straight and she ran her fingers through her fringe.

"I'm here anyhow if ya ever need to unload again – and don't worry – anything you tell me goes no further. Well, I might tell Midnight but that'd be it."

She laughed. Midnight was his much-loved black horse. At seventeen hands he was terrifying, Sandra thought.

"Actually, there's a thought," he said. "Why don't you come up to the yard in the morning for a lesson? You're always saying you'd like to learn. You've been telling me for bloody years that you'd love to have a go. I know you'd love it. There's nothing like it to clear your head." He pushed his blond hair from his eyes.

"Jesus, Dermot, it's one thing saying it but the thought of getting up on a horse scares the living daylights out of me – besides, I haven't the time to shave my legs these days let alone horse-ride!"

"Lovely, thanks for that!" He made a face of disgust. "You seem to have time to swim in the mornings, though, and this is better for yer head. It's the fresh air you need – you're pale under that lovely brown skin of yours." He took a long drink from his pint.

"How did you know I swim in the mornings? Are you spyin' on me in my sexy spotty Penney's cossy?" She was genuinely shocked that he had seen her swim as she had never seen him in there.

He winked at her. "Some pins on you, I can tell you that much!"

She laughed out loud. It had been a long time since she had received a compliment and she enjoyed it. "I dunno, Dermot." She took a long drink from the cold fizzy beer. "What's it all about? Where do the years go? What happens to fun and freedom? I used to have fun, I used to laugh. I used to get drunk and dance to cheesy Kylie hits."

Dermot leaned in close to her and she could smell the mix of mild aftershave and beer from him. "It's a life choice, Sandy. Society tells us we will only be happy when we're married and have kids and a mortgage. It doesn't say that we have to be married to the right person or there's no point to it. It just says do it regardless or you will be miserable. It says that single people are lonely and sad and unfulfilled and that's just not true."

She nodded as she looked at him. His eyes sparkled back at her and his floppy blond hair fell over one of his eyes. "You're right, Dermot, I suppose I always did feel like I had to get married and have kids . . ." She trailed off and picked up her pint. "Aah, just like you said, the marriage bit, *paha*!" She waved her hand in the air and checked her watch.

Dermot was nodding. "I can't say I felt I had to do it when it wasn't totally right," he said. "I always knew I was a free spirit. I adore my sister's two kids but I don't think family life will be for me. I don't think . . . I did . . . well, not now anyway . . ."

"What if you had met someone you just couldn't live without? What then?" she pushed him.

"What? Just like when you told me that Friday night in here that you could never live without Neil Darragh?" He stared right at her.

"Point taken." She picked up her pint and looked into it, the tiny bubbles racing each other to the top. Just like sperm, she thought.

Their silence was a comfortable one until Dermot broke it.

"So, why don't you come down to the yard in the morning before work? Wear a pair of leggings or jeggings or whatever it is you call them these days and I will sort you out. If you hate it I won't ask you again. Deal?" He drained his pint and put his glass down with a bang.

"Okay. Deal," she said, "but go easy on me now! No ride-'em-cowgirl or any of that danger-devil stuff!"

Dermot grinned. "I'll have ya in Jordan's horsey gear in a few months."

Sandra tilted her head to one side, pretended to shift a massive bosom but more in a Les Dawson way and winked at him. They laughed, easy in one another's company.

"Can I get you another drink?" a lounge girl asked them.

"No, thank you," Sandra told her.

When Dermot also shook his head, the girl left them alone again.

Sandra turned to Dermot. "As much as I'd love another drink, I'd better not. The house is in a state and I need to talk to Neil. I can't run away from my problems either. Thanks though, Dermot, I really needed that pint – and see you in the morning so – giddy-up, shave a bullock and all that jazz!" She drained her drink and stood up. Leaning her hand on his shoulder, she squeezed it hard before she left the snug.

She pushed open the bar door and made her way into the chilly night. She was glad of the walk. The beer had gone to her head but she supposed she hadn't eaten any lunch with all the crying. Dermot hadn't asked her any questions and she was glad. He was just there for her, as always, a true friend. Dermot could have his pick of lots of the single girls in the village, she knew that. Tara who ran the salon adored him and she was sure that something was going on there. She never asked. She wasn't nosy.

She waved at Tiffney who was in the doorway of O'Dwyer's Shop & Post Office buying turf. She passed the loft tea rooms and thought of how she'd love a warm scone and a tea and an *OK!* magazine for an hour and a natter with The Apple.

Neil would be in bed again watching DVDs no doubt. She was at a loss as to what to do but thought she'd try and talk to him again this evening, so she upped her pace.

Be brave, Sandra, she told herself. You need to find out the truth. Whether you like it or not.

* * *

Sandra knocked on the bedroom door as it was silent inside this time, the much hated surround sound blissfully quiet.

"Yeah?" came the voice of her husband.

"Neil? Can I come in?"

"It's your room. Why are you asking?"

She gently pushed down the skinny chrome handle and opened the door.

She immediately felt like retching. The smell in the room was a dead giveaway of where he had been all day.

"Jesus, Neil, the smell of drink and aftershave in here!" She put her hand over her mouth and pushed open the window.

"Close it!" he shouted.

She flicked on the light. His eyes were glazed and he was pissed. He could barely keep his bloodshot eyes open.

"What's going on, Neil? Please, love, talk to me?"

The bed that they had jumped up and down on the day they moved in was alien to her now. The bed they had spooned in at night and made love in every morning following the move.

"Neil, I know we're going through a bad patch. I was thinking maybe we could go and see someone – you know, a professional – maybe they could help us?" She tried to touch him but he moved away.

"Leave me alone, Bill Cullen!" he sniggered now as he pulled the pillow over his head.

"What? What does that mean?" she asked, confused.

"I will talk to you tomorrow, I promise. I'm wrecked now and I really cannot take another second of your nagging." His muffled voice was barely audible to her.

"Neil! I need to talk to you! Take the pillow off your face, please?" she shouted.

"Get out!" he shouted back, throwing the pillow onto the floor and turning his head to face her. "Seriously, you are wrecking my head. I need you to get away from me, please, just leave me alone for a bit, will ya? I need some space!"

His glazed eyes told her a hundred different things. What had he been up to all day? Who had he been drinking with? She stood her ground.

"Neil, please, this can't go on. We have to talk!" she pleaded.

"Ah, man, will you ever stop talking? Just get out, Bill!" He turned over and put his face into his pillow, roaring laughing now, his body shaking.

He was too drunk to talk to now. She sat on the edge of the bed and called his name. He wouldn't answer.

"Bill Cullen?" She repeated his words aloud. Oh, right – he

was trying to say she was ambitious like the self-made millionaire Bill Cullen? Didn't he understand she was working all the hours God sent for *them*? For this home?

"Asshole," she whispered to herself as she made her way out of the room but not before quickly grabbing his jacket and jeans as she left.

Chapter 6

Cara was glad to get into bed with her notes, a cup of tea and the top layer of a box of Milk Tray which she had bought in O'Dwyer's on the way home. She had seen Tiffney in there buying her turf and Sandra passing by. It really was a small village. It was so pretty and the locals were all so friendly. It was just the type of place she had always wanted to live. It was idyllic. She thanked her lucky stars she had been offered this job. At long last things were starting to turn for her. Esther had been over the moon for her. Proud of her. It was a wonderful feeling.

Now she wanted to focus on the wedding that was coming up and the big wedding anniversary party next year. She really wanted to impress Jonathan. He'd been so great to her, never once breathing down her neck but just letting her get on with it. He was so calm and relaxed. He had also set her up with her own email address – hospitalitymanager@themoritz.ie – and she was thrilled with it. He had even given her a small laptop and now she was set up in the back office and felt even more official. Next week she was going to order some business cards. Jonathan said she could design them herself and the hotel would pay to print them. Her fabulous briefcase even had a pocket for business cards.

She popped a hazelnut swirl into her mouth. She'd gone a bit heavy on the Elizabeth Arden 8 Hour Cream and the smell was really overpowering her taste buds. "Hmm, true what they say," she said aloud. "Smell really is taste. Won't stop me from eating them all though." She laughed and caught her reflection in the new bedroom mirror at the end of the bed. She sucked the chocolate hard to reach the hazelnut. She looked at herself in the mirror for a few minutes. Then she nodded at herself and went back to her notes. She was going to do her darned best to get Phyllis's family back home for this wedding anniversary party. She jotted the numbers Phyllis had given her into her book. They had compiled quite a good list and she was going to call every individual in the coming days to confirm existing addresses before she went shopping with Phyllis for the invitations. The older couple lived in Dublin and had only another four days' break in the Moritz before they went back, so she had a lot to do. They deserved a fabulous party. What would it be like to be with someone for that long, to share every day and night of your lives for fifty-five years? To be that comfortable with another person? She felt like that around Esther but that wasn't what she meant. She popped a strawberry chocolate into her mouth without looking, bit into it and put it straight back into the box. That was one good thing about living alone, she mused as she took up another hazelnut swirl – you could spit the strawberry creams back into the box. She was turning into her mother. She laughed quietly to herself now. She had booked in the party in for the end of January so she had some time to play around with. She would look into the fashions in fabrics and furnishings around the date of their wedding. It would be great to see some old photos of their day and try to recreate some of that look. She flicked the heavy quilt away with her foot and wrote some ideas down for the upcoming wedding – she did not have so much time on this one. She liked the idea of crystals and white beading. She wanted the Brophy-Burrows wedding to be a great success.

Her own wedding had been a great success. The three people there had all told her so. Pity she spent the entire evening in the bathroom bawling her eyes out.

* * *

"I don't say this easily, believe me, Cara, but I am falling for you, really falling for you." Alex Charles looked into her eyes as they sat holding hands over a small intimate candlelit dinner in the Unicorn restaurant.

She blushed as her heart began to race. It had been such a whirlwind. In the last few months since he got home from Dubai he had wined her and dined her. Alex Charles had literally swept her off her feet. He was so romantic and sometimes she felt she hadn't time to catch her breath he was so close. He was completely smitten with her, of that she had no doubt.

He rubbed his soft thumbs across her hands repeatedly.

"Alex," she whispered, "this is mental, isn't it, but I feel exactly the same way."

She twirled the diamond earrings in her ears, a present from Dubai. She wore an emerald green shirt with tight white skinny jeans and green wedges, her red hair piled high in a messy bun on the top of her head. She felt really beautiful for the first time in her life when she was with him. She was crazy in love with him; how could she not be?

His piercing blue eyes lit up and he leaned across the table and kissed her full on the mouth. He was the type of man she had always fantasised about. She had never had a man in her life like this. She had dated of course, but this relationship was so intense. He was so powerful and manly and real husband material. He was so protective of her. A real gentleman: he pulled out her chair before he sat, he opened doors for her, he sent her flowers, he complimented her at every opportunity.

She had begun to think she might never get married. Of course she wanted a life, and one with children, but she was a realist. She wasn't getting any younger. She also had her mam to think of and, although Esther told her again and again to get out and get her own place, she wasn't comfortable with leaving Esther on her own. Although her mother was only sixty-nine she was old beyond her years and vulnerable in so many ways. Anyway, Cara liked living with her mam and wanted to look after her. They got on so well and enjoyed each other's company.

But now Alex had come along and she was head over heels in

love with him. He made her feel like she was the most unique woman in the world. The sex had been amazing, still was. The night after O'Donoghue's they had made love. Drunk on G&Ts and adrenalin. She hadn't ideally wanted it to happen on the first date, of course, but it had. They had gone back to his hotel room at the Shelbourne and the chemistry had engulfed them. He had opened the door for her and she had gone in ahead but stopped and put her back to the wardrobe. He closed the door, dropped the key card on the table and turned to face her, the room only illuminated by the street lamps surrounding St Stephen's Green. Their bodies seemed to close together like two exceptionally powerful magnets. The passion was mind-blowing. He had an incredibly toned and muscled body and was tanned and taut. Cara ate up every second with him and was in seventh heaven. She pulled her T-shirt over her head and he groaned as he felt her breast roughly, then unclipped her bra as his head fell to taste. She arched her back as she unzipped her denim skirt and wriggled out of it.

He raised her arms above her head and held them there as he stared at her body. "You are so perfect. No other man will ever be here again," he whispered to her as he lifted her up and she wrapped her legs around him. They made love hard and fast and noisily standing up against the wardrobe.

As they lay in bed afterwards, cocooned in each other's arms, she knew that it was something different this time. This was no one-night stand. The way he looked down at her face and smoothed her skin with his hand. She knew this was special.

"I'm suddenly jealous of every other boyfriend you have ever had – I hate them all!" Alex laughed and kissed her gently on the mouth over and over.

"There haven't been many." She kissed him back. "What about you? Have you been in many serious relationships?"

"No, not really. I have always been too busy and too focused on getting my career going. I have never been in love, well . . . before . . ." and he whistled out loud as though to stop himself from saying another word.

Cara's heart skipped a beat and she nestled into his warm chest. His smell was incredible. She wished she could bottle this moment. Open the bottle and feel and smell this very second whenever she wanted to. The chemistry was intoxicating. She didn't want the moment to pass. She took a long deep breath and sighed quietly.

"Do you want to shower first?" he asked, breaking the silence.

She was just falling into a wonderful cosy sleep. "Ah no, thank you, I'm okay." She nuzzled deep into his chest again.

"Really?" He sat up on one elbow, cradling his head in his hand.

She moved and sat up too.

"You don't shower after sex?" he asked.

Suddenly she felt a bit dirty and very awkward. "No, of course I am, I mean I do, I always do – I was just nodding off there, sorry."

"No worries," he said, pulling the covers off her.

She slid out of the bed and padded naked into the en suite, aware of his eyes boring holes into the back of her. She closed the door behind her and looked at her burning red face in the mirror. She reached in and turned the dial to red on the shower. That had been embarrassing to say the least.

She stood under the strong jets and thought about the night. Madness. However, she couldn't get over how attracted to him she was. She rubbed the hotel shower gel all over her body. What would happen next? He obviously thought she was gross not hopping straight into the shower. Did this mean he had one-night stands all the time? Was she falling for ridiculous one-liners when she had never ever done before? She supposed she really should get dressed and go – that's the way it went, wasn't it? Was she reading too much into it? Maybe the shower idea had been to get her out of the room. Of course it had! He hadn't actually asked her to stay the night. How could she be so stupid?

She quickly dried off and rolled her hair up into a high knot. She opened the bathroom door and immediately heard his snores. She glanced around the wardrobe and sure enough he was fast asleep. She pulled on her clothes which were all in one messy pile by the door, grabbed her bag, found her shoes and closed the door behind her as gently as possible.

Chapter 7

Sandra wasn't sure she'd get used to the smell of horses so early in the morning. It was a bit too stinky for her liking. Dermot was tacking up Bolto as she stood by the door watching him.

"Now this fella is as quiet as a lamb. I promise you he will take care of you so don't worry – he'll show you what to do. He'll follow Midnight of his own accord."

He expertly double-clicked his tongue on the roof of his mouth and the small brown horse obediently followed him out of the stable, shavings flying up behind him. He had a white stripe down the centre of his nose and it reminded Sandra of icing on a brownie.

"Lorna? Lorna!" Dermot shouted. "Get Midnight out of the box for me, will ya?"

Lorna popped her head out from inside one of the stables and shouted back, "Sure, Dermot, just putting a new salt lick in for Bubbles!" Seconds later she led his big horse out.

Sandra had never been this close to Midnight and she was terrified. "Holy Mother, Dermot, he's so massive!" Her mouth fell open.

"Yeah, he's my big baby all right. I broke him in myself so he's all mine. Like I said to you in Hines, I tell him everything. He has a book in him, this fella." The horse threw its head and whinnied as Dermot rubbed his nose hard. "He's a bit fresh so don't mind his carry-on. Now I want you to put these on."

He handed her a back-protector which she put on carefully, pulling the straps tight. Then she strapped the hat on – it was slightly too big.

"Now put one foot in the stirrup and over you go," he said, fastening the strap of his own hat under his chin.

"Eh, Dermot, I have never been on a horse in my life – is there not an easier way to break me in gently? Fork lift, perhaps? How am I supposed to get my foot up there?"

"Get up, Sandy!" He held Bolto's rein tight and she put one foot into the silver stirrup. He placed his hand firmly under her bottom and pushed her up.

She managed to throw her leg over and plopped down with a bump.

"Now find your other stirrup," he said.

She did and he adjusted the length of them. Then he showed her how to hold the reins. It felt wonderful. He was right. It felt exhilarating. She felt like she was twenty feet tall.

"Thanks, Lorna!" he called after the stable hand as she left, dragging a pitch fork along the gravel and making an awful sound.

Dermot hopped up on his horse easily and with a soft kick of his heels Midnight threw his head round and danced on the spot before moving into a slow walk. As Dermot had promised her, Bolto followed the larger horse obediently. Sandra held on tightly as they walked slowly out into the sand ring. This was so freeing. The morning was just breaking and the floodlights were on in the ring. The sand looked a soft yellow under the artificial light.

Dermot turned back to her. "You okay?"

"Perfect!" she shouted back, tipping the too-large hat back up out of her eyes. She was holding on tight with her hands and legs. She would pay for this tomorrow, she guessed.

As they walked Dermot came back and his horse fell into step beside hers. "Today is just about getting the feel for the horse. Getting to know your own seat and enjoy the experience. I will teach you then all the technical bits of how to ride properly, about being on the right leg, about the craft and we can go on hacks and you'll love it."

She nodded and they walked on for a while.

"How was Neil when you got home last night then?" he suddenly said.

"Awful," she confided. "He was pissed again, Dermot. He's up to something, I know he is. He needs a job badly to keep him on the straight and narrow."

There had been no sign of Neil's mobile phone in either the jeans or jacket she had taken to search, so he had been sober enough to remember to hide it. She had discreetly opened the bedroom door later that night and thrown them back in onto the floor.

Dermot digested what she had said and chose to ignore the 'up to something' comment, though Sandra noted he looked uncomfortable.

"What about that despicable poser brother of his – Tom? Can't he help out, give him a few days' work in that poncy clothes shop of his?"

"No, I called him already and he had absolutely no interest in our situation whatsoever."

"Is Neil mad? Sorry, Sandra – I mean, what do I know, it's nothing to do with me, is it?"

The two men had never been friendly. "I don't know, Dermot, maybe he is mad. I honestly don't know. The going to bed every time he walks in the door just means he wants to be as far away from me as possible because I can smell perfume a mile off and because he doesn't care enough to run straight to the shower."

Dermot looked straight between Midnight's pricked-forward ears.

"I have been so caught up in my own world too, though, since I took on the full-time position at the hotel and we have had . . . well, we have tried . . ." She coughed now but wanted to go on. "Well, we have had issues getting pregnant – we've been doing IVF and I suppose it has taken over our, well, *my* life in a way. To be honest, Dermot, I can't really remember the last time I talked to Neil properly." She was glad the words were out but felt awful for betraying Neil's trust. He had begged her never to tell anyone they were doing IVF.

Dermot just nodded. "So I'm presuming it didn't work, the baby-medicine stuff?" he asked softly.

"No, it didn't." She shook her head and the hat fell over her eyes again.

"Do you think he's depressed over that?"

She pushed the hat up. "You know, I don't, I really don't think he cared too much either way. It was mainly me. I really wanted . . . I still really want . . . a baby . . ."

"At any cost? And I don't mean financial?" Dermot pulled up Midnight and Bolto halted too. The floodlights from the arena shone brightly in Dermot's face. His blond hair was blowing under the back of the hat.

Sandra paused and thought about his question. "Yeah, maybe."

Dermot clicked and they were off. They rode in silence for a few minutes. She felt she was getting some sort of hang of it.

"See what happens with time, I suppose," he said then. "There's not much else you can do and maybe things will work themselves out soon enough, what?"

He looked at her and she plastered a smile on her face.

"Yeah, I'm sure you're right." She pulled at Bolto's reins. "So a question I suppose I should have asked ages ago . . . where are the brakes? Like, how do I make him stop?"

* * *

Cara took her seat at her laptop in the back office. Sandra wasn't yet on reception and she wanted some quiet time before the other woman's start. The scent of Sandra's perfume filled the small office, not overpowering but sweet. Like grapefruit. Jo Malone, she guessed. She too had bought into the Jo Malone hype until it just became too expensive to condone.

She had to make a lot of decisions today with the wedding couple, Jenny and Max. She wanted this wedding to be a sign of things to come. She wanted to talk to Jenny and then Jonathan about using it as a tool for the new website. She had spoken to Mr Paul Power at The Park Studios in Dublin and they were willing to come and take some video clips for a really reasonable price to embed into the site. They had a wonderful reputation so she was thrilled. She knew the Moritz website needed a better wedding page and a video of a wonderful Christmas wedding would bring in many more bookings, she knew. She also wanted the day to look fantastic and for Jenny and Max to give them a rave review for the site. She was meeting with them at ten this morning to finalise monies and get stuck into details. She had priced the crystals and beading via a wedding website that morning, she had emailed Louise in the village about making the wedding cake, and she had priced four bands that she wanted the couple to take a look at. Then there was the wine and champagne. They would do a taste this morning before they met with Delphine the chef and try some sample dishes that she had made for them. She was presenting a variety of options and Cara knew they would all be of the highest quality.

Yes, her list for this morning's meeting was long.

She decided to go to the staff room and pour herself a large coffee first. Jonathan was already in there.

"Good morning, Cara! Lovely morning, isn't it?" he said cheerfully.

"Morning, Jonathan, it is – cold though." She smiled at him as she made straight for the coffee pot.

"It's nice, strong. Mrs Reilly put it on this morning for us. You're in early?"

He leaned against the wall, his red Nestlé coffee mug in hand, his black suit and white shirt crisp and very professional-looking. He looked every inch a hotel manager, she thought.

"Yeah, I have a meeting with the wedding clients and I want to make sure I'm up to scratch." She added some cream.

"I'm sure you will be. Do you need me for anything?" He was blowing into his cup now, short raspy blows.

She had to ask. "How is that too hot? The temperature of that coffee machine is always so perfect – it's why I love it so much. Top of the range, Big Bob tells me every time he pours a coffee."

"Ah, it's a habit I picked up from the hotel I worked at in London. I'd always put my coffee in the microwave. I'm afraid we didn't have as good a machine there. I never even taste things any more – just reach for the micro. I have to stop."

She smiled and sipped her coffee, enjoying the Robusta flavour.

"Actually I wanted to talk to you about an idea I have for the hotel website?"

"Sure, drop up to me in my office later?"

She nodded.

"How is Mr Peter's cottage working out for you?" he asked.

"It's good, yeah. I have a lot to do to make it homely but I'm really happy."

"Oh, yeah? What's he got you doing, the old miser?"

She laughed. "Ah, he's fine – he basically said I could decorate it any way I wanted."

"Yeah, I'll bet he did. I've been on at him to do that place up before I agreed to put it on my accommodation list for the hotel staff. Listen, let me help. Let me give you some of the hotel supplies we have in the storage room – paint, brushes and that. And I can lend some muscle if you like?"

She was suddenly shy and slightly breathless.

"Well, when I say muscle . . ." he made a feeble attempt to squeeze his biceps, "I mean I can lend a hand." He dropped his arm, extended his free hand and winked at her.

"Honestly, that's not necessary, I can manage on my own . . . I . . ." Then she stopped herself. "Actually, Jonathan, thank you, I'd really appreciate the help."

"Sure thing – let me get my diary and we can see when we can do it."

"Excuse me, please, Mr Redmond?" Tiffney leaned over the reception desk on her tippy-toes and called in. "I need to ask you to come and look at the dish of the day – there are two choices and Chef is in one of her mean morning moods."

"Later so?" Jonathan said to Cara, then picked up his red cup and made his way out to Tiffney.

Cara was pleased with herself. Jonathan was a lovely man

and she had to learn to move forward. She wanted to make new friends and start afresh.

* * *

"Delivery!" Steve shouted through to the kitchen. "There's a delivery man here for a Miss Cara Byrne! Anyone know a Miss Cara Byrne?" he joked.

Cara wiped her hands on her red chequered apron and pushed the door open with her foot. There stood a man holding the biggest bouquet of red roses she had ever seen in her life. It covered his entire upper body. She could feel the rush of blood to her cheeks as the bar went quiet. Curious regular customers on the bar stools craned their necks to get a better look. Aoife and Hanja oohed and ahhed.

"Thanks," she muttered as she shakily signed her name on the electronic pad. She fled to the back storeroom with the roses and removed the card. *"Dear Cara, I so hope we can see each other again. Sorry I was so jet-lagged! I had a fantastic time. Please, please, call me. Alex. xxx"* She was so flattered. No one had ever sent her flowers in her life. Wait until Esther got a load of these! She smelled one after another as she twisted the massive bouquet in her hands. His mobile number was written clear and concise once again so there would be no messing up any digits. She still had the original piece of paper folded neatly on her bookshelf in her bedroom.

She ran water in the old paint-splattered sink and gently stood the flowers up in it. Then she returned to the bar, her face less flushed now.

"Hmm, someone musta had a good night?" Steve teased but she could tell he was a bit put out.

"Who are they from?" Aoife pushed her stud back into her nose as Cara just waved her question away.

The bar was really busy.

"We need mixers quick and the bar's a foot deep so I can't move to get them," Steve said.

Glad of the job, Cara grabbed the large bunch of keys off

him. She had thought Alex would like to see her again but you could never really tell, could you? It had been over two weeks since she had left him in that hotel room but she knew he was in Dubai so didn't worry too much. But the whole shower episode rattled around in her head and she didn't quite know what to make of it. Was it odd or perfectly normal? It didn't really sit right with her but it wasn't the type of question she could ever ask Esther either.

Esther had been peeping out her bedroom net curtains as Cara arrived home in a taxi the night of the Shelbourne episode.

"All I want to know is, were ya with the pilot?" she called down the stairs, rollers studded through her hair.

"Yes," Cara hissed back up. "Now get back into bed, Mam!"

"I'll sleep well tonight so." Her mother closed her bedroom door quietly but Cara could hear her laughing.

Cara grabbed a box of mixers and hoisted it up onto her knee and then onto her shoulder. Her heart was beating fast and she felt great. He must really like her. Alex Charles must really like Black Magic.

* * *

"Do you never wear trousers then?" Alex asked casually as they strolled up a busy Grafton Street towards the Gaiety Theatre.

She suddenly felt very self-conscious as she had debated on whether or not the H&M blue skirt had been a little short. She pulled at it now.

"Oh, I mean, it's a great little skirt – it's just I never really understand how women in relationships can still go out in tiny skirts. Oh shit, that sounded so bad! I don't for one second mean us, mean you . . . oh, please, tell me you know what I mean?" Alex was blushing now and Cara stopped him just at the top of the street.

"It's fine, Alex, really, and I do understand. In fact I wasn't sure about this skirt myself this evening. My wardrobe isn't great. In fact, I ran out during my lunch break up to Henry Street and grabbed this."

"No, Cara, please, you don't need to explain. The skirt's amazing on you. I guess I'm just a really old-fashioned guy. Sorry. Sometimes I speak before I think." He pulled her in close now and his body was taut against hers as his lips found her mouth.

He smelt of Joop aftershave and cigarettes. She wasn't really one for public displays of affection but for some reason when she was with Alex she just wanted to please him all the time. She found his physical presence so intoxicating. They kissed long and hard opposite the doors to the St Stephen's Green Centre as passersby stared.

They had spent every weekend together since his return from Dubai. He had been on dailies to the UK since and he was due to return to long haul soon.

"I'm going to miss you so much," he mumbled.

He pulled at her hand now and they continued towards the theatre.

Cara wasn't really looking forward to the next two and a half hours if she was really honest. Opera wasn't her thing. *Fidelio* wasn't on her list of things she wanted to see.

"Alex!"

The leggy blonde air-kissed him as Cara stood in the background on the steps up to the theatre. "How fantastic to see you! It's been forever. How have you been?"

Cara took in her open fur wrap and tailored white trouser suit with massive pearl earrings and black stilettos. She was so polished, so chic.

"Hi, Glenda! All good, thanks, and what about you?" Alex responded.

"Oh, same old same old, darling! I'm still company manager with Roctas Modern Dance Company, been touring Berlin, heading to NY in the morning. You must catch a show soon? Dying for this production of *Fidelio*, aren't you? Their *Rigoletto* was simply out of this world. *Stunnnnnnning*!"

Glenda leaned in close to Alex and Cara shifted uncomfortably. Alex didn't seem to notice.

"Are you here alone?" Glenda asked.

"Em, no, no," Alex wrung his hands together, "I'm with my friend." He turned and his eyes found Cara's as she stepped forward.

Glenda looked her up and down. "Hello, I'm Glenda Woodcock, how nice to meet you."

"I'm Cara, and yes, same here." Cara wanted to run. She felt so awkward and didn't really know why. She tugged hard at her skirt.

Alex reached for her hand and led her to the doors as people spilled in all around them.

"I haven't seen Beth in so long . . . not since all the stuff . . . you know . . .?" Glenda was still alongside them as Alex handed their tickets over to the usher.

"Oh, really?" said Alex.

Clearly he didn't want to talk about this Beth, Cara thought – or perhaps it was just that he wanted to discourage Glenda?

They made their way into the auditorium and suddenly Glenda was lost in the crowd.

"Sorry about that," Alex whispered into her ear. "An old friend of someone's, I don't really know her too well, ex-model turned company manager, knows everyone." He squeezed her hand.

They found their seats and Alex sat back and read the programme. Cara pretended to read it along with him. As the lights went down and the music started and surrounded her, she found herself drifting. Opera definitely wasn't her thing. She hadn't a bloody clue what was going on. One minute someone was happily singing and the next it seemed some tragedy had occurred, only she didn't have the foggiest idea what it was. Try, she urged herself and sat forward on the red velvet seat. She couldn't: her mind was all over the place. Alex's friends were absolutely nothing like hers. Were she and Alex the right match, she wondered? What you really mean is, are you good enough for him, a little grinding voice echoed in her head. She shifted in her seat and Alex placed his hand gently on her thigh – to stop her fidgeting, no doubt.

She sat back and tried to relax. She was thinking way too far ahead.

Chapter 8

Sandra sat in Louise's with a guest's left-behind copy of *U* magazine and a hot chocolate. She flicked the pages as she sipped her drink. Young Irish models stared back at her, posing in great couture gowns. Louise hovered around, whistling as she cleaned tables and served. Sandra just couldn't face going home yet.

She had cooked again last night when she got in from work – his favourite Irish coddle – and called him to come down. He had come down after a while, starving no doubt, and tried to be friendly to her.

"How was work?" he'd asked as he spooned some hot gravy from the coddle into his mouth.

"Fine." She'd looked at him.

"What?" he'd asked. "Why do you keep staring at me, Sandra?"

She couldn't bring herself to say the words.

"Look, I'm sorry I'm so narky – it's just this hanging around with no work is killing me." He coughed and put his spoon down, gravy spraying over the glass table. "In fact, I'm thinking I might have to go up to Dublin again this weekend and see if I can make any new contacts."

The rain came down and pelted off the skylight, the only noise between them.

"Whatever." She'd pushed back her seat and tried to swallow the lump in her throat.

"Want anything with that, hun?" Louise's voice broke into her thoughts.

Louise slipped into the empty brown-leather-backed chair beside her.

"Ah, I don't think so, Louise, thanks."

"Everything okay?" the older woman asked as she rearranged the white matching salt and pepper set on the table. She pushed up the drooping end-of-day fresh flowers in their cream vase with its logo of two entwined letter L's for Louise's Loft.

"If only!" Sandra sighed.

"I'm always a good pair of ears, you know that," Louise said, lowering her voice to a whisper.

Sandra nodded. "I know that only too well, Louise."

"Are you trying for another round?" Louise slid her hand over Sandra's.

Another round. The dreaded IVF. She remembered the days when another round meant a round at the bar! She almost wished that was her only problem right now. "No, I think I'm done." She shook her head. "It's Neil . . . he's . . . well, I'm not sure but . . ." She dabbed her finger into the pink marshmallow on the side of her plate.

"Oh no, chicken, do you mean what I think you mean?" Louise asked.

Sandra had confided in Louise the last time and the older woman had been amazing. "Well, yeah, but like I say I have no proof . . . I'm only guessing really . . . and to top all that off we are flat broke. I spent every penny we had on the family home and the two rounds of IVF and now we have no money, not a smelly cent. We're in debt. I'm working every hour God sends but Neil doesn't appreciate my efforts. I think he wants out, Louise." The words tumbled past each other now. "We have no marriage to speak of any more, no money and we still have no baby."

Louise squeezed her hand. "He's a bad one, Sandra, if he's doing this to you again. But you need to find out for sure. You've both been through so much, but you in particular. Confront him, it's the only way. I know I told you before that we all make mistakes – I felt his pride was wounded over the IVF. But to do it twice is not on, you know that, love?" Louise's kind eyes were serious.

Sandra didn't think Neil was in the state he was in over the baby, not for a second. She drained the chocolate as Louise got up to serve Cara who had just come in. She carried her empty mug up to the counter and smiled at Cara as she left. She hadn't spoken to Cara much and she felt bad about that but she just had no time lately.

She strolled slowly over the bridge and walked down towards the estate. Funny, she thought as she stopped to let some loud American tourists take their photos, she hadn't thought about her baby in weeks now. The first time in so long. She always said 'her baby' even though there had never been a baby. There had been a pregnancy though. A very brief one. The pregnancy she had longed so much for. Her mouth quivered as she tried to smile her best friendly 'top o' the mornin'' Irish smile at the tourists. Knocknoly needed these tourists and so did the Moritz.

She heard a Vespa pulling into the estate over the hill as she crossed the field. It must be Neil – he possessed the only Vespa on the estate. She would ask him outright after dinner. Sandra wouldn't be a doormat any longer.

Chapter 9

Cara hung up the phone and sat back relieved. She had just finalised the menu with Jenny who was delighted with the final choices. The starter was a homemade vegetable soup or filo prawns in a sweet brandy sauce. For mains it was a thirty-two-day-aged sirloin of tender Aberdeen Angus steak, served with a Béarnaise sauce, skinny fries and roasted tomatoes, accompanied by sides of tender-stem broccoli and spinach with garlic and lemon – or Salmon Teriyaki served with grilled bok choi, ginger, chilli and coriander shoots with jasmine rice – or the vegetarian options of a Tofu Teriyaki served with the same grilled bok choi, ginger and chilli on a bed of jasmine rice, or a mushroom-and-pea risotto. Cara had pushed Jenny on a traditional dessert selection of Christmas pudding with custard or a Crème Brulé. Cara thought it was a great seasonal menu suited to this couple and their guests.

Jenny seemed to be handling everything on her own and it was a lot. Max had come to the hotel last week to meet with her and Cara had found him to be very pleasant but a little under Jenny's thumb. He had spent most of the time sipping his red wine, relaxing and checking sports results on his iPhone.

"So, Max," she had pointed to the menu samples, "I won't keep you much longer, I promise. We're just looking at some samples Chef has put together if you would –" He had cut her off.

"Listen, it's just a bit of grub – whatever she wants is grand by me, Cara. I'm happy if she's happy."

At that Jenny had stood up and thrown her cream leather bag over her shoulder. "Thanks, Cara. I'll ring you during the week."

The two had left, Max shrugging his massive shoulders at Cara as they disappeared out the door.

Jenny definitely wore the trousers in that relationship. Good for her, Cara thought.

She had begun to compose an email to thank Delphine for all her hard work and confirm the menu when Jonathan entered her office.

"Cara, I'm going to need you to go on a conference for couple of nights. You know what the Americans are like – they want us involved in all these conferences. They're hosting a large one and I'd like you to go for us. I'm just waiting on the date. I'm not sure what exactly is going on but they seem a bit on edge. Can you manage that okay?"

"Sure." Cara twisted her hands together. "Once it's after the wedding that should be fine. The anniversary isn't until the last Saturday in January."

He was running his fingers over the mirror in the back office. "Seriously, Sandra's make-up powder stuff gets everywhere. What does she do? Shake it around the place before she puts it on? Sandra really doesn't need to wear that much make-up – she's way prettier without. Actually, I might need her to go on the conference trip too. It might be an idea to put up a local notice in Louise's for some temp staff over Christmas and New Year, what do you think? There are a few locals we use – they'll reply if they're interested."

He approached her now. He came right up to within inches of her face and gently pulled a small piece of paper from her hair. "Paper." He flicked it away.

Cara stiffened. "N-no problem, I c-can do that," she stuttered back at him as the bell at reception rang out and Jonathan left the office.

* * *

When Sandra arrived home Neil was outside, down on his leather-clad knees locking up his bike. The leathers were always a bad sign. It was only a Vespa after all not a Harley Davidson.

"Hi ya, Neil!" Sandra called out to him as she put her key in the hall door.

"Hey, how's things, love?" He pulled his retro helmet off, put it under his arm and followed her inside.

She looked around the hall. "Did you put the washing on the radiators?" She felt the clothes which were still damp. All his clothes.

"Yeah, this afternoon." He balanced the helmet on the knob of the banister.

"Why?" She turned to him.

"Why? Because it was in the machine and I dunno but I guessed it wasn't going to dry in there all by itself," he answered her, too quickly and too smartly. Defence.

"You need something dried?" She kept her focus.

He shuffled from one foot to the other. "Yeah, like I told you, I need a few bits if I'm going to Dublin for the weekend. I need a job, love, you know that." He took her hands.

"Of course you do – silly me." She couldn't do it. She just couldn't face it yet.

"Anything for dinner? I'd eat a scabby man's leg," he asked.

It was the first time in God knows how long she hadn't left out a prepared evening meal for the two of them.

"I'm afraid not. I keep cooking and it keeps going in the bin. I hate wasting good food that we can ill afford. There are tins of beans and fresh bread in the press – that's about the height of it. I'm going up for a shower." She pulled her hands away.

"It will be okay, Sandra, I'll get sorted. Things are all a bit mad right now but I will sort it."

He made his way down to the kitchen and she watched him reach up and open the press and pull out two tins of beans.

"Take your time!" he called from the kitchen. "I'll heat these up and pour us a glass of wine. At least we can still afford wine, I see."

She climbed a few steps of the stairs then halted but continued to make the sound of footsteps, gradually trailing off. Then she stood perfectly still, feeling really ridiculous. His coat was hanging up and she tip-toed back down the few stairs and over to it. She pushed her hand deep into his pocket. She felt around and froze. Her hand gripped his mobile tightly. She heard him slam the kitchen drawer as he read out the ingredients on the tin to himself like he always did. She grabbed the phone and pushed it deep into the leg of her high brown-suede boots. Her heart was racing. She didn't care if he came looking for it in the slightest – she was just terrified about what she was going to read. She crept back up the stairs and headed for the bathroom.

She closed the door, ran the shower and turned the key. She closed the lid on the toilet, sat down and reached deep into her boot. What if it rang? She switched the button on the side to silent and stared hard at the running water. She guessed right. Password four nines just like the house alarm and their old bank pin number. She stared so hard her vision was blurred then she traced her index finger over the little green box with the white bubble inside it. She tapped it ever so lightly. It opened on all Neil's messages. Her breathing quickened. Keith Paul. Sandy Baby. Bert. Terry. Doggie. Marina R. Samantha D. She stopped.

She opened the message box. **Hi, Marina, if you are ever looking for an electrician on the B&B I'm free, here's my number just in case.** Her reply was simply: **Thank you. I will keep you in mind.** Same message to Samantha D. She scrolled down and down. Nothing looked suspicious. Her breathing was returning to normal. Dentist. Hines. Phone company. Pat. Erik. Lucy McKenna – she opened it. **Hi Lucy, how's tricks? If you know of anyone looking for an electrician pass on my number, would you?** A simple reply: **Of course. Hope Sandra and you are well?** She hit the bottom button and returned to the main menu. She flicked across the screen to find the green button with the white phone symbol inside. She hit this and clicked down the bottom on recent. It was cleared. No recent calls. Why was that? She clicked on Missed calls. This was cleared too. He was entitled to clear his call log, wasn't he? But if he was clearing that, wouldn't he clear his private text messages too?

She heard him at the door now and jumped as he pushed the handle down hard. "Sandra?" he shouted above the water. "Why is the door locked?"

She pulled her boots off frantically, pulled down her skirt and wrapped a towel around her head. "Hang on!" she called as she turned off the shower and reefed her shirt off, unclipped her bra and grabbed a towel around her. She opened the door. "Sorry, habit from work, I guess, after my swim. Is it ready?" She pretended to rub the towel around her wet hair as she opened the bathroom door slowly.

"No, but you haven't seen my phone, have you?" He looked hard at her.

She tried to read his face. Poker face. "Your phone? No, I haven't." She continued to rub at her imaginary wet hair, careful not to let the towel slip.

"I thought it was in my jacket pocket but I can't find it now."

Suddenly she felt like such a tit. "I'll help you look now – just let me dry off."

He backed out the door and she shut it behind him.

She had no proof. So he was trying to take care of himself by wearing aftershave and dressing well? So he was spending days in pubs? The man had no work. He had nowhere to go. For better or worse was a laugh. So much for her practising *The Secret* – she was about as negative as a person could be. She was absolutely no support to him. This was crazy. She needed to move on.

There was only one thing for it. She opened the tiny bathroom window ever so slowly and, dangling her arm out with his phone in her hand, so she could position it correctly, she dropped the phone out and it fell right outside the back door beside his tool shed where it smashed to pieces.

* * *

Cara had left the Moritz early this evening. It had been quiet and Jonathon told her she could head off if she wanted to. He knew she was eager to get her place in shape. She opened a tin of chicken soup and left it simmering on low in the pot. After she tidied all around and put on all her lamps and lit her candles she stood back and looked at the walls of her living room. She was thinking the bright yellow that was in Room 16 for this room. When she told Jonathan that she would go ahead and actually make a start on her DIY this evening he had been really helpful. He had kindly given her loads of paints and he was dropping them by later on as they were far too heavy for her to carry. She had seen a beautiful pale blue that the dining area in the hotel was painted in and she wanted that colour for her bedroom. She padded into the kitchen and turned off the hob. She poured the soup into a bowl, ground on some black pepper and got a spoon. She carried it back into the living room and sat on the couch. As she blew on the hot liquid she remembered painting their apartment in Sandymount. It had been a beautiful two-bed overlooking the sea. Someday when she felt strong enough she'd go back and have a walk on Sandymount Strand. It was a beautiful place. She dropped the spoon back into the bowl untouched as she remembered the day they had viewed it.

* * *

"So do you like it?" Alex had asked.

She'd turned around and faced him. "It's just too amazing, Alex. There's no way I could ever afford to live here."

"Well, you wouldn't have to. I can afford it for both of us!" He grinned at her.

"I can't, Alex, really. I mean, I'd love to, but apart from the money I have to think about Esther."

"Hasn't Esther her own house to live in?" His blue eyes narrowed now.

"Of course she does, but you know what I mean. I'd feel better if she sold the house and got a small apartment of her own. So I thought she could put the house up for sale now and stay with us, just for a few months, until we find her a perfect place. Obviously I'm not saying she has to move in with us, Alex

. . . but just for a little while maybe? I'd just feel better about it? Is that crazy?"

Alex dug his hands deeper into his pockets as Mia, the woman showing the property, recognised the tension and backed out slowly into the hallway.

"It's all getting a bit tiresome, Cara – all this mammy stuff if you don't mind me saying."

"I'm sorry, I know it seems stupid, I can hear it when I say it but she needs me, I'm all she has really and I just want her to be happy. You knew that when you met me." She was feeling slightly annoyed now.

"I didn't actually, Cara. I didn't ask your mother out on a date, I asked you."

"Well, you must not have been listening to me, Alex, because I told you that very first night how important my mother's happiness is to me, that I need to look after her. She did everything for me and it's the least I can do for her. I don't want her to live with us, Alex, I just want to make sure she's comfortable and secure, that's all." He didn't answer her. Trying to make a joke of it, she added, "Or maybe all that altitude has you slightly deaf?" She gave a half-hearted laugh as she walked to the window and stared at the waves crashing on to the sea-front wall.

He moved into her face so quickly she started back in fright.

"Never speak to me like that. I'm not a fucking doormat, Cara, and you will not walk all over me!" His words spat into her face.

Cara stood stunned. Alex's piercing blue eyes were blazing anger and his breath was heavy and fast. He was still right in her face. She didn't move. Her heart was pounding.

"What's wrong, Alex?" she whispered, conscious of Mia out in the hallway – but she was on her phone and laughing, so probably unaware.

He didn't answer her. She had never seen this side of him. How had she provoked this reaction? Clearly he'd had it with all the Esther talk. Maeve the chef had told her to "wise up" when she'd talked about worrying about her mother when she left home. "Don't be a head-the-ball – you have to move on! Esther's grand! Next you'll be telling me you want to move her in with the sexy TFC or TDF or TCP or whatever you call that pilot. Cop on, Cara!"

She didn't want to move Esther in with them but she did feel an enormous guilt about moving out and leaving her all alone. She couldn't help it.

"Sorry." He leaned his head on her shoulder now. "It's just . . . God, I know she's your mother, Cara, so this is stupid but –"

His words were interrupted by Mia who had returned to the front room. "So then, do you want to have some more time? I have another couple due in now but, sure, I can meet them down at the car and give you a few more minutes?"

"No, we're done," Alex replied. He took his car key out of his pocket and flicked it open.

Mia had seen it all before. "No worries. Great to see you both and sure you have my number at Clover Auctioneers if you need to speak to me about anything."

Alex left and Mia winked at Cara.

She'd best be honest. "Sorry, Mia, we just had a stupid row."

Mia nodded and held up her hand. "Seen it all before – nothing unusual there. It's hard work looking at places to live – it's such an important thing that people find it very pressurising."

"Occupational hazard?" Cara managed.

"Yes, something like that." Mia laughed. "Listen, Cara, moving house, whether you are renting or buying, is one of the most stressful things in the world. Take your time. You have my number. I'm here if you want to call me."

Mia smiled and Cara was struck with how pretty the other woman was. She felt herself blush. "Thanks, Mia."

Cara made her way down the winding stairway and out to the navy Volvo. He was sitting in the driver's seat, engine running.

"Can we talk?" she asked as she sidled in and the overpowering heat hit her hard.

"Sure," he nodded meekly and turned off the engine.

"What was that all about?" She was beginning to feel really

angry at him now. How dare he speak to her like that?

"Ah, listen, I don't know, I'm just so mad about you . . . and my parents . . . you see . . . well, put it this way . . . there were three people in their marriage . . . and not in an in-law way, you know what I mean?"

"An affair?"

"Yeah, an affair, and a very serious one."

She moved her hand onto his knee now. "I'm sorry, Alex."

"Ah, listen, I'm over it, I really am. I'm a big boy. It's just that it broke my mother up and I've never been able to forgive my dad. He said it wasn't an affair, that he really was in love with this other bitch."

The word *bitch* bothered Cara even though she agreed the other woman more than likely was a bitch.

"Okay, it was just that I want it to be the two of us, no hassles. I know Esther isn't a hassle but I just envisioned looking at my first home with the woman I love being a joyous occasion."

"What happened, Alex?"

"Ah, it was a nightmare. I was young, seventeen, I was doing my Leaving Cert. Dad was always a free spirit, so being a pilot he moved us all over the place." He paused. "Then he met her one day and that was it. He decided it was okay to conduct an affair. Imagine that! She was a scrubber and he was willing to risk his marriage to our mother, our wonderful mother, for her. Sometimes I wonder why I ever followed in his footsteps – in the job, I mean. Who wants to be like him? He's a total fuck-up and now so am I."

"Alex! You are not a fuck-up!" Cara said and meant it. The poor guy, she thought. How parents can ruin children's lives!

"We used to try and hide it from Mam. We were so worried she'd be disgraced. My sister found out about it first and told me. Mam eventually found out but the scrubber had kicked him into touch by then. She didn't want to know him. He was devastated but only that Mam had caught him out. But she forgave him, if you can believe that."

"And took him back?" Cara asked.

Alex ran his fingers through his thick black hair and leaned his head on the back of the driver's head-rest. "Yeah, Cara, she took the dickhead back."

The car was silent. Alex rarely used language like this and Cara was slightly shocked. She didn't really know what to say but at least she was starting to understand Alex a bit more. His behaviour made a lot more sense now. His jealousy. She'd never really admitted it to herself before but Alex was very jealous. He'd pushed and pushed her the other night to tell him all about her exes and her sex life. She had refused for ages and he had tickled her until she was honestly going to cry. She gave in and told him. His face had instantaneously clouded over and he had gone to bed early citing a headache. Jealousy was the one trait Cara hated in people yet here she was madly in love with this man. Now she knew where it was all coming from.

"Seriously, Cara, I'm a nightmare."

She laughed and fished on the floor for her bag. Her lips were so dry. She removed her Kiel's lip balm and rubbed it all over her lips before tying her loose hair up into a knot on her head. "You're not, Alex."

He stared at her, his piercing blue eyes melting hers. "I'm so sorry I spoke to you like that. It will never happen again. We don't have to live there. We can get Esther settled somewhere first and then look at places again, if that's what you really want."

"No." She shook her head defiantly. "It's not fair on you. I love the apartment. I will speak to Mam this evening and I know she'll be over the moon for us. We'll get her sorted after. Let's do it."

He leaned over and kissed her hard on the lips.

Chapter 10

"Cara?" Jenny was standing at her office door in behind reception. "Can I talk to you for a second?"

"Sure." Cara left her seat and made her way out.

Jenny's blonde hair was in a high ponytail and dark-brown eye shadow sat on her pretty slate-grey eyes. She looked worried as she fished a tissue from her small white clutch bag.

"Are you okay?" Cara asked.

"Yeah, I'm fine, but it's Max – he doesn't want to make a speech on the day." Jenny's eyes filled up with tears.

"No? Well, come and sit down and we can have a chat."

Jenny took a seat and blew her nose. "I mean, why would he want to ruin my day like this, Cara? It's a little speech, a few words, that's all."

"What has he said?"

"He says he doesn't want to stand up in front of all those people. He was a tennis pro, Cara, for crying out loud! He's played in front of thousands of people, he reports on television and now he's nervous of this! Give me a break!"

Cara wanted to say leave him alone, so what? Let him enjoy his day. It's not about the silly speech, it's about the rest of your lives together. But she didn't. She couldn't. "Would it help if I called him maybe?" she offered.

"Would you, please? Tell him he has to speak – it will ruin my day if he doesn't." She blew again and stood up. "Okay, I'm meeting the girls in Hines bar for a few drinks now. Here's his number, Cara." She scribbled the number down on the back of a beer mat and hugged Cara. "I owe you!"

"Well, I can't promise you anything but I will try." Cara picked up the beer mat and twirled it between her finger and thumb.

"You can do it – as Jonathan said to me last week, you are very special."

Cara wanted to know more.

* * *

Sandra answered her phone on the third ring as she returned from the stables after her break. "Hello?" She peeled her hair from her mouth as she slipped in the staff back door. The wind was wild out there today and her lip gloss was not for the outdoors!

"Is this Sandra Darragh?" a female voice asked her.

"Yes," she answered as she headed to reception, nodding at Mike as they passed in the corridor.

"Neil Darragh's wife?"

Oh, here we go again, she thought and stopped to lean her back against the wall. I knew it, she thought.

"This is Sister Theresa from St Catherine's hospital in Knocknoly. I'm afraid he's been in a motorcycle accident, dear."

* * *

Sandra sat by the bed and held Neil's hand. His fingernails were spotless. She held a white plastic cup of water in her other hand. He was asleep. He hadn't been too seriously hurt, thank God, but he was still out and she was waiting until he woke. She was still his wife after all, and although she knew she had to speak honestly to him now wasn't the right time. He had a broken wrist and badly bruised ribs according to the doctor. He was bruised and battered all over.

She stared at him sleeping. He was so unfamiliar to her lately and she just couldn't pull him back. He was slipping away as her husband and the man she looked at now was becoming a stranger. It was a deep feeling inside her gut that she knew he was seeing someone. How could he? After all they had been through? What kind of a man was he really? What sort of judge of character was she to have dedicated her life to him? Sandra would never have cheated on him, ever. She took her vows and she meant them.

She sipped some tepid water. She thought about the fact she had called Dermot as soon as she hung up after the call from the hospital. Why had she done that? He had been so kind to her lately, she supposed. "I'll drive you over," he had said. "No, it's fine," she'd answered. "I'll call you from the hospital."

Dermot had always been so kind to her. He was just always around, always close by.

Her parents lived on the outskirts of Knocknoly but she was no longer close enough to them. Since they had both retired their lives had literally been taken over by golf. Every morning, every afternoon and every evening. Her mother had always been there for her growing up and had been very supportive in the beginning with the IVF but now that support had dwindled. "Is it time to maybe move on, love? Explore other options?" her mother had said not so long ago in Louise's over coffee. Dressed in her bright yellow V-neck polo shirt and chequered purple trousers she was becoming a woman Sandra didn't really recognise any more. Her mother Vera used to always be at home. Cooking, laughing, listening to music, tending the garden, doing stuff in the house, painting her stills: she was always just there. Present. It wasn't that Sandra wanted her mother stuck at home by any means but she also didn't want a relationship with a golf club and that's what it was now. Vera was a different woman. Robert, her father, had always played golf – it was where all his business deals were done, he used to say. So he would be gone all week and all weekend. Unknown to Robert, Vera started golf lessons herself and then one day, after a full year of lessons and after taking to it like a duck to water, she asked Robert if she could tag along. He looked at his wife like she was crazy but agreed. As he teed off he turned to humour her. "Your go, dear. Just try and make contact with the ball!" Vera had taken out her driver and hit a shot that made Robert make a sound she hadn't heard in years. It was a cross between an orgasm and acute fear.

So Cara hadn't called her parents when she heard Neil was in an accident.

No doubt the Knocknoly grapevine would be in overdrive by now. An ambulance outside the new builds, which was big news. The accident had happened right outside their house. A young learner driver, who was practising in the estate without an accompanying driver, hadn't seen Neil pull out and had reversed into him, sending him and the Vespa flying across the road into the side of a house. Where had he been off to, she wondered. He had told her as she left for work that morning he would be doing stuff in the house all day.

Sandra rubbed her eyes. She was truly shattered. Emotionally drained.

"You still here, dear?" A matronly type nurse shuffled in in her white plimsolls and lifted Neil's wrist. She placed her finger on his pulse and checked the watch attached to the pocket of her white uniform. "Why don't you head home, dear? He seems pretty much to be still in a deep sleep. It's almost eight o'clock at night. Come back tomorrow?" She fluffed the covers at the end of the bed and took up the chart.

"I have to work at seven in the morning. I'd really like to be here when he wakes up."

"I'm on until eight, love, twelve-hour shift, so I can tell him you waited and waited but had to go. I can bring the hospital phone in and you can call him when he wakes? Write down your mobile there and leave it by the locker in case he's still a bit out of it. His phone was smashed to smithereens by the way. I have left it in the green plastic bag along with his clothes. Bring some clothes up tomorrow so we can hang them in the wardrobe for his discharge." She scribbled on the clipboard, replaced it at the foot of the bed and clicked her pen.

Sandra nodded in agreement. He hadn't told her he had found

the smashed phone. Had he been going to try and get it fixed? She stood and stretched and felt her limbs ache. She hadn't realised she had been sitting with so much tension in her body. She left the cubicle quietly. She hated hospitals. They just smelled of disappointment to her now. Ever since the first round of IVF.

* * *

Neil held her hand tightly. He had come home from work early, ran to the shower and he was now all clean, his hair still wet, dressed in his black jeans with a green T-shirt and light blue runners.

"Are you okay? Nervous?" he asked her.

Business was flying and she knew it was hard for him to take the time off.

"You know, I'm not really that nervous," she lied.

She had changed her outfit three times, as ridiculous as that sounded. She wanted to look nice today. Because today she would be pregnant. Eventually. She was ecstatic. They had been trying to get pregnant for the guts of two and a half years now. Before the marriage. From the second they returned to the hotel room the night of Tom's wedding she'd dumped her pill in the hotel bin. It was something they both wanted. She didn't have the time to hang around. When her period came as usual at the end of every month she hadn't panicked for the first year and a half. It took time getting pregnant, everyone knew that. She'd been to her GP for a check-up, she monitored her temperature and charted it and she bought the ovulation sticks, but still her period came. After two years she began to panic and slowly sank into despair. She just knew deep within something wasn't right. She couldn't put a word on it but every time they had sex and she held her legs up in the air for half an hour, sometimes an hour, she never felt like anything was happening. She knew this was ridiculous, that no one felt anything, but it swam around her head constantly. She went for more tests and bloods and nothing seemed askew. Her phone seemed to beep constantly with news of friends or friends of friends who were pregnant. People would ask her over and over, "So, any news?" "Are you two ever going to get a move on?" "You can't put it off forever, you know." So insensitive. So ignorant.

It had actually been Louise who had stepped in one day as Sandra was close to tears. It was a comment made by another customer in the Loft. "It's all right for you career women," she said as she pushed her double buggy past Louise and Sandra who were chatting at the counter. "I'd love to have the time to gossip but this pair want their bottles now!" A simple enough throwaway comment but as Sandra moved in to let her past her eyes darted down to the precious little girls in their buggy, holding their security blankets up to their tiny faces, and her heart dived into her feet. It must have been pretty clear on her face.

"Not happening for you, pet, is it?" Louise whispered when they were alone again. Sandra had kept it together but had confided in Louise and Louise had dragged Sandra straight through to her back kitchen.

"Ring Doctor Morris and make an appointment," she said.

"Oh, I've had lots of appointments, Louise, but nothing is showing up." She wiped her wet eyes.

"Then tell him it's time to refer you both on to a fertility clinic!"

The relief of sharing had been great. She was fed up pretending she just wasn't ready for kids. She was fed up fielding the insensitive comments. Most of all she was fed up when she still wasn't pregnant after all the trying they were doing.

She had gone to talk to Doctor Morris again and he had been wonderful. Very understanding and helpful. He referred her to a specialist in Holles Street first where she did rounds of tests and after much discussion decided to begin taking the fertility drug, Clomid. It was a really successful fertility drug, the doctor had told her, especially in her case where the reason why she wasn't getting pregnant was unexplained. They had wanted to see Neil. She had told them no, told them he had been checked elsewhere. Anyway she was sure it was her, it had to be. Sandra just knew Neil would react very badly to going for tests so she wanted to put that off for as long as possible. The drug hadn't worked.

She pressed on. Next Holles Street referred her to the HARI unit in the Rotunda Hospital in Dublin. Sandra had secretly started to look into IVF months before. On quiet days at the hotel she would Google it. It was pricy but they had the money. They needed this procedure and that valuable time was ticking away. As she expected Neil hadn't been too keen at first.

She remembered the night she had informed him of their situation so well. She had been at work on her half day in the Moritz, Neil was putting in extra sockets at Louise's. She left and popped into O'Dywer's and got some wine and ingredients to make a lasagne. O'Dwyer's sold all local fresh produce including the meat so she always shopped in there as did all the locals of Knocknoly. Back home she had skipped around his old bungalow and pulled fresh flowers from the garden.

"Smells amazing!" Neil shouted as he opened the back door and headed straight for the toilet to scrub his hands.

"It's ready when you are!" she called back.

"Fancy a few pints in Hines after dinner, love?" he'd asked.

She was slightly nervous but only slightly – surely he would react okay? He knew how badly she wanted to have a baby.

He ducked his head as he emerged soapy-clean from the bathroom and kissed her on the lips as she ladled the lasagne onto two plates.

"Wine on a Monday? Do ya not want to head to Hines for a pint after, so?" He looked at her as she put the plate of food in front of him. He tucked in without waiting for her.

"Yes, we can – well, we're celebrating, sort of," she said.

"Oh yeah?" He looked up at her.

"Well, yeah, the hospital rang. It seems those tests I had done all came back clear."

"That's really good, love," he mumbled through a mouthful of hot food, his fork dangling precariously now from side to side.

"So the thing is, Neil," Sandra poured him some red wine, "well, the thing is you will have to go and get tested now." She would tell him everything on a need-to-know basis. She sat down and pushed her fork deep into her lasagne.

"What does that mean exactly? Spit it out now, Sandra." He dropped his fork now with a clatter on the edge of his plate, picked up his napkin and roughly wiped his mouth. "I can't say I like the sound of this. You already have me half demented ringing me at all times of the day to come home because you're ovulating or whatever. I feel like a fucking baby-making machine you just plug in when the time is right!"

Sandra stared at the lasagne-stained napkin before she took a deep breath. "Okay, well, basically it's pretty easy for you," she laughed. "All we need you to do is to go into a room and give a sample." God, he didn't look happy.

"A sample? A sample of what?" his eyes darkened.

Could he really be asking this? "Well, Neil, come on . . . a – a sperm sample obviously." She had read up so much on the subject over the last few months it seemed impossible he wouldn't know this.

His cheeks were red and blotchy now. "Are you asking me to have a wank in a hospital room, Sandra?" His expression was zombie-like.

"Don't be so crude, Neil. It's not a – a wank, it's to test your sperm. It's sperm analysis. No big deal."

"So basically you're saying it's my fault you can't get pregnant?"

"Not me, Neil . . . we . . . *we* can't get pregnant. It's both of us. No one's to blame. We just need a bit of assistance, that's all. It's very common. This is all you have to do. I can take care of all the rest."

He pushed the full plate of steaming lasagne away now and got up, his body towering over her. "Tell me where to go, when, whatever! I'll fucking wank anywhere to shut you up, Sandra. I am sick to my back teeth of all this baby talk. It's so boring!" He dug his fingers into his wet hair.

"I'm the one doing all the work here! Do you not want a family?" she shouted now. He was so frustrating.

"I do, Sandra, well, at least I did, but it hasn't happened yet, has it, and let's face it we've been pretty hard at it and zilch. It's not like we haven't been trying our hardest, now is it? It's a military operation every time you're ovulating. Once I see those ovulation sticks out I know I'm on duty! The fucking pressure is on. I can't stand it any more. Let's face it: we might never have kids and so what? Is it the be-all and end-all? Where are you in there? Is Sandra in there any more because if she is she's covered in baby-fucking-mania and I can't see her!" He spat the words at her as she stared up at him.

Her eyes filled up with tears. Was he right? Had she become obsessed? Well, she couldn't help it. She couldn't stop it either. In fact, the one thing she was sure about was that she hadn't even started yet.

On the first hospital appointment she had her tests done through her belly button and Neil begrudgingly had had his semen analysed but nothing untoward came back. "Unexplained infertility," they were told rather clinically.

The next suggested route was IVF, if they were interested. She so was. She didn't even ask Neil if he wanted to go down that route. As far as she was concerned they didn't have a choice. She had called the NISIG, a fertility support group, and they were fantastic and told her a lot of patients had moved on to the SIMS clinic in Dublin, so she turned to them too. They explained so much more about IVF. She was so familiar with the procedure anyway but they spelled it out in simple terms. She had dragged Neil along, his hands stuffed in his pockets and his head bowed. The nurse sat them down and pushed leaflets and pamphlets and a DVD in front of them, and then she went on to explain the technicalities.

"I know the whole world is familiar with IVF now but just to run through it quickly. IVF is an acronym, another word we use for *in vitro* fertilisation, *in vitro* meaning *in glass*. Simply put IVF is adding Neil's sperm to your eggs, Sandra, in the laboratory, to produce embryos. In vitro fertilisation is an option for you guys as it seems for whatever reason you cannot conceive through conventional therapies. These embryos are put back into your uterus, Sandra, or more commonly we call it the womb, and after three to five days of being in the incubator, hopefully they will then grow into a baby. Any questions so far?" She smiled over at them both and they shook their heads. "Okay, great. Then, just to add so you know, the first IVF baby was Louise Brown, born on July 25th, 1978, at Oldham General Hospital, England, through a planned Caesarean section. She weighed five pounds twelve ounces. Doctor Patrick Steptoe, a gynaecologist at the hospital, and Doctor Robert Edwards, a physiologist at Cambridge University, had been actively working on finding an alternative solution for conception since 1966 so she was, and is, a miracle. IVF is just an incredible thing. Make sure you watch the DVD: it shows a conventional insemination with the egg surrounded by coronal and cumulus cells and sperm swimming around the egg."

Louise, Sandra repeated the name: a good omen she thought.

Sandra was booked in for a laparoscopy and a D&C. They gave her a prescription for the pill. The outline of her IVF cycle was standard. On the day she got her period she was to call the nurse to discuss when to commence her pill. She would start the pill and continue as directed but without taking the normal seven-day break between packs. Then she would begin taking the Buserelin nasal spray, two sniffs three times a day, to prepare for treatment to artificially stimulate ovulation.

They bought her meds up in Dundrum in Dublin at the Medi Pharm.

It hadn't been too bad a day. She had been trying really hard to cheer Neil up, cooking his favourite meals, renting his favourite DVDs and in fairness to him he had come around a bit and was actually starting to look slightly interested.

"Sorry if I was a prick but it's just all so unnatural, isn't it? I don't want to be like this. I just can't help it," he had said when they sat down outside Mao in Dundrum Town Centre for lunch.

"It's our only option, Neil," she said carefully as she read the menu.

"Yeah, well, at least this is it, I suppose. What you fancy here?" He held his menu in front of his face, studying each dish carefully.

"Hmmm, so much looks nice," she said and then added, "It

will be grand, Neil, don't worry about it."

But his interest was gone as he was looking around for a waiter or waitress. Neil was always so impatient in restaurants it drove Sandra mad.

"Neil?" she called him back to the conversation.

"Yeah, I know, it's just not something I thought would ever happen to us, did you?" He was waving wildly now.

"No, I suppose I always imagined I would, or *we* would I should say, get pregnant just like everyone else, but I am that bit older, I suppose, so let's just hope and pray with all we have that this works."

He was biting the top of the menu now. "It might not work?" He looked bewildered.

She held it together. "Did you not read the leaflets, Neil? Listen to the doctor?"

"Not really, no. I just wanted to get the fuck out of there, to be honest, Sandra."

A pretty Asian waitress arrived now to take their order and Neil beamed at her.

"Can I have the Chilli Chicken Ramen with an extra portion of noodles and a Tiger beer, please, love? Sandra?" He handed the menu back when the waitress had taken down his order and she stuffed it under her arm.

"I'll have the Nasi Goreng with a sparkling water, please, and can I get a side bowl of pickled ginger?" Sandra said.

They people-watched in silence as they waited for their meals. Sandra was afraid to say too much about the IVF as she knew he was still freaked. She wanted to keep the mood light and happy. She laughed inwardly though – you'd swear it was Neil who had to go through the needles and drugs insemination.

The waitress was back quickly and dropped two steaming plates in front of them.

"Can I get a decaffeinated coffee too?" Sandra asked her. She turned to Neil. "I'll drive back to Knocknoly so you can have another beer if you like?"

"Go on the Sandra, you mad yolk! Two whole bottles of beer and you are letting me? Lord above, things are looking up!"

He was making a joke, she knew that, but it just hurt her. She was about to put her body and mind through so much. She couldn't have caffeine. She couldn't have alcohol. She would be afraid to get off the couch and he hadn't even read the information?

She studied the leaflets like the Holy Bible when they had got home as she memorised each step. She had opened each leaflet and laid them out on the kitchen table and poured a large glass of bottled water.

Step one: wash your hands.

Step two: line up medication vials to be taken.

Step three: open all vials by snapping off the cap.

Step four: attach green needle to your syringe, push the needle through rubber stopper and draw up all of the medication fluid.

Step five: repeat as necessary until all allocated ampoules are drawn up.

Step six: if applicable, inject medication fluid into medication powder, the Menophur. The Menophur should dissolve instantly. Using the same needle and syringe draw up all the dissolved medication. If using more than one ampoule of medication repeat steps five and six.

Step seven: carefully recap the needle. Gently twist off the needle and replace with the smaller orange, blue or grey needle. Secure needle tightly to prevent leakage.

Step eight: gently tap syringe, needle pointed up to remove air bubbles. Gently push plunger until a tiny drop of medication is at needle tip. You are now ready to administer the injection.

She would memorise every letter. It was all so important. It had to be done perfectly. He hadn't read it. She couldn't wait to get started.

That evening, when they returned home, Neil was slightly tipsy as the two beers had turned into four but he was being really good to her. He was at last asking lots of questions and being supportive. They had even begun laughing together again and had a cuddle.

They started their first round of IVF on the twenty-first of March. She had started her pill on the first day of her next period and had been so full of hope. She began on the Buserelin nasal spray, taking her two sniffs three times a day. The first appointment at the clinic she had her vaginal ultrasound to check her ovaries and her uterus, to ensure she was 'down regulated' prior to starting her medication. She decreased her sniffs to one sniff daily and continued her folic acid. She took her low-strength adult aspirin daily with her lunch. She injected the Luveris and Puregon into her tummy and the Gastone into her bottom and used her Cyclogest suppositories.

Neil had even helped with some of the injections. "So what do I do exactly?" He had stood in the kitchen with the needle filled with meds.

"Okay, so just stick it into me!" Sandra laughed, pulling up her T-shirt. "I'm a big girl – I can take it! I do it to myself for crying out loud!"

"I hate you having to do this!" He sighed and concentrated on the job in hand.

"I don't mind at all. If it gets us our baby I would have a million needles stuck into me. I'd even stick them in my eyes." She lay back on the couch when he was done, still laughing at his squirming.

One week later she was back for an ultrasound. Her medications were increased slightly and she stopped the aspirin and continued her other meds as directed. Four days later she was back for another ultrasound and it was confirmed she was ready for her egg retrieval. She stopped her simulating drugs and had an injection of Pregnyl for the final maturation of her eggs.

Two days later she arrived in for the retrieval. She had nothing to eat or drink since midnight. Neil had to give a fresh semen sample but this time he didn't make too much of a fuss. It took thirty minutes and the next day the embryologist called with fertilisation results and a time for her embryo transfer. She was petrified but giddy with anticipation.

On the day, she did her meds, went to the loo two hours before the appointment and drank the required two litres of water. It wasn't painful. In fact she welcomed every step of the procedure. Every needle, every tablet, every scrape, every invasive moment was pulling her nearer and nearer to her baby. She could almost smell that perfect soft pink baby skin.

When it was all done she started to relax but the two-week wait was a nightmare. The fourteen long days ahead looked like Kilimanjaro. She even called the clinic to check they couldn't fall out. "Uterus embryos do not fall out," the nurse had kindly reassured her. Sandra had a feeling it wasn't the first time she'd been asked that question. She had obeyed every law: no heavy lifting, no over-exertion, no hot baths.

Neil had been great. She had been so delighted with his reaction. He cooked and cleaned and didn't go to the pub after work.

"You know what, Sandra?" he had said one week later as they sat in the bungalow with the front door open. It was unusually warm for March but the warm breeze flowed through their living room. "I'm thinking it's going to be a little boy. I have a really strong feeling."

Sandra felt a warm bubble of air rise within her and she smiled "Please God, Neil – wouldn't that be amazing?" She rubbed her tummy gently for the hundredth time that day, willing their baby to grow.

"If it is, and you can say no now, I don't mind, but if it is could we call him Neil, do ya think?"

A huge smile broke out on her face and she reached her hand across to take his. "Of course we can. I think that's really lovely actually – I love tradition."

He jumped up and rubbed his hands together and started to jog around the couch where she was sprawled. He was kicking a piece of rolled-up paper. "And it's Big Neil Darragh heading for the goal – but, hang on, it's little Neil Darragh coming up behind him – he slips the ball through his dad's feet and heads for home and it's a goal! Little Neil Darragh scores again! This lad will play for Ireland one day, no doubt about that!" He ran in slow motion now, his hands above his head, and his face full of joy.

Neil was also very happy to be able to drink again.

"Can I get you anything?" He knelt down beside her and kissed her on the lips.

She held his chin in her hands. "No, I'm good, thanks. Are you heading back to work?"

"Yeah, if that's okay with you? I've left the lads with no scaffolding so they can't do much until I put it up." He stood up and went to get his high-vis jacket. "Funny though . . ." he stuck the Velcro across his chest to hold the high-vis jacket together, "you know John O'Dowd? Well, his brother's this hot-shot economist and he says that the building trade is going to be hit so hard we won't know what's happened. He said we'll all be left spinning." Neil looked at his wife.

Sandra laughed. "Neil, you're such a worry wart. Don't be listening to the scaremongers like John O'Dowd. We'll be grand. People will always need electricians!"

He grunted. "See you tonight. I thought we could go to Louise's for tea and have a pint in Hines on the way home?" He pushed his yellow hard hat under his arm.

"Well, I don't think I will get up and walk much today, love, if you don't mind, but you feel free to go." Sandra was happy to look at the laptop and browse her favourite internet sites. Mainly all baby and pregnancy ones.

"Okay, great, sure. I'll see you later tonight so, love."

Sandra felt a little disappointed. She'd rather hoped he would stay home with her but she was being selfish, she supposed. What was the point in both of them lying around? It had been a whirlwind of medical procedures and she was wiped out. She hadn't really expected it all to be so hard and she especially wasn't prepared for the hair growth all over her body and on her face. It was awful.

When the phone rang out two weeks later Sandra screamed for Neil who was washing his new Vespa in the garden. He ran in. Instead of doing a home pregnancy test they had chosen to do blood tests in the clinic.

"Hello?" Sandra's voice was crackling.

Neil pushed his head in close to the handset so he could hear even though it was on loudspeaker. He grabbed her hand and squeezed it tight.

"I'm sorry to inform you, Mr and Mrs Darragh, but you are

not pregnant on this occasion."

Their doctor droned on and Neil let go of her hand. She couldn't believe it. She burst into gulping tears. They had retrieved all those eggs and yet she wasn't pregnant? She was beyond devastated. Neil took the phone as she sat on the kitchen chair.

"Okay, thanks, doctor." He hung up and put his arms around his wife. "It's okay, love, what can we do? At least we tried. Come on, grab your coat and I will take you for a pint. You must be dying for a pint."

A pint. She didn't give a shit if she never had a pint again in her whole fucking life! She wasn't pregnant. This couldn't be happening to her! After all that? How could this be? What kind of a woman was she? The tears wouldn't stop flowing and came hard and fast, her breath rasping.

"I can't believe this!" she sobbed as he stared at her.

"It's okay, you're not dead, it's okay, Sandra. Come on now, pull yourself together."

"Pull myself together? What the fuck, Neil?" she screamed now and he stood back. She screamed at the top of her lungs. A wild crazy noise.

"That's your hormones, love, all that shit you're injecting into yourself can't be good for your head, never mind your body."

She was numb. He was not. She reluctantly pulled on her cream jacket and he linked her arm as they strolled to Hines.

"I can't believe it after all that," he said as they headed over the bridge.

"I know."

Neil fished for something that had blown into his eye. "Well, that's that, isn't it? You know, we can maybe just look to go on a nice sun holiday. We could go back to that same hotel we loved in Nerja – aah, wouldn't that be bliss, Sandra? Remember strolling around the Balcon? The cocktails in The Dubliner? That Robbie Box who sings in there is deadly."

She started to cry again on the Knocknoly Bridge. The water whooshed under them and she looked up at Neil through her tears. He looked really uncomfortable.

"I can't give up. I want to do the IVF again."

"What?" His eyes narrowed rapidly as he looked at his wife in disbelief. "Why?"

"Why? Because it will work. You remember what they said at the first meeting in the clinic – that the first time is almost a trial."

Neil suddenly hung his head and dug his hands into his pockets of his leather jacket. "Come on, I cannot talk about this now. I need a drink!"

Hines was heaving on that Friday evening and the tables outside under the heat lamps were packed. They went inside.

"Two Bud, Charlie, when you're ready!" Neil shouted to the barman who was pulling pints faster than people could drink them.

"Hi ya, Sandra." Jonathan Redmond stood beside her. "Feeling better then?" He grinned at her.

"Oh hi, Jonathan, yeah, one of those twenty-four-hour things, you know the type. Actually, Jonathan, I wanted a quick word with you. I'm looking for full-time work now and I was wondering if the Moritz could use me full time?"

Jonathan shook his pint of Guinness gently, the black taking down the remaining cream, and then started to nod his head. "Actually, Sandra, your timing is perfect. I could use you full time on reception if you are happy with that? I'm also looking for a new hospitality manager but that will be down the line."

"Great, Jonathan, I'd be delighted to do full-time reception work!"

Neil arrived back just then and handed her pint across to her. She tipped her pint off Jonathan's.

"Cheers!" they all said and then Jonathan excused himself.

"What was all that about? Is he freaking you took time off?"

"No, sure I was off anyway the last few days – I only took yesterday – told him I had a bit of a bug. Anyway, I'm due a load of days. It's quite the opposite. He's offered me a full-time job!"

Neil's eyes lit up. "Brill, did you accept, love?"

"I sure did. You are looking at Sandra Darragh, full-time receptionist at the Moritz! Well, we have to sit down and work out hours and money and all that but he said he wants me full time."

"Well, well, well, you know what this means . . . with us both having full-time jobs and all that I can upgrade me new Vespa already!"

Neil laughed hard now and Sandra realised it was the first time he had really laughed in quite a while. His handsome face lit up.

"Well, I did notice the brand-new Vespa brochures on my bedside locker, then one on the breakfast table, and lo and behold there even managed to be one in my car! What are you like? You only just bought one!" She laughed now too – he really was such a child.

"I love you, Sandra. We will be all right. I'm sorry . . . I'm a bit at a loss for words right now. Your reaction just freaked me out a bit. Scary Mary."

She leaned up and kissed him weakly on the lips. "It's totally understandable. I love you too, Neil." She felt sick inside.

They took their drinks outside and as they leaned against the wall Sandra thought he looked sad for a brief moment, until a young blonde girl walked past him with her glass of wine in her hand and he followed her every step with his eyes. She was full of charm with her sunglasses balanced on her bouncy blonde hair. Skin-tight jeans and brown leather jacket.

"*Over here, Kelley!*"

Sandra saw another pretty girl with a sleek bob wave at the blonde.

"Sorry, what?" Neil turned back to her now but she shook her head.

"I didn't say anything. Isn't that one of your work lads over there? I know you are dying to sit with them so go on. I want to fix my make-up anyway, be back out in a bit."

He rolled his eyes but quickly nodded in agreement as he took in the young blonde again, her head thrown back and her giddy laughter carrying on the now cool March evening air.

Now that Sandra had taken on the full-time job so she could save for another round of IVF. She wasn't about to tell him that right now. Let him have his flirt with the young blonde, she thought, as she shivered. She picked up her pint and made her way inside. As she looked back over her shoulder her husband was already chatting up the other woman.

* * *

"I want to move house, Neil," she suddenly announced as she sat on the toilet.

The negative pregnancy tests, all six of them, lay scattered on the bathroom floor. She had started doing tests before her period was due as she just couldn't wait. If it really was just unexplained infertility there was still every chance they could get pregnant naturally. They were still having sex when he came home from the pub. It took him longer and she had to put a hell of a lot of foreplay into it.

He stood at the bathroom door but didn't answer her.

A lump the size of a tennis ball was lodged in her throat. "Did you hear me? This house is too small – we're sending the wrong signals to the universe – how can we raise a family in here?"

"Is this your little orangey *The Secret* book talking again because to be honest I find it a little disturbing." He used his fingers to make inverted commas when he said '*The Secret*'. He took her hands. "Stop doing all these tests, Sandra. It's all becoming a bit too weird for me, to be honest, it's all freaking me out. I'm finding it difficult to be around you, love. As my mate Bucko said, if God wanted to send us a baby he would have sent us one naturally the way nature intended it to be."

Her mouth went as dry as a desert. "How dare you! How dare you say all that?" She stood up, her knickers and trousers around her ankles, and pushed him so he almost lost his balance.

"What the fuck? Are you gone mental? Have you seriously lost your mind?" His eyes blazed at her.

"*Get out, Neil! Leave me alone!*" she screamed at him as he stuck his two index fingers into his ears. "*The Secret* is only a book, it's only words, it's the message I take from it that is important. I want to be positive. I want to live thinking I will get good things from this life. I don't for one second think a book is going to do that for me! There is nothing new or revolutionary in what *The Secret* says – it's common sense. I believe that negativity brings you down. End of."

He shook his head at her and left the bathroom. She couldn't move. She was beyond devastated. Tears started to fall and she had no desire to stop them or even brush them away. Why could she not get pregnant? Why? Why? Why? How could Neil have just said those words to her? They had hurt her almost as much as the negative tests scattered aimlessly on the cold tiled floor.

"Did you hear me, Neil?" she shouted now as he came back. "I want to move house!"

"Sure, whatever you want!" he shouted back.

That calmed her a little. She did love this cosy little house but it wasn't big enough to raise a family. Also it never really felt like *their* home, it always felt like Neil's place. He had one arm into his leather jacket now. "If you don't mind I'm heading to Hines to meet Bucko." He kept his head down.

"Fucking Bucko!" Sandra shouted. "I'm sick of Bucko! Will he ever grow up and find a girlfriend? What does Bucko know about life or babies? This is the third night this week. You don't see him for nine years and now suddenly you're best friends again?"

"What's wrong with you lately?" Neil shouted now "Leave me alone! You're constantly on my back and I can't deal with it. It's hard for me too, you know. Pull up your knickers, woman." He looked disgusted at her.

"*Woman?*" she spat the words at him. "What are you, seventy-five?" She reached for her knickers and jeans, pulling them up together.

"Sometimes I feel like it with your constant nagging. My head can't cope, Sandra. You're turning into someone I really don't know. I am so sorry you're not pregnant, I really, really am, but there is nothing I can do. You can't let this take over your whole life. You used to be a bit of *craic* – that's why I married you! What happened to you? Did you trick me? Was that fun lovin' Sandra all an act to get a ring on your finger?" He looked deflated now, his frame too thin for his leather jacket.

"Stay, please, don't go – let's go to bed early?" She stood up now.

He turned to go but came back, his finger pointing wildly. "Sandra, the only reason you want to have sex is to get pregnant. It ain't happening. I don't care that they say it could happen any time. I won't live my life timing sex to your fertility needs! I do all I can do to get it up these days!"

"Oh, *my* fertility needs is it now? Do you not want this baby?"

"I do . . . I did . . . I dunno any more . . . but I won't let it take over my life, no, and . . . and other people don't think that makes me a bad person!"

"Other people? What others?" She knew she was losing control now but who had he been talking to about their private life?

"Never mind." He put his hand on the door handle.

"No, I want to know exactly who you have been talking to about me. I thought you didn't want anyone to know about the IVF?"

"I don't!" He was really mad now. "Look, you married me, not the baby – the baby was never a given."

"Those words so aren't out of *your* brain, Neil Darragh! Who is filling you with this shit? Paul bloody Buckland?"

He let go of the handle now and put his back to the door. "You took all the good out of sex because it's an obsession now. Shortly after we got married you developed a bad case of baby-brain baby-mania. You drive me crazy. I thought you were fun yet quiet and calm and that you'd be good for me. Not this – this psycho stuff! You might need to talk to someone – because I tell you one thing – if you don't lighten up I'm out of here!" He turned, opened the door, bent his head to go out and slammed the small bungalow door behind him.

Sandra screamed. She went to the fridge and grabbed the wine bottle. What was happening with them? What was wrong with her? Why couldn't she just let it go for a while? Okay, she did want a baby so badly it hurt. She couldn't help that. It was deep inside her. She wanted him to want the baby just as badly too but she just didn't think he did.

She grabbed a glass, opened the laptop on the kitchen table and flicked on her moms-to-be website. She had been on it a lot lately – she would check it a few times daily. She poured a huge glass of wine.

Nicky Moore was online. She was also in the trying-to-conceive group.

Hi. Nicky's words popped up. **How are you?**

Not good! Sandra whacked the keys in response. **You?** She waited for the reply as the computer told her Nicky was typing.

Not feeling too great but started the IVF again today so fingers crossed this time.

Sandra leaned in closer to the screen, her bare feet cosy in the rug under the wooden kitchen table. **Good luck, Nicky. I didn't know you were trying again so soon?** She waited.

I'm not telling anyone this time! Nicky hit back. **I'm too nervous.**

Sandra banged the keys hard again. **Keep me posted, OK?**

Will do. When are you starting again?

Hopefully soon! Sandra bashed the words out and drank a long bitter gulp of wine.

Nicky was suddenly gone offline. Sandra found that with this site: it was all cloak and dagger. Good luck, Nicky, wish I was in your shoes right now. She knocked back her glass of wine and stared out of the cottage window. She could see old Mr Peter's cottage across the field – it had been empty for so long now. She'd always loved it as a child.

She rose from the table, reached for the phone and slowly dialled the number she knew off by heart.

"Hello, Doctor Brady's office."

"Hi, it's Sandra Darragh here. I'd like to talk to the doctor about starting another round of IVF as soon as possible. I'm thinking of July?"

Chapter 11

Cara closed the door behind her, her red hair wild and her face red from the cold night air. Esther was sitting in the hall, on the phone, no doubt to Ann.

Cara had gone to dinner with Alex in The Gresham Hotel again. It was one of his favourite old Dublin hotels and it really was still stunning. Alex knew a lot about the place.

"It was my dad's favourite haunt," he explained as he pulled out the big soft armchair for her. "Did you know, Cara, that a Thomas Gresham bought 21-22 Sackville Street and started up his own hotel? I know how much you like hotels so I thought you'd like this story." He sat down opposite her. "Thomas Gresham is a fascinating person. He was a foundling child, abandoned on the steps of the Royal Exchange. Thomas Gresham came here to Ireland and as a very young man obtained employment in the service of William Beauman of Rutland Square in Dublin. After some time, though, and he was still really young, he became a butler to the family. Now remember, Cara, this was an important position in the Georgian household with its complicated domestic structure. In 1817 Thomas left Beauman's household to open this hotel. How he acquired the capital to undertake an enterprise of this size has never been known." Alex opened his eyes wide now, making her laugh. "Today Gresham Hotels is a privately owned company and has six properties around the world."

"Wow!" Cara was impressed at his knowledge. "Brainy boy! Alex Charles on *Mastermind*: specialist subject The Gresham Hotel!" she laughed. "How did you know all that?"

"Easy," he smiled as the waiter approached them. "I read the writing on the plaque under the picture of Thomas Gresham behind you!"

Now Esther smiled at her and she could see the brown toffee of the éclair wave at her too.

Cara unravelled her white scarf and took off her fluffy Dunne's fleece. Her sheep gear, Alex had called it, laughing, but she knew he didn't really like it.

This was going to be so hard and she was dreading it. She loved Esther with all her heart. She thought of her sitting out there on the phone, sucking on her sweets, feet still in her dark tan tights stuffed into her old battered pink slippers with the backs stood in on them – no matter how many pairs of slippers Cara bought her for various Christmases she always went back to them.

Cara looked around the small house now with new eyes. Since meeting Alex she realised her little life had changed a lot. It was all about fancy restaurants and eating out every night he was here, and now lately the house-hunting. Cara had been thrilled when he brought up the possibility of them moving in together. He hadn't exactly asked her to move in with him – he'd more or less just announced they should look at places. She hadn't realised Dublin was so big. She was used to just going to and from work to their little semi-detached in Harold's Cross. Her life was very predictable. Esther would have the evening's TV circled in red pen in the *Evening Herald*. They would watch everything she had chosen, back to back, until it was time for bed. It was only with her new eyes that she could now see that the little house was well and truly looking shabby. The net curtains she had always liked looked so old-fashioned to her now, the living room with its dozens of assorted ornaments and almost antique television the same – and the same old brown squared patterned carpet they'd had forever. But the house was spotless: Esher was a very clean person. She had her routine. Starting every morning in the kitchen she mopped the lino and scrubbed the surfaces, then into the front room where she would vacuum and then the Brasso and Silvo or damp cloth would be out for each individual ornament. She was meticulous with her cleaning. The stairs were vacuumed and the Shake n' Vac sprinkled lightly on each step and in the bedrooms. Esther always sang the Shake n' Vac ad tune when she did this. Every day. The bathroom always took her the longest: it was bleached and scrubbed within an inch of its life. The brasses on the hall door would then be shone and the step scrubbed in disinfectant.

Cara had been just fifteen when her dad had passed. Her parents had tried for children for years, only having her late in life. Esther had to find a job quickly. Esther, who had got married at seventeen, straight out of school, and never worked a day in her life outside the home, had gone out to work in Rosie's Café by the airport. She had to be in work at five o'clock in the morning, making fries and breakfast rolls for the airport workers and builders who passed through. She worked hard until five in the evening, six days a week. Esther had never once complained. Esther had never once missed a day. She had earned the right to eat as many éclairs as she wanted and to wear her worn-out slippers. Cara had left school with a good enough Leaving Cert and got a job in Rosie's too. She loved working with Esther. It was a really busy café and a fantastic place to learn her trade. As with The Law Top later, she was often envious of the glamorous air stewardesses and business people who passed through.

Esther had never wanted to marry again but there had been a short-lived romance when Cara was still in school with a man she had met in Rosie's. She never spoke about him too much, only to tell Cara her heart just wasn't in it. That was good enough for Cara. She remembered the night her mother was getting ready to go on a date with him to a hotel in town. Esther had looked very strange with the bright-red lipstick and the high-heeled shoes. Cara had thought she didn't look like her mother at all. Esther had even painted her nails. Her Auntie Ann was over to sit with her and Cara had started to cry. Ridiculous at her age but she couldn't help it.

Her dad's sister had hugged her close as Esther closed the door behind her. "Your mother is entitled to a life, love – she's still a relatively young woman."

Cara never asked what happened that night. She was just glad when Esther returned home later, spoke in hushed tones to Ann but never went out looking like that ever again.

Yes, the house looked shabby, Cara thought as she held the net curtain in her hand. She realised guiltily she didn't like these new eyes of hers very much.

"What on earth are you wearing, pet?" Esther shuffled in and flopped on the couch. Cara stood up on the grate around the fireplace and gazed into the mirror above it. "What? What do you mean what am I wearing?"

"Well, ya look like a man, that's what!" Esther swallowed now.

"Get lost, Mam!" Cara laughed but Esther was right – indeed she did feel a bit like a man today. "It's called *smart casual*, if you must know!" She smoothed her hair in its tight bun with her hands.

"Well, in that case ya look like a smarty casual man then." Esther picked up the remote control and did the usual pointing it at the TV as though it was a loaded gun, squinting her eyes as she held on to it for dear life.

Cara stood down off the grate and gazed into the mirror again. She had bought a white shirt in PINK on Nassau Street that had cost her a week's wages and she'd teamed it with some black pants from Dunne's stores and black patent pumps. She had wanted to look the part for the Sandymount viewing. Alex had mentioned they needed to look like serious clients and not a couple of loved-up messers. It wasn't really her, she admitted. She'd done her best to meet his standards but she'd seen the way he'd looked at her fleece which she wore over the shirt.

"I'm just going to change so." She stuck her tongue out playfully at Esther who was now swaying from side to side on the couch, pressing buttons like a trigger.

"Don't forget to shave!" Esther laughed at her own joke as she eventually found her favourite *Friends* repeats and let out a gasp of surprise like she had every night for the last three years. "It's on!" she squealed and immediately fished into her cream cardigan pocket for an éclair.

"Mam, seriously, you've seen every episode at least fifty times – enough with the *Friends* repeats!" Cara sighed – she really was sick and tired of *Friends*.

"It's Ross Week on Comedy Central, ya know. I love Ross, he's me favourite."

Cara rolled her eyes – she knew what was coming – she'd heard it all before on a daily basis.

"It's funny, ya know, Cara – it was Joey for years, wasn't it, and then suddenly – well, I think actually it was the episode when Ross had to roller-skate to work between the two campuses that just turned it for me. From then on it was all Ross. '*We were on a break! We were on a break! No more, How you doin'*.'" Esther shouted her best Ross impression and began to roar laughing. "Could Chandler *be* any more hysterical?" She popped the sweet into her mouth now and folded her arms contentedly.

"Yes, okay, listen, Mam, I'm going up to change but I need to talk to you when I come back down. Will you be going to bingo tonight?"

Esther didn't look up until she had chewed enough to be able to speak. "No, it's too windy. I'll stay put, I think. We could put on a few of those Tesco sausage rolls later if you fancy that?" She chewed some more.

Cara nodded and closed the front-room door behind her. She leaned down and pulled off her pumps and held them in her hand as she pulled her body up the stairs by the old wooden banister. She flopped down on her single bed. She suddenly felt like she was being pulled in two different directions. She glanced out at her streetlight as it shone brightly and she could see the betting shop Pete's Punters opposite, with Mr Courtney leaning against the wall smoking his roll-up.

"You are too old to live here any more," she whispered out

the window and pulled her curtains across. She knew she was. It really was time she made a life for herself. She was thirty-three for crying out loud and so excited at the thought of starting a brand-new life with Alex. All she wanted was for Esther to be happy too. She wanted Esther to sell up here and get an apartment close to them. She wanted her mother to live nearby so she could see her often. If that was mad then, so be it, she was mad. As much as Alex had listened and nodded on their early dates when she told him how lost Esther was emotionally when Lar had died and how she needed her, he wasn't making it any easier for Cara now. Did this make him a bad person, she wondered as she unbuttoned the starched white shirt. No man wanted his girlfriend's mother living beside them, she got that, but if he just got to know Esther he'd realise she wasn't like anyone else. She wasn't needy or nosy. She wouldn't pry into their lives in a million years – she'd just get on with her own while minding her own business.

She took her brush from her dressing table and let down the tight bun. The relief was wonderful. She brushed out her long red hair before scooping it up again, this time into her trusted messy knot on the top of her head. "What am I to him?" she asked the mirror. "His girlfriend, yeah, but is it going to be more? Do I want to marry Alex? Does he want to marry me? Oh, why can't I ask him any of the really important questions?"

She pulled off the black pants now and stood in her bra and knickers. She actually had matching underwear. For the first time in her life she was paying attention to what was on under her clothes. She grabbed her orange T-shirt off the chair and put it on. As she pulled on her grey leggings, soft socks and fake Uggs she gasped out loud. "Ah, comfort at last!"

She was madly in love with Alex and she believed that he was madly in love with her so why was this odd feeling hanging over her? It was guilt, she nodded her head – that uneasy feeling was pure guilt – she felt awful leaving Esther alone. She grabbed the bedspread and threw it back as she did every night. A habit her dad had got her into. Let the bed know you will be up soon, he used to say laughing. He was always laughing. So she still did it every night.

She made her way downstairs.

Esther was humming the *Friends* theme tune.

"Mam, I need to talk to you."

"Of course you do, love." She muted the TV with a generous overly heavy-handed press of the red button. "I've been waiting for you to tell me: you want to move out and live with Alex, am I right?" She smiled warmly at Cara.

Cara couldn't read her face. "Yes, Mam." She slid into the comfy blue sofa beside her mother. "It's just that it's probably time, don't you think?" She swallowed a lump in her throat.

"Oh, absolutely, love!" Esther grabbed Cara's hands and held them tightly.

Cara watched the familiar purple veins in her hands rise.

"I'm delighted for you, love. I have only met Alex those two times but I thought he was a lovely, lovely man and you know I'm over the moon with the whole pilot thing!" She was joking now to ease Cara's obvious tension. "But, seriously, if it feels right then I am more than thrilled for you. I know it's time you lived your own life and I have never tried to stand in your way. I know you want a partner in life and maybe children – so go for it and you have my full support. Your happiness is all that matters to me, be it you are happy here or happy living with Alex or happy to go bag-packing in Outer Mongolia. Once you are happy?"

Cara squeezed her mother's hands tightly. She had to admit she did feel badly that Esther hadn't got to know Alex very well. He had come for tea one night when they first met and they two had got on really well.

Cara had nervously led Alex into the small kitchen where Esther had her back to them, engulfed in steam from their non-fan-assisted oven. She had turned when Cara called her name.

"Mam, I'd like you to meet Alex."

Esther had an unusual look on her face. One that Cara hadn't seen before. It was a cross between shock and excitement.

"Well, heeeello there, Alex, and how noice of you to come to tea!" She sounded like Audrey Hepburn in *My Fair Lady* now.

"It's my pleasure, Mrs Byrne." Alex extended his hand and they shook.

Alex also looked nervous. Wow, Cara thought, these two have put a lot of thought into this meeting.

They sat as Esther fussed around them. Alex had complimented her lamb stew and had eaten every last drop only telling Cara after that he couldn't stomach lamb stew! How sweet, she thought, that he just got on with it and ate it.

The second occasion they met, Alex took herself and Esther to The Gresham for Sunday lunch. Esther had got dressed up in her good woollen pink suit but Cara didn't think she'd really enjoyed the day. When Cara had told her where they were going her face had paled slightly and she'd shaken her head.

"Ah, here, no, Cara, not The Gresham. It's . . . it's too formal, is it not? Why don't we just go to the Kylemore and grab a nice fresh cream cake and a cuppa tea?"

Cara assured her The Gresham was not too formal. They had taken Alex's favourite window seat and ordered drinks first and Esther had spilt her sherry the second it arrived and a little had run off the table onto Alex's suit trousers. While Alex didn't mind in the least, Esther had been mortified and on edge the rest of the day. They watched the passersby on O'Connell Street and chatted sporadically. The lunch had been delicious and Cara had stuffed herself with a roast beef and Yorkshire pudding full roast dinner. The beef had melted in her mouth and she had stuffed her roasties with knobs of butter – the greens she hadn't touched. Esther had gone for the ham and chicken with jasmine rice while Alex had the Salmon Roulade.

It was probably fair to say that Esther and Alex didn't have a lot in common but then again they were from very different worlds. He had spoken very little that day about himself, paying much more attention to Esther's life story. While most women would be flattered by this attention, deep down Cara knew Esther would think he was being nosy. Mind yer own, mister, she was probably saying in her head right now. Cara had tried to change the subject several times but Alex had always been keen to get back to Esther's life story, obviously thinking that this was the courteous thing to do as this was Esther's day out.

That evening Alex had dropped them both home but declined

to come in as he had an early-morning flight.

"He's very nice, Cara." Esther had reefed her neck free from the pink woolly jacket as though it had been choking the life out of her and kicked her kitten heels off her swollen feet. "Nice man, decent too," she added as Cara looked at her from the seat under the window in their front room.

"Are you really happy about him or are you just saying that because you know it's what I want to hear, Mam?"

Esther put one finger on her lips. Then she removed it cautiously as though she was holding back her words and choosing them very carefully. "I think he is a very nice man, Cara. I don't know him very well so that's as good a judgement as I can make right now, okay, love?"

"Yes, Mam, I understand, but he is great and a real gentleman, what?" Cara got up and headed for the kitchen. She ran the tap at the sink and filled up a pint glass with water.

"Does he make you laugh?" Esther was beside her now and as Cara turned her head she stared hard into her daughter's eyes.

Cara thought for a second. "He's not like Dad, Mam, he's much more serious. I like that about him." She put the glass to her lips.

"Yer dad was serious too, young lady, when he had to be. There has to be a happy medium – a person can't be serious all the time or it would drag you down. Your father was serious about the right things but he was funny and loving mostly and that is why I loved him so much and that, my dear, is why you loved him so much too. Qualities and characteristics. Watch out carefully for them both, love. They are what make a man." Esther turned on her heel and headed for the make-believe world of Central Perk.

Cara got up from the couch now and went to the kitchen. She didn't trust herself to speak another word to Esther yet for fear she'd burst into tears. She filled the kettle and flicked it on to boil and stood at the sink for a while as she remembered Esther's words. Qualities and characteristics. She wasn't sure what they meant exactly but understood that Esther was supportive and that was all that mattered. She was relieved at her mother's reaction although she hadn't expected anything less than total support. It was out in the open now, she was officially moving out. She took the teapot out from the press and threw three tea bags in. Again Esther's words came back to her. Yes Alex was serious but there was nothing wrong with serious in her opinion. She wanted a serious relationship, then marriage and children. He was very different to Lar in every way but she hadn't met a Lar, had she? She wasn't twenty-one anymore and she had to understand that if she wanted all these things then she had to grab them when they came along. She couldn't sit back and say, no, Alex wasn't all this or all that. He was a good man and she was over the moon he had come into her life. He could give her the marriage and the children and the life she was supposed to be living at this age. He was her ticket to *normalness*. She would be like every other thirty-something woman now.

Esther came into the kitchen and removed the sausage rolls from the fridge as Cara filled the teapot with boiling water.

"Anyway, Mam," Cara bounced back to the moment as she stirred the teabags around and then popped them on the draining board, "I hate the thought of you in this house all alone."

Esther shook her fist at her. "Now, now, now! Don't start all that crap! Sure I'm absolutely grand here!" She stabbed the plastic packaging with a fork and removed the sausage rolls.

"No, hear me out – this is what I'm thinking," said Cara. "What about if we sold up here and I gave you my share of the house and you bought a nice apartment somewhere close enough to myself and Alex around the Sandymount area? You'd love Sandymount – the sea close and bingo in Ringsend at your doorstop seven nights a week! I know we're only renting now but it's an area I think we'd love to buy in when the time is right." Cara was clutching at straws here, she knew. She got some cups and poured the tea, watching the steam rise.

"Listen, lady, this is my home and your home. It will always be here for both of us as long as we are alive. We have both worked damn hard to pay off this mortgage and it's our little sanctuary. I'm delighted for you to go and live with Alex – in fact, I approve of that more than you jumping into marriage with him this fast, so go and see what each other are all about. Want to know me, come and live with me. I will not move from this house. Lar is here, all around me, I will never be alone. Now I'm starving after that lunch. I could barely find that measly piece of chicken, and what about those peas – they were a teaspoon-big! And call that ham? It was more like spam and, as for the rice, tasted more like lice! And certainly not the portions that they used to give years ago. Ah, here, I'm putting on that Sloppy Giuseppe I got from Tesco as well – I hope there's a bit of coleslaw left in the fridge."

Cara handed her a cup and Esther took a sip and put the cup back down on the counter. With that Esther bent to put the sausage rolls in the oven and the conversation was over.

It was official. Cara was moving out. Esther was not.

Cara took her cup of tea from the draining board and headed to her bedroom.

"Be back in a few minutes," she told Esther. She needed a few minutes to herself. Sometimes she felt like she hadn't had time to digest any of this. She had met Alex, he had swept her off her feet, and because of his job every time they were together was extra special – trying to grab time – the sex was amazing, she was infatuated with him and he was a perfect gentleman . . . but somehow she wasn't sure she knew him all that well. Something wasn't perfect.

"Why, oh why, are you picking this apart?" she asked her reflection in the mirror. "Congratulations, Cara Byrne, you are shacking up with your boyfriend!" she whispered. She smiled broadly at herself and stood there until the smile faded away.

Then she drained her tea and went back downstairs.

Chapter 12

Sandra grabbed a cab easily enough outside the hospital and gave the address. "You got rightly stung in them houses, didn't you, loveen?" the older driver started.

She really wasn't in the mood. She got this in every taxi she got into. She tugged at the ancient seatbelt in the back seat and clasped it shut.

He reached into the glove compartment now and pulled out a bag of peanuts. He drove with one hand as he threw nuts down his gob with the other.

"Excuse me one moment, would you?" She pulled her phone from her brown leather Mango bag and discreetly flipped it on to silent, then pretended to answer it. "Hi, Sandra!" She began a pretend conversation with herself that lasted for the short drive.

As she paid her driver who was now silent she noticed the lights still on in the front room. It was such an unusual sight of late to see the house lit up at all that she welcomed it. Dermot must have popped around like he said he would but she hadn't expected him to still be there.

He opened the front door as she rummaged in her bag for her keys.

"Are you all right, Sandy?" He was in his stocking feet, in his grey jeans and a light blue shirt open to the third button. His blond hair flopped over one eye and he now pushed it back with both hands.

"Dermot, I didn't expect you to still be here!" Sandra was mortified as she entered the warm house and saw to her utmost surprise the open fire crackling away in the front room. She hadn't been in that room in months. She couldn't light the open fire herself and those easy-light fire logs were just too expensive now. There was a smell of food too as Dermot took her coat and hung it up behind the hall door.

"Listen, it's no problem, I wasn't doing anything. I got your spare key at reception like you said. I was about to leave you a note and head off. I just didn't want you to arrive back to a cold, empty house. I hope that's okay?" He looked concerned now as he tiredly rubbed at the light stubble on his chin.

Dermot, Sandra surprised herself with this thought, was really very sexy. What is wrong with you? she shouted at herself internally. Your husband is lying in a hospital bed!

"Did you hear me, Sandy?" Dermot placed his hand on her shoulder and she jumped.

"No, sorry, Dermot, what was that?"

"I said I threw a few logs onto the fire to keep it burning for you. This is one cold gaff." Dermot leaned against the banister and the space in the hallway suddenly seemed small.

Sandra coughed even though she didn't need to. "Who are you telling?" she said as she gestured to him to follow her into the kitchen. She immediately opened the shiny red American-style oversized fridge and reached for a chilled bottle of white wine. No matter how tight money was she couldn't live without her bottle of wine. There she was avoiding the expense of a fire log but buying alcohol. This was where she was in her life right now: that she'd rather sit in the freezing cold kitchen with a bottle of wine than in her front room alone and wineless in front of a cosy fire. She might have a problem, she thought. But, hang on, other women had husbands who loved them, children, gym memberships, hairdressers, facials – all she had was her bottle or two of wine. Right now she wasn't giving that up for anyone or anything.

"Want one?" She offered a glass to Dermot.

"I'd rather a beer." He was draped over the chrome counter now.

She laughed. "If I only had a beer to offer you."

"Go on then, you've twisted my taste buds." He reached out and took the glass as she filled it. "So how is Neil doing now?"

Sandra took a very long drink and refilled the glass immediately. She had sent Dermot a text when she arrived at the hospital to tell him of Neil's condition. "Ah, I don't know really, no change after I texted you. He was asleep pretty much the whole time. His wrist is broken so that's not good for work, if he was to get any work, and his ribs are bruised. But maybe he can claim something now? His face is fairly battered but he was lucky, I think." She swallowed the white wine slowly.

"That's good, Sandy."

There really wasn't much else to say about the accident. There was a lot to say about why she had called Dermot, she thought, but he didn't ask.

"I cleaned everywhere by the way. It's perfect now if I do say so myself." He took a mock bow, twirling his hand as it pointed down to her feet.

"You didn't?" Sandra pulled out one of the tall stools from under the island in the middle of the kitchen and sat on it. She spotted her scarf on the counter. "Where was that?" she asked him.

"On the floor there." He pointed under her stool.

She looked hard at Dermot. "Thanks, Dermot, you're so good. I'm sorry I bothered you. I really shouldn't have – I mean, I have other friends and of course my parents are here. Somewhere." She rubbed away an imaginary stain from the counter top with a clenched fist.

"It's no problem. I'm glad to be here. I want to be here for you." He looked over at her as silence engulfed the room and the clock ticked loudly.

His blond hair fell forward again and the moment was broken. "I really do need to cut this mop, don't I?" He laughed now as he drank the rest of his wine in one go.

"I like it, it's different. It's you," Sandra said. "By the way, what was cooking? The smell is divine."

"Oh shit, yeah, sorry, Sandy, I ordered you a chicken curry and fried rice. I remember you saying you love a chicken curry. It's in the oven – here, let me pop the oven back on to warm it – you must be starving?"

"No microwave?" she asked him.

"No, never put a Chinese takeout in a microwave – it just dries it out." He put his glass in the sink and busied himself at the oven.

She was starving. "Do you mind if I get out of my uniform? I'll be back in it in a few hours."

He shook his head. "I threw down those switches on the immersion but turned them off again later – however, the water should be hot enough for a shower."

"Oh, that would be amazing. See you in a few minutes so." She took her wine and headed for the shower.

She grabbed her towel and shower gel from the main bathroom. She hadn't dared enter Neil's bedroom, as she now called it, to use the en suite shower in weeks. The spare room had become her room. As she stepped under the showerhead the water hit her hard – that was probably the only good thing about this horrible house – the power shower. She rubbed the tea tree and lime gel all over her body and scrubbed at her hair. She was washing months of this life away. In one way she was glad to get Neil out of the house, as awful as that sounded. She couldn't cope with him any more. She hadn't been coping for ages. It wasn't just the fact she was suspicious of him, that he'd had an affair before, the failed IVFs, the recession, the lack of money and piled-up unpaid bills. It was something else. It was that they hadn't been close in so long now, Sandra could barely remember it. Was she a horrible wife? She didn't really think she'd done her best. Done the wifely stuff. Her duties. Paid heed to her vows. Did she still even love him? She honestly didn't know the answer to that. If he wasn't seeing someone else, what then? Would she feel this suspicion for the rest of their lives? Really this came down to the fact that she still wasn't over the affair with Kelley. Poor Kelley. She had been beyond devastated when she'd found out they were still married. She'd immediately stopped the relationship as she called it, or "fling" as Neil called it, and also left her job and gone back to the US.

Sandra had dialled her number on Neil's phone. "This is Neil Darragh's wife, Sandra Darragh. Who is this?" she had asked with shaking voice and hands.

"Oh my God, he's married still, isn't he?" came the heavily drawled accented reply after a long pause.

"He is, to me, yes. Who are you?" Sandra had whispered before the tears came.

"I'm Kelley. I am so sorry. I had totally no clue. I believed he was separated. I believed that was why we had to be secretive – because he said you were still very upset and he didn't want to hurt you any more. I'm such a dumbass!"

"Kelley, he's lying. We are still very much married."

She didn't have to warn the girl off, or say stay away from my man or else. Kelley had sobbed and apologised over and over and told Sandra she would leave the village as soon as she could put arrangements in place. Sandra didn't tell her to stay.

Sandra stepped out of the shower now and, as the smell of the curry wafted into the bedroom, her stomach rumbled.

"I'm going out the back for a smoke!" Dermot shouted up as he heard her move about.

"Righto!" she shouted back as she heard the patio doors slide open and bang shut again. She pulled out the hairdryer from under the bed and as she stood back up she looked up at the pictures of her and Neil on the wall of the bedroom. One of their wedding day. The pictures were taken on Knocknoly Bridge after they got back from the Registry office. The sun was shining warmly and was bouncing off the water underneath the bridge and the two of them were smiling so brightly. She had been so happy that day. She walked closer and examined the other pictures. The first year of marriage captured in stillness. A trip to Nerja in Spain with them on a horse and cart, both tanned and laughing. As she made her way along the wall she was struck by the difference in their body language. Early pictures saw them squeezed up tight together, and as it progressed to the last picture when Neil had a bit of a thank-you-and-goodbye party in Hines for three local lads he'd had to let go, they looked very much apart. Neil's eyes looked clouded over and she looked miles away. She had been miles away that night, she now recalled. It had been during the second round of IVF. She was pretending to drink from her pint glass all night and now and then Neil would swap it for his under duress. Their communication was at an all-time low. She remembered now that a few nights before the going-away party they'd had to have sex to check for blockage, to check that the sperm were swimming freely, and it was torture. They weren't even speaking. It took forever and she almost cried.

She moved away from the pictures and blasted the hot hair from the dryer all over her body now before slathering Aloe Vera Vaseline cream on, and then dried off her hair with her paddle brush.

She supposed Neil had a point: she had been a very different girl then – or woman, which was it? It had all been so easy. He liked a beer and football and he wasn't a complicated guy. Then her hormones began to rage when she kept getting her period like clockwork each month. It was out of her control. In all the magazines around the hotel, celebrities were popping them out like pills from a plastic packet. Pop. Pop. Pop. Life wasn't fair.

Sandra turned off the dryer and shook her dark hair. She pulled on her white Gap track suit and went barefoot down the stairs just as Dermot was entering from the garden.

"Give up them old fags, Dermot!" She shook her finger at him.

"Never, Sandy, I love my fags. They take ten years off your life and as far as I'm concerned they're doing me a favour. Eighty years is enough for me to live. My entire family live well into their nineties – I don't fancy that. Now sit there till I dish this up for you." He washed his hands and dried them with the tea towel as she took a seat.

"Wow, Dermot, you are a man of many hidden talents!" she said as he scooped a massive portion of chicken curry onto her

Paul Costello plate and placed it in front of her. “How can I eat all that at this hour? I meant a nibble!”

“Eat it!” He gently ripped a piece of kitchen paper off the roll and put it beside her plate. “Listen,” he started as she scooped a mouthful into her mouth, “I’m off now.” He grabbed his Husky jacket and found his shoes under the table. “But don’t you come in until nine in the morning. I’ve Lorna lined up to do the feeds so I’ll mind the reception for you for two hours. Big J will be gone to Dublin for another secretive meeting, whatever the hell he’s at, so he won’t know. He's very unlikely to phone reception and if he does I'll wing it. I doubt very much he’d mind if I told him but I know you won’t let me.” He pulled his tweed cap from his pocket, straightened it out and pulled it down onto his head, his blond hair sticking out from under the peak.

“I can’t do that.” She dabbed her mouth with the paper towel.

“You can and you will. Eat that all up now.” He reached over and poured her another glass of wine. “See you at nine bells and sure I can spin you up to the hospital on your break if you want?”

She picked up her wineglass and looked at him. He smiled.

“Okay,” she whispered and she didn’t know why she whispered.

He walked to the front door and didn’t look back, closing it gently behind him.

Chapter 13

The room looked amazing. Cara smiled to herself. She was bush-tired and it was past midnight but she had wanted this all done before she got back in the morning. She had let Tiff and Mike go home as she was happy to attend to all the little extra touches herself. Jenny had chosen red roses and the scent filled the small room wonderfully. Cara went from table to table now with her wooden ruler and measured the distance between each plate and each glass. Then she measured the distance between the tablecloths and the floor. It had to be exact on each table. She was slightly anal in this department, she acknowledged. The tables were set with eight chairs, and there were six tables in all. The main table was a long trestle under the long window with the sea peering in at their backs. Jenny had chosen crisp white linen with small red bows – the exact colour of the roses – on the back of each chair, and red velvet ties on the menu scrolls. The area would be cleared for the band after the reception, a Beatles Tribute act, and Cara had the table for the cake already set up in the corner. Louise had made the most incredible four-tiered cake. It really was a work of art. She had one hundred candles to place yet and then she was done. She needed a strong coffee for her flagging energy levels.

"Oh, hi!" She was startled as she left the room and walked straight into Jonathan on the corridor.

"Cara? You're still here? I think we should get you a room here!" He fell into step beside her.

"I want to get as much as I can done before tomorrow, just to be sure to be sure. It's okay doing all this in an essay but in practice it's different. People's lives, you know. It has to be perfect for them."

They headed for the back kitchen and Jonathan took two mugs down off the stack. "It will be wonderful, I know it. Coffee?" He held the almost empty pot up.

"No, sure you go ahead – I'm happy with a glass of water," she said.

"No, come on, I insist. Please have the coffee. You'd probably be doing me a favour – it's like my tenth cup today and you know any second now old Mrs Reilly will make a fresh pot and I'll have to drink a cup. She's my Mrs Doyle of Coffee-pushing." He pretended to have the shakes in his hands. "Listen, I'm sorry I didn't make it over to your place with the rest of the paints last week – something really important cropped up here and I just couldn't leave. Story of my life I'm afraid. I'm still more than willing to help you paint but I was thinking it's probably even better if I loan you Big Bob – he's a brilliant handyman and will have that place painted in a weekend for you." He sighed hard, handed her the coffee and bent down to open the small staff fridge.

She nodded. "Would it be okay if I took a few tins of that blue too?"

"Of course, work away – just leave me a little post-it on my desk of what you took, okay? But it's all there for you to use."

His smile was so warm. Then she noticed what he had in his hand.

"No, please! Not Red Bull?" She laughed at him.

"Afraid so." He smacked his left hand with his right one. "I can run you home tonight with the blue paints in the boot if you want? Carry them in for you – at least you'll have them there for when Bob arrives?" He leaned against the back wall.

"Thanks, Jonathan, actually that would be great. I am really keen to get the place looking well over the next few weeks."

Cara sipped the coffee as Jonathan opened his can and the potent smell of raspberry from the Red Bull filled her nostrils even over the strong coffee.

"Okay, how much have you left to do here, do you think?" He pushed his body away from the wall and stood tall.

"Well, I just want to place the candles and do final checks, so half hour should do me?"

"Cool – sure I'll drop into the room in half an hour." He moved towards the door and she followed out with her coffee cup between her hands. "I have a last pile of invoices to put through and there are still some guests in the residents' bar so I want to check on the level of drink flowing in there, make sure the new barman Christy's all right on his own. I'm so ready for my *leaba* then!"

"See you then." Cara strolled down the corridor as the lush dark carpet welcomed her pumps.

In the wedding room she placed her coffee cup on the window sill. She bent down to take the first of the silver candlesticks out of the cardboard box and, as she unwrapped the old newspaper from it, she remembered her own day in oh-too-vivid detail.

* * *

The apartment in Sandymount was beautifully laid out. Alex had brought most of his own furniture and it was all very modern.

He still found it funny that Cara had never had a DVD player let alone an iPod. "How is that possible?" he said, chomping down hard on his nicotine gum.

Cara was still working at The Law Top but Alex was always on and on at her to give it all up.

"I like it – it's my job!" she had protested as he picked her up one evening and made a face at the place when he got out of the car to greet her.

"It's an absolute shithole, Cara! Come on, you know that surely?" Alex crinkled up his nose.

"Actually, now that you mention it, funny I have never asked you this. What were you doing in the bar the day I first met you?"

Alex opened the passenger door for her as his hazards flashed red in his eyes. "I was meeting a friend, that's all." She got in and he closed the door with a bang.

"Who was he, the guy you were with?" she asked. "I mean, he didn't look like a friend. Tristan, wasn't it? I remember the name as I thought it was so posh! It all looked pretty official. I remember the table was scattered with a lot of papers?"

"No one interesting. *Gee, Officer Krupke!* Okay, now listen, I have had a great idea – guess where we're going?" He eased the car into the traffic, the engine purring so softly sometimes Cara thought the engine had cut out.

"Where?" she asked as she clicked her seatbelt on to shut up the bloody warning signal beeping relentlessly at them.

"To the DSPCA. I thought it would be a nice idea to get Esther a little dog for company."

"Oh Alex, that's so nice of you!" Cara was instantly delighted with him once again. Esther did love dogs and, although she said they were too much work, Cara knew she'd be secretly delighted now that she was going to be on her own.

They drove to the shelter for the Dublin Society for the Prevention of Cruelty to Animals, listening to some obscure classical music. Cara would have loved a bit of Beyoncé. When eventually they arrived the gate was closed and Alex pressed the buzzer.

"Hi, there." A tall man approached them with a gang of yapping dogs close at his heels. His green Hunter wellies were well nipped, she noticed. "Hush a minute!" he called down at them and patted a couple of them on their heads. "Can I help you?"

"Yes, I called earlier. I'm Alex Charles. I said about looking for a dog for my mother-in-law?"

Cara made a noise. An involuntary one but a noise nonetheless. Both men looked at her.

"You okay?" Alex asked.

"Yes." She smiled a huge big smile, her mouth now so dry her tongue was stuck to the roof of her mouth.

"In you come, in you come! "The man opened the gate and they followed him into the yard.

Cara walked carefully as the muck was slippery in places. *Mother-in-law*, she said over and over again in her head – he had called Esther his *mother-in-law* and he hadn't made any deal about it. It was matter of fact. In fact he hadn't really realised what he had just said. Cara put her hand on her heart and it was beating wildly. She tried to concentrate on the task at hand.

There were rows and rows of dogs and she found it all very upsetting.

"I'm Colin Creedy by the way, district manager. Just take your time and give a whistle if you need me – they're all beautiful animals." He left them to it.

Cara peeped into each box. Big dogs, small dogs, old dogs, puppies, they were all so adorable. Time passed as she scrutinised each one, moving slowly from cage to cage. Then she stopped at this one cage. It was the low almost introverted whimpering sound that got to her. She bent down slowly and there she was. A small black-and-white Shih Tzu dog. Cara felt sure she was a female. She looked at the little dog and she immediately stopped the whimpering.

"Good taste there, Missus." Colin was back now, hands clasped low behind his back. "Expensive dog, that one, but she's been here over three months now and no one has come looking for her. We reckon the couple broke up and neither wanted her so they just let her out."

"You are not serious?" Cara was appalled.

"Yeah, happening a lot lately. Couples move in together, playing house, get the dog and then it doesn't work out. Especially these days with the money gone and couples having to leave the country. The need to emigrate always means horrendous times for animals. People just open the door and let the dogs go. You want me to let her all the way out, Missus?" He jangled the largest bunch of keys Cara had ever seen, which were attached to a chain on his army belt.

"Yes, please." Cara fell to her knees now as the cage opened and the little black nose emerged first, then the head, two tiny front legs followed by the black-and-white body and two tiny back legs. She was wagging her stumpy tail wildly. Her breathing was snuffled and loud.

"Hello there, little one," Cara whispered and she clicked her tongue. "A girl, yeah?"

"Indeed she is," came the reply. "She's a bitch – neutered though."

"Hello, girl," Cara said again.

The little dog took her time. She sniffed at Cara's outstretched hand, no doubt smelling today's corned beef and cabbage off her clothes.

"Hello, my pretty, aren't you the best girl?" Cara rubbed her head ever so softly. "Aren't you a beautiful little thing? Yes, you are, yes, you are!" She was besotted. Alex, leaning against the whitewashed wall, laughed out loud. "Looks like she's the one – so what do we need to do now?"

Cara jumped up and hugged him tightly. "We can't just take her now, can we?" she asked both men, her eyes darting from one to the other. They both nodded and she clapped her hands.

They headed for the Portacabin office.

After all the paperwork was signed Cara picked the little dog up gently and placed her in the curve of her arms.

"What you didn't know," said Alex, "is that I already had a visit from the DSPCA when you and Esther were out shopping in that woeful TK Max last week. Esther's little house was inspected for its suitability to care for an animal and checked out thoroughly, and they will be back to make sure all the safety gates and lists they left me are done next week. Isn't that right, Colin?"

"'Tis right enough. And just so you know, we call her Victoria, after that Posh Spice one, because she was the most expensive animal in here. She's a thoroughbred, that one. I've a soft spot for her. Bring her back to see us on occasion, won't you?"

"I will of course, Colin, I promise. Well, hello, Victoria, and welcome to the Byrne family!"

The little dog's tail wagged but she didn't move at all as she took in all of Cara's face. Cara didn't know why but she put her nose right up close to Victoria's nose and said, "I love you, yes, I do."

Alex laughing made her blush.

"Seriously, Cara, you do know you have to give her away?"

"I know, but she's just so gorgeous, Alex."

They said their goodbyes and walked back to the car.

"Thank you, Alex," Cara said as they reached the car and she eased into the passenger seat gently with the little dog on her knee.

* * *

"What on God's green earth is that?" Esther half shouted as Cara entered the kitchen and put the dog down.

Victoria skidded as she ran on the lino.

"This is Victoria, Mam," Cara laughed. "Your new housemate!"

"Hello there, Alex." Esther looked flushed. "Cara, you really should have told me you were calling! Would you look at the pure state of me?"

She did look a bit the worse for wear. Mismatched soft rollers in her hair, face cream not fully rubbed in, the old grey nightgown Lar used to call her "haunt-the-house robe" and her old pink slippers. Cara did feel a bit bad about not warning Esther now.

"Sure I'm family now, Esther!" Alex laughed awkwardly and pulled out a chair at the kitchen table. He fixed the padded cushion on it before he sat down.

"Well, she is cute," Esther said.

She got a bowl from the draining board and half filled it with water. She placed it by the back door on the brown-and-grey non-slip mat. Victoria wasted no time and lapped it all up.

"Well, what does she like to eat?" Esther asked now as she popped on the kettle and tried to discreetly pull a few rollers out and shove them into a kitchen drawer.

"There's a whole pile of papers on her here – what she does and doesn't like, what jabs she's had, what she may need, all that sort of stuff," said Cara as she flicked through the pages in the large folder the DSPCA had given them. "Are you happy with her, Mam?"

Esther smiled down at the little dog. "Sure I am, I suppose, but they are an awful lot of work. I mean, what happens when I'm away with the bingo after Christmas?"

"We will take her for you, won't we, Alex?" Cara turned to him now as he had stood up and was looking at pictures that adorned the kitchen wall.

"Sure," he said, not turning around. Then he added, "We really should go, Cara, it's late." He grabbed his coat off the back of the chair.

"Will ya not have a cuppa tea, Alex?" Esther said, pouring the boiling water into the old teapot.

"No, no, thank you, Esther – we'll have a nightcap at home."

Cara was a little shocked. It was quite rude as the tea was already made but she didn't make a fuss. "He's right, it's too late, Mam. You enjoy the tea." Cara patted Victoria who had settled herself nicely on a cushion that Esther had thrown down by the back door.

"Okay, if yer sure?" Esther said and walked them to the door as Victoria jumped up and tottered slowly behind her new mammy.

* * *

Back at home Alex poured them each a glass of Hennessy brandy and they sat back on the stiff leather couch. Cara was trying to like the taste of brandy but she'd have murdered a chilled white wine or even a cup of her mother's tea. Alex wasn't one for television either.

"I'll be gone now for two weeks, you know that," he suddenly said, "and here's the thing . . . well . . . I don't want to you to stay with your mother while I'm gone." He cupped his oversized glass in his hand and looked at her.

She looked back at him, her feet curled under her and her red hair flowing free. "Why not?" she asked, puzzled.

"Because this is your home now, Cara. You can't run back to Mammy every time I'm on a long haul – it would be ridiculous. It looks ridiculous. Promise me you'll stay here, in our home. It's the reason we moved in together, to set up a home. I mean, come on, you're a grown woman!"

The leather creaked as she shifted her position. "Okay, if you feel that strongly about it. I won't stay over with her, I promise."

They drank their brandies, each lost in their own thoughts.

"Say something," Alex said after a while. "I hope this isn't you sulking now, is it, after all I've just done for you and your mother?" He drained his glass and put it on the wooden floor at his feet. He insisted on no rugs. He hated rugs.

"No, of course not . . . it's just a big change for me, that's all," she managed.

"Listen, Cara, I don't want to upset you but I think you need to make a clean break, I really do. If you keep running back to Mammy every time I'm away this will never work."

She knew he was right but she didn't know why she felt so bad about it. It just seemed silly that she couldn't spend time with Esther while he was away.

He leaned over and kissed the side of her face with soft, soft kisses. Then he pulled her close and they made love hard and fast on the couch. Alex wasn't a gentle slow lover, he didn't take a long time over sex, but Cara liked it that way.

He was leaving at four in the morning so she wouldn't see him now for two weeks. As she showered before bed she thought about what he had said. She supposed he was right: this was her home now.

"I'll call you every night around ten, okay? You'd better be in," he whispered in her ear as she crawled into bed beside him, exhausted now.

"Okay," she mumbled and immediately fell asleep.

* * *

She wasn't due in work until twelve the next morning so she enjoyed a nice lie-in. Alex wasn't one for lying on in bed in the mornings: he was always up at the crack of dawn. He didn't really like Cara lying in either. Cara liked her sleep.

When she awoke at eleven she stretched out on the expensive sheets. If she was really honest she didn't find them as cosy as her old pink, blue and green-striped cotton sheets. She sat up in the bed, and threw her hair up in a bun. She knew Alex liked it down best so she tried to leave it down when she was with him. She found all that hair around her face all day tiring.

She hopped out now, dressed quickly in her work clothes and headed for the kitchen. She would make the bed tonight.

Alex had left a note, written in huge black block letters, all coloured in to perfection with a red biro. "I LOVE YOU, CARA . . . FOREVER." He was so romantic. He was always leaving little notes around the place for her. Sometimes in her bag or even in her purse. When she mentioned this to Esther the other woman had simply said, "A man shouldn't go through a woman's bag." She was so old-fashioned at times, her mother.

She boiled the kettle and took a green-tea bag down from the clear glass jar and popped it into a mug. She really had to remember to buy regular tea bags. Her mother always bought the tea bags at home so she never remembered them. She grabbed the phone from the wall and punched in Esther's number.

"Hi, Mam!" she called as she poured water on the lonely tea bag.

"Morning, love, I'm just brushing Victoria. She's a little baby, not a bother on her!" Esther was chewing.

"Mam, will you leave off the éclairs! It's too early! I know I keep saying it but really and truly you won't have a tooth left in your head!"

Esther was silent and Cara knew she had her hand over the mouthpiece and was chewing furiously.

"So what time are you coming over tonight?" Esther asked eventually.

"Actually, Mam, I can't come this evening after all. I know I told you I would as Alex is away but I'm working today and back in on an early shift tomorrow morning so easier if I just head back to Sandymount."

There was a brief pause but no chewing. "Sure, love, that's fine. When will I see you so?"

Cara could hear the disappointment in Esther's voice, though she tried to hide it, and she listened to Victoria's snuffly breath. She pinched the bridge of her nose. This was crazy. "Ah, actually, listen, Mam, I will come after work and stay the night. Will you make some dinner or will I bring two of Mary's Chicken Kievs?"

"No, love, I'm more than happy to cook if you're sure you wanta come over? There's no pressure, you know, I'm grand here."

"I'm sure, Mam." Cara closed her eyes.

"Lovely so. Okay, I want to take Victoria for a walk now and I'll pop into the supermarket for us. It's bloody ridiculous though, Mrs Canavan who had the poodles told me that I have to tie her up outside while I shop. Sure what harm can she do in a supermarket on a bloody lead? It will break my heart to leave her outside in the cold. Only God knows what she's been through and she'll probably fear every time I go into the shops that I'm not coming back. There should be supermarkets for dogs!"

"She'll be fine, Mam, or maybe she'd feel more secure if you just left her at home when you go shopping?"

"That's true."

"Mam, make sure you have tea bags in – I'm gasping for a proper cup of Barry's tea!" Cara smiled as she crinkled her nose at the smell of the green tea.

She hung up and went into the bathroom to apply her make-up. As she put on her mascara she suddenly felt a little nervous. Would Alex be mad with her? He did say she should promise him she wouldn't go back to Esther's.

"Don't be ridiculous, Cara!" she chastised her reflection. "He won't mind, why would he?"

Okay, so she understood his point. They were newly in love and newly living together, but she still felt it was all a bit of a dream. Alex had taken on the majority of the rent, insisting she pay only what she could. It was an expensive property even in this current rental climate. Alex had even suggested they look into buying the place but Cara had said a firm no. Not yet.

She sat on the toilet now as she tied the laces on her runners. Alex hated her runners. She smiled. She really wasn't his type at all. They were like chalk and cheese. She stopped smiling all of a sudden and she didn't know why. She was so very out of sorts. Maeve had asked her yesterday as she sat in the steamy kitchen of The Law Top tucking into a Shepherd's Pie if she was okay.

"You don't seem your usual bubbly self, missy!" the other woman had said as she tested her carrot and coriander soup from a huge black ladle, made a face and then added more sea salt.

"No, I'm good, Maeve, just a bit tired."

Maeve had made a guttural noise. "There isn't a fire burning under yer arse, Cara. Take your time, don't rush into anything," she said before moving on to chop the living daylights out of a turnip.

Here was the thing, Cara thought. Alex never spoke about himself, apart from that awful story about his father's infidelity. She still hadn't met any of his family. She was concerned about this at this stage. She had tried to bring up the possibility of her meeting his parents a few weeks before.

"They are getting divorced," he said. "It's really not a good time for them, Cara. Try not to be so selfish."

That stung. It was nothing to do with being selfish. "Well, okay, maybe I could meet them individually then?"

"I don't speak to my father." He stared at her. "And I just told you it's not a good time for my mother. The last thing I want to do is push a happy relationship in her face. Think about it? Can we drop it now, Cara, please?"

Deep down Cara knew this wasn't good. She stood again now and jogged on the spot. She always did this to test the tightness of her laces. She flicked off the light in the bathroom and then flicked it back on. At the very top of the boiler in the bathroom she had noticed a small black box. She had never seen it there before but she had noticed it during the move. Alex had laughed and called it his "box of tricks". Right this second she was really curious about what Alex had in there. It must be something to do with past relationships – otherwise why hide it in the bathroom? It was way too high for Cara to reach – she doubted if she could reach it even standing on a chair with a few books or whatever on top. Now that she thought about it Esther had a small stepladder. She would borrow it tonight and take a look at that box tomorrow. She needed to know more about Alex but for whatever reason she couldn't bear to upset him by asking him again. He was so good to her. She just needed to get to know him better, she needed to know more about his life before her. She locked the door behind her and headed for a busy day at The Law Top.

* * *

"Ah, listen, it's very sad, I'm not saying it isn't, Aoife," Steve was saying to Aoife as Cara pushed open the bar door. The smell of bleach was overpowering, as always at this time of the day. The two were stacking the mixers into the bottom fridges. "What's very sad?" she asked as she joined them behind the bar.

"Ah, yer man Seán Hackett. Overdosed in prison last night."

Cara's hand flew to her mouth. "Ah no, is he dead?" she managed.

"Dead as a doornail," Steve flicked his white teacloth at a fly as he stood up.

Cara was sickened. What a tragic life Seán had! She would go to his funeral. "Poor Seán, he never stood a chance," she said, more to herself than anyone else.

"What are you on about, Cara?" Steve said. "He was a thieving druggie bastard for God's sake! Let's not make him into some poor martyr now he's popped his clogs, please. I took you for being smarter than that!"

"You didn't know him, Steve." She bent her head and tried to walk past him.

"Neither did you. You really are gullible, aren't you, Cara? Seán Hackett would have robbed the eye out of your head given half a chance."

She turned on Steve now. "No, he wouldn't, Steve, you've got that all wrong. He was my friend."

"Ha!" Steve shook his head wildly. "Your friend? Get off the crack, will you? You are too trusting, that's your fault, your biggest fault! Be careful of it, Cara – it could be the ruination of you!"

She was angry now. "What's that supposed to mean? Leave it out! I am entitled to my opinion and you can't push yours on me. You didn't like him, fine, you didn't trust him, fine. I did. I liked him as a person, I took the trouble to get to know him a little bit. In fact I'd have trusted him with my life!"

"Well, more fool you because you'd be stone dead!" he said and walked away into the kitchen.

She pulled her apron out from under the bar and turned to Aoife, catching her breath. "So, busy morning?" She composed herself now.

"Ah, ticking over – there's a big rape trial on in the court today so I'd say we'll be packed."

No sooner had Aoife spoken the last word when the door opened and a bunch of customers piled in. It was obviously a very serious trial by the look on the faces of all of them. She hated these days when the bar was wracked with tension as members of each side sat as far away from each other as possible. They spoke in hushed tones. Violence was always a threat.

Cara grabbed her notebook and slid her biro into her messy hair-knot. She dropped clean beer mats on all the tables and checked the salt and pepper sets were full before finally checking to see who looked ready to order. As it was usually a one-hour break the pressure was on.

She approached a corner table, where three men and one older woman were sitting. They were whispering urgently, so obviously were part of the trial.

"Are you ready to order?" Cara asked quietly.

The woman spoke. "Wot is zee soupe of ze daz?" Her French accent was hard to understand.

"Soup?" Cara checked.

"*Oui – soupe?*"

"It's carrot and coriander," Cara answered.

"That okay with you all?" one of the men asked – he was obviously Irish – and the other three nodded. "Four soups so with some brown bread, please, love."

The woman looked up at Cara again and then back to the three men sitting around her. She looked sad.

Cara wriggled through the crowd. Steve was back in behind the bar and their eyes met. "Sorry," he mouthed at her.

"It's okay," she mouthed back. Who knew which one of them was right? But Cara always saw the good in people. It was a legacy her father had left her and she meant to honour it. "Docket down, Chef!" She rang the bell with the palm of her hand and they were off.

Chapter 14

Sandra crawled out of the bed at eight o'clock, padded naked out to the landing and flicked down the buttons for a shower. She found her bag on the floor by the bed and fished out her phone. She dialled the hospital. Neil had had a peaceful night, had woken for water and painkillers and had gone back to sleep. The nurse said she could come in at any time so she told her to tell Neil she would be there at lunchtime. She pulled on her white fluffy robe and went downstairs.

The house was bitter cold and she shook as she poured the dregs of the semi-skimmed milk on her Crunchy Nut Cornflakes. Not the real deal, but who could tell? She stood eating as she gazed out the window. How she hated this house! But they were stuck in it. Stuck paying over the odds for it. What would happen to them? There would never be any more money for another round of IVF, she knew that. She threw the bowl into the sink and turned on the tap to wash it. She couldn't think about that. She couldn't believe that it was all over. That she would never have her baby. A tear dropped onto her cheek. She wiped it away guiltily as she hadn't really shed a tear over her marriage. Funny how the tears just came now without her really ever getting worked up. It was like they dropped onto her cheek to let her know they understood. They were supporting her sorrow but in an understated controlled way.

She ran back up the stairs and hopped into the shower before dressing quickly and fixing her hair. Downstairs again, she pulled on her green Oasis coat and slammed the damned front door behind her.

As she approached Louise's Loft on her way to the hotel she upped the pace – she wasn't in the mood for talking to anyone today. As she passed the Loft she saw faces staring out at her so she lowered her head and hurried on. Sandra hated gossipers.

She slipped in through the fire escape at the back of the Moritz and walked briskly through the kitchens to reception. There was Dermot. He had put on a tight black shirt with his jeans and black shoes for the morning and Sandra barely recognised him.

"I could get used to this work. Easy." He pretended to type with his long fingers against the edge of the reception desk. "How is he this morning?"

As she slipped in behind the desk the phone rang. "Hang on," she said to Dermot, putting her finger to her lip. "Good morning. The Moritz Hotel. Sandra speaking. How may I help you?" She sat and pulled her office seat in under her. "Oh hi, Jonathan!"

She pointed frantically to the phone and Dermot pulled pen and a hotel notepad from the drawer and wrote quickly. He pushed the note in front of her. It said: "*He hasn't called this morning.*" She let out a slow breath.

"No, everything is fine – well, actually, Jonathan, I have two calls on hold. Could I call you back in a few minutes?" She hung up. "Okay, that was close. He'd have a fit, wouldn't he, if he thought you had manned reception for me?"

Dermot just laughed and shrugged his huge shoulders. "I doubt if a *fit* is the correct word," he said.

She made a face. "I know he is your friend but still he's my boss and he's uber-paranoid about this wedding. I better get back to it." She started to read through the list of messages Dermot had taken.

He was looking at her strangely now. "Yeah, J's one of my dearest friends, Sandra, and yep he runs this ship like clockwork but you –"

"Most of these messages are for Cara – is she in?" she said, ignoring his comment.

"Cara is indeed in – she actually offered to do reception for you. I didn't tell her why you weren't in but I should warn you, Sandy, the whole village knows about Neil." He looked away now too quickly. "I mean . . . I mean . . . not about . . . well, about Neil's accident . . ."

She had known that. It was the reason she'd flown past Louise's window – she'd seen the customers stare out at her. There was no way a small village like Knocknoly wouldn't be eating into that kind of gossip like a fresh gooey-in-the-middle chocolate cake. Anything drama-related and it was a fun day out. But it was the gossip they really knew that was bugging her the most. The gossip that Dermot had just tripped himself over. She tugged at her fringe. It wasn't fair to involve Dermot – gossip certainly wasn't his thing.

"I'm going up to see him at lunch if that offer of a lift still stands?"

"Sure. I'll drop back for you then," Dermot said. "Must go tend to my horses."

"See you then."

Sandra caught up on the messages and only then remembered to call Jonathan. He sounded dog tired and rather tense. After a brief exchange with him about a few matters. Sandra turned back to her computer.

"Hello."

Sandra looked up to see a couple standing at the desk.

"Hi, welcome to the Moritz," she said, greeting them with a big smile. "Have you a made a reservation booking?"

"Yes, Mr and Mrs Crowley and Baby Rose," the woman said and bent down to pick the baby up from her snugly Maxi-Cosi.

Sandra stared at the baby. "She's so . . ." she paused, "she's so perfect." She reached over the desk and took Rose's tiny pudgy hand in her larger one.

"Thanks," said the woman rather snappily. "Well, you can have her! She's hard work, she doesn't sleep at all and we are totally wrecked. That's why we are away – thought we could get a sitter and try and have a quiet dinner together for once. No one warns you about the tiredness – she just never shuts up and we are just totally exhausted all the time – she's such a hard baby."

Sandra rubbed the soft perfect pink skin. "So soft, so perfect," she whispered and the Crowleys stared at her. "Sorry," she said hastily. "But you have something so precious, you should be over the moon." She stopped herself just as the printer whirred into action and printed the booking form.

Mrs Crowley stared at her then signed the form. Tucking her long brown hair behind her ears she said, "I'm guessing you don't have children so you wouldn't understand." She pushed the completed form across the reception desk.

Sandra swallowed hard and forced a smile on her face.

"Will I book you a baby-sitter for Rose tonight then? We have quite a few on our list from teenagers to older mammies – it's whatever you'd prefer yourselves?"

"We'll get back to you later, thanks," Mr Crowley said, giving her a funny look. He took the key cards as Sandra pointed out the lift and they left.

She shook her head. "Oh Sandra, that was very unprofessional," she said under her breath.

The rest of the morning flew by with bookings for the Brophy-Burrows wedding and the hotel was buzzing.

Jonathan returned just before lunch as Sandra was getting ready to go and see Neil. He came through to the back office as Alice the relief sat down at the desk.

"I heard about Neil, what the heck happened?" He sat on the swivel chair, leaning forwards so his hands hung loose between his legs. He did look exhausted.

"One of the kids from the Bracken's Road decided to take a driving lesson in her dad's car, without her dad!" She applied some Coconut Vaseline to her dry lips and then put it back in her handbag.

"Yikes, is he okay?" he asked softly.

"Yeah, I think so. It only happened last night and he hasn't been awake much. I'm going down now. Broken wrist, bruised ribs and his face is cut but I'm sure he'll live." She didn't quite know why but suddenly she couldn't make eye contact with her boss. Embarrassment perhaps.

"Don't come back," he said. "Take the day off. I'll ask Alice to stay. Just leave a detailed list of the wedding reservations for her."

"Are you sure?"

He nodded. "Yes, certainly. I'm really sorry, Sandra. If there's anything I can do?"

She smiled at him as Dermot approached, the yard keys dangling between his fingers, and they left.

* * *

Jonathan sat in the chair for a few minutes as Alice settled herself into reception. Sandra had always been such a lively happy girl. Now she was a shadow of her former self. It saddened him deeply. He had heard the latest rumours around the village about Neil Darragh. He wasn't one for rumours. If he paid too much attention to the biggest rumour they would all be in trouble. The rumour that was haunting him. That the Moritz was going up for auction. The conference had been cancelled so a decision must already have been made. He had a meeting to attend with the board and he was dreading the outcome.

* * *

Dermot pulled up outside the hospital front doors and told her he would park up and wait. He had plenty of calls to make to the blacksmith and food suppliers and he had brought all his phone numbers with him so she should take her time.

Sandra nodded and turned to enter the hospital, then halted. There was a big sign in red lettering on the door: VOMITING BUG. DO NOT ENTER.

Why had the nurse not told her this earlier? Sure she had to enter, she had no choice. She'd have to argue her case if they tried to stop her. She tried to dispense some alcohol rub onto her hands but the dispenser was empty.

Inside she was surprised not to be confronted with some kind of hospital security barring entry. Shrugging her shoulder she headed for St Anthony's Ward.

Neil was sitting up, pale and gaunt but sipping some water through a blue straw. He half smiled when she approached the bed and he put the glass down on his silver bedside locker.

She pulled the plastic green-and-orange curtain around them and sat.

"It wasn't my fault." He turned his face to hers.

"I know," she said.

"I can't cope any more, I can't cope with any of it."

She slid her hand over his. "With what, Neil?" she asked him slowly.

"This is just the icing on the cake. I can't stand my life right now, Sandra."

She removed a crumpled tissue from her pocket and blew her nose. She felt numb. "I don't know what to say." She pushed the tissue up her green coat sleeve. "Is it the house?"

He shook his head and stared at her. "The house is the least of my worries, Sandra. I would have liked that new house if you'd given . . . I mean . . . it's you."

"Me?" She hit her chest hard. The words, however true, still stung.

"Yeah, you. I cannot take you any more."

"Well, okay, Neil, you can't stand me any more. I get it. Then leave me. What do you want from me? A separation? A divorce? What?" she dared him, really wanting to hear his honest answer at last.

"Maybe some time?" He looked out the window, wincing as he turned his head.

"Time? Time for what exactly?" She wouldn't play this game.

"You are so sympathetic, Sandra, aren't you? I am lying here in a hospital bed in case you hadn't noticed!" He turned away from her.

"I am sympathetic, Neil, but I don't know what to do any more. I'm hardly life's greatest advertisement for happiness now either, am I?"

The silence hung over them now.

Why couldn't she ask him? Why couldn't she just say 'Are you seeing someone else again – is this what this is all about, darling? Is your dishonest body cheating on me again, you bastard?'

"You have worn me down. I no longer feel like a proper man. That's all because of you. From the moment I knew I couldn't give you babies naturally, I felt like half a man but you just wouldn't let it go. Then the business went belly-up and that other half went with it . . ." He trailed off, then added, "You just don't get it."

Sandra stared at the holy picture above his bed. By God, she was lost here. "I do get it, Neil, I really do. I am so, so sorry the IVF didn't work. But I never meant to hurt you. I never meant you to feel like half a man." Somebody in the next bed cried out for a nurse and Sandra felt the urge to get up and help him.

"Leave it – he's a nut-job." Neil pulled his sheet slowly up under his chin.

She shifted uncomfortably on the seat. "So, what? What happens now then?"

He didn't answer her. The two of them were so far apart it was hard to know what to say next.

"So how are you feeling?" was all she could think of now. She knew she could just get up and walk away but it wasn't the way she operated.

"Brilliant, Sandra, top notch." He ground his teeth and tried to lift his bandaged wrist. "There is fuck-all work I can do now."

"What can I do, Neil? I don't know what to do! I have never been in this situation before. I am hurting too, you know."

"No, you're not!" he hissed at her. "All you care about is your baby – baby, baby, baby! I can't give you that so I'm worthless to you, I can't pay our mortgage, I can't do anything. I'd be better off dead." He started to cry now, horrible heart-wrenching sobs that had the nurse flinging back the curtain and asking Sandra to leave.

"No, please, can I just stay one more minute?" She implored Neil with her eyes.

The young dark-haired nurse shook her head firmly. "Come

back tonight. He needs to rest. He's been through a lot, he is very badly bruised and we just got the repeated X-rays back and he has broken ribs also. No more visitors today. And how you both got in I don't know – there's a vomiting bug in this hospital. How did you get past security?"

"There wasn't any," Sandra protested.

The nurse looked puzzled but just gently ushered Sandra out.

Sandra half ran to the ward door, almost knocking a young woman in a very short red dress over as she went. Unusual attire for a hospital visit, she thought, as she reached the door, her eyes running tears. What was she going to do? She looked back but knew she had to go.

Dermot was sitting on the bench outside writing in a notebook, a free newspaper on his lap. She headed for him and as he rose she collapsed into his arms.

"I'm a horrible, horrible person, Dermot. He hates my guts and he's right – I'm a shadow of a woman. I've been so selfish I hate myself!" She sobbed on his shoulder as he rocked her.

"*You* are not the horrible person." Dermot's head flicked back to look at the hospital doors and he stared at them for a moment before saying, "Come on, let's go back to mine. Big J texted me to say he'd given you the afternoon off. I can ask Lorna to take the hacks out. Come on."

Sandra let him lead her to his pick-up truck in the multi-storey car park. As he leaned across and strapped her seatbelt down, her tears subsided. She thanked him again as her chest still heaved.

"Seriously, Dermot, you don't need all this. I can manage. Just drop me back."

"No way." He stopped and gestured to let a wheelchair-user pass and then drove on. Dermot glanced at her. She was staring out the window, lost in her own world. So she hadn't noticed the lounge girl in the red dress, thank God. Dermot sighed to himself as he headed for the main Knocknoly road.

Chapter 15

The Law Top had been busier than Cara could ever remember as she ushered the last of the punters out. "Goodnight now, mind how you go!" She closed the door behind them and pushed up the huge old-fashioned rusting bolt. She leaned her back against the cold door.

The current court case sounded completely horrific. The people from the earlier lunch table had stayed late into the night drowning their sorrows as the case had been adjourned. From what she could make out a relative of the French lady was the victim of the rape and she was the main witness. The accused was pleading not guilty. It was awful. Cara wondered where the poor girl was. Her life could never be the same again. It was too dreadful a thought and she shuddered.

Cara had been due to finish at nine but it was too manic so she'd stayed on. She texted Esther to tell her that she was now working late and she would pop her meal in the microwave later. Esther never minded when this happened and it happened all too frequently Cara thought now as she fished her mobile out of her bag.

Eleven missed calls. Her heart started to race. "Oh God – Esther!" Had something happened to her? She pushed the button to retrieve information on the callers. It was Alex. All eleven calls. She heaved a sigh of relief that it wasn't her mother.

But why would he have called her eleven times? What the hell was wrong? He must have had a scare on the flight. She quickly dialled her message minder as Steve pushed a huge glass of red wine in front of her and lay out on the bench opposite her in the now blissfully quiet bar.

"Thanks, lovey." She smiled at him, pressing her ear tightly to the phone as she listened. No new messages. She hurriedly dialled Alex's number. She heard it connect but not on a different country ring tone. Her heart continued to race? Was he okay? He must have had to return home early for some reason.

"Where the hell have you been, Cara?" he answered in such a strange voice that she laughed at first, thinking he was joking.

"Aah, man – phew, I got a fright! Are you okay?" Silence. "Oh what a night, Alex! Is everything okay? You gave me a scare when I saw all the missed calls. What's happened?" She picked up her glass and swirled it, warming the red liquid in her palm. Steve knew she hated cold red yet he always served it to her.

"Where are you, Cara?" Alex asked.

She put the glass back down. "I'm in work, Alex, where are you?"

"Why are you in work still, Cara?"

"Ah, we had a mad busy day here – it was non-stop – so I stayed on. Jeez, Alex, you frightened the daylights out of me when I saw eleven missed calls!"

Steve made a snorty laugh now and Cara glared at him and covered the mouthpiece.

"I told you I would call you at ten o'clock. What are you doing, Cara? I mean what the fuck is going on in that pub?"

Steve leaned up on his elbow now, chin resting on his hand but ears pricked like some kind of sausage dog. He was obviously able to hear Alex's loud voice. He opened his eyes wide and Cara blushed.

She coughed. "Just work, it's been mad – em, so how are things in sunny Dubai then?" He didn't answer but she could hear his breath hot and heavy. It sounded like he was pacing around a room.

"Don't take me for a fool, Cara Byrne. I'm no fucking fool!"

She really needed to get up and walk away from Steve and the others but if she did it would look bad.

"Never!" She tried her best to laugh.

"What are you laughing at? Are you laughing at me? Me? Is this some sort of fucking joke to you? Are you fucking laughing at me?"

She had to hang up now. She couldn't do this in front of everyone. It was obvious now she was having a row with her boyfriend on the phone. She pressed 'end call' but kept talking. "Are you messing, you loony?" She laughed loud now and held the laughter for moments. Just as well she'd pushed the silent button on the side of her phone as it was lighting up now, no doubt with Alex calling back. She turned her back on the bench where Steve was. "Okay, listen, I have to go . . . I do too . . . stay off the vino, ya nutter . . . okay, bye, love you too!" She threw the phone into her bag and with slightly shaky hands picked up her wine. He palms were so sweaty now she'd warm her wine in seconds.

"Everything okay?" Steve sat up and looked at her.

"Fine, yeah."

"Was that Top Gun himself? Is he Maverick or Goose?"

"His name is Alex, Steve, and yes it was. He's just a bit of a messer – been on the wine, I think." She painted on a huge smile.

Steve looked at her for a few seconds too long and then shook his head. "Another?" he asked, nodding at her empty wineglass. She had knocked it back.

"Why not?" She handed the glass to him and as he made his way over to the bar she grabbed her phone out of her bag again.

"Want crisps, Cara?" Aoife asked her.

"Hmm, yeah, cheese and onion, please, Aoife – the black Manhattan packet." She had another six missed calls. What was he doing? He was beginning to scare her. She checked her watch again and dialled Esther – she'd be finished watching *Downton Abbey* now.

"Hi, love, I'm on the land line to Ann here. Can I help you?" Esther's phone manner was most odd.

"Yeah, I'm sorry – hope you got my text about how manic we

got – I just couldn't leave. I'm starving so I won't be too long but I might have a couple of drinks to clear my head of work. I'll just heat up my meal when I get home. That okay, Mam?"

"Yes, dear."

What was it with everyone tonight? Esther never questioned Cara's time keeping. If she was home she was home, if she wasn't she wasn't, but Cara liked to check in with her anyway, especially since she'd specifically asked Esther to cook for her tonight.

"You okay, Mam? You sound a bit weird?"

"I'm grand, love. I have to go – see you in a while so if I'm still up."

"I could just head back to mine?" Cara tested her.

"Ahh no, sure I've a lovely dinner for you and I got the making of a fry for us for the morning, take your time and have a drink with Steve and the rest. Goodbye, Cara dear."

Cara turned off her phone and stuffed it into her bag. Jesus, Alex had been mad. She didn't even know if he was home or not. If he was home he'd be expecting her back but she'd promised Esther now. She rubbed her eyes then dragged her hands down both cheeks. She was beyond shocked at his reaction. A bit of healthy jealousy was one thing but that had been close to insane behaviour.

"So how's the new place, you lucky sod?" Aoife asked. "Sandymount, aah! I just love Sandymount Green. I used to work in a pub there and loved lazing in that green on my break. Then Borza would open and the smell of freshly cooking chipper chips was amazeballs!" She threw a bundle of assorted crisp packets onto the table, kicked off her red Adidas runners and curled her slim legs up under her.

"It's great, Aoife, thanks – yes, it's a really nice place to live." Cara copied her and curled up on the big bench now too.

"Wow, that was all so quick, wasn't it, though?" Aoife asked and gently drank the creamy head from her pint of Guinness.

Cara looked at her youthful face. "I suppose, well, really . . . I mean we met and a few months later we moved in together but it's what we both really want. We aren't twenty-something after all. Time isn't on our side." She was protesting a bit too much, she knew, but Aoife just nodded.

"Must be nice with him being a pilot and all – you get to travel all over the world."

"No, not really. I mean the last thing he wants to do is get on a plane when he's off duty, you know."

"Ha, yeah, a busman's holiday, wha'?" Steve chipped in as he popped open a bag of salt and vinegar Tayto crisps and began to crunch them very loudly.

Steve did not like Alex, Cara knew that now for sure. On the few occasions Alex had come into the bar to collect Cara he had been very quiet. The first time Steve had extended his hand to shake and Alex had reached for his ringing phone in the inside pocket of his suit jacket and ignored the other man completely. Steve had thrown the red tea towel over his shoulder and turned his back.

"Who wants to play getting completely sloshed?" Steve asked now as he licked his fingers and Cara sensed he was aware of her sudden discomfort.

"I'm on!" Aoife squealed.

Aoife squealed a lot. An awful lot. Cara found it seriously annoying. Aoife also had a little crush on Steve, Cara observed. With her pixie peroxide-blonde haircut and numerous facial and body piercings, Cara didn't think she was Steve's type. But what did she know?

Steve hopped up and grabbed the bottle of red wine off the bar counter along with the sambuca bottle and removed his lighter from his pocket.

"Okay, let's play getting shitfaced, my tired overworked little bar friends!"

Anto and Phillip, two part-time barmen came over with glasses and joined the little group. Steve lit a round of flaming sambucas and they all began to drink.

"I really shouldn't!" Cara protested as a fiery shot was pushed into her hand to the chorus of "*Drink! Drink! Drink!*" . . . so she did . . . otherwise she'd have been burnt. She blew out the blue flame and knocked the bitter-sweet drink back in one go. It had been ages since she'd had a bit of a blow-out. Since just before she'd met Alex, in fact.

The conversation flowed and Steve got up and put *The Best of Duran Duran* on the surround – so that was it: Cara was off. Up on the tables she let her red hair fall loose and drank her wine as she swayed to Simon Le Bon's wonderful voice, the row with Alex not forgotten but parked for now.

Later, as she headed for the toilets, Aoife followed her.

Cara locked her cubicle door.

"Cara?" Aoife knocked gently. "Do you think Steve could fancy me?"

Cara smiled inside her cubicle, curling the white toilet roll up in her hands. "I don't know, Aoife, to be honest, but you really like him, don't you?"

"Yes," Aoife whispered very loudly. She must have moved to the mirror now as her voice was further away.

Cara flushed the toilet and went out.

"I'm kinda only like mad about him, Cara. I think he's fab."

As Cara washed her hands she watched Aoife put water on her hands and spike up her hair in the mirror.

"However, I don't want to make a move in case I'm wrong as I need this job and that would just be too awkward. Would you have a sly word with him for me? I know how close you two are." Aoife scrubbed at her teeth in the mirror with her index finger and then smiled broadly at herself. "Were ye ever, like, together?" She turned to Cara.

"No! Never. God, no, Aoife. Sure, okay, I will have a quiet word with him, maybe before I hit the road, yeah?" Cara laughed.

"You are a Star Bar. A right good Creme Egg!" Aoife grinned at her.

They made their way back to the bar and Cara took her seat as the music became a bit more hard core. Suddenly she wanted to hit the road. It was past one in the morning and she was wall-fallen. She gathered up her bag and pushed her feet into her runners which barely fit at this late hour.

"Steve, I'm gonna hit the road!" she called to him. He was

behind the bar again, this time putting money in the till for the wine and sambuca after the whip-around.

"Ah no, are ya?" He looked disappointed.

Aoife winked at her.

"Oh, yeah." Cara nodded at Aoife. "Sorry, Steve, would you walk me out, please?" She pulled on her fleece and then her jacket and said her goodbyes. She would not be missed by everyone judging by the air-guitar playing going on now between Anto and Phillip.

Steve unbolted the door and opened it wide as he let her out. She stopped in front of him on the street under the lamps.

"Steve . . ." she started.

"Cara." He put his hands on her shoulders. "What is it?"

"Well, little Aoife asked me to suss out if you might fancy her a wee bit?" She laughed. She was drunk, she realised, as the cold air hit her. Her head was spinning a bit.

He shook her gently. "Me?"

She now put out her hands and rested them on his shoulders and shook him back. "*Who, me? Yes, you. Couldn't be. Then who?*" she sang to him now and laughed harder.

"Honestly, Cara, how long have you known me? You really think Aoife is my type of girl? Don't get me wrong, she's so sweet and an absolute gem to work with but no, not like that."

They both stood looking at one another now.

"Ahh look, you know well I've only got eyes for you." Steve swallowed hard and tightened his grip on her now and she lay her head on his left arm.

"Ah, Steve, you never said . . . I didn't know, well, not really . . . but it's too late now . . . I'm with someone else, so let's not go there." She dropped her arms and looked into his kind eyes.

"I'm sorry I had a go at you over Seán's death this morning. It's just I worry about you. You are too trusting. Regardless of my feelings towards you, I don't like that Alex guy, Cara – he gives me the willies."

She smiled at him and rubbed his cheek, then blew him as kiss as she turned and wobbled and then steadied herself.

"Here, let me hail you a cab. We can talk about this again.

When we are both a bit more sober? What?"

"No. We can't talk about it again, Steve." She raised her hand now and kept it in the air. "I think I need a bit of a stroll, okay?"

"Be careful, Cara. I don't like you wandering the streets at this hour."

She turned and walked back towards him now and hugged him tightly. "I think you are a great guy, Steve, I really do." She kissed his cheek and turned away again.

Steve was searching the empty Quays for a taxi light.

"I think I'll be okay!" she yelled back now, arms still waving in the air, and happily headed down the Quays, hiccups now arriving to walk with her. "I do think you are a great guy, Steve, but your timing sucks!" she said out loud to herself and she laughed and then snorted as she wobbled along her way.

Chapter 16

"Okay, so the meeting today is as always to keep the lines of communication open." Jonathan sat under the twinkling red fairy Christmas lights in the elegantly decorated conference room. He had no intention of mentioning the possible auction of the hotel until he was one-hundred-per-cent sure. These things could change up to the very last minute. He had a meeting in London with the conglomerate in a couple of days. He had to ignore the rumours. He needed to concentrate on the here and now. He couldn't take in what could happen; it was too hard for him right now.

"December is upon us at last and the festivities are planned so I'm pretty confident we are all on the same page."

"If I may, sir," Big Bob spoke up. "I was wondering why the rota for Christmas Day isn't posted in the back office yet?" He was chewing on a piece of paper like he always did.

"Well, okay, there is that!" Jonathan laughed now. "I need volunteers to work that day. I hate asking you at all, I really do, but as you all know it's the nature of the job."

To Jonathan's utmost surprise Big Bob's hand went up, immediately followed by old Mrs Reilly's, then Tiff's and then Mike's.

"I'm free too," Cara said.

"And me!" Sandra piped up now, waving her chocolate-shortbread biscuit in the air.

"Really?" He laughed again. "Well, that's just fantastic, lads and lassies, and I will as always ask Delphine to prepare all our Christmas dinners and we can sit down later on in the evening once the band starts and celebrate, okay? Cara posted a notice in Louise's and O'Dwyer's so we have a load of locals to work bars, kitchen, room service and so on, but I do need my core team as we are full to capacity and with a waiting list. Very well – that's settled.

"Now on to other business. As you all know the Brophy-Burrows wedding is today. I know Cara has it all in hand but, just in case, we all need to watch her back. They will all be here at one o'clock for the pink champagne reception. The rain is sleeting now unfortunately but the forecast is to clear so I have left the red carpet in the reception area, rolled up. We will leave that until the last second." He poured some cream into his coffee cup now and Mrs Reilly leaned across and stirred it for him.

Cara's palms were sweating and she was suddenly nervous. Her reputation depended on the success of this wedding. She didn't think she had left any stone unturned. She had been up half of the night going over and over her checklists. Jonathan had dropped her back home with the paints and had left them at the side of the house for her. She hadn't asked him in. He had been exhausted too. He had yawned a goodbye to her as she thanked him and told him she'd see him tomorrow.

Jenny was upstairs in the bridal suite getting ready and Cara was going up to her after this meeting.

"We need a load more champagne glasses, Jonathan," Mike said, looking at his list in front of him.

"I'm on that, Mike. I'm waiting for a delivery from Hines. We have to buy more though – I was shocked we had such a small supply. Anyway, Charlie's dropping them up later." Jonathan sipped his coffee. "Cold," he mouthed to Cara and she laughed before pulling out her notepad and jotting down some notes.

"Okay, that's it then, I think?" Jonathan said and they all nodded in agreement and pushed back their chairs. "Good luck today, everyone. Let's make it the best day of Jenny and Max's lives."

Sandra looked miles away, Cara noted, when the two women fell into step as they headed for the door of the conference room.

"After you!" Sandra smiled at Cara.

"Thanks." Cara slipped out first, although the doors were wide enough for three people to get through, and Sandra followed.

The rich carpet was soft and silent beneath their feet.

"You okay, Sandra?" Cara looked up at the other woman as they walked.

"Don't ask, Cara!" Sandra replied without looking at her.

Cara tightened the bobbin on her low ponytail and decided to say no more. She knew what it was like when people kept asking her if she was okay. Sometimes people just wanted to be left alone.

"Good luck with this event – I hope you rock it," Sandra said now as she slipped in behind the reception desk.

Guests were streaming down for breakfast, and by the look of some of the heads they must have had a really late night last night. Cara couldn't understand that. The night before a wedding? I mean, surely it ruined the big day if you had a massive hangover?

She quietly made her way into the breakfast room and spotted Jenny's mam and dad, John and Mary.

"Good morning, Father and Mother of the Bride!" She crouched down beside their seats and gave them a huge confident smile. "Everything okay with your stay so far?"

"Ah, it's super, Miss Byrne." John wiped his mouth with the white linen napkin. "Really super, love. She couldn't have asked for a better hotel. I asked for an iron at eight o'clock this morning, thinking I'd get it after breakfast sometime – it arrived at six minutes past eight, didn't it, love?" John turned to his wife who was smiling.

"It did, love. It was truly a miracle." Mary kept a poker-straight face and Cara stifled a laugh. "The staff have all been amazing, Cara." Mary poured more tea into John's teacup.

"Lovely!" he acknowledged his wife's action gratefully. "And another thing – the free newspapers, nice touch."

"Well, I'm popping up to see Jenny now so enjoy your

breakfasts and, please, John, call me Cara."

Cara stood and said good morning to some of the other guests as she made her way to the lift. The gold doors opened and she was about to press the button for the second floor when Jonathan stepped in.

"Third, Cara, please." he leaned against the gold bar in front of the mirror as the doors closed.

His presence was all-consuming this morning, Cara felt. He was so calm and so masculine. He smelled divine. She sniffed the air – inconspicuously, she hoped.

"You're doing great, Cara," he said.

"Thanks, Jonathan – you're so kind."

"Things are a bit crazy my end at the moment, Cara, but –" His phone rang out in his pocket and he dug it out and answered it.

"Ah, how's tricks, Dermot?" he said as the lift door opened on the second floor and Cara got out.

Jonathan was smiling at her as the lift doors slowly closed.

She rapped on Jenny's door three times.

It was opened by Angela, her sister and only bridesmaid. She looked stunning in a beaded one-shoulder emerald-green dress with a simple thin green satin hair-band in her shoulder-length curly brown hair. "Come in, come in, Cara!" she called, full of excitement.

Must be wonderful to have a sister, Cara thought. She entered the room and stopped in her tracks.

"Da-*da*!" Jenny stood up and took Cara's breath away.

She looked so beautiful. Her blonde hair was scraped off her beautiful young face in a tight bun with white glittering diamante beads spread throughout her hair, and her make-up was subtle and fresh as her face glowed with happiness. She wore a halter-neck crystal-studded wedding gown that made her waist look tiny and then fell in gathers and gathers of white lace to the floor. She lifted the gown to show Cara her magnificent sky-high white strappy sandals. She had small diamond earrings and a small diamond bracelet on her left hand and that was it. She was perfection.

"Oh my God, Jenny, you are absolutely stunning!" Cara said as her eyes filled up with tears.

"Go on out of that with the tears, you mad thing!" Jenny gathered her skirts up and made her way over to Cara. "Thanks so much for talking Max into making the speech. I can't tell you how much it means to me. It was so important. Here, get a picture of us both, Angela, will you?" Jenny draped her arm over Cara's shoulder. Cara took a deep breath. This moment was much harder than she'd anticipated. There was a knock at the door and Mary entered the room.

"Oh, love!" Mary was sobbing into her hankie before the door closed behind her.

Angela poured more champers.

"Go easy on that, Angela Brophy!" Mary told her as Angela handed a glass to her. "You remember what happened to you at Uncle John's fiftieth!" She shook her finger at her younger daughter. "Made a holy show of us, she did!" she told Cara.

"Ah, give it a rest, Mam, will you? I didn't know there was already vodka in the orange mixer, did I? Otherwise I would never had been ordering double vodkas with it. Easy mistake to make." Angela made a grimace at Cara.

Mary sipped a little now with shaking hands. "I didn't know if I would ever see this day!" She was choking back tears now.

"It's okay, Mam!" Angela put her arm around her mother. "I told you it would all work out, didn't I?"

Jenny handed her mother a fresh tissue and they all looked at each other.

"I had breast cancer last year, Cara," Mary explained as Jenny rubbed her arm. "All I could think about when I was diagnosed was would I make this day for either of my girls? Would I ever be well again? Could I beat this? And here I am now feeling better than I have done in years! Yeah, a boob lighter, but I needed to lose a few pounds anyway, didn't I, girls?"

They all laughed and the tension oozed away.

"That's terrific, Mary, I am so pleased for you," Cara said.

"Oh, she's a trooper, this one!" Jenny said. "That's why I

wanted Max to make the speech so much. I wanted the guests to know how wonderful she has been but, as the bride and her daughter, I knew I wouldn't make it through a speech about her. I just wanted Max to praise her and thank her for being so brave and to tell her how happy I am that she is here today . . . ah no, here I go, see . . . this is exactly why I needed Max to speak!" Jenny opened her eyes as wide as she could and fanned them to try and stop the tears.

"Stop that this very instant, Jenny Brophy!" Her mother put down her drink and was fanning now too. "This is the last thing we want – all that expensive MAC make-up floating down your face!"

"I think we all need another drink," Angela said and the other three women shouted "No!" back to her at the same time.

When they had pulled themselves together Cara said, "I will run now, but how are you feeling? Is there anything at all you need me to do for you?" She grabbed the used breakfast tray from the table beneath the large window.

"I am totally happy, Cara," said Jenny. "I'm just on cloud nine. It's the most wonderful, amazing feeling in the entire world and I can't wait to become Max's wife."

Cara nodded. "That's just as it should be," she managed as she stood back to let Angela open the bedroom door of the bridal suite for her. "So see you in a little bit, after everyone has left. The cars are coming at two forty-five sharp so I will have everyone out of the bar and en route to the church by then."

"Thanks, Cara, for everything," the bride said as the door closed slowly on its automatic release. "You have been utterly amazing. I will be recommending you and the Moritz to everyone I meet!"

Cara stood outside for a moment and thought how wrongly she had judged Jenny because she had wanted Max to make a speech. She had rendered the other girl slightly superficial in her head but had got her completely wrong. She swore standing there that she would never judge people again. She looked at the shining gold letterings on the door. *Moritz Bridal Suite*. The letters gleamed. Don't think about your wedding day, don't do this to yourself, Cara, close that closet! She took a deep breath and headed for the kitchen with the breakfast tray shaking slightly in her hands.

* * *

Sandra was up to ninety at reception. There was a massive problem. Two young couples checking in wanted their rooms very early to get ready for the wedding. She had told every last guest that had booked in for the wedding that it was not guaranteed they could get into their room before one o'clock, so she was at a loss as to what to do now. The two bare-faced girls clutching their make-up bags and dry-cleaned dresses for dear life stood beseeching her to get their rooms ready.

She hated to bother him but she needed Jonathan's help. She dialled his office, no answer. She dialled his mobile.

"Hi, Sandra?" He was obviously in the stables as she heard horses whinnying in the background. "I need you, Jonathan, I have a big problem here." She explained the situation and he said he would come to reception at once.

She put down the phone and ran her hands down her cheeks. Then she held her hands up to the waiting guests. "I am so sorry about this but I did tell you that check-ins weren't guaranteed until one. There are still guests occupying the rooms, I'm afraid. The manager is coming right now so you can speak to him. I need to deal with the other hotel guests behind you now, if that's okay?"

"This is a joke!" one of the annoyed male guests piped up. "Seriously, I wasn't told about this! We are just off a flight too after a long tennis tournament in Beijing. We are wrecked!"

"I told everyone," said Sandra. "I am the only one taking the bookings so you must have known! I would never take a booking for this wedding and not have told you check-in wasn't guaranteed until after lunchtime – never! Even when Alice the relief receptionist is on the desk she doesn't take bookings, just messages, and I call you back." Sandra tried to keep her cool. She never lost her cool with guests but these were really trying her patience this morning.

"No, I spoke to a man on reception when I booked early the other morning, not a woman. I got an email from the cancellation list we were on to call the hotel immediately if we still wanted a room."

"So did I!" the other girl practically shouted at Sandra now.

"Please, with respect, I understand you are upset but please do not raise your voices at me," Sandra said – and then her heart stopped. Oh shit, she said to herself as she suddenly realised. She closed her eyes for a second. It must have been Dermot when he was helping her out the other day. He must have taken these bookings. She was responsible for this after all.

As she was about to speak to the guests Jonathan and Dermot arrived in the door. "Hi there, I'm Mr Redmond the manager – may I help you?" Jonathan spoke in an authoritative yet understanding tone.

"Well, she doesn't have our rooms –"

"And we were not told about this late check-in –"

They spoke over each other.

"One at a time please, ladies and gentlemen. Let's move over here for a moment if we may and sort this issue out." He ushered them to the side to allow other guests access to Sandra. "Now, you must have been informed – that's our policy." Jonathan looked quizzically back over his shoulder at Sandra and then back at his disgruntled guests.

Sandra was just about to open her mouth when Dermot butted in: "Here, now I've an idea. Grab yer gear, lads, and I'll grab a sliced pan and some freshly baked ham and cheese from the kitchen and I'll take the four of ye back to mine. The girls can get ready and ye can make a few ham and cheese toasties and a pot of tea. I think the Man United highlights from last night are on. I'm just behind the hotel here – three seconds' walk, ladies! Come on, let's go!"

"A pint of Guinness even?" one of the lads replied, looking brighter now.

"No problem, whatever your fancy is – as I said, I'm only at the end of the stables here. So come on. Actually, Jonathan, can you get Big Bob to grab a full-length mirror from the conference room for me so the girls can see themselves in all their wedding glory?"

Sandra sat back on her chair. Dermot had saved her. She had also put him in a terrible position of lying to Jonathan and she felt awful about that. She knew Dermot would have come clean to Jonathan, no problem, but he was just protecting her. Again.

The couples seemed pleased enough and gathered up their belongings.

"And there will be a bottle of champagne on ice at the bar for you when you get back," Jonathan said to them. "I'm terribly sorry about that mix-up."

They were completely won over.

"Will you be at the wedding later?" the taller girl with the high ponytail plait asked Jonathan. "I want you for a dance."

"Watch it, Clare Hinch!" her partner said. "We are still engaged, aren't we?" He laughed though as they all left in a trail of conversations about fake tans needing to be washed off and a forgotten eye-liner sharpener.

Jonathan was standing in front of the desk as Cara approached to ask Sandra a question about the wedding car's arrival. The driver was to call reception when he was leaving the garage.

"What the heck happened there, Sandra?" Jonathan asked.

Cara had never heard Jonathan use that tone with anyone before so she hung back.

"I don't know." Sandra rubbed her eyes and her mascara smudged under them both.

"You took a booking and didn't tell them the check-in time? On the morning of a wedding?"

Sandra was just about to admit her mistake when Cara piped up. "That was me, actually, Jonathan. I manned reception for Sandra the other morning when she stood over the photocopier man to make sure he fixed it properly once and for all. Sandra did tell me to tell the guests. I'm terribly sorry. I just forgot." Sandra opened her mouth and Cara rushed on. "I'm new to it all, you see, Jonathan. It was just a teething problem." She clasped her hands together prayer-like under her chin. "Forgive me?"

He looked at Cara for what seemed like a long time, taking in every inch of her face. "Okay, fair enough but, seriously, don't let a mistake that big happen again. That's the one way our reputation gets ruined. Something as simple as that." He patted the desk hard twice with his right palm and then walked away down the corridor to the kitchen.

"Thank you, Cara," Sandra said as Cara fished in her pocket for a clean tissue.

"Your mascara." Cara nodded at the piece of tissue as she held it towards Sandra.

"Oh thanks. Seriously, though, I feel really shit letting you take the rap. Why would you do that for me? It's not as if I've gone out of my way to make you feel welcome."

Cara laughed. "I'm new, it's okay. It was Dermot on reception the other morning, wasn't it?"

Sandra slowly nodded. "It was a stupid thing to do . . . I just have so much going on . . ."

The phone rang and she answered it. It was the wedding-car driver telling her he had just left the garage for the hotel.

"Okay," Cara said. "I have to get Jenny down the stairs but first I have to clear that bar. I'm not looking forward to this!"

"It's not that I didn't want to get to know you," Sandra blurted out, "to welcome you here, Cara, it's just . . . I . . ."

Cara raised her hand. "Another chat for another day, maybe?"

Sandra nodded gratefully.

"Now this bar . . ." Cara said and the two women craned their necks to look into the bar where a chorus of *Olé Olé Olé Olé* had already started up and full pints of Guinness were still being passed over heads from the bar.

"This is one thing I can help you with!" Sandra said as she licked the tissue and rubbed hard under her eyes. "Gone?" she asked and Cara nodded.

The two headed into the crowded bar.

"Come on now, folks, please – it's time to leave – the church starts in fifteen minutes," Cara pleaded.

The church was a five-minute walk into the village. The rain had long since moved on and the sun was shining. It was cold but bright and beautiful.

"We're on our way, girls!" one of the jolly guests threw back, taking a seat by the fire, obviously with no intention of leaving the bar.

Sandra strode forward. "Folks! Leave now! Come on! Drink up! Get ye to the church on time!" she shouted really loudly.

Cara burst into giggles. They caught one another's eye and it was game on.

"Leave! Get out! Go forth!" Cara said loudly, her and Sandra falling around the place laughing now.

"*Go, go, go!*" they yelled in unison, now clapping their hands, and were beside themselves with laughter when Jonathan and Dermot arrived. The two men stood there looking at them, bemused, as the guests filed out one by one.

* * *

When Jenny had been settled into the car and waved off, the staff took a ten-minute break in the round conference room.

Old Mrs Reilly had made another pot of coffee and sliced up some of Delphine's banoffee pie for them all.

"There's fresh cream in that stripy blue bowl if anyone wants extra cream. I'm watching my waistline!" she said and patted her ample tummy.

"Bit late for that!" Big Bob winked at her as he licked the back of his pie-covered spoon.

Old Mrs Reilly wiggled her hips at him.

Sandra and Cara arrived in.

"I haven't laughed like that in months," Sandra said, still wiping her eyes.

"Me neither." Cara blew her nose as they sat. "God, I enjoyed it though!" She stuffed the tissue up her sleeve. It was badly needed and way overdue!"

"What was that all about?" Jonathan asked her as he set out the white coffee cups on white saucers.

"I don't know really," Cara said. "We just took a fit of laughing. Sorry."

"Looks like you both enjoyed it," Dermot noted as he

spooned sugar after sugar into his coffee and then plopped a large dollop of the whipped cream on his pie.

Tiffney and Mike walked in and sat together in the corner, taking their coffees and pies with them. Sandra and Cara looked at each other. The two women had hardly spoken in all the time Cara had been at the Moritz but they both sensed now that they had each found a new friend. They just got each other. Kindred spirits. It was crazy. It was as though, just like that, there in that bar, they had known each other all their lives. They had just suddenly and immediately clicked.

"Sugar?" Dermot asked Sandra.

"Yes, my sweet," Sandra answered and Cara spat her coffee all over the table and the two women roared laughing again.

Chapter 17

"Oh my God, Cara!" Sandra was flopped over the reception desk half an hour later and beckoning Cara manically with her right hand, fingers dancing to a frantic beat.

"What?" Cara pulled at the cream bobbins in her hair. They were too tight.

"You will never guess who just tried to check in?" Sandra was flushed.

"Who?" Cara was opening her jacket now as the morning's activities and all that laughing had left her hot. She couldn't remember the last time she'd laughed like that. It was an incredible relief. She was up to her eyes now though and hadn't the time to chat any more.

"*Jamie Keenan.*" Sandra said the two words ever so slowly, releasing them from her mouth like a tortoise from its tracks, before adding, "You know, the famous English tennis player?"

"Oh, yeah," Cara said. "Jenny mentioned he's a friend of Max's all right. Max is a tennis pro, well, a coach now, a very successful doubles player apparently. What do you mean *tried* to check in? Didn't you have a room for him?"

"No!" Sandra hissed and held her hands up in the air. "Can you believe it? I'm so pissed off. He's going to drop his bags here and see what happens. They don't know he's coming. It's a surprise."

"Ah, what a shame! What can we do for him?" Cara asked, moving away from Sandra toward the dining room.

"I know what I'd *like* to do with him!" Sandra laughed and then immediately stopped, her face suddenly pale.

"What is it?" Cara came back towards the other woman.

Sandra bit her lower lip.

Cara reached over and laid her hand on Sandra's. "I'm here if you ever want to talk."

"Ah, I'll tell you later sometime, whenever. If you have the energy. It's long, it's depressing and it's not looking brighter any time soon." Sandra licked her lips, now horribly dry and in need of some lippy no doubt.

"Well, I see your tragic story and I raise you mine!" Cara gave Sandra the thumbs-up. "Let's do it later. I'll bring the wine to yours."

"But I'm on here till very late," Sandra said.

Cara nodded. "I will be here until the death as well so we will need a drink and Big J says we can both have a late morning. Oh, and bring tissues!" Cara made two fists with her hands and twirled them in front of her eyes. They both burst out laughing again. "Okay – a little wedding reception to organise, Sandra. Later!"

Sandra smiled as she reached for the ringing telephone. It was her bank manager.

"I asked you before not to call me in my place of work!" she hissed down the phone to the unfortunate man. "I will have the mortgage money next week."

"I'm sorry, Mrs Darragh, but we really need to see you urgently. It's not about the mortgage repayments – it's about the transfer of the mortgage to a Mr Tom Darragh."

She stood for a moment and let the words sink in. Then she let out a slow breath. "I will be in later this afternoon after I go up to the hospital, Mr Kilroy," she said and went back to pour herself a large glass of water from the cooler in the back office. She held the plastic cup under the nozzle. She couldn't pinpoint her feelings right now. She was afraid to think too deeply, but not because she would upset herself more but because she knew she'd uncover her true feelings and she was deeply guilty about this one emotion. *Relief.* As she stood gulping the cold welcoming water, she remembered.

* * *

Sandra was dressed in a canary-coloured yellow T-shirt and cut-off denims with her white flip-flops. She stood in the kitchen of her new build, Number 11 Cherry Hill. The papers were signed and sealed and it was now theirs. She couldn't believe it. They were going to IKEA in Dublin that afternoon to buy lots for it. It was so big. They had some furniture from Neil's bungalow but somehow it didn't suit this big house. The bungalow had been bought by a local so they had left a lot of stuff for her. She glanced out the window at the builders working away furiously to finish the rest of the houses. "Going like hot cakes!" the auctioneer had told her as he left. "There's a waiting list for the others, and them not even built yet." They were so lucky. She hadn't mentioned the baby again since all the moving-house stuff was going on around them and neither had Neil. They were repairing their marriage slowly and she didn't want to rock the boat. She knew deep down he was hoping she had moved on. Forgotten about it. As if. She was going to bring it up this afternoon. He couldn't say anything about money because she had it saved for the most part herself. It was the same procedure all over again.

Sandra headed to their master bedroom. They had bounced on the bed last night until they couldn't breathe. She had worried, but only slightly, that all that bouncing could kill off any good sperms. They had even christened the new house.

Neil had nuzzled into her ear last night as they made love in the empty curtainless front bedroom on the hard wooden floor – for the pure enjoyment of it! It was the first time in so long that sex hadn't been purely to procreate. Sandra hadn't found it all that comfortable to be honest but she wanted to make Neil happy. She wanted the marriage to work.

She turned on the power shower and stepped out of her

clothes. Their life was a routine. Work. Bar. Dinner. Work. Dinner. Bar. She was tired. She had been working full time the last few weeks and, although she was enjoying it, it was a means to an end. As soon as she got pregnant she knew she would give it up. She couldn't work full time anyway when the baby was born, but she fully intended to go back part time if Jonathan would have her, to help with the bills. She stepped under the shower jets and poured some Coconut shampoo into her hand before washing her hair really well. Sandra was a double hair-washer: she washed it and then washed it again, always had done. Would Neil be freaked out when she asked him if they could try again? She had mentioned it only that one evening on Knocknoly Bridge when they had received the negative result. He hadn't wanted to discuss it then but she'd understood it was way too soon. What if he said no now though? She scrubbed harder and looked down at her flat tummy. All she wanted to see there was a big growing baby bump. She'd welcome the stretch marks and piles and varicose veins. Was it too much to ask for?

She should invite her parents around this evening, she thought as she heard Neil come up the stairs – they hadn't even seen the house yet. She had asked her mother last week but she was in the final of some golf competition and couldn't make it.

"*Mmmmm* . . . someone's wife all showery and naked in there?" He tipped the glass shower door with his index finger.

Sandra laughed. "Come in if you want!"

He didn't need to be asked twice. He stripped off his work clothes and stepped under the hot jets. "You are so sexy, Sandra!" he gasped as he took her all in.

"Hmm, I wonder will you think that when I have a huge baby bump?" She opened her mouth to kiss him.

"What do you mean, a huge baby bump?" His eyes nearly popped out of his head. Oh God, he thought she was pregnant! Naturally.

"No! No! I'm not pregnant, Neil, I just mean . . . well . . . I want us to try IVF again this month."

His eyes clouded over. His mouth pursed closed. A light went out. "No, please, Sandra, not all this baby business again! I thought we agreed?" He slowly dragged his hands down his wet face.

"No, Neil, *we* never agreed. I want a baby, Neil. You know that. You have always known that."

He put one hand over his private parts and slid the shower door open with the other. "I didn't always know that, to be honest. I knew it was probably what you wanted but I didn't know it was the only thing you wanted."

"Where are you going?" She pushed the button to turn off the power shower and, dripping all over the floor, walked naked through to the bedroom after him.

"Sandra, put something on! The curtains are open in this room!" he hissed at her as he pulled on his boxer shorts. He padded to the landing and dragged his jeans off the banisters.

"Why are you so against trying the IVF again?" she implored him, trying to remain calm. She pulled her robe from the chrome hook behind the bathroom door and slipped it on.

"It's not so much the IVF, Sandra, it's you . . . it . . . it's what can I do to make you happy? I got you a house I can't really afford and as soon as we move in you are on to the next thing. Tom warned me you were high maintenance!"

"Tom? He doesn't even know me and I assure you, Neil Darragh, I am so not high maintenance!"

"Forget IKEA, I can't be arsed now, I have a lot on so I'm out of here. You know, Sandra, if you ever bothered to ask, work is drying up. I am pricing every job going out there but I am losing it all. No one is employing me, Sandra. So I'm fucking shitting it that the construction industry is going belly-up after us buying this mansion I can't afford!" He pulled on his jeans.

"Neil, please sit down for a few minutes. We need to thrash this out. You have me all wrong – a baby isn't all I want, I want us too."

He poked his head through his grey T-shirt and ignored her as he left the room. He ran down the stairs, taking them two at a time.

"*Shit!*" she shouted to the empty bedroom. She couldn't do it without him. If she could, she would.

He slammed the front door hard behind him.

* * *

They sat among other hopeful couples in the clinic again five weeks later and Neil was handed the cup to do his thing.

"This is the last time," he growled at her as he left to make his way, shoulders hunched, down the grey carpeted corridor.

The last few weeks had been awful. Neil was pissed off with her and barely speaking to her. She knew in her heart he wanted her to cancel the IVF, she knew he didn't want to do it but she just couldn't stop. He was never in any more and she never asked him where he was.

As soon as she became pregnant it would all change. It would all be better, back to normal. She had to be cruel to be kind. She watched him follow the nurse and she prayed a silent prayer it would work for them this time.

Neil's electrical business had slowed dramatically in a matter of weeks and she knew he was really worried about their finances. He had been in foul moods and nothing she did was shaking him out of it. She had kept her head down and gone to work and come home, made his dinner which most nights he just pushed around his plate before telling her that he was going out.

When he returned from wherever he'd been he went straight upstairs to watch DVDs in their bedroom, shutting the door behind him. The house was still as though they had moved in yesterday. There was a huge snag list to be attended to but they were having problems pinning the builder down. He had been off site for a week now and Sandra was losing patience. Their bedroom was the only one furnished and the rest of the rooms remained bare. That IKEA trip had never happened and although Sandra saw some great pieces online the funds were not there, Neil had told her. "Don't buy a thing until I say it's okay," he said. "Now I have to let the lads go too."

She had managed to save quite a lot and it was all going on the IVF. Her mother had not offered her any funds towards it which she was fine about even though she knew her parents had money to burn.

A nurse approached Sandra. "Now, as soon as Neil is back we will take you through," the nurse told her. A different nurse this time. A different baby.

Neil hadn't spoken to her again about how he felt about the IVF. He refused to get into a conversation about it so she had gone ahead and made the appointment.

He returned very soon after and handed the cup to the nurse. He was bright red, his face all blotchy, and he looked really uncomfortable as though he was willing the ground to open up and devour him.

"You don't need me any more, Sandra, so I'm going." He zipped up his black bomber jacket.

She could not believe this. "Are you joking?"

"No, there's a massive problem at work," he muttered, casting a glance around the waiting room – no one met his eye but he knew they were all listening. "Ben Ashmore, the contractor, is reported to have done a legger to Spain. If it's true and he has, we are completely screwed. He owes me over thirty thousand euro and if that's gone I don't know what I will do. I won't be able to afford to pay for that house, never mind a plastic baby."

"What is that supposed to mean?" she hissed. God, he was getting on her last nerve. She was the one who had to go through all the invasive procedures.

"You know, your test-tube baby or whatever it is, whatever it will be – more than likely nothing but a period." His voice had risen and glances were thrown in their direction.

The nurse coughed loudly. "I will give you two a moment but kindly keep your voices down," she said to the pair of them and backed away.

"It's not a test-tube baby, Neil, it's IVF," Sandra said, making a great effort to speak calmly. "And it's our only chance to have a baby of our own."

"But it's not natural. We can't have children and if I am perfectly honest with you I don't agree with all this IVF – it's going against God's plan, it's totally unnatural. I tried to tell you how I felt about all this but you never listened. Soon man will invent a womb and women will no longer be needed to produce babies. Do you think that will be natural? It's all about money, medics making money!"

Sandra couldn't believe he was ranting like this in the waiting room. Other couples buried their heads in old dog-eared magazines while one girl looked up and Sandra knew she was biting her tongue.

"Just go right now!" Sandra hissed at him.

He didn't need to be told twice. She watched him go as the nurse returned and she was brought into the treatment room.

She returned days later for the transfer. Alone. After, the nurse called a taxi for her. They were confident this time. She was too.

She lay on the couch after she got home from the hospital. When Neil came in she got a shock when she saw his face. "What is it?" she managed even though she was fuming with him.

"It's my worst nightmare. Ben Ashmore is gone. The site is closed down and all the money owed to me and future work is gone. I have nothing." He was devastated. He slumped onto the armchair. "Why on earth did you make me buy this place?"

She couldn't get up, she had been told not to. She wanted to comfort him but she knew she couldn't get up. "He can't just do that, Neil, he can't just leave us high and dry owing us thirty thousand euro! There must be a way to get the police involved?" She craned her head to try and make eye contact with him.

"There's not. He can and he did. Jesus Christ, Sandra, are you just going to lie there? Are you not even going to get up off the couch and come over to me?" He looked totally shocked.

"It's not that, Neil – I do want to, but I can't – they told me at the clinic not to –, it's best if I –"

He got up as she was mid-sentence. "I don't want to know, I honestly have no interest. I'm going to bed. Don't disturb me." He slowly dragged his tired feet across the room.

"I'm fine, by the way, thanks for asking!" she called sarcastically after him even though she knew she shouldn't.

* * *

Sandra re-played the events of that evening clearly in her mind as she made her way into the hospital. The "I'm fine, by the way" conversation was probably the last one they had ever had of any meaning. She hadn't moved off the couch except to make tea and toast and pee. Neil passed her by like he couldn't even see her lying there. He never asked her a question. If she was pregnant it would shake him out of it, she knew that.

She got up and dressed early two weeks later and drove to the chemist outside the village. She bought three pregnancy tests. She tucked them in the glove compartment in the car as she drove past the Moritz. The timing was excellent as the hotel was undergoing renovations so it was closed temporarily. It would reopen next week and she would be back to work full time.

She parked the car and headed straight into the house and up to the bathroom. Neil was out. She opened the first box and pulled the plastic off the white stick. She grabbed her bag and pulled the water bottle out and drank loads. Then she stood and looked at herself in the mirror.

"Please, God, please, please let me be pregnant. Let us be pregnant." She slowly unbuttoned her jeans and pulled down her pants. She sat with the stick between her legs and peed, taking care not to wet the window of the stick. She pulled the stick out and laid it on the side of the bath as she prayed and prayed over and over again. Her hands clasped so tightly together her veins were popping. She couldn't look. She didn't want to look. She wanted to save this feeling. She might be pregnant. There was every chance she was growing her baby inside her right this minute.

Then she grabbed for the stick. She stared hard at the little window. It was there. A very faint blue line but a blue line nonetheless.

"Jesus Christ!" She jumped up and with her knickers and jeans around her ankles as she shuffled across the bathroom to grab another test. Her heart was racing. "Oh dear God, oh dear

God, please, give me another one!" She drank more water, sat back on the toilet and gritted her teeth as she pushed her bladder and stuck another stick under her. Again when she was done she left it on the side of the bath. She stood up now very slowly and fixed herself. Slowly she pulled up her pants and buttoned her jeans. She thought her heart might jump out of her chest. She washed her hands thoroughly before picking the stick back up. She looked down. It was there again. The wonderful, exciting, incredible, fantastic, surreal, mind-blowing, out-of-this-world amazing little blue line.

"Yes! Yes! *Yesssssss!*" She punched the air and danced a gentle dance around the bathroom. "Oh thank you, God, thank you, Mary, thank you, Jesus!" she shouted, wet tears streaming down her cheeks.

She sat now on the edge of the bed and tried to calm herself. It wouldn't be good for the baby, all this hyper stuff. The baby. She lay down gently. She said the words out loud now: "The baby. My baby." She stared at the ceiling without its light fitting for ages. It had all been worth it, every last miserable step of the process. She felt wonderful. She felt at ease and completely happy. She felt like a proper woman. A proper wife. Finally she would be a mammy. At long, long last. She smiled at the image of her baby growing inside her. Then she got up slowly and searched for her phone. She dialled Neil's number quickly with panting breath again now.

"What, Sandra?" he answered on the last ring.

"Neil! I think we're pregnant. I mean, I have done two tests and they are both positive – we are – we are pregnant!" If she smiled any wider she was afraid her teeth would fall out.

"Oh . . . seriously, Sandra? That's really . . . wow . . . amazing . . . well done, you. I don't know what to say to you really . . . now. I need to tell you something though . . . I'm . . . oh look, Sandra, I'll come home right now."

She felt it there and then. Felt it trickle down through her and flow into her pants. The oh-too-familiar feeling of an unwanted period. It couldn't be, she'd just done two tests. Two positive tests. She reefed down her jeans and pants and there it was. The red stain. The red stain. The red stain. She hung up and threw the phone onto the bed and grabbed her car keys.

She drove to the clinic in Dublin in a record-breaking fifty-three minutes. She parked at the doors knowing well she would be clamped.

"You need an appointment, Mrs Darragh," the receptionist told her quietly. She was hysterical.

"I need to see my consultant *now*!" she screamed at the poor unfortunate girl. "I am bleeding! Do you hear me? I am *bleeding*!"

"Okay, please calm down and take a seat, we will do what we can as soon as we can. It really won't help you if you become hysterical." The receptionist handed her a plastic glass of water now.

Sandra drank it and clutched her car keys and crossed her legs tightly as she sat. She was well aware that everyone was trying not to look at her. Don't fall out, baby, please, stay, stay, stay with me. I need you. I love you. I want you so much. I just want to hold you and smell you. I can't bear this, I just can't lose you . . ." She rubbed and rubbed her stomach and then her tears turned into loud sobs as she was escorted to a treatment room by a lovely kind-faced nurse.

"It's okay, my love, try and relax if you can at all. We will do a quick blood test and the doctor will be in to take a look at you, okay?"

As she held her arm out and the needle sank into her vein she knew in her heart it was over. Her pregnancy was gone.

"Can I get you a cup of tea?" the nurse asked as she gently patted a small brown plaster down onto Sandra's vein.

"No. Thank you."

"As soon as we run the bloods we'll be back, okay? Can I call anyone for you?" Sandra shook her head.

It seemed like hours before her consultant came in with a chart in his hands. He smiled at her before putting on the ultrasound machine. She lifted her shirt and he squeezed the ice-cold jelly onto her tummy. She stared at the screen. Then he asked her to raise her knees, put her feet together and spread her legs.

He put a camera up her now, and then he said softly, "Sandra, the bloods are negative, I'm afraid . . . just having a little look here . . ."

A little black dot swam before her eyes as his machine picked it up.

"There was a pregnancy, okay, but I'm afraid it's no longer viable. I am so sorry." He removed the camera and put the scanner back into its holder with a final click and handed her some rough grey tissue paper to wipe her tummy. "I will need you to come in for a D and C, okay?" He helped her up by her elbow.

"Yeah, okay." She fixed her top into her jeans. "I wonder what it was?" she asked.

"Too early to tell," he answered gently.

"I think it was a boy. I'm going to call him Neil Junior."

"Can we call anyone to take you home?" He opened the door for her.

"No, it's okay, my husband's meeting me outside," she lied.

She left the building. She wasn't clamped. Now that was a miracle.

"False alarm," she managed when she got home and he was standing at the door.

"False alarm?" He looked at her like she was crazy.

"Yeah," she said simply as she went inside.

"What do you mean *false alarm*? I've been ringing and ringing your phone! Are you pregnant or not?" He glared at her.

She really didn't need this. "No, I'm not," she told him, then she made her way up the stairs.

"That's it? You ring me and tell me you're pregnant and I rush home. I can't find you anywhere, you won't answer your phone, and now you tell me you're not? You need help, Sandra, you know that? You're losing your marbles. Don't call me again!" He left, slamming the door behind him.

She crawled into the spare bed and she cried and cried and cried herself to sleep.

* * *

She supposed she hadn't noticed the marriage dissolve away as she had been so caught up in her own world. She had thought that it would blow over. But it didn't. Look where she was now. As she entered the hospital ward she saw his brother Tom sitting by the bed.

"There she is: Wife of the Year!" he scowled at her.

Neil didn't bother to say hello to her.

The young dark nurse from yesterday was changing the water in the brown hospital vase. Fresh flowers, Sandra noticed. Who had brought those?

"What's going on?" she asked.

She looked at Tom and he held her stare.

"Can you explain why Mr Kilroy, my bank manager, has called me to say you are taking over our mortgage, Tom?" She kept her dignity and didn't yell as she sat on the opposite side of the bed on the white plastic seat. She even laid a brown-paper bag of Louise's white chocolate-chip muffins that Neil so loved on his locker.

"Cheers," came his monosyllabic reply.

"I can't stay long because we have a wedding up above in the hotel and I have to get back to reception. Alice is covering for me for the hour. What is going on?" She looked from one to the other.

"Okay, Sandra, Neil called me in here today for a reason. I drove down this morning." He turned to the nurse. "If you don't mind, sweetheart, this is private business." He pointed to the curtain and she left, pulling it across behind her.

The guy in the next bed called out for the nurse but she didn't come back.

Tom turned back to Sandra. "Basically I am going to buy the house off ye – well, off the bank, I suppose. The shop's doing really well and I always wanted a place back home in Knocknoly for summer holidays and all that. He can't afford it and you can't afford it on your own. Simple really." He shrugged. "Glad to help out. Generous of me, I know – but that's the kind of guy I am."

Sandra looked at him, her jaw dropping to the floor. "Can he not speak?" She pointed at Neil. "Can you not speak any more, Neil?"

"What can I do? I can't afford it! Don't you get it?" he hissed.

Well, that was quick. Tom had wasted no time. Was it all going? House and marriage? Even though they were married she would never dream of taking a penny off Neil – it was his money as far as she was concerned. She knew she'd have to think differently if children were involved. But they weren't. The horrible house would soon be gone but along with it her marriage and her life as she knew it.

"Excuse me, can we have some privacy, please, Tom?" she asked.

He ignored her. "He has no focking money, Sandra, he can't keep up the mortgage repayments – you have the poor fella fleeced. Do you not understand the money is gone? His job is gone? All you care about is yourself. Seriously, all ye eejits who got stuck in Knocknoly, who never moved on, there's something wrong with all of you! Inbreds!"

They both stared at Neil now. He was obviously tanked up on pain medication by the blank look on his face.

"Tom, that's our home you're talking about, and Neil is my husband." She took Neil's limp hand in hers.

"Not any more, sweetheart." Tom pulled a black-covered notebook from his back pocket.

"What do you mean 'not any more'? Neil, come on, I need you to speak to me here!" Sandra fought back the huge tears.

"No waterworks, please." Tom was flipping over pages.

Sandra swallowed hard. She didn't know what to say. Neil let go of her hand and turned his head on the pillow to face Tom. She felt like she no longer knew this man. It was insane. She was deeply saddened.

Tom continued. "Look, Sandra, it's settled. I've spoken to a contact at the bank and, as Neil is bankrupt, I'll be able to do a deal with them – pay the mortgage off at a much reduced price.

All going well in that regard, I should be able to pay you a lump sum to compensate your loss – say, one hundred thousand – enough to put a deposit on a place of your own – that is, if you don't want to just move back in with your folks out on the hill."

"What?" she shouted. "Neil?" She took his hand again. "Say something, please! Is this what you want? Can we not at least talk in private for God's sake?"

He looked into her eyes now, his watery and weak. "What can I do, Sandra? I can't afford it, we can't afford it. And there's something else I need to tell you. I don't know how to tell you but if I don't I know someone who will." He pulled himself up on his one good arm in the bed and lowered his voice. "I'm so sorry but I've been seeing someone else. I'm really sorry, Sandra, but I'm going to move in with her for a while. You reduced me to this. Sure you know our marriage is over."

She was completely lost for words. What a coward to tell her in front of his brother!

"When it's over it's over, I suppose, what?" said Tom. "What's that quiz show that used to be on the BBC? '*They Think It's All Over – it is now!*'"

"You prick! You horrible, mean-spirited selfish prick!" She stood up. "I hate you, Neil. I will never forgive you for this." The tears were running down her face now. "I didn't deserve this!"

Tom butted in. "He's not a prick – you're a witch!"

Sandra couldn't believe this was happening. So just like that he was selling their home from under her and moving in with his mistress. "This marriage is definitely over, Neil Darragh, you got that much right!" She stared hard at him.

"Why would you think that?" he answered sarcastically, staring back at her, making a pathetic face. "Don't lay all the blame on me, because I won't accept it. You changed the second we got married."

"For fuck's sake, Neil, you had an affair a few months into the marriage! I forgave you!"

"The chap is miserable with you," Tom butted in again now.

"Fuck off, Tom, you total tosser! It's nothing to do with you!"

Her eyes were blazing with temper now as she took in his ridiculous overly tight black-leather jacket with his pot belly bulging out and his purple skinny jeans along with his cream winkle-pickers. Tom might have an exclusive clientele and his shop Be Bang Be in the middle of Grafton Street in Dublin but he hadn't a clue how to style himself. He looked like a packet of Opal Fruits had puked all over him. He had looked like a total tool at their wedding party in Hines, as Dermot had so rightly put it.

"You wouldn't wait, would you? Typical Knocknoly girl, so narrow-minded, get married at the drop of a hat! Sure ye had fuck-all in common! I tell you, my Scarlett would put manners on you!"

Sandra snorted at the mention of Tom's ridiculous wife Scarlett. "Scarlett, or Bridie as she was originally christened, does not live in the real world, Tom. Bridie married you for the money and don't kid yourself about that. Sure wasn't she about all the hot spots in Dublin chasing the rich and the famous? She'd put manners on me? Ha, don't make me laugh!"

Tom opened his mouth to protest, his overly bleached teeth blinding Sandra. She continued, "What do you know about me, Tom Darragh? Nothing!"

"I see a woman who is infertile and can't give this man kids!" he spat back at her.

The air hung heavy around them as the sick man in the next bed called out, "Nurse! Nurse!"

"Yeah. I guess that's what you would see." Sandra stood and slung her bag onto her shoulder.

The nurse opened the curtain and looked at Neil. "You okay, Neil?" she smiled at him.

"You might spend more time checking on the man in the next cubicle – he's been calling for you." Sandra turned on her heel and walked away.

As she made her way for the last time down the corridor Tom's words rang loudly in her head. Was it all her fault? She felt like she was walking in a dream. It was all over just like that. It had been a whirlwind of a couple of years and she didn't know how she felt. She passed a girl sitting at the end of the corridor and then stopped in her tracks. She walked back slowly. It was the girl from the other day in the red dress – the one she had nearly knocked over. She was holding a fresh bunch of flowers tightly in her hand, her head down. Sandra stood in front of her and she raised her face. The new waitress from Hines. The nurse's words rang in her ears. "There's a vomiting bug here – how did you both get in?" You *both*. It had been her.

"I'm going. I won't be back. He's all yours," she told her and suddenly realised she meant every single word.

Chapter 18

The wedding was in full flow now and Cara was over the moon. She checked her appearance in the mirror at reception. Her Stella McCartney suit was teamed with a tight red vest and a red rose was pinned to her lapel. Her hair was scraped back into a low ponytail, hair sprayed into place and her make-up was a little more extreme than usual. She had gone heavy on the black liquid eyeliner for the evening and had added some MAC face and body foundation of Sandra's and even some red lipstick. She had even managed to get into a pair of black high heels.

"You look really pretty. And tall!" Jonathan came up from behind her and she jumped.

"Sorry – and thank you!" She turned to face him.

"Still so jumpy?" His eyes narrowed.

"Yes. I'm afraid so. Can't help it." She rubbed her hand across the tip of her nose and sniffed. "Better grab a tissue, the speeches are coming up." She had to turn sideways to slip past him as he stood his ground. She supposed he was wondering why she was so closed off with him all the time?

She had wanted to offer him a nightcap the other night when he dropped her home but she was so scared he'd start asking her questions that she just didn't want to answer. She didn't want to make him uncomfortable. She just wanted to be Cara Byrne, Hospitality Manager, and not poor unfortunate Cara Charles. In any case they had both been exhausted that evening.

She stopped in her tracks as she gazed at the people at the top table eating and chatting happily, the backdrop of the mountains and the sea a bride's dream setting. Jonathan had added some white outside fairy lights to the trees and it was a complete fairytale. Her top table hadn't been anything like that. She leaned against the wall at the back of the room. She hadn't had a top table. The mixed sounds of all the different voices was hypnotising as Cara became lost in her old world yet again.

* * *

Cara strolled on down the Quays that night after leaving The Law Top and continued hiccupping to herself. It had been a fun evening. Steve was a great guy but just as Aoife wasn't his cup of tea, romantically he wasn't hers. It was too late to test it now anyway. They had a great rapport but Cara didn't know if it would translate outside the job. The Law Top was a really nice place to work. She actually laughed out loud now thinking about it – the drink was painting a rather rose-tinted image of her job and not the reality of the blood, sweat and tears that were the stuff of most days.

She was so lost in thought that she didn't hear the person come up behind her. Suddenly she was punched in the back of the head and fell to the ground screaming. A hand went over her mouth immediately and her face was pushed hard into the concrete path. Her attacker smacked her head three times off the ground and she was completely dazed as she tasted the warm blood that flowed into her mouth. He pulled her wallet from her bag and her mobile phone and then he ran. She heard the footsteps receding and then there was silence. She couldn't move. She tried to cry out but her voice wouldn't work. She was simply paralysed with fear. Her head was pounding and she was terrified.

Cara didn't know for how long she had lain there when she heard heavy footsteps approach. She felt a hand on her body and she screamed. Loud.

"Shush, it's okay, I'm a guard, please try and stay still," came a warm voice. He didn't move her. She heard his radio beep and interference piercing the line as he called for an ambulance, gave their location and then she must have blacked out.

* * *

Alex stood over her in the hospital, with Esther on the chair beside her, as Cara opened her eyes.

"Oh . . . I'm so sorry, Mam . . ." Her lips stuck together as she saw Esther's pale worried face. Her speech was slurred as it hurt her to speak – her tongue felt the size of a house.

"Don't be sorry, love – sure you have nothing to be sorry about and it's all going to be fine," Esther replied and held her only daughter's hand.

Alex moved up and took her other hand. "There's a policeman outside who wants to take a short statement," he said just as the nurse and policeman entered the room.

"Sorry, Alex," Cara whimpered.

"Hey, stop, it's not your fault." He rubbed her arm and then smoothed her hair from her face.

"Just a few quick questions, Miss Byrne, and we'll be out of your hair." The guard pulled up a seat at the side of her bed.

She tried to sit up but the pain in her lower back was piercing and she cried out.

Alex jumped up, "Is this really necessary right now?" he asked.

"I'm afraid so, sir," the guard said as he flipped over a new page on his tiny hard-backed black notebook.

Cara told him all she remembered and was embarrassed that she had put herself in such a vulnerable position. She was embarrassed she was so drunk and mortified when he asked her just how much alcohol she had ingested on the night in question. "Can you remember anything – any physical attributes about your attacker at all?"

She shook her head. "He came at me from behind," she whispered.

"We had a Steve Brady in for questioning this morning. I

understand he was the last person you came into contact with on the night?"

"Oh no, please don't, Steve would never do this, he –"

Alex interrupted her. "He what exactly?" He was standing again. "He fancies you, you know he does, you told me as much yourself on our first date. He's jealous. If I find out he did this to you so help me God I'll –"

"Thank you, sir, that's quite enough." The guard closed his notebook, folded the black elastic around it and stood up, replacing his hat slowly. "We can take it from here."

He left the room, saying he would be in touch.

"I want you out of that job," Alex said.

Before Cara could respond the doctor entered and took the now-empty bedside seat.

"Well, Cara, you have severe bruising to your lower back," he said, "so no lifting for a few weeks. You needed three stitches in your lower lip and your tongue is split but this will heal itself. We also had to put a stitch into the top of your left ear as this was split also."

Esther started to cry.

"You were very lucky. The MRI revealed there is no swelling on your brain though your head did take quite a pounding off the pavement."

"He could have killed you!" Esther wailed. She blew her nose, the noise almost comical in this heavy atmosphere.

"But he didn't. I'm okay, Mam, really I am. And it was not Steve, absolutely no way in the world. I'm the idiot getting pissed and walking the Quays at one in the morning alone. Steve had offered to call me a taxi. I wouldn't let him."

"I'm sure we'll be able to discharge you later today. Plenty of TLC for her now," said the doctor to the other two and left.

"How did you get back so quickly?" Cara asked Alex now.

"That's the thing, the reason I was calling you – I wasn't needed. The airline double-booked me and Officer Keily so one of us was free. I called and called you but you didn't answer and then you turned off your phone so I just headed home for an early night. I made you a supper and left it on the table. When

I woke at the crack of dawn this morning and saw it still there I reckoned you must have stayed in Esther's after all so I called her and she didn't know where you were. Because you had no wallet the hospital had no ID for you. It's just as well I called every hospital and I found you quickly. They told me what had happened. I drove over and I collected Esther and here we are."

"That explains it – when I rang you I didn't get a foreign ring tone."

"Why did you turn off your phone?" he asked softly now.

"Ah, here, does that matter now really, Alex?" said Esther. "All these questions and she needs to rest." She folded the clothes she had brought up for Cara and placed them neatly in Cara's locker. Cara could smell her mother's washing powder from them. Comforting.

"No, Esther, it doesn't matter, you're so right." Alex smiled and pulled up the bottom of the old window – the cold air came whizzing in.

Esther got up and pulled it halfway back down. "And there was me thinking I was having a night of it! Someone tried to poison poor Victoria – when you called me that time I was running out the door to the bloody vet. I didn't want to worry you so I kept schtum. I let her out the back but she ate some rat poison. Now here's the thing, I have never in my life laid rat poison." Esther had her best Miss Marple face on.

"Oh no! I did, Mam, ages ago. Mr Dolan next door told me he had seen a rat and I didn't want to freak you out so I just put some poison down and I forgot about it, but it was like a year ago?"

Esther Byrne chewed on a nail. "Ah, right, just as well you told me. I was about to knock and blame Dolan because he had shouted over the garden wall for her to shut her yapping trap yesterday morning. The poor little darling was only doing me the favour of yapping at the birds who were shitting all over my freshly hung towels."

"Wow, what kind of person would poison a helpless animal?" Alex asked as he smoothed the sheets on Cara's bed with the palms of his hands.

"But is she okay?" Cara asked.

"Ah, she's grand now but I'm smashed! Them vets are not cheap!"

Cara closed her eyes. That had been the worst experience of her sheltered life. How had she been so bloody thick? She deserved it, she thought.

"Cara?" Alex said.

She opened her eyes.

"I'm going to drop Esther home and come back." Alex stood and brushed down his light denim jeans with the palms of his hands, his blue eyes shining bright.

"What?" Esther asked. "No! I mean . . . I'm grand. I'm stopping here." She folded her arms.

Alex put one arm though his sports jacket. "No, I think you should go home, Esther. You need to see to Victoria, don't you? I will stay and take Cara home as soon as the doctor says she's good to go."

So just like that, after thirty-odd years of minding Cara single-handedly, Esther was ushered out the door. Esther did not look happy but she let Alex take control. Cara looked longingly after her mammy and felt like such a stupid child. She really just wanted to get home to her own bed and have a nice cup of tea and cheese on toast. Alex didn't do nice tea or indeed carbs.

She flicked through the magazine Esther had bought her but her head was spinning. What a terrible thing to have happened to her! Funny, she always thought she'd fight back if she was attacked. She'd assumed she was stronger that she was. She wasn't strong at all. She was weak.

* * *

When Alex returned he had a takeaway hot chocolate for her. She was dressed thanks to the help of the nurse and was sitting on the edge of the bed.

"Oh, are you discharged already? That's great. Here you go, extra hot just the way you like it!" He handed her the drink.

"Thanks, Alex. Yes, the doctor says I can go. Was Mam okay?" She opened the lid and blew at the drink. It shivered under her breath.

"Totally fine, glad to get back, I felt." He picked up her orange plastic hospital bag with her bloodied ripped work clothes peering out at her.

"I'm so embarrassed, Alex, it was just such a silly thing to do. But, believe me, it was not Steve who did this – please never accuse him of it."

"Let's see what the Guards have to say on the matter first, shall we? I told you that place is dangerous, Cara." Alex knelt in front of her. "Promise me that you won't go back?" he pleaded as she sipped the hot chocolate.

"Well, I can't go back to work for a month or so anyway so I probably don't have a choice. "The bar trade isn't like other jobs – they can't afford to have staff out of work so they'll need to employ someone else." She took another drink and this time let the liquid burn the cut on her battered tongue. "I'll ring them tonight and tell them I won't be back."

"Good girl!" Alex took her drink as she eased her sore body off the bed. She didn't want to speak any more, her speech was becoming more slurred due to her tongue being sliced and the stitches in her mouth.

"Let's get home and let me take care of you," he whispered.

She made baby steps to the door then stopped. "Why were you so cross with me on the phone, Alex? You were like a bloody madman."

He squeezed her hand. "I know and I'm so, so sorry. It's just I needed you, I really needed you. I couldn't understand why you were ignoring my calls. I was afraid you had gone off me, Cara. I just couldn't bear it, I am so madly in love with you. I'd die for you, Cara. I can't believe my luck that I found you."

His eyes filled up with huge teardrops and she gently wiped them away as they fell. "It's okay, Alex, I will be fine. I love you too and you can trust me. I would never do anything to hurt you. I'd never have an affair, never! But you need to start trusting me – you can't behave like that – I won't accept that."

He nodded. "I understand. I will. I do."

She turned and left the hospital room.

Chapter 19

Sandra cried all the way back to the hotel but there were no actual tears. She made the sounds and her body shook but her eyes remained completely dry. Next on her list was to call a good solicitor. She wished she had someone to talk to. She kicked the wet leaves as she walked. She had been right about Neil all along. She had known. He had said someone was going to tell her? Who could that be, she wondered. A few people popped into her mind. It was such a small village she wasn't surprised. She just hoped it wasn't her mother. God, please don't let it be her mother! Could Tom do this? Could he just push her out of her own home like that? All her savings were long gone. She couldn't afford it on her own, he was right about that. Her green Oasis coat was always warm against the weather but now she was shivering with the cold. She had to pull herself together before she went back to work.

She still had half an hour so she took a few deep breaths and opened the door into Louise's Loft. The little coffee shop was warm and there was low relaxing music on the stereo. Crowded House. Sandra recognised "You're Not The Girl You Think You Are". Ironic. She shook her head.

She grabbed a seat in the corner and took off her coat. The smell of freshly baked bread and Louise's famous cheese-and-ham croissants filled her nostrils but she had no appetite.

Without really thinking she opened her bag and took out her phone.

I am in Louise's if you have 10 minutes? She pressed send.

"What can I get you, darling?" Louise stood over her, her light-brown hair tied back in her familiar brown hairnet and her white apron tied tightly. A welcome sight.

"Can I have a pot of tea? And I'd better try and eat so a white cheese and smoky ham croissant, Lou, please."

"Coming up!"

Louise headed for the kitchen, stopping briefly at tables as she went to check the customers were all happy.

Sandra watched Louise chat to the customers. Sometimes she wondered how she did it all on her own: ran a really successful business, did the book-keeping, did the ordering, did the cooking and at the end of a long hard day went up those stairs alone. She had never really asked her if she minded being alone as the last thing in the world she wanted to do was to hurt Louise's feelings. Someday she would though because she wished she could live like Louise.

A few minutes later Louise was pleased to see the door open and Dermot make his way over to Sandra. She looked like she had the weight of the world on her shoulders, the poor lamb. Louise wouldn't push her. She wanted the Loft to be a comfortable place for people to come and eat and drink and be left alone. That was always her policy. She knew when to back away and just be a hostess. It had always been her dream to own her own place. Other women had different dreams of what life happiness meant to them. It was this to Louise. She never had any desire to marry, she had travelled and read all the books she ever wanted to read, she had Salt and Pepper, her two Pekinese dogs, to take care of, and she was in a walking club. It was exactly the life she had always wanted and she was exceptionally grateful.

"Well?" Dermot sat, pulled off his tweed cap and pushed his blond hair back out of his face. It didn't stay and flopped back down over his eyes.

It had grown wild over the last few weeks, she noted. "Well,

Dermot, my gut instinct was correct. Neil is having an affair. Not only that but he wants out of the marriage and out of the house. Tom's going to do a deal with the bank and pay off the mortgage. He's going to 'compensate me for my loss' by paying me one hundred thousand. It was all settled before I even got there. I had no say and no choice in any of it."

Dermot was quiet as Louise put the pot down with two cups. He winked at her. "Thanks, Apple."

She smiled at him and moved off.

"Can he do that though, about the house I mean?" He took the lid off the pot and stirred the tea leaves with the teaspoon.

"I don't know. I need to see a solicitor, I suppose. But Neil can't keep up his payments and I can't do it on my own. I don't want to be in that house anyway. It suits me to leave if I'm perfectly honest. I want out but where am I going to live, Dermot?"

He twisted the ceramic lid several times before it slotted back into position. "And what about the marriage?" he asked.

Sandra put her head in her hands. "It's been over for ages, Dermot. I feel like I've been living in some sort of bubble. I fell in love with Neil and, yes, we married very quickly but I was sure, totally sure. But now that I think about it, I just saw the future. The family. I saw the house and the children, the family Christmases, the family holidays. I never in my wildest dreams just saw me and Neil – that was never in my mind. So stupid of me, I know, but that's the truth."

Dermot poured her tea now as Louise placed the food down and slipped away again. "So no kids equals no marriage, is that what you mean?" He spooned sugar into his tea.

Sandra watched it dissolve as it hit the hot liquid. "It's as though there was always something missing. He had an affair very early into the marriage and I forgave him. I know what was wrong – I should never have married him. We had been already trying for a family but, you know what, Dermot, I didn't do it on purpose. I just didn't think. I was supposed to get married. I was the right age. I didn't want to be the odd one out."

He sipped the tea and broke an edge off her croissant and

handed it to her. She nibbled at it.

"But now, Dermot, he's doing it again and this time it is the deal-breaker and he knows that. In fact it's as if he did it on purpose to get away from me. He had no shame in telling me, not like the last time. He said he had to tell me – that if he didn't there was someone else who would. I feel, I don't know, somehow guilty."

"You feel guilty?" he asked, kind eyes wide open.

"Yes, I feel guilty. I know a lot of it is my fault because I wanted the baby so much. I wanted the big house and I didn't ever think about the money aspect. I was pregnant, for a very, very short moment and when I lost the baby I barely told him about it. You see, Dermot, it was only ever about me the second time we did IVF. He really didn't want to know. I used him."

Sandra dropped her head and Dermot didn't answer. He sipped his tea, giving her time.

"I mean, he was horrible to me." She lowered her voice now as Mike and Tiffney came in. "He was really cruel about the IVF and he turned off a switch in me. I just never imagined he could be so nasty, but then again he didn't want it and I forced him."

"But you wanted it, Sandy. It's okay to want kids – that is okay, you know? And it's okay to do whatever it takes to try and get what you want out of life."

"Yes, but what if your partner really, really doesn't want what you want? He loved me, Dermot, I know he did. He was perfectly happy with just the two of us but I wasn't and I drove a wedge between us and it's too late now. I would never go back to him."

"Two affairs doesn't say 'perfectly happy' to me, Sandy." Dermot cut the rest of the croissant in half now and the steam rose up. He handed half to Sandra wrapped in a white serviette. "Let's walk." He pulled on his cap and he helped her into her coat. "I'll grab that bill later, Apple, okay?"

Louise waved him away.

"No, Dermot, here let me!" Sandra rummaged around in her bag.

"Your purse is behind reception." He smiled at her.

"Of course it is!" She pulled her long black hair out from under her collar and had to laugh. She'd left it there after she nipped out to buy the cakes for Neil earlier. "I am such a scatterbrain these days. Thank you, Dermot."

They fell into step and walked towards the Moritz. The birds were singing and it was a beautiful clear December day. Dermot had the right idea living the outdoor life, she thought as she took a welcome bite from the warm croissant.

"I don't think you have been in love with Neil for a long time, Sandra. I don't think you ever knew Neil. I did. I've known him since we were boys. He's always been a tough guy. Don't get me wrong – he's a good man, but he was never honest with you. I saw the way he treated women here in Knocknoly back when you were busy flying around the world. Tom came up and set up Darragh Electrics for him when their old man retired. I knew he was seeing that au pair Kelley behind your back and it killed me." He took a deep breath in through his nose and exhaled slowly out through his mouth. "It was me who knew about this latest affair too, I told him before the crash to tell you or I would. I went to the house that morning. I guess he was going to tell his fancy lady they were caught out when the car hit him in the estate. He's always been . . . a bit of a boyo. That's why I was so taken aback when you started to fall for him."

"I guessed it was you all right. Thanks, Dermot. How on earth did I not know this about him though? It makes me look like the biggest eejit in the world. I'm not saying I wouldn't have still married him – I know I would – it's just I'd have seen a very different side to him and I could have treated it differently. I wouldn't have pushed the baby on him, I –"

Dermot held up a hand and stopped her. "Like I said inside, there's nothing wrong with trying your damnedest to get what you want, and if that was IVF or something else I say you had to go for it. Don't blame yourself, Sandra. I think you should happily wave that gaff and Neil goodbye. I just think you'll be happier. You deserve better. You deserve the best and there is a place at mine for as long as you'd like until you find a new place of your own."

They had reached the end of the driveway to the hotel and he stopped and looked at her.

"Are you serious?" She looked up into his kind warm eyes.

"I am totally serious. Come and go as you please. I have a spare room. It's not the tidiest house in the world but sure you can solve that!"

She playfully swiped at him and he jumped out of the way.

"You are saving my life again," she said. She let out a slow sigh of relief.

"Anytime. Now come on, it's time you were back on the desk – there's a wedding in full flow up there." He leaned in and gently picked a piece of pastry from her chin.

"What would I do without you, Dermot?" She looked up at him as she put a hand on his arm.

He looked uncomfortable before he said, "G'wan outta that!" and they walked on.

Chapter 20

The weeks after the attack had been hard for Cara. She relived it every night in her sleep. Alex, true to his word, had looked after her and he had been amazing. He had asked for personal leave and was given three weeks off work. He did everything for her. He waited on her hand and foot.

"I thought we could go for a spin today," he said as he gave her breakfast in bed again. "Get you out of the house."

"I'd love that," Cara smiled. "Maybe we could drop over and see my mam?" She hadn't seen Esther all week as it was quite a distance by bus from Harold's Cross to Sandymount. Esther had come over on the buses the week after she left hospital but the journey was hard on her and Cara told her not to do it again.

"Do not come all the way on the bus!" she had warned her mother as she spoke to her on Alex's phone. "We will drop in to you next week. I am fine. I just want to stay in bed and rest my back." They hadn't dropped in though.

"No, I was thinking we could drive out to Dalkey, have lunch in the Queen's and take a walk along the beach after?"

"Sure, okay, that sounds lovely." Cara cut into her scrambled egg with salmon drenched in lemon. If she was honest a bowl of Rice Krispies was all she really fancied. Alex went to so much trouble when he cooked breakfast for her but sometimes it was all too exhausting.

She dressed carefully after breakfast and slowly made her way down to Alex's car. He helped her in as she was still really sore. They put some classical music on and she enjoyed the warm relaxed drive. She wondered how Esther was. She had still not got a new mobile since the attack and she desperately missed texting her mam. She smiled as she remembered the lessons every evening teaching Esther to text. They would light their little fire and lessons would begin. "Go easy with me now," Esther would say as she whacked each letter on the phone. "Gently, Mam, stop over-pressing!" Eventually to her credit Esther had stuck with it and got it. She always sent texts in capital letters as though she was always shouting which was odd as she did really shout down the phone. Cara would ask Alex again in a little while if they could drop in to visit her on the way home.

"How's the pain level today then?" he asked as he kept his eyes on the road.

"Ah, I think it's improving a little but still sore."

"We'll be getting a visit from Guard O'Neill this evening, you know."

"Really?" she asked, eyes wide open. "Why?"

"Well, it seems that asshole Steve had a credible alibi – an Aoife Someone said he was with her from the moment you left – they left the bar together soon after you went and he spent the night with her in her flat on Dorset Street."

Cara looked out the window. Men. Hilarious. It didn't take Steve long to get over her, did it? Minutes in this case.

"So they haven't a clue who attacked me then? I guess they wouldn't though, would they? Attacks like this happen every day – it's just when it happens to you . . . well . . . you want to know who did it."

"Well, we can talk to him later and see. In the meantime relax and enjoy the day, yeah? I will never let anything happen to you ever again. Ever." He leaned over and rubbed her thigh.

"Yeah, I know, you told me," she nodded and tried to relax.

Alex ordered for her as the waitress rushed from table to table in the busy pub. Cara missed work, she realised. She felt very much out of her own body and mind lately and she hated the feeling. She just wanted to get back to normal.

It was a warm day and the tables outside were full also.

"Can we have the garlic mussels to start, please, and two medium-rare steaks?" Alex asked the waitress.

Cara grimaced as she shifted on the seat.

"That sound good, Cara?" he asked her as the waitress jotted it all down. She nodded.

"And to drink?"

"We'll have a bottle of Faustino V red, please. Mainly for you, Cara, but sure I can have a glass with all the food."

"Ah, just get a half bottle then," Cara suggested but Alex shook his head and the waitress moved away.

Alex cupped some crumbs on the table in the crook of his fist and swept them to the floor. "Listen, Cara, I really want to talk to you. I know how tired and upset you have been. Not that you don't know it at this stage but I just want to tell you again how madly in love with you I am and that I admire you so much. I wish I could have you at home with me 24/7 like this all the time."

She looked at him. He was gorgeous and generous and kind but the possessive streak was still worrying her. "I've enjoyed it too, Alex, but I do really want to go back to work again." She rushed on before his mood changed. "Oh, not to The Law Top but maybe, you know, a different career. Actually, I always wanted to – to go to college."

His blue eyes lit up. "What a fantastic idea! You would be a great student. I can just see you now in your cords and cowboy shirts and cool Converse runners!" He laughed and leaned back on his seat.

The waitress brought the wine and Alex tasted it expertly.

"That's lovely, thank you," he said. "You can pour away there." He dazzled her with his blue eyes.

She stood motionless for a few seconds. "Oh right, yes." She poured now then placed the wine on their table and slipped away.

"So any idea what you would like to study?" He warmed his wine in his hands.

"I always thought the hotel business would be something I'd love to learn about. I think I mentioned that to you before, did I not?" She began to feel happier now for the first time since the attack.

"Yeah, you did, of course you did. I could really see that would suit you perfectly, Cara." He pushed the salt and pepper to the side as the waitress laid the garlic-smelling bowl of mussels on the table. "Hmmm, smells divine!"

"My dad always said it would be something I could do well." She sipped her wine.

"I wonder which college runs courses in hospitality?" Alex said as he dipped in for a mussel.

"Would I even get a place, I wonder?" she asked him as he handed her a mussel and she leaned back in her chair.

"Of course you would, you'd be incredible. I know that much! You have to go for it, Cara!" He nodded at the uneaten mussel in her hand as he swallowed one.

She decided to be honest. "Sorry, Alex, I know I ate them with you before in Dun Laoghaire but I really didn't like them at all."

He grinned at her. "I'm so sorry, Cara, how bloody rude of me to order them! I just thought after the last time you oohed and ahhed when I got you to try them that you loved them."

Cara pushed her hair out of her face and tried to knot it out of her way. She crossed her jeaned legs and opened the top buttons on her overly starched green shirt. She felt uncomfortable. Why was she always so uncomfortable lately? "I did. I tried, Alex, but . . ." She shivered now and he burst out laughing. "The thought of them sliding down the back of my throat again – *urhgh*! I can't bear it."

Alex put his hand up and the waitress was back like a cannon ball.

"Sorry, would it be possible to get a portion of spicy chicken wings as soon as possible?"

"Sure, not a problem," she nodded.

"Thanks, Alex, you're so good," said Cara. "I suppose I should speak up. I'm just getting used to all this boyfriend stuff and I'm finding my own feet, I suppose. It's all been so fast, hasn't it?"

"Quite all right. It has been ridiculously fast but we are in love and that's the way love happens. Don't forget we are still getting to know each other. I'm no expert on this either, you know."

The chicken wings and the main courses arrived together but Cara didn't mind and she picked at her wings and the underdone steak. Cara liked her steak well done.

She began to relax as the wine took hold and they chatted easily. Alex wasn't looking forward to going back to work.

"You know, I might have to do a long stint in Dubai soon. It will mean I am away for a few months." He looked hurt and she took his hands.

"Don't worry, it's your job. I understand that and I will be fine. I won't move back in with Esther if that's what you're worried about."

"No, you should if you want to. It's just this job is so unsettled at the minute, that's why I'm so concerned about our relationship. I saw it all with my dad being away so much, how much my mam missed him and when I think of him carrying on with other women it just hurts me still so much, Cara. Sometimes 'absence makes the heart grow fonder' quickly turns into 'out of sight out of mind'."

She understood. Alex needed full commitment from her and she was ready to give it.

He refilled her glass.

"I love you, Alex." She leaned over now and through the back pain kissed him softly. They had a terrific afternoon. Cara enjoyed his company and the wine just as she had on that very first date. He wooed her all over again. When Alex drained the last of the bottle into her glass he looked at his watch.

"I have an idea! Why don't we order another bottle and book into Fitzpatrick's Castle for the night?"

"No, don't be mad!" Cara looked at him. "Sure I've had enough and to be honest I'd like to drop in on Esther on the way back." She really hoped this didn't bug him. It didn't seem to.

"And don't we have to be back for the guard calling?"

He raised his hand. "I insist. The Guards can wait. We can take Esther for lunch tomorrow to make up for it. Call her when we get to the hotel and have a good ole yap with her." He took her two hands in his now as he looked up and ordered a second bottle from their waitress. "I'm a bit of a force of nature, Cara, I know that only too well. I know I haven't opened up to you about my family but I will. Ask away?"

She sat bolt upright now. This was worth staying for. "Well, okay, I suppose I want to know how many brothers and sister you have for starters."

"One sister."

"Are your parents divorced now?"

"No, not yet, but like I said Mam has decided to divorce him after all these years – it's under way."

"Do you see him?"

"No."

"Where does your mam live?"

"Here in Dalkey."

"Here?" Cara was amused for some reason. "Are we going to see her today?"

"Absolutely not." His blue eyes sparkled with the wine and he was having fun. "Cara, I don't get on with my family – well, okay, I do get on with my mother but she's the only one. I have no time for my sister."

"Name?" she interrupted.

"Beth." He drank some wine before placing it back down carefully.

Beth. Beth. That was the name that woman, Glenda, had used outside the opera at the Gaiety that night.

"Do you still see Beth?"

"I don't. I don't think this makes me a bad person or a weirdo. I just don't get on with her. I want to live my own life and to be happy. Just because we are blood-related doesn't mean we have to like each other. Beth isn't a very nice person, Cara."

She understood. She had never had a sister to give her the right to say that she couldn't imagine not speaking to her.

"Okay, I get it, I won't ask again but I would really like to meet your mam soon."

"Done," he smiled.

"There is one other thing . . ." The wine was obviously going to her head now. "The day in the Sandymount House when you flipped at me, it scared me a little, Alex – in fact, it scared me a lot." There. She had said it and she was pleased with herself. No secrets.

"I know. I scared myself. It was my dad all over again. I was him. I have his temper. Oh Cara, I wish I didn't, I wish I was perfect but I'm not. It's just I have never felt this way about anyone before and I am truly obsessively in love with you and I can't help it. I think about you every second of every minute of every day. These feeling are all new to me. I look at you and I just want you by my side 24/7 and I know that's crazy but I can't change how I feel. If I could I'd lock you up in a box and take you out whenever I wanted to look at you."

She was blown away by his honesty. At last. It was all overly emotional but she really felt she was connecting with him.

"Oh Alex, I feel the same, I really do, and believe me these feeling are new to me too." She leaned over as far as she could without her back aching more and kissed him hard on the mouth.

"Bill!" he only half-pretended to shout.

Cara looked around the bar at happy diners chatting easily and eating great food. Esther would love it here. She would bring her out here tomorrow like Alex suggested. She was over the staying in bed and over the patient stuff – it was time to move on. No doubt the guy who attacked her was one of the Seán Hacketts of the world, dragged up and with no real chance in life. It wasn't personal. It wasn't her. It was drugs, she imagined. Well, she hoped he hated himself for what he had done to her and she hoped more than anything it made him get help. Maybe she had made a difference to his life. She hoped he didn't end up like Seán.

The waitress came with the bill and Alex paid. Then he stood and held her coat out for her. "Shall we?"

He took her by the hand and led her out the door. They strolled in the warm evening breeze up Dalkey Village, stopping to look in an art shop at some incredible prints in the window.

"Oh, I love that!" Cara was admiring a sketch of the front of the Queen's with people shown drinking pints outside in the sunshine.

"Do you?" Alex pulled her toward the door.

"No, Alex, I just mean it's pretty." She tried to dig her heels into the path.

"Can I help you?" the art dealer asked. He was dressed head to toe in black and smelled of wet paint.

"The Bedford print in the window, how much?"

Alex could hold his own here, Cara was sure of that.

"That is two thousand five hundred, sir," the dealer informed him. Not a sales pitch – just a matter of fact.

"We will take it."

"Indeed," came the reply as the dealer headed for the window.

Cara's chin hit the floor. "Are you nuts?" she hissed at him.

"You like it, and it will forever remind us of this wonderful day." As the print was delicately wrapped in brown paper and bubble wrap Alex paid by card and asked if it could be held over until the next day. It was agreed and they left the shop.

They walked and walked and talked and talked.

"Oh look, I like that car!" Cara joked as she stopped beside a Ferrari outside a house on Sorrento Terrace. "Aren't you going to buy it for me?"

She put her hands on her hips and he laughed before wrapping his arms gently around her and kissing her.

They reached Fitzpatrick's as it was starting to get slightly nippy. Cara took in the magnificence of the building while Alex booked dinner for eight o'clock.

"I will need a snooze first," she joked as they got out of the lift on the top floor. "Let me guess – the room's a biggy, isn't it?"

"After you!" Alex opened the door and she entered the room.

She gasped. Then screamed. "What?" she gasped again and spun around.

He was smiling more broadly than she had ever seen before.

"What's this?"

The huge suite was covered in pink rose petals, dozens of tiny lit candles adorned every shelf and available surface and the words **WILL YOU MARRY ME?** were written in red lipstick on the huge window.

She couldn't speak.

She turned to find him but he was already on one knee.

"Cara, will you marry me?" He had an open box and a cluster of diamonds sparkled up at her.

She dropped to her knees now, all back pain forgotten. "Are you sure? I mean it's been so quick?"

His eyes glazed for a split second.

"I mean yes, yes, yes, Alex, I will!"

He removed the ring carefully and it slid perfectly onto her ring finger. She stared at it. It was the most beautiful ring she had ever seen in her whole life.

"I love you so much!" he said.

He kissed her and she kissed him back, completely carried away in the moment.

"Do you like it? Because if you don't I can change it. I got it in Dubai but I can show you the brochure. I honestly won't be offended if you want to change it. I just really wanted to have the ring to propose to you with."

She put her index finger on his mouth. "It's perfect, this is perfect, I adore it – but how did you plan all this?" Tears pricked at her eyes.

"It wasn't easy but my mam helped. In fact she's downstairs. Will I have her come up?"

"What?" Cara was astonished. "Oh yes, yes, please do, and I have to call Esther – she will be thrilled!"

"Of course but not just yet. I have another surprise."

He walked to the minibar and opened it. All the small bottles had been removed and an ice bucket housed a large bottle of Moët which Alex was now popping. He poured two glasses as she took in the romantic sight that was their room.

"Here's to us!" he said. "I want to marry you as soon as I can, not a big long engagement, okay? Let's just do it!"

They clinked glasses and sipped slowly. She looked at the magnificent ring again. She was truly overwhelmed. Her heart was racing madly.

"Oh sit, please," he said. "You have to mind your back."

As she did he pulled off his jacket and tucked his white T-shirt into his jeans. "Let me buzz my mam."

He did and she sipped the champagne, almost bursting at the seams to ring Esther. She didn't want to ask him again. Damn, she missed having her own phone.

A few minutes later there was a knock on the door.

"Come in!" Alex yelled from the bathroom and the door opened.

"Hi, I'm Marie," Alex's mother said, smiling at Cara. "Well, congratulations!"

She embraced Cara who immediately liked her. She was warm yet reserved.

"Are you responsible for all this?" Cara asked, pouring her mother-in-law-to-be a glass of bubbly.

"Well, sort of – I did have lots of help from the wonderful staff – but Alex was very clear about what he wanted. Alex is always very clear about what he wants."

"Oh Marie, it's so beautiful, thank you for all your time and effort."

"May I see?" Marie lifted Cara's hand. "Amazing, may I have twirl?"

Cara took off the ring and handed it to her to twirl around her finger three times towards her heart and make a wish. She wondered what Alex's mother would wish for.

Alex emerged, smiling, from the bathroom.

"Darling!" Marie kissed him.

"Thank you for everything, Mam."

"I'd move the moon for you, you know that," she responded. "Please stay in touch now. I am so happy for you. Mind yourself, dear. Look after yourself." She took his hands in hers and squeezed them tightly, her eyes never leaving his.

The moment seemed to Cara a little intense.

"I am always here if you need me," Marie said, "but I have to go now and leave you to it."

"Okay, Mam, thanks – and sorry – I know it was short notice!"

"Please stay a little longer, Marie," said Cara. "Have a drink with us. It would be nice to talk a while."

"No, no – I won't, dear – it's your time – enjoy – and I look forward to seeing you sometime . . . again soon, Cara." She hugged Cara and left the suite, her son walking her out the door. They had a conversation in hushed tones outside the door before he came back in to Cara.

"Well, well, well, here we are!" He pulled the white T-shirt over his head. "Alone at last."

His eyes were heavy with desire as he stood in front of Cara. She put down her glass and moved to him. She slowly unbuttoned his jeans. Their breathing was heavy in the quiet room. He unbuttoned her shirt slowly while kissing her neck and then he moved faster, almost ripping the shirt off, and carried her to the bed. He stripped her completely and entered her very quickly and she tried to block out the pain in her back. He kissed her hard and repeated her name over and over and over.

When he finished he flopped beside her and smiled. "Got you!" He held up her left hand. "This is the best day of my life."

Chapter 21

Jamie Keenan stood over the reception desk, a twinkle in his eye. Although Sandra knew well she should not be in this frame of mind, she could have gladly stripped off there and then and done him dirty. She almost laughed. Almost.

"Can I help you, sir?" she asked in her poshest voice.

"Well, yeah, I was in earlier. Jamie Keenan is my name. I was wondering if you had a cancellation by any chance."

Sandra pretended to type at the keyboard, knowing full well there were no cancellations. She knew all about Jamie Keenan's career. She loved tennis. Not to play but to watch. She used to try and take the two weeks of Wimbledon off work when she flew and she'd spent the entire time engrossed in the tennis. He was always big news at the event.

He continued to drape himself over her reception desk. He was built like a male supermodel. Over six foot four and so tanned. He had short brown wiry hair and wonderful green eyes. He was a worldwide pin-up, a God to the athletic advertising world not to mention absolutely loaded and single as far as she could remember.

"I'm so sorry, Mr Keenan, but nothing has come up."

He was smiling at her.

"Ah, that's a disappointment . . . Are you married?" he said in his clipped English accent.

He had the cheekiest look she had ever seen.

"What sort of a question is that now?" She had removed her wedding ring that afternoon.

"An honest one." He grinned at her.

"Oh, I'm . . . well, to be honest, I don't know what my status is right now . . . is that information enough for you, Mr Keenan?"

He was still smiling.

"Well, that's not married then, is it?" He moved his head in closer toward her.

"If I told you the facts, Mr Keenan, you would run a mile."

"Try me?"

"Well, thank you, but I'm working." She pushed a few pieces of paper around the desk.

"What time do you finish?"

Was he serious? This was turning into some day.

"I finish late." She willed the phone to ring.

"In that case I'll be back at late." He leaned right in and gently flicked her name badge. "Sandra, my favourite name in the whole world." He laughed loudly as he turned and moved his tall frame back into the wedding reception.

Cara had been watching this little scene from a couch nearby. Sandra hadn't even noticed her so she now coughed loudly. "Eh, hello, what was that all about?" She stood up and walked over to Sandra.

"Holy Mother, Cara, but I'd eat him alive so I would." Sandra made chomping noises.

"And you a happily married woman!" Cara said, deadpan.

"Ah, I wish, Cara, I really do – or do I?"

The two women went into the back office and sat down opposite each other. At the same time both kicked off their shoes. Timing. They both laughed.

"What are we like?" said Cara. "Tell me everything later? I have two bottles of wine in Mike's small back-bar fridge with our names on them." Cara rubbed her feet.

"How's the wedding going?"

"The cutting of the cake is next and then the wedding band is setting up."

"I never had a wedding band," Sandra said quietly and there was a silence.

"No? Neither did I." Cara looked up slowly.

"You're married?" Sandra looked shocked.

"No, I'm divorced," Cara said as Jonathan called out her name. She fished for her shoes and slipped them back on.

* * *

"I cannot wait until we're married!" Alex had enthused as they woke in the hotel the next morning.

"Me neither!" Cara had stretched slowly and arched her stiff back. Alex was actually so excited she began to laugh. He looked so sexy this morning, his black hair ruffled and his shadow of beard growth suiting him. He needed to chill out a bit, Cara realised, not be so immaculate and proper all the time. She would help him.

In fact, there was no rush to the altar, she thought. They would take it nice and slowly.

They should organise a trip away actually. It would be fantastic to spend some relaxed time together.

"What do you say, my darling wife-to-be?" He positioned himself on top of her and she scratched his bare back gently as he leaned on his elbows.

"To what?" she asked as she continued to run her nails down his back.

"To this," he said and kissed her over and over and, as he kissed his way down her body, he said, "Ears, I own you now. Neck, I own you now too, and these hands I nom nom nom . . ."

She tried to laugh but it didn't come out and Alex groaned as she continued to touch him.

He stopped now, his mouth inches from hers. "Actually I have another big surprise planned for you. Will I tell you now or keep it?"

She kissed him. "Seriously, I don't think you can top the last surprise so keep it. I like surprises now." She ran her hands through his hair and he groaned at her touch. She really only had to tip Alex and he was aroused.

"Shall we take this into the shower?" he asked and she said yes even though she didn't want to she was so comfortable and sex in the shower really didn't do it for her. Alex washed her hair, another thing she didn't really like as he never gave it enough welly and she liked to dig into her scalp. One time she rewashed it and he had been really offended.

As they stood under the jets after making love she glanced down at her left hand. The cluster of diamonds was enormous. A little too big, she thought guiltily, but she'd never change it. He had picked it and that was enough for her.

"Okay, let's get packed up and out of here." Alex slid open the shower door and began to dry off.

"Packed up? Sure I only have the clothes I came in!" She slathered the lemon hotel moisturiser all over her legs.

"You know what I mean. Are you bothered having the breakfast – all that fried crap?"

Was she bothered? She'd eat a scabby man's leg right now. "Ah, I'm starving, Alex, aren't you?"

He nodded. "Yeah, but let's go somewhere and get something light instead, if that's okay with you – or do you want that fry?"

That fry. That said it all. How could she stuff a pig into her now with him shaking his head. "Fine," she managed and finished dressing – it was becoming easier so she must be healing.

"Come on, chop chop, let's go!" He bundled her out the door in seconds.

They checked out and left.

By the time they reached the car she was really curious.

"So what's the secret?" she asked as they got in.

"You'll soon see, my dear Cara-Byrne-soon-to-be-Charles, you'll soon see." He checked his rear-view mirror as he always did.

He hit the M50 and Cara's tummy rumbled.

"Can you believe we're engaged?" He was looking straight ahead. "You are all mine now, Cara Byrne."

She shifted her weight. "Well . . . I'm still me, Alex, but yeah I'm totally happy, over the moon." Cara stared at her fiancé. Such a slow careful driver you'd never think he flew Boeings.

Where on earth were they going? She still hadn't called Esther. "Alex, can I borrow your phone and call my mam?"

"Ah, shoot, my battery died and I didn't bring a charger! Sorry, love. We can grab a payphone when we get there." He kept his eyes on the road.

"I have to buy a new phone today, Alex, I can't stand this." She fiddled with the huge engagement ring.

"Seriously, Cara, would you ever just sit back and chill out – it's just weird that you have to call your mammy all the time. I mean, grow up!"

His hands gripped the wheel tightly. She could see his fingers turn white as the blood drained out.

"No, Alex, it's not that at all. I have just got engaged! Of course I want to tell my mother! How is that weird? In fact, I am bursting to tell her!"

"Okay, sorry, it's not so weird when you put it like that." He took a deep breath now and steadied his voice. "I do understand that. It's just we will be married soon and you have a new life – I should be your priority not your mother. All this texting and calling all the time – don't you think it's all a waste of life and of precious time? I mean, I said nothing the night we went to the theatre but after in the bar you sat there texting your mother. It's just bad manners, Cara, well, in fact it's really rude." He had been aching to say that for ages, she knew. She really didn't want to upset him.

"I'm sorry if that was rude, Alex, but she is on her own and she is getting older – she likes to get texts – it's a little novelty for her. I don't see it as that big a deal."

"Another thing, Cara, you really shouldn't put your phone on the table when we go out to dinner – that's also horribly bad-mannered."

"Well, excuse me if I wasn't pulled up in Dalkey but I am working class and my manners come from my parents who were good, hardworking, decent, loving people and I am proud to take after them." She was aghast. He had really insulted her now. She sat back, afraid that he was going to freak at her.

He was very calm. "You are really taking this all too

personally. All I'm trying to say is that it is possible to enjoy the company of your husband-to-be without having to have a phone on every second of the day. Don't you agree?"

She ignored him now, feeling weak with the hunger and from taking tablets on an empty stomach, but also feeling an overwhelming relief that she hadn't put him into a bad mood.

He put his hand on her leg. "Okay – imagine *I* did it. Imagine I was always texting under tables while we are supposed to be watching a movie or listening to some perfect music? What does it say to you? It says that I'm bored, doesn't it?"

"Okay, point taken," she admitted.

"I think we should just not carry mobile phones any more." He laughed now.

She really hoped he wasn't serious.

She had been so engrossed in the conversation that she hadn't been paying any attention to where they were going. So when they pulled up at Dublin Airport her mouth fell open.

"Oh, what? Where are we going? But I've no clothes or passport!"

Alex rolled down the window and collected the ticket for the short-term car park by pressing the small black button. "Don't worry, I have everything sorted."

He parked and then popped the boot and removed two small suitcases.

"How did you get that?" Cara peered at her much-loved M&S red-and-white plastic-covered suitcase.

"Esther! My wonderful mother-in-law-to-be!" He slammed the boot, beeped the alarm and picked up the two cases, grinning wildly. "Come on, we're cutting it fine."

He trotted and she followed.

"But when?" she huffed – she really wasn't that fit yet.

"I'll explain all – just keep up," he said, beginning to jog.

As they checked in she noticed all the flights were to the UK so they weren't going too far.

There was no time to look in Duty Free – straight onto the flight. As the captain greeted them he told them the flight time to Scotland would be one hour. "Scotland?" She was feeling really tired and sleepy now. They had stayed up until all hours last night. She closed her eyes and fastened her seatbelt. Even the hunger had worn off.

She must have nodded off before take-off as they were landing as Alex woke her. His porridge and coffee remains were still on his tray. A car waited to collect them and drove for over an hour with Alex snoring away beside her.

The Scottish scenery was breathtaking, Cara thought, as she watched it fly by.

"Here ye are!" The wonderful lit of the Scottish accent woke them both. She'd fallen asleep again for the last half hour.

"Good luck now, Mr Charles, and thanks for the tip."

They got out and he dropped the cases before he drove away.

"How did you pay him and tip him already?" She was puzzled.

"All done over the internet, my love."

They stood in front of a waterfall and a redbrick building. *The Mill Forge* was written on the building in black slate. It was surrounded by green gardens and beautiful flowers.

"So here we are!" He did a turn to take it all in. "The beautiful and very famous Mill Forge Hotel!" He took her hands. "And this very evening, Cara Byrne, we will become husband and wife here!"

She stared at him and he laughed.

"Welcome to Gretna Green!" He laughed until tears poured down his face. He was sobbing and laughing at the same time. "Come on, darling! The others are inside!"

She was frozen, dizzy from lack of food and shock, and she could not take any of this in. The others were inside? How had Esther got here? She noticed the old timber roof as Alex almost sprinted ahead and headed straight for the bar. There was noise and cheers and she slowly made her way up the three steps behind him.

"Cara, this is Fred and this is Pattie, my best friends." Alex presented them to her.

"Congratulations!" They looked like twins. Both were dressed the same in black polo necks and black jeans. Both extremely tanned and blonde. American accents seemed to shout at her as she looked around frantically for Esther.

"Where's Esther?" she asked and Alex's face clouded over. He literally went grey. "Who's Esther?" Pattie asked, drawing the name out as she reached into the silver bucket for the champagne.

"Are you serious with this 'where is Esther' question?" Alex squeezed her hand too tightly.

"Sorry, Alex, no. I'm just a bit in shock and I haven't eaten since yesterday, I'm taking all these tablets on an empty stomach. I need to lie down." Cara thought she might faint.

"She was attacked recently," he explained to these strangers.

"Oh no, you poor dear, how awful!" said Pattie. "Come and sit here beside me and tell me all. Here's a delicious bar menu. We ate some great hamburgers and some fries. It's all really good." She pulled Cara into the seat.

Alex and Fred hugged like men hug.

"Are you just like so hyped right now?" Pattie couldn't stop talking.

"Yeah, I suppose, but it's a bit of a shock . . . I . . ." Cara tried to gather her thoughts.

"I know, right? Alex told us it was a surprise, you lucky rubber ducky! I wish I had been given this!" She popped the cork and poured champagne into the four champagne flutes. "So you were attacked, right? Where? When was this? What happened? I want to know everything? Shoot!"

She put the glass to her mouth and Cara wanted to ram it down her neck. She knew this wasn't fair and began reliving the night of the attack as she told the story yet again. She was on autopilot.

"You okay now?" Alex leaned in. "Put a smile on your face, please," he whispered and flicked her under her chin as she downed the champagne in one go. "That's my girl!" He punched the air.

Cara wanted to throw up.

"More?" Pattie asked.

Cara held out her glass to Pattie and she poured.

"Awful, just awful!" Pattie shook her head as Cara finished the story. "Really awful for you, kiddo!"

"So how do you all know each other?" Cara said to change the subject.

"Well, long story. Fred met Alex on a flight-training month in New Mexico. I was going out to see Fred for a week and we all just hit it off so well that Alex ended up coming to stay with us in LA for six months. Well, I'm sure you know all about that!" Pattie slid her black-framed Armani glasses onto her blonde hair, using them as a hair band.

Cara didn't know. She never knew Alex had even been to LA, let alone lived there. She flung the champagne down her neck.

"Hey, easy, Tiger, we gotta go get you a dress, am I right?"

"A dress?" Cara looked at the woman's huge voluptuous lips. Were they implants or was she naturally blessed with amazing Angelina Jolie lips?

"Sure." Pattie nodded. "I took the liberty of making an appointment at Tartan Spirit down the road as we don't have much time." Pattie handed the menu to Cara again "Why don't you eat and then we can go? I know Alex has said we need to be in the ceremony room by four forty-five so we will have the dinner around seven, I'd imagine? What about your beautiful red Irish hair? Will you have it done? Up or down?"

"I dunno." Cara ordered the cheese-and-bacon burger and chips but when it came she couldn't get a bite down her. She lashed tomato ketchup all over the chips but the taste was somehow alien.

"Come on now, eat up!" Alex tried to feed her chips by his hand.

She politely laughed. "Alex, could we maybe check into our room so I can freshen up before we go dress-shopping?" She desperately wanted to speak to Esther.

"Good idea." He was so happy. Beaming. "We'll be back down in twenty minutes, guys."

"That all it takes you these days, Charlie-man?" Fred gibed and they laughed.

"Ha, no chance, buddy, I'm still a well-oiled love-machine!"

They passed reception and Alex collected the key cards.

As they entered the lift Cara turned to him. “Alex, seriously, I don’t know what to say here – I mean I don’t think I can do this, I can’t just get married like this . . . I . . .”

He ignored her as the lift doors opened and she trailed off. They found their room. It was really pretty but Cara didn’t notice much as she flopped on the bed. The champagne now giving her a banging headache. There was a phone by the bed and she reached for it.

“Darling,” he took the phone from her hand and replaced the receiver, “listen to me for two minutes. You are tired, I understand that but I have worked tirelessly on organising this wedding for the last month: birth certs, forms, legal issues, passports, accommodation, restaurant bookings, and it’s been a lot of work. I had you sign what you thought was the lease for Sandymount when in fact it was all these forms.” He opened his case and took out a large yellow folder. He got on his knees in front of her now. “This is meant to be. We didn’t want a big old fuss. Your dad isn’t here so I thought this would be what you wanted – a happy day instead of looking at an empty seat. None of my family would come except my mother and it would have been an all-over disaster. Can you see that, my love?” He pushed a loose strand of red hair from her eyes.

“But I don’t even know those people and they will be at my wedding! They will be the only guests at my wedding!”

“We needed witnesses,” he said abruptly now.

She was terrified to ask the next question but she did, her mouth dry as a bone. “What about Esther? She must have known when you asked her for my birth cert and passport?” She licked her lips.

“No. I told her they were for the lease and she dug them out the day I dropped her home from the hospital. Those documents really should have been in the purple box file I gave you at the Sandymount place – I told you to put all your important things there. I asked Esther for her patience over the next few days as we would be away. She didn’t seem in the slightest bit interested.” He ran his hands over his stubble.

"So you didn't tell her we were getting married?"

He stared hard and then his eyes closed slightly. "I told no one except our witnesses. Who the fuck did you want to invite? Steve fucking Brady?"

She was obviously beginning to rile him. "No, of course not, Alex, of course not," she said.

"Well, you don't seem to have any really close female friends that I could have asked, I wasn't dragging an old lady all the way over here, so here we are. Have I done the wrong thing again as usual?" He got off his knees and flung the yellow folder across the room, pages scattering everywhere.

"No, of course not, I'm fine, honestly I am – I suppose I'm just in shock – well, I mean I got a major shock."

She dropped to her knees and slowly began to gather all the documents. "Here!" She held them up to him and he grabbed them sharply from her hand.

"Get dressed! We are going back down right now!" he barked.

Tension hung heavy over the room.

She opened the suitcase and rummaged through the clothes he had packed. It was very little. Her pants rolled up and four white bras. He had packed two pairs of black trousers and two shirts, one cream and one brown. Old clothes. Clothes she never wore. Nothing sexy or pretty. The shoes were runners and her black work pumps. He hadn't packed her make-up bag. No toiletries. Not even her toothbrush. She dressed and felt drab and completely outside her own body.

"You look lovely," he said and pulled her hair down over her shirt collar. "Now here's my card – go and buy yourself an elegant wonderful dress. You must be back in Pattie's room for, say, no later than four o'clock. I will send up champagne and orange juice for you girls as you both get dressed. Then I will see you in the ceremony room at four forty-five, okay? They are very strict on time-keeping. We need to be ready to go on the dot of five."

"Okay," she meekly replied.

"Cara, are you happy? Are you okay with all this?"

She couldn't read his face and she knew there was only one answer. "Yes, Alex, I'm happy." She smiled as brightly as she could and they left the room.

* * *

"This is awesome, honey!" Patty shouted as she held up a tartan satin gown.

Cara shook her head.

"Not really your thing?" the assistant said. "I'm Elaine Kidd, the dress designer – what are you after?"

"Oh, something really plain, simple, and I'm going to need shoes. I'm a size five in shoes and I guess a ten to twelve in the dress." Cara walked along the line of dresses and picked some off the hangers and quickly replaced them. This was never how she had envisioned shopping for her wedding dress.

No Esther. She really couldn't get her head around it. She was marrying Alex today . . . she wanted to marry him, didn't she? Well, yes, but not like this. But what could she do now? She was in too deep and couldn't back out now. What would Esther say? 'Run a mile, love!' she guessed. 'What's the rush?' She agreed with her mother's imaginary words. Too late. She was going to do it.

"How about this?" Elaine held up a knee-length off-white silk dress. It had capped sleeves and a high round neck and was totally plain.

"Yes, I like that. Can I try it on?"

"Well, now, that's just dainty!" Pattie drawled.

Cara pulled the heavy purple velvet drape across and stripped down. She pulled the dress over her head and slipped her feet into the shoes Elaine had pushed under the drape for her. She looked up. She stared long and hard. She no more looked like a bride than the man in the moon.

"It's perfect. I love it!" she called out to the two waiting women in a voice she hardy recognised as her own.

"Well, come on out and let us have a gawp then!" Pattie shouted.

Cara had no intention of coming out. "No, actually, Pattie,

I'd like to keep it as a surprise if you don't mind? Until I put it on in the room . . . later . . ." she trailed off.

"Shall I just take a quick look at the fit on you, lovey?" Elaine asked.

"Okay." Cara opened the curtain a tiny bit and Elaine stepped in.

"Are you okay, lovey?" she whispered into Cara's ear, her scent sweet and her breath warm.

"Yes thanks, Elaine." Cara swallowed hard and smiled at her.

"Okay then," she whispered back.

Elaine never even looked at the dress.

* * *

Back in the hotel room Pattie fussed over Cara. She was in her bridal dress and shoes and Pattie was clipping some wild daisies into her hair.

"I can't believe you didn't want a pro hairdresser! You just need that little something extra and I think these will do it!" Pattie said as she clipped in the dozen long-stemmed daisies she had handpicked on the way back to the hotel.

Cara had borrowed Pattie's make-up bag but the colours were all far too dark for her pale skin. She had washed her hair and let it dry naturally. She had no jewellery apart from her huge glistening engagement ring.

Cara then asked Pattie if she wouldn't mind lending her phone to her?

"I'm afraid I don't carry a cell. I don't agree with 'em. All that radiation going into your brain," Pattie replied, turning Cara's head back towards the mirror.

Cara had seen a phone box across the road but as she had no English money she had no change to use it.

"I can ask Fred for his?" Pattie offered.

Fred was with Alex.

"No! Please! It's fine, really it doesn't matter." She drank more champagne and made small talk with Pattie, her head beginning to pound again.

"Honey, don't you think you should have shaved your legs?" Pattie looked down at Cara's growing stubble.

"No, it's fine," Cara replied and, standing up now, pulled the dress down over her legs.

"Well, then, we are ready I think, and don't you look so pretty! Are you just wildly in love? Is it just all too much right now? Are you just like *woowwwwww*?"

Cara tried to move away. Pattie was nice enough, she supposed, but she was just all too much for Cara right now. She was emotionless.

They made their way down the stairs, with other guests oohing and ahhing at them, and straight into the ceremony room.

The female celebrant stood at the top of the room dressed in a cerise-pink trouser suit. Alex and Fred looked great in their tartan suits and before she knew it Cara was saying her vows. It lasted all of fifteen minutes including the signing of papers before Alex picked her up and twirled her around.

"Hello, Cara Charles!" He kissed her hard as Fred and Pattie threw multi-coloured confetti over them. "Let's celebrate!"

The four of them linked arms and Cara was half dragged to the restaurant.

* * *

"Isn't it such fun!" Pattie clinked her glass against Cara's in Blacksmith's restaurant, overlooking a green wet landscape. The rain had started to fall heavily. "You are a lucky woman, Cara Charles! Alex is besotted with you!"

"I know." Cara had had a smile plastered on her face for the last two hours. While she was drinking just as much as the other three she just wasn't getting as drunk as them. She begged for drunkenness to take over her mind.

Alex and Fred were singing some song by Aerosmith and Pattie was constantly doing her lipstick by holding up the candle holder to see her reflection.

The meal had been tasteless to Cara – she picked at as much

as she could. Alex had ordered for each of them. It was mainly fish and, although she liked a fresh cod from the chipper now and then, she really didn't care for fish. "I'm just too excited," she explained, her full plates going back each time the waiter cleared.

When they were finished and before they took to the residents' bar, Cara excused herself to go to the toilet. She shut the cubicle door and slid down it until her already sore back hit the hard ground and she cried her eyes out.

Chapter 22

"Wasn't it all just a bit too fast, though, Cara?"

Esther had stood gripping onto the back of her chair tightly as Cara told her the whole tale while trying to keep her voice steady. The kitchen table was set for tea and Cara was sitting at it. Alex hadn't come with her.

"I suppose it was, Mam, but I love him and he loves me so why wait? I'm only sorry you weren't there. I'm so sorry you weren't there." Cara was trying to convince herself as well as her mother and well she knew that.

"God, I can't believe it, love. You are married." Esther took an éclair from her apron pocket but put it straight back in again. "I wasn't there to see you get married. It was the one thing I always held out hope for. Lar couldn't be there but I always hoped that I could. And you never even rang me!"

Cara couldn't bear the hurt look on Esther's worn face. "I didn't plan it, Mam – as I told you he surprised me. I still have no phone and it was all so fast. What could I do – say no?"

The two women looked at each other. Esther moved towards Cara now and tried to smile. Her fake smile. "Of course not, love, and I wouldn't expect you to do that for me. I'm just disappointed, that's all. Sure I'll get over it – all that matters is that you are happy." Esther turned back to the cooker and began fussing with the frying of her sausages. "Are you not going to go back to work then? Or what about that idea of college you were so excited about?" She lifted the sizzling sausages onto two plates and scooped on her home-made chips.

"I'm not sure yet, Mam. I'm looking into lots of different options for myself right now." Cara peeled off her fleece.

"Eat up now, love. Jesus, Cara, but in such a short space of time I've seen you fading away before my eyes!" She pulled her apron off and sat down.

Cara was suddenly starving and started to wolf down her mother's home cooking. The chips were burnt and crunchy, just the way Cara loved them. She laced her sausages with vinegar and ketchup and she wrapped them in a slice of thickly cut white bread.

"I'm really sorry, Mam – and I couldn't call or text you as I still have no phone." Cara struggled to swallow.

"Shush now, love, eat your food and let's relax for a while, yes? I'm sure it was a beautiful day and that you looked stunning. That Pattie woman sounds really nice. You have photographs, I presume?"

Cara nodded.

"Sure you can tell me all about it after dinner. I've a lovely flaky pastry rhubarb-and-apple pie we can take into the front room."

Cara glanced at her watch. Alex would be waiting – she didn't have the time. "No, Mam, I don't really have the time for dessert. Alex is waiting for me to get back. But I do want to tell you all now while I'm on my own with you."

Esther clicked her tongue off the roof of her mouth, sausage flying everywhere.

"What, Mam?" Cara asked but really didn't want to hear the answer.

"It seems to me, missy, your wonderful Alex is a tiny bit bossy. I don't mind telling you I think this is a mistake – it's too rushed!" Esther wasn't able to control her tongue a minute longer. She folded her arms, glad she had spoken her feelings at long last, and pushed her plate away.

Cara wasn't upset at her mother's words. In fact she found

them strangely comforting. "He is, Mam, a bit, but he really means well. He is kind and generous and caring but, yes, a bit bossy and possessive." Cara stuffed the food into her now as she was running out of time. She knew Alex was cooking for her at home and she had to be back by six o'clock on the dot. She couldn't tell him she had eaten in Esther's so she'd have to eat two dinners. Alex's idea of a good meal just wasn't hers. He had made a comment that they both needed to lay off the junk as they both had too much junk on their trunks after Scotland. Now Alex was a gym maniac so she knew deep down he was referring to her weight and not his own. He was watching her weight. He was making a Chicken Caesar Salad tonight so she'd manage to eat that too. Cara had never really watched her weight before. This was all new to her and she hated it. It was so bloody boring. Counting the calories on this and the fat content on that. Her usual chocolate after dinner was no more and Alex still didn't "do" bread despite her protests so that was gone from her diet too.

"See, you're starving! Why are you horsing the food into you like that? Relax and eat slowly. Jesus, he has ya like a nutter! Surely he can wait until you've finished your tea?" Esther pulled her plate back in and stabbed four chips with her fork. "I don't want to be the overpowering mother-in-law, Cara, but I need you to be open with me. Please, love, please stop shutting me out. It's just so unlike you that it concerns me greatly. He needs to chill out a little, don't you agree? Whatever you do, start as you mean to go on – don't be running after him like a gobshite. Stand your ground. Do not let him walk all over you because as far as I can see that is exactly what he is trying to do, young lady!"

Cara felt a massive lump rise in her throat. Of course Esther had noticed she wasn't in contact as much as before. "Mam, I love you and I am sorry you weren't at my wedding." Tears fell down her cheeks and now they fell down Esther's too. "It was wrong but I couldn't stop it and . . ." Cara sobbed and sobbed now and Esther pushed back her chair and went to comfort her daughter.

"Now, now, come on, love, it's okay. I'm sure he's going to be a great husband, don't mind me. And don't you have loads of pictures you can show me? And I was talking to Ann who suggested sure maybe we can do a little celebration here? I mean, maybe you could bring the pictures and we could have a few drinks?" Esther handed Cara a paper towel.

Cara nodded and wiped her nose. "Yes, I'd love that, Mam."

Esther hugged her daughter tightly and Cara didn't want to leave.

She ate the pie too afterward and was so sorry she had to rush off.

"Ring me later, won't you? Just borrow his phone!" Esther waved her goodbye at the door with Victoria nestled cosily in her arms.

* * *

As she entered the apartment she felt stuffed. Her stomach must be shrinking.

"In here, Cara Charles!" her husband called out from the kitchen and began whistling.

He was wearing his grey Paul Smith tracksuit. His pilot's uniform hung in the dry-cleaner's bag in the living room. He was set to go to Dubai in the morning and she was slightly relieved she would have the place to herself.

"Where were you?" He turned, licking his home-made Caesar Salad dressing off his fingers. Virtually no calories in it.

"Oh, just looking for – looking for gloves," she stammered. Why was she so afraid to say she'd been to Esther's? It was ridiculous.

"Gloves?" He approached her and made a look of revulsion. "Cara dear, you have cake all over your chin."

She wiped at it frantically and went bright red. She tried to laugh although his expression told her not to.

"You let me cook all this and you have already eaten?" He waved his spoon at her. "So I'll dump all this food then, shall I?" He went over to the cooker, flicked off the gas and pulled the baking skinless chicken out from the oven.

"No, seriously! I dropped into Esther's for five minutes and had a tiny slice of her rhubarb-and-apple pie – I'm still starving." She made smelling actions around the kitchen.

"Why did you lie to me? Why didn't you just say you dropped in on your mother?" He was angry now and she was nervous.

"I don't know, Alex. I suppose because I know you don't like that."

"Why on earth would I not like you dropping in on your mother? What do you think I am?" He wiped his hands slowly with the white tea towel and threw it into the sink. She followed him out into the living room. He stood staring at his uniform for moments before smoothing, the plastic making a crackling sound. Then he turned and went back into the kitchen. Again she followed.

"I'm sorry, look, it's me, I don't know . . ." She couldn't think of what to say next.

The silence was deafening. He was mad but was he mad because she had seen Esther or because she had lied? His hand was around her neck before she had time to ask. He pushed her from the kitchen to the end of the living room. She couldn't breathe.

"What else are you lying about?" His blue eyes were no longer beautiful but menacing and bulging. The veins in his forehead were a dangerous blue too and trying to escape the confines of his skin. She pulled at his hand but he didn't release his grip. "What else? A little affair with Steve perhaps? Is that where you've been? Fucking barman Brady?" He smelt her neck now.

She pulled harder at his hands and he loosened his grip as she wheezed and coughed hard and fell to the ground. "Stop, Alex! Please!" she gasped as he backed away. "What are you doing?" She crawled along the floor. "How dare you!" She burst into huge sobs, gulping to catch her breath.

He stood still over her, looking down at her. "You aren't all that special, Cara, you know that? I don't know the real you. Who are you? Why do you lie? Liar! Filthy liar!" He spat the words at her as she sobbed again and again.

She screamed now as he pulled her up by her hair and dragged her to the bathroom, her feet trailing along the wooden floor. He pushed her face right into the bathroom mirror.

"See? You are no fucking beauty queen, are you? I could have had my pick of women out there but I picked you. Look at yourself, covered in fucking cake and your arse the size of a fucking house. You're not in Harold's Cross now, Cara, you are my wife. Take some pride in yourself for fuck's sake!"

She didn't try to move – his grip on her hair was way too tight.

"Well? Say something? I suppose you think I'm overreacting and I suppose you're going to try and run a mile from me now? Well, don't, because you'll be sorry. I can hurt you in more ways than this. In more ways than you can ever imagine. I can do more than just poison a dog, you know!"

Time stood still.

He eventually loosened his grip and she slumped to the toilet seat. He didn't move. She cried until she could cry no more. Then she looked up at him and pulled herself up slowly and painfully by the cold black tiles. She stood by the bath. This time he wasn't sorry, this time he was still angry.

"Fucking lying whore!" he started again and his face reddened once more and his blue eyes changed colour. He came at her now, his foot high in the air and it caught her straight in her stomach and knocked her flying over into the bath. Her head smashed off the taps and she could see the white of the ceramic turn red from her blood. If she blacked out he could kill her.

"Alex!" She tried to reason with him as she tried to get a breath. "I love you! Come on, stop all this nonsense!"

He towered above her, his breath like a speeding train and white spittle gathering at each side of his mouth. She knew she needed to calm him down. "Please, love?" She held her shaking hand up to him, her engagement ring glittering in the light, and after what felt like a lifetime he took it. She was becoming dizzy and seeing white flashing lights but she had to stay with him. She suddenly thought of her loving father. She hoped Lar wasn't watching this from wherever he was – it would break his heart.

He'd kill Alex stone dead, she knew that for sure.

He pulled her out of the bath now roughly and held her in his arms – if he let her go she would collapse. She tried to breathe slowly.

"You're bleeding." It was as though he suddenly snapped out of some sort of trance and came back to reality with a bang. He held his hand in front of his face and examined the warm blood, turning his hand round and round.

"Yeah, I think I caught my head off the tap. Can you help me?" She smiled at him. "It's okay, Alex, I deserved that. I lied to you, it's not on, you are completely right."

He took a deep breath in through his nose and scratched his head viciously. He picked her up and carried her to the bed and ran for water. He held the cup ever so gently to her face as she sipped. Then he soaked a wet towel and pulled it tightly around her cut head.

"It's not too bad – not as bad as it looks actually – the blood loss, I mean," he said. "It will stop as soon as I apply pressure here."

She nodded.

They sat in silence for a while. Cara could hear children laughing and playing outside the window down on the green. Life was normal out there.

"I need to use the toilet, Alex," she said now and he gently helped her up.

She moved slowly to the bathroom and he closed the door behind her. She stood and ran the cold tap. She washed her face and hands and tried to slow down her breathing. What was she going to do? She had to run. She had to get out of here. Who was this maniac she had married? She stood rooted with fear. He had nearly killed her, she knew that, and he had threatened her mother. Had he really poisoned Victoria? But why? She gathered her thoughts: because he's a fucking psychopath. He knocked on the door now as she cowered. He opened it slowly, tears streaming down his face.

"Go, you should go, leave me, I'm no good!" He fell to his knees now, sobbing. He rocked back and forward on the bathroom floor, hitting his head hard off the wall every time.

She wanted to run but she knew she shouldn't. Not yet – he was too dangerous.

"I can't leave you, Alex, I just can't," she managed as her heart almost leapt from her chest. She hesitated and then asked: "Did you really poison the dog?" For some reason, to her that action was worse, more vicious than the attack he had just carried out on his own wife. She remembered distinctly his words that night: "Wow, what kind of a person would poison a helpless animal?"

"Yeah, well, I couldn't get you on the phone so I thought you must be at Esther's. I crept over there and that stupid dog kept barking when I tried to peer in the windows. I flew down to Tesco and got some rat poison." He said it all so matter of factly.

"But you were the one who suggested we get her in the first place." She smiled at him.

"I know but just to keep the old biddy happy and hopefully keep her away from us."

She nodded, struggling to conceal her feelings.

"I'm cancelling my flight chart, I can't go now!" He jumped up.

"No!" she almost screamed and then tried to cover her panic up. "Don't be a ninny! I'm fine. It's all fine, love. You go – it's your job, love!"

"Are you sure?" He held her face in his hands. "I am so, so sorry, Cara! I want to kill myself for doing this to you. It will never, ever happen again. Is that okay? You believe me, don't you?" He stood up.

Damn right it will never happen again, she repeated over and over in her throbbing head. "I know that and I do believe you, love." She reached up and kissed him on the lips, swallowing the bile that crept into her mouth.

Chapter 23

"Big cake!" Jonathan hid his laugh and Cara giggled as she looked around the crowded room full of smiling faces.

"Yes, well, only the best for our Jenny, and actually, Jonathan, she's a pet."

The wedding cake stood tall and proud on its silver podium.

"If you must know, the tiers are as follows. Bottom tier: carrot cake. Next up: chocolate biscuit cake. Next up: lemon drizzle cake. And the top tier is traditional wedding cake. Louise really is a wonder in that kitchen of hers!"

"Ah yes, the Apple can really cook and put away copious amounts of cider and yet I have never seen her drunk!" he said. "Excellent. Great day, Cara. They are having such a good time. Well done!" Jonathan put his hand on her shoulder and she jumped.

He stood back, bemused.

"Sorry, Jonathan!" she said and then she slowly put her hand on his shoulder with a mischievous grin. He held her eyes for seconds. "Are you dating?" She shocked herself with her question and removed her hand hastily. She felt her colour rise as Jenny and Max cut into their new life and a riotous round of applause exploded. Max's speech had been wonderful, heartfelt, and he was beaming with happiness now.

"No." He clapped with the others and then looked back at

her. "I don't date staff, Cara, I'm afraid . . . it's just . . ."

She burst out laughing. "I wasn't asking you out, Jonathan! I was just wondering, just being nosy."

He laughed now too. He shuffled from one shiny shoe to the other. "You know what, Cara, I've given up, I honestly can't be arsed any more – comes with age, I imagine."

She nodded, staring at his shiny shoes. "I agree. In fact I feel the exact same way. I won't ever . . . well, what I mean is . . . I don't want a relationship with a man ever again." She was starting to blush now – what on earth was she talking to him like this for?

"Oh!" His eyes bulged. "Oh, are you . . . you're a . . . so you like . . ."

She raised her hand and laughed. "No, Jonathan, unfortunately I'm not a lesbian – just happy to be on my own, that's all. Well, not on my own. I'd love to have my mother down here with me. I have asked her time and time again but she doesn't want to impose on me and no matter how many times I tell her I want her, that she would not be imposing, she doesn't believe me. So I'm going to get settled into the job properly and then look around Knocknoly for a place for us to buy – ideally I want to buy Mr Peter's cottage."

"Are you serious? You want to settle here for good?" he said, looking slightly shocked.

"Why do you say it like that?" She looked into his kind eyes.

"It's just that I imagined you putting in a good year here and then hitting the big Dublin hotels with your CV."

"Really?" Cara pushed a strand of hair behind her ear.

"Yeah," he answered.

"So do I have a chance of getting my yearly contract extended then or not?" she asked cheekily, surprising herself that she was enjoying his attention.

"Oh . . . absolutely . . ." But Jonathan looked less than convinced.

"No?" she pushed, disappointed to a level she was shocked by.

"It's not you, Cara, honestly you are brilliant – it's just, well,

I can't really say yet, okay?" He extended his arm and directed his index finger around the room. "Look at this, though – you have created the most incredible wedding for these people, it's beautiful, perfection, you really have the touch. You are fantastic at this." He dug his hands deep into his black suit trousers.

"Okay but do keep me posted, won't you, Jonathan? I have fallen in love with Knocknoly now and can't imagine settling anywhere else." She suddenly realised how true this was.

"I will, don't worry," he said.

They stood, surveying the happy guests.

"Must be wonderful though," he said, gesturing towards the newly married couple.

"What? Marriage?" she said scornfully.

"No, not marriage exactly but to feel so deeply in love. I've never had that."

"No, neither have I," she said and their eyes locked for a brief moment.

He gently took her elbow and led her to the bar where Mike greeted them both. "What would you like to drink?" Jonathan asked. "I think we deserve one?"

"Really? On the job? Okay, you're the boss! White wine, please," she said laughing.

"Two sauvignons, please, Mike – the New Zealand one." He turned back to Cara and said quietly, "What is it you are looking for then, Cara Byrne?"

"Ah, I don't know, Jonathan. I completely lost myself some time ago. I suppose I'm just trying to find me again." She dropped her face into her hands, "Oh man, that sounded so corny! What I mean is I got into something that was so awful I can't even tell you. I actually surprised myself at how stupid I was. I became that woman that I always thought was an idiot, I suppose. I became that what-was-she-thinking-of woman!" She tried to laugh as Jonathan handed her the freezing cold white wine. Thank God he hadn't ordered champagne. Cara never wanted to taste champagne again as long as she lived.

"I understand. I think I did the same myself – well, am still doing it, I suppose. In London I lost myself in the hotel. You see,

I always wanted to own my own hotel and at the Kingston I knew that the owners were in trouble so I worked my ass off and applied for a massive loan. I wanted to buy it off them. However, it didn't work out and I didn't get to buy it, so here I am back with my tail between my legs. Massive loan still promised to me and still sitting in the bank whenever I need it." He sighed and his eyes took in the room.

"Surely there's still an opportunity to do it? Buy somewhere else?" she asked.

"Maybe, Cara, we'll see. We'll see soon enough actually."

She looked up at him and wondered what he was thinking that very second. There was something in his words that was hidden. A hidden message. Was he trying to tell her something? His dark brown eyes were miles away as he watched the wedding progress. Suddenly Cara wanted to know everything about him. He was so calm, she mused as she sipped her wine. So trustworthy. Or was he? Was any man what he seemed to be? She honestly didn't know if she'd ever again be able to trust another man. It was true what she had just said to Jonathan: she didn't want another relationship. Alex had seen to that. She had been perfectly happy and contented before Alex and she was planning on being like that again. She watched as Max tucked into a plate of what she knew was the chocolate-biscuit tier. It had been about the only thing to do with the wedding cake that he was interested in. Max was a good guy. Her dad had been the greatest guy in the world. Maybe she should lighten up. She laughed now at her own thoughts.

"Cara, could you watch the desk for me?"

Sandra's voice dragged her back to the present and she noticed the other woman was slightly shaken-looking.

"Is everything all right?" Cara asked.

"It's Neil, my husband. He's just called to say goodbye – he's at the house, our house – he's packing. I need to see him. I can't just let him go like this and never have said goodbye. We owe each other that much. He must have been discharged after I saw him this afternoon. I just want closure."

Cara didn't have the first clue what Sandra was on about but she just nodded and made soothing sounds.

"Go on," Jonathan said, "I can do it. Cara needs to be in this room for Jenny and Max."

"I'm so sorry, Jonathan," Sandra whispered. "This is the last time I will let you down. I don't know what else to do."

"Go, it's fine – take the time to sort out whatever you need," he said and made his way to reception, leaving his wineglass now empty on the bar.

Cara opened her arms and Sandra stepped into them. Cara hugged her tightly. "Good luck. We will have that chat soon, don't worry. Do what you have to do, hun."

* * *

The porch light was on and the front door wide open. It was being held open by one of the large grey suitcases Neil's granny had given them as a wedding gift.

Sandra stepped over it. "Neil?" she shouted.

"He's upstairs!" came a reply.

She turned to see Tom standing in the doorway to the kitchen, eating a sandwich. "Can't say I like what you've done with the place, Mrs Darragh. All a bit bare, isn't it?"

She just ignored him in his lycra orange jacket and took the stairs two at a time. Neil was in the bedroom folding T-shirts into a small black Samsonite suitcase, the other large one already filled and waiting patiently by the door. She pushed the case back slightly, closed the door behind her and sat on their bed.

"Where are you going to live? Will you stay here in Knocknoly with her?"

"We're going to Dublin. She's from Enniskerry but her dad has flats in Rathmines so we are going to rent one of those." He folded the sleeves inwards and then popped the dark shirt into the case.

She loved that shirt on him. They used to joke about it. "Love that shirty on you!" they would say in unison whenever he put it on, and laugh like school kids.

"Are you in love with her?" she asked the question and didn't really want to know the answer.

"Oh, God knows, Sandra. I don't know. All I do know is she's easygoing and just wants to enjoy life." He looked uncomfortable.

"Just like you, hey?" She paused and then said, "So that's it, Neil, that's it. It's all over. I don't quite know how we got to this place."

"I do. It just all took off way too fast and as far as I'm concerned you just lost yourself in this obsession to have a baby. Do you really honestly even care that it's all over between us, Sandra?" He lifted his head and stared at her.

"No," she answered honestly. "Do you?" She didn't really know why she was here or why she was asking him this. It was what it was. It was completely and utterly over so what was the point?

"A bit." He shrugged his shoulders and whistled a sigh of relief into the air.

"Can I help? I know how much you hate to pack." She tried to laugh and so did he.

"Ah, I'm nearly there now. You know me, Sandra, not much to pack. Never was much of a shopper, was I? I'm just clearing out my clothes, and CDs and a few DVDs . . . em, the other stuff . . . I guess we'll need professionals to get involved at some stage? As far as I'm concerned you can take it all. I want nothing except the armchair from my cottage that was my Granddad Frank's." He reached over and took her hands and her eyes welled up. "Sorry." He rubbed her cheek. "I loved you, Sandra, I really did but we're just not the same people any more."

"You are the same," she managed and he nodded and smiled widely.

"I'm guessing that's not a compliment, now is it?" he laughed.

It was the first time she had seen him laugh freely like that in such a long time.

"What were we at? I realise now we didn't know each other at all."

"I think it was probably an age thing for me. I was in my thirties I had no boyfriend and all I really wanted was a family. Simple as that. I didn't want to be left on the proverbial shelf.

My biological clock wasn't slowing down so I had to do something to keep up with it. I wanted to give myself that chance and you were great, I had so much fun with you . . ."

"But all you ever really wanted me for was babies?" he asked quite calmly, without malice now.

"I didn't think I did. I mean, underneath it all, even on our wedding day, I was thinking babies, christenings, birthday parties, but you were always there. I should never have rushed it. We should never have married so quickly."

"We'd never have married had we waited though, would we?"

"No, probably not," she admitted.

"So what is it you're looking for now then?"

"Nothing, Neil." She stretched her arms high above her head. "I'm not looking or wanting anything any more. I can't, it's too exhausting. I just want to live my life now and whatever happens, happens."

"Pity you didn't think like that a year ago," he said.

Sandra took a breath. "There is one other thing. It might mean absolutely nothing to you but I feel I need to tell you. I *was* pregnant that day. We were blessed with a very brief fleeting visit by our baby."

His eyes stared at the floor. "Shit," he managed and stood up.

"Take care of yourself – I am always here for you if you ever need a friend," she said and she meant it. She was no longer in love with him but she did love him. When she had fallen out of love with him she would never really know. She couldn't answer that question herself. "You were a great husband to me, Neil, and you were a great friend. I put you through so much with the IVF and I am sorry."

"Come on, Neil! Are you roight? I need to hit the frog and toad fast loike!" Tom yelled up the stairs in his pretend Dublin 4 accent.

Neil let go of her hand. "Sorry about Tom. I know you hate him but I need him right now. So, is John Wayne chasing you already with his lasso?"

"*Now*, Neil! Move it! The M50 will be getting crazy if we

don't leg it now!" Tom's annoying voice pierced her ears yet again.

She didn't understand the John Wayne reference but just waved him aside to go.

"I guess that's that then." He clicked the silver locks down at the same time. The noise was somehow very final and as he picked up the case their marriage dissolved. He lifted the case to the door. "Has the bank been in touch?"

"I'm in with them in the morning – what am I to expect?"

"It's pretty straightforward. Tom had his solicitors meet with Mr Kilroy and all you need to do is sign all the papers and the money will be deposited into your account." He paused now. "Will you want to claim maintenance from me and all that?"

"No. No, Neil, I don't want anything. Half the house will be perfect. Half the house will be really great, thank you. I don't want anything in it either, but yes I guess we will have our solicitors sort that one. I will go in and sign what needs to be signed in the morning. Maybe put everything in storage for a while." She let out a long slow breath.

"You can live here until you find a place of course," he said as he stood at the door.

She stood up. "Can I ask you one final favour? The extra cases we had, are they still in the attic?"

He nodded.

"Can you get them down for me before you go? And my red rucksack too? I am going to pack now too. I never want to set foot in this house again."

She stood and watched as her soon-to-be-ex-husband pulled the attic stairs down and got the cases and her bag out. He folded the stairs away again and shut the trapdoor. Then he took the two cases down the stairs into the hall and left them at the front door. He pulled on his jacket and put the two large cases in Tom's car and came back into the hallway. The breeze blew the junk mail and flyers from the floor down the hallway. They locked eyes and he gave a half smile as he took a look around the house and with a snap of his wrist picked up the small case and put his foot on the doorstep.

"Take care of yourself, Neil," she said from the landing.

"I will," he replied. "Be happy, Sandra, you're a great girl altogether." Then he blew her a kiss before turning and slamming the front door behind him.

"See ya, wouldn't wanna be ya!" she said and the tears began to stream down her face. She went downstairs into the cold kitchen and poured herself a pint glass of wine. She took it back upstairs and opened her wardrobe. She began to fold her clothes into the case. She knew she should go back to work but it was almost clocking-off time and she didn't see the point. Honestly, she didn't care about work right now. She didn't really care about anything at this very moment. She cared about getting drunk and getting out of this shithole of a house. She couldn't put into words how she was feeling. How had this all happened? She knew her next visit had to be to her parents before all this news spread around the village.

She clipped her fringe back off her face and pulled her phone out and called the hotel.

"Good evening. The Moritz Hotel. Jonathan Redmond speaking."

Sandra looked out the window. She knew fifty per cent of the responsibility lay at her door, isn't that what they always said? It takes two.

She heard Jonathan say again, "Hello? The Moritz Hotel. Can I help you?"

"I'm not coming back, Jonathan."

"Sandra, is that you? Are you okay?" His voice was concerned.

"Yeah, I suppose I am, thanks." She gulped the cold wine and it stung the back of her throat.

"I can't hear you very well," Jonathan went on. "Do you want to talk to Dermot?"

"No," she replied.

"Are you handing me your notice over the phone?" He sounded incredulous.

"Oh God, no, Jonathan! I just mean I'm not coming back this *evening*! I'm due to clock off in twenty minutes so I don't see the point."

"No, fine, we weren't expecting you back."

She could hear the relief in his voice.

"Listen, Sandra, you just mind yourself. In fact, I was chatting to Dermot earlier – I hope you don't mind but he filled me in a bit. I think you need to take some time off for yourself. Take a nice long week – it's fine, we are fine here. Is that okay?"

She could hear the noise and hustle of the hotel and she felt so alone. "Okay. I will take you up on that offer, thanks," she managed. She heard him move away from the mouthpiece for a moment, then he spoke again. "Sandra, a Mr Jamie Keenan is at reception now. He has no room here but said you were looking after him? What were you planning on doing with him? Did you check if Louise has her spare room free?" Jonathan sounded a bit frazzled.

"No, she's full unfortunately – I rang her earlier." She drank the end of the pint glass. She needed this like a hole in the head.

"Hmmm . . . this isn't great . . ."

"Oh, here, tell him he can stay here in this house – sure there's lots of room – well, I . . ."

She heard Jonathan talking to someone before he said, "Hang on, Sandra, I'll put him on to you."

She heard Jonathan speak and then she heard Jamie's voice. "Hey, Sandra, it's Jamie Keenan. Jonathan mentioned you may have a spare room I can crash down in at your place, is that right?"

"Yeah, sure, no problem. I'll leave the key under the front-door mat for you. I have some personal issues so I won't be back to work. Tell Jonathan to call you a cab later tonight and he can give the address to the driver. I'm literally five minutes away. Please help yourself to anything in the fridge but be warned there isn't very much. And I can call you a cab in the morning."

"Wow, that's so nice of you! Great, thanks so much. I promise I won't be any trouble."

She looked around the empty house. "Anytime," she said and hung up.

She went back down into the kitchen and fished for the spare key in the knife drawer, found it and put it under the mat. She padded back into the freezing kitchen to search for any more alcohol she could get her hands on.

She flicked on the heating but, no matter how long the heating went on sucking up money, the house was impossible to heat. There were so many drafts on the snag list that no one had ever come back to fix. Vent holes that had never been filled. Doors that didn't fit properly. She found half a bottle of vodka left over from their moving-in party but no mixer so she added some tap water to it. She drank a gulp and nearly threw up. It was vile. She drank some more. She trudged back upstairs and started her packing. She would have to take Dermot up on his kind offer tomorrow and stay with him for a few weeks. This would be her last night in this house and the very thought cheered her up somewhat. She thought about Dermot as she lay back on the bed now. He was so good to her – now that she thought back he always had been. He had always been around her.

She sat upright. She wondered. Just as she reached for her phone to call him she heard a knock at the door. Shit! It couldn't be Neil back and it couldn't be Jamie Keenan yet as she'd only got off the phone minutes ago.

"Coming!"

She suddenly knew it was Dermot. Of course it was Dermot. Jonathan must have told him and he came straight over.

She ran down the stairs and flung open the door and there with a bottle of wine in each hand stood Jamie Keenan.

"Need some company?" He walked right in, put the bottles down and threw his black suit jacket over the banisters.

"Did you run?" she asked.

"Not really," he drawled.

"Well, em, I wasn't expecting you until the early hours of the morning, Jamie. I presumed I'd be in bed."

"Why would I want to stay there when you are here? I asked the manager to call me a cab as soon as you hung up the phone but then I got lucky – a cab pulled up dropping off some guests so I just hopped right in."

He stood tall, a power horse in front of her, arms bulging

from his tight white dress shirt. The new physique of today's tennis player. Gone were the wiry bodies of McEnroe and Bjorg and in were the muscles of endless training sessions. He pulled off the navy dickey bow and stuffed it carelessly into his pocket. Then he undid some buttons on his shirt.

"Glasses?" he asked.

Sandra was rooted to the spot. She had watched this man so many times on TV. His temper on court was legendry. He hated to lose. His energy was electric.

"This way," she managed as she tugged the clips from her fringe and, licking her fingers discreetly, patted it down.

"Shit, it's cold in here, isn't it?" He shivered.

"I've only just put the heating on and it's very inefficient anyway." She'd leave it on now all night and let Tom foot that bill.

"Sorry, I'm in the middle of moving out so excuse the mess." She reached into the press and took two wineglasses down.

He unscrewed the cap and poured. "Red okay, I hope? It was all I could manage to steal off the tables."

"What are you like?" she laughed.

"Ah, Max won't mind – he's a very close old friend. It was touch and go whether I could make it to his wedding. I really didn't want to let him down but I'm playing a tournament in London all next week, I leave first thing in the morning so I didn't fancy too late a night."

His eyes never left hers and she knew he fancied her. A lot. There were plenty single girls at the Brophy-Burrows wedding, sure she knew half of them, so why on earth did he want her? And want her he did, she knew that. She was more nervous than flattered for whatever reason.

"Jamie, before you waste your time here, let me get something perfectly clear. I just literally came out of my marriage a few hours ago."

He sat up at the kitchen island and she did the same, her legs dangling like a child's and his flat on the floor.

"What happened?"

"You know, I haven't a clue. I married too quickly, I married someone I didn't really know, so it's over just like that." She laughed now even though she didn't feel like laughing.

"Are you still in love with him?"

She shook her head.

"Don't worry, I'm not going to propose to you!" he laughed. "But, listen, I'm sorry it fell apart for you. Though I can't say I understand because I've never been married." He gave an unconscious shiver.

"No shortage of offers though, hey?" she said, stating the obvious.

The radiators were warming up the house and the alcohol was warming her up. He was unbelievably sexy and he wanted to be with her.

"Yeah. I have had a serious girlfriend on and off for the last few years but never actually proposed to anyone and, like I said, you won't be the first."

"Piss off!" She tilted her head and stuck out her tongue at him. "So is it on or off right now?"

"Oh, it's off. Do you think you will marry again?"

"I hope so, I really do."

"You are stunning," he said and filled up their glasses.

"Stop it, will you, it's wasted on me."

He stood now and circled the kitchen. "You like tennis?"

She wasn't going to lie. She wasn't going to be one of those girls who stood in front of Brad Pitt and said, "So what do you do for a living?"

"I do, Jamie, I love it. I love watching you play," she admitted.

"Really?" he smirked. "Why, thank you!"

"Must be a fantastic lifestyle – all that travelling, the glorious weather, not to mention the outrageous prize money." She tipped her glass to him.

"Well, I'd beg to differ. Here's how it really is. Training. Really, I train all the time and it's mind numbingly boring. My father coached me from the time I was five. I have never had a life. He never let me just be a normal kid. That's why my temper gets the better of me on court sometimes. I'm angry with tennis. Actually, Sandra, I hate tennis!"

"No, you don't!" She banged her glass down. "Do you?"

"Hate, hate, hate it. Hate it with a passion. I can't wait to get to thirty-five so I can get the hell out of it. It was never my choice, you see – it was always my dad's dream." Sandra had read all about Albert Keenan, a force to be reckoned with. The Guru, they called him.

"The Guru," she said now.

"The Grinch," he answered.

"So what is it you really want to do then?"

"Well, mainly get out of the constant pain I am in. My knees ache every second, my back aches every second – it's all too much for me sometimes. The pressure to win. I do have a plan though. I'd love to get into the restaurant industry. Well, something like that. I'm a mean cook. I'd love to run my own kitchen after I'm done with all this.

"Wow, that's nuts!" She sipped more wine and knew she was drunk.

"Why?" He came closer to her. "Gordon Ramsay did it – he was a footballer – it can be done."

"I don't know – I suppose I feel you have this god-given talent but yet you don't appreciate it," she answered truthfully.

"I do appreciate it but it's far from god-given, Sandra, it's bloody hard earned."

She stared into his brown eyes and realised that for one night she wanted to forget her life. She wanted to be free. No worries, no hassles, no desperately wanting what she couldn't have. As she once was. Sandra Loughnane.

"Go for it, Jamie Keenan," she said. "I know you can be whatever you want."

He stood in front of her now and she knew it was wrong but she reached over and took his hand in hers.

"Really?" His innocence appeared in his eyes.

"Yes, totally, you are special."

"So are you . . ." he took the come-on line and ran with it. "I think you are so beautiful, I really do."

He kissed her then. Softly. It felt so strange. Like trousers that didn't fit but you really wanted them to. His tongue felt too long for her mouth and she couldn't get her arms around his back. He was not Neil. But she would never do this with Neil again. It was time to break the mould.

"I really shouldn't do this . . ." She pulled away.

His eyes were heavy with desire. "Why not?" he breathed heavily at her.

She couldn't answer that. She stood now and he stood close. She could do whatever she wanted, she was a free woman. He smelled of mild aftershave mixed with wine. "Come," she said and turned and headed for the spare room.

She took each stair slowly and he followed. In the bedroom she stood in front of him and peeled off her uniform before his eyes. He stood illuminated by the moonlight through the bare window. She was horny as hell for him – as wrong as that was, it was the truth. She stood in her black bra and pants.

He took her all in. "Holy shit, you have a body to die for!" He kicked off his shoes and removed the belt from his suit trousers.

She unbuttoned his shirt very slowly, remembering in vivid details Jamie Keenan's body at the side of the court every time he changed his shirt, the girls whistling in the stands going wild. She removed it slowly. The body of a professional athlete. Torso to die for. Somewhere deep inside she felt like giggling. It was like a teenage fantasy. He kissed her hard and she kissed him back harder. He no longer felt so strange. She squeezed those ace-serving arms with all her might and he unclipped her bra. The passion was exceptional, those first touches that can never be recaptured. It lasted forever and she was not unsatisfied when he flopped beside her, sweat on his forehead and upper body.

"My but you are fabulous altogether, Jamie Keenan!" She rubbed at his face with her hand as he pulled her in close. It was fantastic raw unabashed sex and she had loved it. She felt free and sexy and wanted and she wanted him just as much.

"Sandra!" he whispered.

She should have videoed it, got a fortune for this sex tape. She laughed out loud now and he mistook it for a reaction to her previous pleasure.

"Oh I know!" he agreed. "Come with me to London tomorrow morning, you can watch me play from my player's box and I can take you to dinner and treat you like a princess."

"Oh, I'd love that, believe me, but let's be realistic here." She counted each point out on her red-painted fingernails. "One: I live in Knocknoly. Two: I'm about to go through a divorce. Three: I have no home to live in –" She suddenly stopped, hand in mid-air and folded down each finger, one at a time. She thought about every word she had just said. "Actually, Jamie, I have the week off work. I'd love that – let's do it!"

"Really?" He leaned up on one elbow and smiled widely at her. "You'll come with me?"

"I will and here is the deal. I don't want anything from you except some fun for a week. I need a week off, a week off my life and a week to just have fun before I have to join all the dots back up again."

"You're a wonder." He kissed her again "To be honest that's all I am capable of. That's what happened with Carolina Valenticka, you see – she wanted more, I was happy the way we were. She wanted both of us to retire and for us to start a family. Marriage isn't for me, Sandra."

Sandra understood Carolina only too well. Funny that deep down, no matter how famous or how rich you are, deep down most women just want the same things from life. Must Have Husband, Must Make Baby, she chanted in her head. It's embedded in some type of computer program in women's brains. She pictured the fantastically stunning Russian blonde pro-tennis player and thought again: I hear you, Carolina!

"Do you miss her?" She rubbed at his chest – she just couldn't help it.

"I do sometimes but not enough to beg her back. She's very, very stubborn. She hates the game too. She won't come back to me until I agree to what she wants." Sandra couldn't believe it: these athletes put their total lives into this game and they hated it.

"I'm starving." He sat up.

She couldn't believe this but she wanted to have sex with him again. Right now.

He got up and she got up after him and both stood naked in the room.

"Hang on there, Mr Tennis Pro, I'm feeling a little –"

"Sandra!"

She jumped out of her skin and turned to see Dermot standing in the doorway, his face ashen.

"Dermot!" She grabbed for the duvet and pulled it off the bed, wrapping it around her naked body.

"What the –?" Jamie grabbed for his trousers.

"Jesus! I'm so sorry!" Dermot turned on his heel.

"Dermot, wait!" she called, her face burning red with embarrassment.

He turned back but didn't look her in the eye. "No, sorry – it's just that Jonathan said you sounded really upset so I was worried – I knocked but you didn't hear me and I didn't want to keep knocking or ring and wake you if you were asleep . . . but I didn't want to leave without making sure you were okay . . . and then I found the key under the mat . . . I'm sorry . . . I shouldn't have come in . . ."

He ran down the stairs and slammed the hall door shut.

"I'm confused," Jamie said. "I thought you said your marriage was over?"

Sandra dropped her head into her hands. "That wasn't my husband – he's just my friend." She was horrified. What was she doing? So what? a voice in her head cried out. What's it got to do with Dermot?

"Oh? So you are okay – like we haven't just been caught doing something really dreadful?"

"Dermot saw my boobs," she answered him.

"And that is lucky for Dermot, is it not?" He was pulling his trousers off now and climbing back into bed.

She couldn't think about Dermot now, she couldn't add him to her guilt list. Her head would explode. Sandra wanted a week off guilty and that was exactly what she was going to get.

Chapter 24

The Four Seasons in London at Canary Wharf was out of this world. The magnificent ten-storey hotel was located in this vibrant section of London and it had views of the River Thames that Sandra couldn't take her eyes off. It was a superb hotel, she thought, all the staff attentive and smiling, all the guests happy and the hotel shining. Jonathan would love the atmosphere here. It almost smiled at you, it was so happy. She was sitting in reception, her small suitcase by her feet, sipping a white wine spritzer as Jamie waited on his entourage to check them in.

"This way, please." Jamie's exceptionally tall and pretty PA Nicola Pawley politely directed her boss and his flame of the month towards the glistening lifts. Nicola was all business, in a deep purple suit, blinding white shirt, flesh-coloured tights and black patent flats.

The doors opened and Sandra placed her small case on the brown carpeted floor. She fixed her pale-pink silk blouse and tugged up her black Karen Millen trousers. She knew she looked good. She couldn't remember the last time she had worn killer heels.

The lift stopped on the tenth floor and Jamie stood back to let her out first. The Executive Suite. Sandra actually said the word "Wowser!" and then bit her lip hard as she entered the suite. It was incredible. The huge window framed London like a painting. A soft grey couch ran the whole length of the window. The king-size bed was scattered with fresh rose petals and the chaise longue was of the deepest, softest reddest velvet she had ever seen. She sat deep into it and it embraced her tired bones as she kicked off the heels.

"So I'll be back in half an hour," said Nicola. "Jamie, you have an interview with Sky News at three o'clock and then an interview for *The Daily Mail* at four o'clock and then . . ."

He lifted his hand and her voice trailed off. "Please don't depress me, Nicola – just come and get me and tell me on a need-to-know basis." He gave her a weak smile as he flopped his huge frame onto the bed and Nicola left the room.

He patted the bed for Sandra to join him.

Reluctantly she peeled herself off the chaise longue. She should have felt a little dirty in front of Nicola but she didn't. She was starting to feel happy. She was past caring about other people's opinion of her right now.

She was hungry, she realised, as her tummy rumbled. Jamie had made the most amazing fluffy cheese omelettes with onion and tomatoes in her kitchen this morning.

"Damn, you are good, Keenan," she had muttered through a full mouth, savouring the tastes. "If you could make anything with the ingredients in my kitchen, what a man you are! In fact, I am completely gobsmacked that there are ingredients in my kitchen!"

"Well, I did have to use tinned tomatoes but needs must." He'd blushed with pride. "I'd spend all day in that kitchen. I love it." He'd cut into his omelette and folded it into his mouth.

She had made a mad dash to her parents on their way to the airport and dropped her big suitcases off. Her mother looked aghast as the words spilled from her mouth, unable to absorb the situation with Neil, and now Sandra running off to London with a professional tennis player. That was until her father pitched in. "Does he play golf? Usually these tennis players are fantastic – will you ask him what he plays off?"

Her dad had craned his neck to get a look at Jamie who was playing a video game on his iPad in the waiting taxi. She knew her dad would have loved to meet him but she wasn't getting into all that. It was still hard to accept that her parents loved a stick and a little white ball more than her these days. Piss off, she thought in her head. Golf off! I hate golf. Suddenly she realised how much she did hate golf. Golf had stolen her loving parents. She knew it was immature and that she shouldn't think like this now she was a grown woman but she did. She found it difficult to understand their obsession and that was why she had married Neil.

It hit her like a bolt of lightning.

She had been spending all her time at home alone. He wanted to spend time with her. She had sat in her parents' home on her days off and nights off alone as they played golf. The home she once loved was now cold and lonely and she hated it. The clubhouse was their new home. She wasn't of interest to them any more. They had a new life, their job as parents pretty much completed as far as they were concerned.

She got it now. Neil had just appeared at the right time in her life and she had wanted to be wanted. She wasn't blaming her parents by any means but at least it had clicked in her head now exactly why she had rushed into a marriage so fast. Her parents had changed their lives so she guessed it was time she changed her life too. Well, she was over it now. Other people did want to spend time with her and they should be the people she focused on. Good luck to her parents and their life with golf – they deserved to be happy, they had done enough for her. It was time to let go.

Jamie dragged her back to the moment by kissing her face with soft butterfly kisses that made her want to grab him and kiss him so hard. She didn't. She let him take over and they made love again slowly and tenderly.

"Jamie?" Nicola's Jersey lilt came eventually through the door.

Jamie looked tired. He was hitting thirty and he'd had enough. The wear and tear on his body and mind was now visible on his handsome tanned face.

"Why don't you go and explore, Sandra?" he said. "I don't know if you had time to get cash and all that but here's my credit card – and don't look at me like that – it's not *Pretty Woman.* Like you said, prize money is tops and I am a millionaire – so go out and buy yourself some things if you want? If not, just chill and order room service and drink some wine. I can't drink as I'm on court at ten in the morning but I can have a nice relaxing bath with you later."

"What time do you think you might be back?" Already she knew she couldn't be married to an athlete.

"Impossible to say." He painted a half smile on his face, grabbed his leather jacket and left.

She would never in a million years take his credit card and buy herself stuff. She stared hard at the gold winking at her in the glare of the bright winter sun. Then she did take it. She slid the shiny plastic off the table and into her purse.

She skipped down the corridor and took the red carpeted stairs and went out onto the streets of London's East End. Canary Wharf was buzzing and Sandra took in the lively Arts scene, hip boutiques and the treasure-filled markets. She browsed happily and stepped into a café to buy a hot chocolate. She walked the streets as she sipped her drink. She was taken aback by how busy London was – it was a lifetime away from the sleepy village she loved so much. She would avoid the Tube as distant memories of standing on the wrong side of the escalator on her first ever Gatwick overnight still haunted her.

She started to shop but she bought only for Jamie. She got him new aftershave, vintage sweets and various cookery books.

There was an old Aer Lingus haunt that the staff used regularly in London very near the Four Seasons, called The Gloucester – she would go down and see who was there. Would any of the old girls still be working?

She pushed open the heavy glass bar door and poked her head in. The smell of bleach and coffee burned her nose.

"Jimmy!"

The Scottish barman was still there.

"Sandra Loughnane! A miss't ya! Whit's new?"

She hugged Jimmy tightly and then escaped his always-too-close hugs for a seat at the bar.

"Whit d'ye dae for a livin' now?" He wiped down the bar with his grey dishcloth.

She looked around. A few stewardesses stood in a circle gossiping about the pilots at the other end of the bar. Nothing changes, does it, Sandra thought.

"I'm in the hotel industry now, Jimmy," she replied as she ordered a black coffee and pushed her bags in towards the bar.

"Och! That's guid!" He turned and lifted the coffee pot and poured Sandra a large black coffee.

If her memory served her correctly it was not going to be hot.

"Here ye gae," Jimmy added some sachets of sugar to the side of the saucer.

"Sandra Loughnane?" a voice came from the other side of her. "It *is* you! How are you?" The man stood up and approached her seat. She'd know those piercing blue eyes anywhere.

"Alex Charles! Jeekers, it's been years!"

They hugged.

"I thought you rerouted to Dubai?" she asked as the other man took the free seat beside her.

"I did. I had a few personal issues. I actually have a meeting scheduled in London this week for a desk job, believe it or not. I'm hoping to transfer to the US as soon as possible."

Sandra nodded – she didn't want to pry.

"I came back though and based myself in Dublin again for a year or so. What about you?"

Sandra filled her old work colleague in on what he needed to know and he ordered a coffee too.

"It's still awful coffee," she whispered and he smiled. God, those piercing blue eyes were intense.

"Always was. So, the Moritz sounds like a nice little job then?"

"It's grand and by no means little. I mean, it's not the closeness like I had with the AL girls but it's good – it's a good job, Alex." She added some more sugar to try and mask the taste.

"Yeah, we used to have great *craic*, didn't we? I think it's important to have friends in a job so you can have a laugh." He looked around him. "Do you remember you girls used to fight about who had to work the section of the aircraft with babies – I always thought that was hilarious. Not a maternal bone between you all!"

Sandra laughed despite herself. "Yeah, we did have a lot of banter all right. I do miss that. Well, actually, there is one girl at the Moritz now I have just started to get close to, and Alex," she sipped her overly sweet yet still bitter coffee, "you'd love her! I remember how you always had a thing for the redheads!" She winked at him and he laughed.

"Ah, how well you know me, Sandra, I still do!"

Sandra's face was suddenly serious. "Poor Cara, though – that's the redhead – I think she's been through a very hard time lately so I won't introduce her to you any time soon."

He stared at her. "Cara. Lovely name. Like the matchsticks."

"Yeah, I forgot about that. She is like a matchstick too. Well, the old ones with the red tops, remember them? Non-safety, I think they were called?"

"That's right – they were removed from the market for being too dangerous. So is Cara from Knocknoly dangerous too?" He winked at her now.

"Well, as far as I know she's from Dublin. To be honest we are only getting to know one another even though she's there a good few months. She's rented Mr Peter's cottage, a dainty little place, my dream home when I was growing up. To be honest I'd still love it."

"And that's in Knocknoly too?" Alex chewed on his fingernail.

"Yes, it's just over the bridge and into the large fields – so pretty."

"Here, how rude am I? Can I buy you a drink? For old time's sake?" He dug his wallet out of his back pocket.

"No, I really shouldn't. I have to get back. It's been wonderful to see you though." She drained her cup, not wanting to offend Jimmy, and called her goodbye out to him. He waved back.

"You take care." Alex stood and they hugged before she headed back to the Four Seasons to run a bath for Jamie Keenan.

* * *

It was midnight before Jamie returned and he looked shattered.

"Get undressed," she ordered him as she poured him a cold glass of sparkling water and added ice from the machine right outside the suite door. He did what was asked and padded naked into the bathroom. She added hot to the bath and he folded himself in. There was very little room for her.

She sat on the edge in her fluffy luxurious hotel robe. "So how was it?"

"Ah, the usual, same old questions and same old answers . . . could you get that muscle rub for my neck – it's on the top of the toilet?"

She did and rubbed it in hard. The vapour making her eyes water.

"Ah, thanks, it's so stiff this evening. I can't sit in those interview chairs any more – it's too painful."

Sandra watched as he tried to turn his neck from side to side and he winced. "Quit then," she told him.

"Easier said than done. I want to go out on a winning streak. I want to win all I can, and then I go."

"For the money?" she asked as he filled his hands with water and splashed his face.

"Sandra, I have more money than I could ever spend. It's hard to explain, I suppose. My dad beat it into me literally that winning is everything. I think that's why I like cooking so much – because I can make it perfect. I can cook a winning meal every time. No one can stand in my way. I am in control in a kitchen."

"Oh, I got you some books!" She pulled her dressing gown belt tight around her and stepped barefoot out to the suite where she grabbed the bags from the chaise longue. She held the books up and he oohed and ahhed and genuinely loved them.

They ordered salads and tea and watched *The Talented Mr Ripley* in bed. It was so nice to relax. She was herself again. She felt ten years younger. She didn't want to leave her life in Knocknoly so much as change it. Sandra Loughnane Darragh was of Knocknoly and it was a part of her.

She snuggled down to sleep in Jamie's massive arms and realised she had never really done this with Neil. Yes, they had slept together but she now realised that he usually passed out the second his head hit that pillow. He liked his few pints after work and she understood that. She was the same. He was a decent man.

* * *

Sandra spent a glorious week in the company of Jamie Keenan. True to his word he treated her like a princess. She loved watching him play every day on the tour and on the Sunday she was leaving he won the tournament. He held the trophy high above his head as the crowd cheered and he winked right up at her. Funny, she thought as she made her way through the bustling stands and out to the waiting Limo that was taking her back to Heathrow airport. That win had made Jamie truly happy. For like an hour. It was all about the build-up to that win. All the hard work and misery wiped away for those few short hours post-victory.

They had laughed in bed last night for hours. Like two school kids. She had told him that she was going home. He had told her he was going on to the tour in Oslo. She had told him he was amazing. He had told her she was beautiful and clever and incredible company. It was easy and adult and they had both had a great time. They promised to keep in touch. Jamie Keenan had injected Sandra with life again.

Chapter 25

The hotel was busy as it was Christmas week and it was fully booked. The Christmas programme started today. Sandra smiled at Alice on reception and headed for Jonathan's office. He was on the phone as she went in.

He covered the mouthpiece. "Take a seat."

She sat and looked around his office. It was as tidy and shiny as a new pin.

He hung up and grinned at her. "Welcome back."

She noticed he was pale with big black circles under his eyes.

"I'm so sorry I've been so scatty lately. It's all over now. I am back."

He nodded. "It's okay."

"You look really tired. I feel awful. I can work around the clock now – just pencil me in."

He stood. "There's an urgent meeting now, Sandra. I called it late last night. I'm afraid there is a big problem." He grabbed his keys off his tidy desk and stood up.

She got up slowly from her chair. "What is it?" she asked as she hauled her bag over her shoulder.

"I will tell you all at the same time if that's okay?"

They walked in silence down the corridor.

Inside the conference room old Mrs Reilly was sitting beside

Big Bob, and Tiff and Mike were standing close together, laughing. Cara and Dermot were pouring the coffee.

Dermot gave Sandra a big smile and a wink. "Welcome back," he mouthed at her.

She made a face at him. He waved her away and grinned.

Then Jonathan arrived.

"Okay, thanks, everyone." He sat as the noise level in the room suddenly dropped to an eerie silence. "Can you all please take a seat?"

They all did and the room was completely silent as they waited.

"It isn't good news. I'm so sorry to have to say that the Moritz is going up for auction. There is no guarantee that it will remain a hotel so therefore no guarantee that anyone will keep their jobs. I'm very sorry to have to tell you all this."

A collective gasp filled the room.

Jonathan nodded slowly. "As I said there is no guarantee that, if sold, it will be kept as a hotel. There is talk of interest in turning it into a stud farm, in which case it will be knocked down completely."

"*No!*" Big Bob slammed his hand on the table and old Mrs Reilly put her blue-veined one on top of his and held it there. Coffee had spilled and Tiff covered the liquid with left-over wedding napkins.

"I spent four hours with the heads on a conference on a Skype call last night," Jonathan continued. "They have no funds, and their accountants have advised them that the Moritz is the best place to sell for now, taking the current Irish economy into consideration. They are insistent. I am truly sorry, everybody."

The staff all looked at each other. Sandra looked at Cara and they both shook their heads. Jonathan looked like a beaten man. No one spoke for minutes and then Dermot spoke slowly.

"Big J, can we not buy it?"

Jonathan nodded his head repeatedly. "I have thought about it. I approached the bank that offered me a loan on the Kingston in London and, while unbelievably in this climate they are still willing to help me out, it's not nearly enough any more. This place will go for two million, Dermot. A few years ago it would have gone for five."

"Can we not get investors involved?" Sandra asked.

"We could. I mean, it's an auction and anyone can bid. We can go in and bid for the Moritz, but at the end of the day it will be sold to the highest bidder."

Big Bob pushed back his chair and stood. "This hotel is my life, Mr Redmond." He pushed his glasses up high onto the top of the bridge of his nose.

"I know, Bob, I really do understand."

"It's my life too, Jonathan," old Mrs Reilly added as she too stood up. "*We* need to save it. I don't even care so much if it's sold as another hotel and I lose my job – but the thought of them knocking this old girl down! Over my dead body. I will lie down on the steps of that old mahogany door and they won't move me." She sniffed back the tears and stood tall, her chest heaving in and out.

"I understand how you all feel about this building," Joanthan said, "I really do. Because I feel the same. I had my first ever job here, my first ever kiss here – my heart and soul is in this hotel, it always has been – but unfortunately I am not a millionaire."

"When is the auction?" Dermot and Sandra asked at the same time.

"Two weeks from today in Leontia's auction house in Dublin."

Dermot nearly choked on his coffee. "So we only have two weeks to get this money together and it's Christmas week in a booked-out hotel on a rota of extremely reduced staff?"

"Yes," Jonathan nodded.

"Right so." Dermot drained his cup then he stood up to join the other two. "So my question is: why are we wasting time talking about it? Let's start doing something!"

"Like what?" Cara asked.

"Like raising money!" Dermot clapped his hands loudly.

"Dermot?" Jonathan said. "You're talking about how we're going to raise two million euro? It's not easy."

"It's achievable. Like you said, five years ago this place was five million. That wasn't achievable, we were out, but maybe this is? Let's get our thinking caps on. I mean there has to be a way. I won't give this up without a fight."

Sandra stared at Dermot. He was pumped. The Breena yard was his life, she knew that. She looked around the table and suddenly realised that this was her life too. She was now happy it was her life. She wanted to keep her job here, she wanted to start over in Knocknoly, save money and get a place of her own. "Well, I am getting a cheque for one hundred thousand euro and you can have it!" she suddenly exploded.

They all stared at her.

"Did you win the lotto?" old Mrs Reilly asked, taking her seat again and pulling at Big Bob's brown cardigan to make him sit too.

"No. Neil and I are getting divorced – and Neil can't keep up the mortgage payments on the house. His brother is paying off the mortgage and I am getting a cheque to 'compensate for my loss'. I will put it into the Moritz. Just give me a room here to live in for a while." She sat down, slightly red-faced at her public outburst about her personal life.

Then Cara got up and stood behind her and put her hands on her shoulders. "I have a house I can sell in Dublin. Well, Esther, that's my mother, she's still living in it. It's both of ours. But I want to get her down here. I know she will love this village as much as I do. She will have a better quality of life and we will be together. She will agree. It's time we both moved on. It will only be worth about two hundred thousand though."

Sandra looked up at her and smiled as Cara continued to rub her shoulders.

"I have my home. I will sell it. I'm more than happy to live here too," Big Bob said. "It's on a good few acres so we could do all right out of that. That should see us getting towards the one mill."

Jonathan shook his head slowly. "Are you all serious?" His eyes began to fill with tears and he stood, turned his back to the room, sniffed and then sat back down. "Holy shit, you all are!"

"I have nothing, Jonathan, I'm afraid," Tiffney spoke quietly "but the Moritz hotel has saved my life. I had nothing in Romania many years ago, I escaped my own family and my country and now I have this family and, well . . . and now Mike. I will do anything I can do to help . . ."

Mike blushed and then stood tall, his shoulders pushed back and his head held high. "I have some savings, J, and you can have them all. It's not much and I do still live at home but I was saving for a . . . I am saving for a ring . . . I am . . ." He stopped to swallow.

Jonathan held his hand up. "No, Mike, don't say it again!"

"Let me finish, Jonathan, please. I am saving for an engagement ring for Tiff." He held her hand tight as she smiled up at him. "I have a few thousand euros saved but it's yours."

Tiffney jumped up and hugged Mike as he kissed the top of her head.

Sandra burst out crying, her emotions exploding, and Dermot handed her a napkin. "Wow, listen, Mike, you don't have to do this but thank you so much," Jonathan said. "We will accept. Okay, maybe we can do this after all?" His eyes were bright and his face flushed. "So we still need to raise a cool mill. I'm going to see the bank manager in Dublin now, okay? I'll be back later." He literally ran from the conference room before returning and poking his head back around the door. "Seriously, I can't tell you all how fantastic you are. Now kindly run the hotel in my absence, won't ye?"

The room exploded with laughter and release of tension.

* * *

"Do you think we can do it?" Cara asked Sandra as they headed back to work.

"God, it's exciting, isn't it? Yeah, I don't see why not. What about Mike? Wasn't that an incredible thing he just did? I'm so happy they are a couple – they are so well suited."

"Would we have to live here though? Surely that would be nonsense as we'd take up half the rooms?" Cara wondered if Esther would have fifty fits at what she had just done. She really didn't think so. She knew Esther would love life down here. She knew Esther was pretending that she was fine without Cara but really all Esther wanted was to be with her daughter.

"Yeah, I suppose we would but we could build on maybe? Build staff quarters around Dermot's area?"

"Wow this is mad."

Sandra slipped in behind the reception desk and thanked Alice. "You can go and help Cara today if you want the extra hours? Jonathan's out on business so she might need help with the Christmas activities and all that."

"Will do." Alice nodded and grabbed her bag.

Dermot approached the desk. Sandra still felt mortified about his visit to her house the night she had sex with Jamie.

"So, how was your week off?" He pushed his blond hair out of his eyes and held it off with his hands.

"It was good. I needed to get Neil out of my system. I know that sounds crazy and so selfish but I needed to do it."

"How are you doing now?" he asked, concerned.

"I think I'll be okay. I spoke with Neil last night and he's doing well. He's living in Rathmines with yer one. It won't last but sure he's happy for now."

"That's great, Sandy." Dermot let go of his hair and it covered his eyes.

"Listen, Dermot, I'm sorry that happened last week – eh, when you came to the house . . ." she whispered as he backed away from the desk.

He came back slowly. "Come on, I should be the one apologising for barging up your stairs! I was just so anxious about you . . . imagining all sorts of disasters to tell you the truth . . . No need to apologise. You know me better than that. It's your business, Sandy. I'm just happy you're okay, nothing else is important. I have my own life and you have yours, isn't that right?"

He smiled at her and then she watched him go. His hair had grown so much in a week, she noted. There was nothing between them so why did she feel as though she'd just cheated on him? Dermot was right – she was crazy, she had nothing to feel guilty about.

Her stomach rumbled now and she was suddenly starving. She rang Tiffney in the restaurant. "Could you drop me down a plate of chips with loads of vinegar whenever you get five minutes? And I mean *drench* them in vinegar."

"Sure, no problem," Tiff said and rang off.

The hotel was packed, the guests were all well looked after and the Christmas buzz had opened up. Cara had done a terrific job, Sandra noted, very classy. The reception area twinkled in discreet red and green fairy lights and some soft classical Christmas carols played around her. Poinsettia plants were positioned at the doors and in window boxes. The dining-room roof was circled in white fairy lights that flicked on and off at intervals of thirty seconds. Cara really had the touch.

Sandra dialled her mother's number at home.

Answering machine. "*Hi, it's us! We're on the green! Shush!*" Laughter and a beep. Sandra hung up. Her mother hadn't tried to call her to see how she was. She hit the numbers harder this time as she rang back and this time she left a message: "Hello. Mam and Dad, it's me, your daughter. I will be working all over Christmas so if you would like to see me I will be in the Moritz. Happy Golfmas!" Then she slammed the phone down hard. It would take her a while to mellow.

"You okay?" Tiff asked as she balanced the biggest plate of chips in her right hand and a can of Coke and a bottle of vinegar in her left.

"That's a talent, Tiff!" Sandra said.

"Who are you telling? It took me lot of years to master!"

Tiffney looked much brighter, Sandra noted. She'd had her hair cut into a sleek bob and it really suited her. She seemed to be standing taller, straighter. "How are you, Tiff? I love the hair. I'm sorry I haven't talked to you much lately. I've been, well, busy!" She laughed and dipped her fingers in for a hot homemade chip.

"Yes, I wondered why you never come in for your lunch break any more?"

"Money, Tiff, it ran out," Sandra muttered through a hot chip and immediately grabbed for another.

Tiff shooed her hand away. “Sit and eat. Is better. I understand money running away all too well.” She bowed her head. “Money makes the world go round – isn’t that what the song says?”

“Yeah, I suppose it does, Tiff, but they also say ‘Money Can’t Buy You Love’!”

Tiff took this in and worked it out in her head. “They are correct. It cannot.” She turned on her heel and walked back to her restaurant.

Sandra wolfed the chips down and sipped her chilled coke.

“Chips and Coke? Classy girl, wha’?” Cara poked her head into the back office.

“Shit, can you smell them? Jonathan would freak. I never, ever do this. I am just totally starving.” She handed the can to Cara who drank from it.

“So how are you?”

“I’m okay, Cara. Sorry I bailed on you and our night – everything just happened so quickly. I just had to get away.”

“So I’m taking it your marriage is really over for good?” Cara sat opposite Sandra, redoing her low ponytail.

“Yeah, it is.”

As Sandra filled her in Cara listened intently, nodding her head and taking in every word.

“I’m so sorry,” she said at the end. “I know what it’s like, well, sort of . . . mine is . . . well, another shocking story altogether.” She felt uncomfortable as her past sloshed around her mind and Sandra noticed immediately.

“Will we reschedule that X-rated chat for tonight?” Sandra asked.

“Yeah, I’d love that. Where are you staying now?”

“I’m supposed to be in Dermot’s but I’m not sure the offer still stands.” Sandra looked down at her feet.

“Why not? Has something happened?”

Sandra didn’t answer.

Cara changed the subject – she didn’t want to be nosy. “So what did you do on the week off anyway?” She threw the empty Coke can they had shared into the red recycle bin.

"I'm not sure I can tell you. I'm not really sure I actually did it to be honest. I may have done a Dorothy and just had a very crazy dream."

Cara was looking in the bin. "Who keeps putting chocolate wrappers in this bin?" she asked as she removed some. "Did a what?" she asked then, wiping her hands down.

"Well, basically I eloped for a week to have incredible sex with Jamie Keenan." Sandra licked her fingers one at a time as Cara looked at her, her mouth stuck in a perfect O shape.

"You are kidding me . . . aren't you?"

"No. I'm not."

"Well, good for you!" Cara said at last and closed her mouth tightly. She stood up to leave. "And I hope it was every damn bit as good as I am imagining it was right this very second?"

"And then some," Sandra said.

Cara laughed all the way down the corridor and she could still hear Sandra's giggles as she entered the kitchens.

Chapter 26

With Jonathan away for the day the hotel was even busier. He was now on his way back and they were all so frustrated that he didn't have an answer from the bank just yet. They were to get back to him later that evening.

"My God, now we see how much work he really does!" Cara said to Big Bob as she rang the window cleaner for the fifth time. The weather had taken a turn for the worse, there had been a gale-force wind and the sand ring was now splattered all over the windows.

"I know it's three days before Christmas, Mr Campbell, but that's exactly why I need you today," Cara implored the window cleaner. "Please, Mr Campbell, I will make it worth your while." She smiled and draped herself over the reception desk in relief as he finally agreed to come later on in the afternoon.

Cara and Sandra had passed each other running all day and every time they did they made hand signals, miming glasses of wine being poured down their necks later that evening.

Sandra was just settling Alice in for the night shift when Dermot popped into the back office.

"I'm heading down to the house for a shower," he said. "Can I take anything down for you?"

"Are you still sure it's okay, Dermot? I mean, I understand if it's not now after . . ."

"After what?" He narrowed his eyes. "We are not dating as far as I am aware, Sandy, are we?" He winked at her.

"I know, but you know what I mean – I'm morto."

"Don't be." He started blinking his eyes over and over while staring at her.

"What are you doing?"

"Oh, just looking at those mental pictures I took of your wonderful boobaloobies!"

"Piss off, Dermot!"

He smiled, bent down and grabbed her case. "Is this it? Is this all you have?"

"Yeah, I dropped the rest at my folks' place – I'll get it all tomorrow."

"What time will you be down?"

"Well, actually, I'm going to Cara's for wine after work but you are more than welcome to join us?"

"Nice one, I might. I'll see. I'm away to the train station later to pick up Big J so I will let you know. Will you sleep there?"

"I don't know, Dermot, I might. Depends on how drunk I am."

"Sandra Darragh, what a lady you are!" He bowed as he shifted her case to his other arm and then pretended to pull his back.

"Hilarious as always, Dermot. Oh and, by the way, that horse thing – when am I doing it again?"

He came back closer to her and stood, his blond hair flopping from side to side as he shook his head. "That horse thing?" he asked her, amused.

"Yes, you know, the horse thing I started a few weeks ago?"

"Learning to ride, you mean?" His eyes were suddenly deadly serious.

"Yeah, learning to ride." She looked at him like he was mad.

"D'ya remember years ago, Sandy – you were about eighteen and I was about, oh, twenty-six, and you asked me why I did 'that horse thing'?" He leaned his elbows on her desk. "I told you it wasn't a 'horse thing', it was my life. It still is. I live for those horses. If you took that yard away from me I don't know what I'd do."

She coughed a short uncomfortable cough. Dermot rubbed his eyes and continued. "You told me that night in Hines you understood. You said that you could totally understand how someone would want to be around what they loved all the time. You were drunk. And then you said 'When I get older and I'm having lots and lots of babies then I can bring them down to you. You could teach them to do that horse thing'."

Sandra felt a lump rise in her throat.

"I always remembered that."

Then he left. What had he meant by all that? What was his point, she wondered as she tidied the main desk.

* * *

Cara dashed to Louise's and bought a couple of small homemade lasagnes and then dropped into O'Dwyer's and bought more wine and nuts and crisps. She also bought fresh flowers. Then she trotted on home. It was a dark evening and the wind was cutting her in two but she felt okay. She had her panic-attack alarm in her pocket that she always kept her hand on. She reached the cottage and hurriedly opened the door and slammed it tight behind her. She had set the heating so the cottage was snug and warm.

She popped the food into the oven, ready to be warmed up later. Then she put the white wine in the fridge and picked out some CDs. She was apprehensive but also looking forward to having a girly night in. Sandra would be another hour, so she had time to change and shower before their evening began.

The wind was rattling the windows so she popped on a Beatles CD and turned the volume up loud. "My windows. The noise is my windows," she muttered as she headed for the shower. She would call Esther after.

No doubt Sandra would be shocked to the core by her story later and in a funny way she was looking forward to getting it all out. She had gone over and over the events with her counsellor but never with a friend. She started to undress as she wondered where she would start with Sandra. Start from the end and work your way back, she decided. The end was horrific.

* * *

After Alex had left for Dubai Cara had scraped herself off the bathroom floor. She had no tears, funnily enough, just anger. Ever so slowly she threw some clothes into a couple of plastic bags from the kitchen drawer. She knew there was one thing she wanted to look at before she left this lunatic en route to the guards.

She winced in agony as she stood on the bathtub and grabbed a long bath towel. She wound the towel into a long knotted shape and with a swoop of her hand tried to knock the black box from the top of the boiler with it. She missed and cried out in pain as she wound the towel up again. Blood was seeping from her head again and she knew she had to get out of here quickly. He could come back again. At any second. She wouldn't put anything past him at this stage. She suddenly heard her father's voice loud and clear: *One more try, Cara, you can do it!* She twisted the towel as tightly as she could and she swiped at the box again. This time she caught the edge of it and it tumbled down in slow motion, down into the bath. She slowly released her grip on the towel, dropped it into the bath and climbed down.

The box was made of metal and locked with a small padlock. She rattled the box and items moved around inside it. She took it into the kitchen and opened the kitchen drawers. She rummaged around, throwing things on the ground in her hurry. She tried the small knife Alex used to slice peppers. The lock didn't budge. She rummaged again and found some old silver hairclips at the bottom of a drawer. Alex was always on at her to put them in her bedroom drawers. She opened the clip out wide and pushed the skinny leg into the hole of the padlock. It didn't click. She pushed and pushed again, twisted and turned it and the frustration was mounting in her. It didn't work. She grabbed the box and bashed it off the side of the table and bashed again and again with all she had left in her until she managed to bend one corner of the lid slightly. She grabbed the big navy-handled scissors from the drawer now and slid it into the slit, then pushed and levered with all her might while the lid lifted more and more. She tried and could almost fit her hand in. Almost. She levered it again and suddenly one of the hinges gave way and the lid bent right back, exposing the items inside.

She shook the box and the contents fell out onto the shiny wooden floor of the Sandymount apartment.

There were a number of items, including several long locks of hair – blonde, black and chestnut.

But she really saw only two: her mobile phone and her wallet.

She dropped the box and stood very still, staring at them both as they came and went in and out of focus. She picked them up and held each one tight, one in her left hand and one in her right.

So Alex had attacked her on the Quays that night. For some reason she kissed her wallet. It was as though she had just been handed her old life back.

She wasted no more time. She grabbed the plastic bags and threw the items in.

She opened the door and made her way out to the road to hail a taxi. The state of her, she wasn't sure if one would stop, but one did eventually and suddenly she just wanted to go home before going to the police. She just wanted her mammy. The taxi driver knew better than to try and make small talk and he kindly put his foot down and got her to Harold's Cross in double-quick time. She had no keys, she realised. She hoped Esther was in. She opened her old wallet and the money was still in it. She paid the taxi man with a huge tip.

"You mind yourself, love." He nodded at her as she slowly dragged herself out.

"Oh! I am so terribly sorry – there's blood on your seat! Here!" She pulled notes from her purse.

"Ger away oudda that! Sure I'll wash it down later. Me own daughter went through it, ya' know – slimy bastard got away with it – if only I'd a caught him he wouldn't be alive today."

Cara held her breath, fearful she would explode into horrendous tears, and waved at him as he drove away. She rang the bell. No answer but Victoria was barking. Esther couldn't be gone far. Maybe she was in the supermarket – it was the one place she wasn't allowed to bring Victoria with her. She slid through the half-open back gate and headed for the backdoor. As she got there she could see a shadow moving through the bubbles of glass on the old-fashioned panes of the back door.

The door was flung open and Alex stood in front of her.

"Nice to see you again, Cara. Took your time. I was actually about to leave, thinking you weren't coming. I actually nearly thought you were telling the truth for once in your pathetic life."

Jesus, where was Esther? Cara darted her eyes all around the kitchen as she stepped in but there was no sign of her. She must be out. She had to be out. Please, Esther, be out! Victoria barked again at Cara and Alex kicked the little dog so hard she flew across the room and bounced off the fridge. Whimpering, she fled for safety under the kitchen table.

"What are you doing here, Alex?" Cara leaned back against the kitchen sink.

"What are *you* doing here, you lying bitch? I thought you said you loved me and it was all okay? 'I love you, Alex!'" he mimicked her voice, "'It's okay, Alex. I deserved it, Alex. For lying to you, Alex. Go to work, I will be fine, Alex!' So why did you run back to your mammy? And don't say it was a visit because you didn't even change your clothes, the state of you! Did the neighbours see you like that?"

He spat the words at her and she knew he was approaching his most dangerous again. The games were over. She leaned further back against the steel counter. "Where is my mother?"

He laughed now. "Your mother, she's nothing but a tramp. Did you know that?"

Cara stared hard at him.

"Did you know your precious Esther had an affair with my precious daddy? Did you know that, Cara Byrne? Esther Byrne's the scrubber who my dad had the affair with!"

Cara tried to take in what he was ranting about. "Where is she?" she asked again.

Alex walked to the small white door under the stairs and kicked it violently. "Speak, tramp!" he called out.

Cara heard a muffled voice from under the stairs. She was alive. For a brief moment there Cara had shuddered to think.

"Can I see her?"

"Why?" he asked.

"Because I want to see what she has to say about all this crap you are going on about."

He moved again to the small white door and Cara made her grab. She stuffed the butcher's knife down her trousers, gashing herself as she did.

"Come out, little pig!" Alex chanted as he dragged Esther out.

Cara yelped. Esther's face was bloodied and she was white and shaking like a leaf.

"Oh, Cara, love, are you okay? Oh Jesus, love, what's going to happen to us?"

"Nothing, Mam, we'll be fine." She stood her ground, her heart beating at a surprisingly slow pace.

"*So tell her!*" Alex screamed at Esther and Victoria barked under the table at his voice, "and if that dog barks again. I will kill it."

"*Shhush*, Victoria," Esther soothed her little dog, "go to bed – good girl, Mammy will make your tea soon. *Shhusshhh* . . ." Esther wiped the dried blood away from the side of her mouth and looked at Cara. "Well, love, do you remember that man I was seeing when I worked in Rosie's in the early days? Simon?"

Cara shut her eyes tight.

"Well, it seems he is Alex's father. I did think I knew him the moment I saw him. The thing is, I never knew Simon was a pilot. If I had I might have put two and two together. He just said he worked in the airport. We had a few dates and then I heard from Marina Gleeson that he was married. A friend of hers had seen us in The Gresham. That was it. I finished it and I never went on another date the rest of my life, did I, love?" She trembled. "But now Alex is saying I knew all along – he's saying he took me to the same table in The Gresham where Simon brought me and that is true – but I didn't realise, it was all so long ago."

"I found Esther first, you see, Cara. I asked my dad who she was and he told me. I asked after her in Rosie's and I was so surprised that she still lived in the same house. I presumed it was a sign. I knew I wanted to get back at her and what better way than to hurt the thing that she loved the most – you!"

Cara kept breathing. In and out slowly, trying to keep her head as clear as was possible. Alex was rubbing his hands together in a manner that really frightened her. Constant rhythm. As though he had no control over them. "But then I actually got to like you – I always had a thing for redheads, you see, and I wasn't expecting you to be a redhead, I just wanted to get your trollop of a mother back for wrecking my life. My mother's life. It was no coincidence I was in The Law Top that day. I had followed you for weeks. The guy with me was hired – you asked about him before – he's some actor I got off a forum on the internet."

"I didn't mean to wreck anyone's life, Alex, you have to believe me . . . if I had known . . ." Esther whispered and the blood trickled down her chin again from where she had reopened the cut at the side of her mouth.

"She didn't know your father was married, Alex, so how can you still blame her?" Cara stood tall.

"Because someone told my mother about her and my mother had a breakdown. She couldn't believe it. And then the truth about more and more women came out but, you see, if it hadn't been for your mother she would never have found out in the first place."

It made no sense but Cara was not surprised. She remembered Esther seeing a man but it had only lasted a matter of weeks and Cara, being a teenager, was delighted when Esther had finished it.

Alex smashed his hand off the wall and the bowl of éclairs that Ester had obviously been filling when Alex arrived now fell from the kitchen surface and the sweets scattered all over the floor. Victoria barked out loud. Cara's heart started to beat faster now.

Alex dragged Esther by her hair and shouted, "Get on your knees and drag that dog out now!"

Esther opened and closed her mouth but the words were lost in her throat.

"*Now!*" he shouted and Esther bent and crawled under the table.

"Leave them, Alex, let us go and talk – it's about us now. Please stop this, you need help."

"No, fuck off, Cara! Get the fucking dog out now, Esther!" He was screaming manically.

Esther's sobs were getting louder and louder as she remained under the table.

Cara noticed now for the second time that day that Alex wasn't handsome. It was amazing how someone's looks could differ in your mind according to their appalling actions. His eyes again were that dangerous blue – they were too close together, and his body over-built. Poor Esther! Cara couldn't believe this was happening to her beloved mother. That she was responsible for putting her through all this. She loved her mother so much. Her mam, who still made her a "chucky egg in a cup" on a Sunday morning and brought it up to her in bed on a tray with the big pot of tea. She looked at him now as he was shouting at Esther, white spittle gathering at the sides of his mouth. She waited. Then he made the move she knew he was going to make. His back suddenly turned and then he was on all fours, reaching under the table. A bark from Victoria was followed by a yelp from Alex. He pulled his hand back, snarling at the dog, and Cara saw that Victoria had drawn a little blood.

Cara pulled the butcher's knife out. She saw it in her right hand now, a gleaming get-out. A welcome blade. It was old but still a very sharp large stainless-steel knife. "You can't buy knives like this any more," Esther had so often told her as she sliced her meat. Cara placed her left hand on it now too and turned it twice, making sure she was in control of it.

Alex was trying to grab at Esther while avoiding Victoria's sharp little teeth.

Cara saw Esther's eyes peer out at her through the small hole in the tablecloth, the hole that her mother always complained about. Their eyes locked and Esther suddenly shut her eyes tight.

Cara lifted the knife and with all her strength plunged it into Alex's back. He screamed and fell to the floor on his stomach.

He screamed louder now as he wriggled and wriggled and tried to reach around his back for the knife.

As Cara stood motionless a pounding sounded on the front door.

"The Guards! Open up! We need you to open this door right now!"

Cara fell to her knees and crawled to the door. She pulled herself up by the wall just as the door was battered in and two guards ran into the hall.

"In the kitchen. I think I have killed him," she said in a calm clear voice.

One radioed for an ambulance and the other pushed her up against the wall and put her in handcuffs.

"Mam!" she shouted now, her head beginning to clear a little more. "My mother is under the table."

"Stay!" the guard shouted at her and went into the kitchen.

"Cara, love!" Esther cried out, Victoria tucked tightly under her arm, as the guard gently led her out of the kitchen. "Oh, love, it's okay!" She wrapped her other arm around her daughter's neck. "You had no choice, love. You had to do it. He told me what he had done to you earlier. I thought he was going to kill us both, didn't you?" Esther pushed Cara's hair from her face, her breath fast and raspy.

The other guard emerged from the kitchen. "He's still alive," he informed them. "I can't move him until the ambulance gets here. What has happened here?"

Cara couldn't speak. She had hoped he was dead. Esther was cradling Victoria in her arms now as she explained what had happened.

The guards listened intently and suddenly the one who had pushed her against the wall and handcuffed her roughly, asked, "Are you okay, Cara?" She nodded as the ambulance siren sounded in the distance.

"How did you know we were in trouble? Was it the taxi driver?" Cara asked.

"No, not a taxi driver – we got a call from your neighbour, Mr Dolan. He said something strange was going on and that there was screaming coming from inside the house and it was extremely unusual. He said he heard a male making threats."

The ambulance crew arrived and did their business as Cara and Esther were led outside. Mr Dolan stood at the fence between the two houses.

"Can you mind Victoria?" Esther asked him. "She needs to be fed and there is water in her bowl. They won't allow me to take her. And thank you, Kevin, you have always been a good neighbour." She kissed the little dog on the nose and handed her over.

It seemed the whole of the estate was gathered outside their small house, children standing holding their bicycles and mothers cradling their babies, watching as they were put in the police car.

At the station the handcuffs were removed and they were given sweet tea in polystyrene cups and told they were to be put into separate holding rooms.

"I'm an awful eejit," said Esther. "How was I so blind not to see you weren't yourself? I should have asked you more questions. That's what I get for trying not to be a nosy mother. Well, never again, I tell you. Whatever happens, Cara, I am here and I always will be."

"It will be okay, Mam, just tell the truth," Cara told her as they were separated. Her long red hair fell around her face and she had no tears left to cry. How had her life come to this moment? What a stupid woman she was! She had to be responsible for some of this. She should have run a mile that day when they were looking at the Sandymount apartment and he had turned on her. It was a great big flashing neon warning sign and she had ignored it. Now she could well spend the rest of her life behind bars for murder. But what choice did she have? She had seen Alex earlier – once that switch was tripped he was capable of murdering them both, of that she had no doubt. Of that she was one hundred per cent certain. She did what she had to do. She would stand by her actions and accept her punishment. Her thoughts were interrupted as the door was opened and a woman walked in carrying a file and a polystyrene cup. She pulled up a seat at the yellow plastic table.

"Hello, Cara, I'm Detective Samantha Doyle." She was a pretty slender woman in her early forties. She clicked on a small black recorder and spoke into it: "Detective Samantha Doyle interviewing Cara Charles. Time three forty-two p.m. Cara, just to let you know before we start this interview, Alex Charles is alive. The knife pierced his lung but he will live."

Cara nodded. "Thank you," she said and her shoulders dropped a little.

"Apparently he's conscious and eager to talk to us. I'll be going to the hospital directly after this interview. Now, Cara, can you tell me the events that occurred leading up to you stabbing him?"

Cara told her story and Samantha listened as she stared at the recorder and never once at Cara, nodding occasionally.

When Cara had finished Samantha looked up at her. "Now, Cara, your husband has a criminal record – did you know that?"

Cara shook her head. "No, I didn't."

Samantha opened a light-blue file and removed some old papers. "Yes, he allegedly assaulted his sister Beth Charles in 2007 and put her in the hospital. He broke her arm and she needed fifteen stitches to her face. He slammed her face into a mirror. She dropped the charges. Going back to 2001 he allegedly assaulted his own mother Marie Charles, put her in ICU. She suffered severe swelling to her brain and three broken ribs. She dropped the charges too."

"I met his mother – she seemed to be fine with him." Cara shook her head.

"In the last medical report after he allegedly attacked Beth it says Alex has mental health issues." Samantha held the page closer to her face as she muttered to herself, reading further on down.

"But he's a pilot! He couldn't do that job if he has mental issues." Cara didn't want to hear the answer to this and she put her head on the table. "He's not a pilot, is he?" she muttered.

Samantha Doyle shook her head. "Oh, he's a pilot all right, Cara, that much is true, but he's been on 'gardening leave' for the last few years – you know, where an employee who is leaving a job, or who is fired, is instructed to stay away from work during the notice period, while still being paid. He hasn't flown in over five years."

"Jesus!" was all Cara managed.

Samantha picked up her polystyrene cup and drank as she flipped through another book of notes. "Charles is by all accounts a dangerous man, Cara, but you tried to kill him so you can be prosecuted for attempted murder."

"I had no choice but to do what I did. I firmly believe he would have killed one of us. He was just about to kill Victoria."

"Who's Victoria?" Samantha looked confused.

"Oh sorry, she's my mam's little dog."

Samantha just looked at her in silence and nodded her understanding.

"I was attacked a few weeks ago on the Quays. The attacker mugged me violently, smashing my head repeatedly on the concrete path, and put me in hospital. My phone and wallet were stolen. I found them both in Alex's apartment earlier after he attacked me there again this morning." Tears started to flow now and Cara lost all control as she sobbed through a running nose. "He did it. He assaulted me."

"I'll need the phone and the wallet to run prints for evidence."

"Yeah, but I know he will say his prints were all over them as he's my husband and of course he's picked up my stuff before," Cara sighed.

Samantha Doyle spoke into the recorder. "Interview over at four ten p.m." She stood up. "Okay, I'm going into the hospital to talk with him now. I'll see you again after that." She seemed to hesitate, then said, "Every single suspect is innocent until proven guilty – that goes for you but it also goes for Alex. But, off the record, I do believe you. Alex Charles needs help, and he needs to be made accountable for his actions, whatever that takes. I will not let this happen to another woman." She almost said this last sentence under her breath but loud enough for Cara to hear it and believe her.

* * *

Two hours later Samantha returned. Cara tried to read her expression but failed.

"Well, Cara, the situation has changed," she said. "I've spoken to Alex and he's not pressing charges – but only on condition you don't press any charges and neither does Esther. He says when he recovers he's out of here and moving away from Ireland. He says he knows he is ill. I can trace his passport to make sure he's true to his word. Right now I am setting up a barring order. Now, I must warn you that while I think we should get him, put him away if we can, you would go on trial for attempted murder first and then, secondary to that, we could prosecute him for battery and assault to you and Esther." She paused and looked straight at Cara. "But I'm afraid there is no guarantee that he will go to prison."

It was too much to take in. Cara didn't know how to respond.

Samantha waved her hand. "You don't have to make any decision now, Cara, but the sooner the better. Esther is out in the waiting room. You are both free to go for now. I will be over to see you first thing in the morning and you can then let me know what your decision is."

Cara heaved a sigh of relief. "Thank you, Samantha," she said.

Samantha ushered her out to where Esther sat waiting.

"Let's get home, Mam," Cara said.

"Do you not need a hospital, love, to see a doctor? You're battered."

"No, Mam, all I want is a bath and my own bed."

"Sleep in with me tonight, love, will you?" Esther asked as they made their way to the doors of the station and out into the daylight.

* * *

Cara didn't sleep a wink that night and Samantha knocked on their door at eight. Tying her dressing gown around her Cara led her into the kitchen where she pushed down the button on the kettle.

"So how do you feel this morning?" Samantha asked. "How is Esther?"

"We're doing okay, thanks . . . but I didn't sleep."

"Have you come to a decision?"

Cara didn't answer at once. She put some tea bags in the pot, poured boiling water onto them and popped the cosy on. She sat down opposite Samantha.

"I just want my life back, Samantha."

"I know you do. I can't tell you to press charges but I think you should. If you don't he could do this again, Cara."

Cara poured the tea now and stared up at a family picture from Blackpool all those years ago. Esther smiling wildly with her *Kiss Me Quick* hat on. She'd only worn it for the photo. She had to think of her mother first. She couldn't put her through a trial. She also couldn't risk losing the case and going to prison. Her hands were tied.

"We don't want to press charges either," she said quietly as Esther shuffled into the kitchen and sat down.

"That's perfectly okay." Samantha lifted her cup.

"What's okay?" Esther said as immediately Victoria jumped onto her lap.

"Samantha says it's okay if we don't press charges, Mam."

"So it's all over then?" Esther's eyes were wide and innocent.

"Yes, Mam, it's all over," Cara said through gritted teeth and poured Esther a hot cup of tea.

Chapter 27

Cara jerked under the hot jets as a sudden noise dragged her back to the present. How often she found herself in these total day dreams! It scared her slightly. She stood with her ears pricked for a minute or so but no other noise seemed to occur. "Must be the wind," she muttered to herself. She stood back under the hot water now and focused on the present.

She hoped that Jonathan would get some good news from the bank. She scrubbed her long red hair and added some tea tree and lime conditioner. She heard a bang again and this time she froze as the white suds spilled into her eyes.

"The wind, Cara," she said again as she held her face under the water stream. "Oh!" she suddenly remembered. "It could be Sandra!" She let out a low breath and turned off the shower. She really had to stop being this nervy. She really had to stop talking to herself.

"Coming!" she shouted as she wrapped the big fluffy yellow towel around her and opened the bathroom door.

"Only me!" Sandra's voice piped through the letterbox down the small hallway. "Get me a stiff drink, please!"

Cara padded along the hall. She unbolted, unchained and opened the door.

Sandra stood in front of her, her green coat tight around her, and she held a brown paper bag in her arms.

"Jeez, Fort Knox, hey! Sorry, you were still in the shower! Am I too early?"

"It's fine, I was daydreaming as usual – glasses are in the fridge along with the wine and I have a couple of Louise's lasagnes for later."

"Superb! I am absolutely starving! I've been starving all day."

Cara took Sandra's coat and hung it on the old-fashioned coat-rack by the door. She repositioned her fluffy towel.

"There's still no word from the bank," Sandra said. "I just emailed Jonathan on his Blackberry – Dermot's on the way to get him from the train station. Man, it's exciting, isn't it? It's just what I need – a whole new lease of life! Did I just say 'man'? Okay, I really do need a drink." Sandra flopped on the small couch as Cara made her way into the bedroom to get dressed, the two still chatting through the open door.

"There is red on the counter and white in the fridge so whichever you prefer!" Cara called out, shaking the wet out of her long red hair with her left hand then she turned on the hairdryer to blast it dry.

"You know, when I was a little girl I always wanted to call this place home. I had a bit of a property crush on it! I was only telling an old friend – Alex Charles – about it when I bumped into him in London!" Sandra shouted down the hall as she headed for the fridge and removed the white wine and the chilled glasses. She poured two large measures and popped the bottle back in the fridge before returning to the couch with the drinks.

Cara came out of the bedroom in her blue tracksuit and fluffy red slipper-socks.

"Sorry? Were you saying something? I couldn't hear a word over the dryer."

"Nah, nothing important. Nice outfit!" Sandra said and smiled as Cara curled up on the couch beside her.

"Yeah, I'm a comfy girl, always have been, I'm afraid."

"Oh, me too!" Sandra handed her a glass and they clinked. "Great to meet you, fellow-comfy-girl Cara Byrne!"

"Great to meet you too, Sandra . . . are you still Darragh?"

Cara asked as she sniffed her wine and swirled the clear liquid around the bottom of the glass.

"Ah, yeah, I don't think I will go through all the bother of changing it back to Loughnane. I was Sandra Darragh, I still am. I think I need to just move forwards and not go backwards." She sipped her wine. "Ah, that is so good!" She threw her eyes up to the ceiling. "So then, here we are!" She laughed. "Both with a novel in us, I guess?"

"You got that right," Cara laughed.

"So what genre would yours be then?"

"Oh – horror!" Cara answered immediately. "And yours?"

Sandra paused and looked Cara in the eye. "Well, it's hard to categorise my book really – romantic fiction meets hospital drama maybe?" They both laughed even though they each guessed the seriousness of the other's choice.

"So, fire ahead – tell me all." Cara twisted her red curls up into a knot as Sandra filled her in on all her story.

"What about the babies? Are you giving up on that too?" Cara touched Sandra's arm.

"It's so hard for me to think about it, Cara, it really is. I can't explain my desire to have a baby – it's completely overwhelming. Don't you ever feel like that? If you don't mind me asking – and if I am out of line tell me to mind my own bloody business."

"I don't know. No, not really. Esther, my poor traumatised mother, had me quite late in her life so maybe I'll follow suit," Cara said.

"Why do I get the feeling that no matter how bad my story is, yours is probably worse?"

Cara laughed now. "Because it probably is. The thing is, Sandra, I can be judged by my story. You won't think the same way about me ever again. But I trust you and I feel that if I can't open up and come totally clean and honest about my past then maybe Knocknoly's not the right place for me after all." Cara was suddenly really nervous. Why didn't she just bury Alex Charles instead of thinking about him all the time? And now she was going to talk about him.

"Shoot!" Sandra picked up her glass, kicked off her runners and tucked her feet under her.

So Cara shot. She began with that afternoon in The Law Top when this absolute ride of a man invited her to take a drink for herself.

Sandra's facial expressions over the next half hour were priceless but she never once made a sound, never tried to interrupt or ask a question – she just listened.

Just before Cara got to the last piece of her awful tale she stood up. "Hang on." She stretched her arms above her head. "First – where's that vodka?"

"Really?" Sandra's eyes were on stalks. "It gets worse?"

Cara shrugged her shoulders. "Depends on what you see as worse."

Sandra dragged the bottle straight through the paper bag which ripped in two clean halves as Cara grabbed two new glasses from the kitchen and a two-litre bottle of Diet Coke. She popped a glass in front of each of them and added vodka and some Coke. "The Coke's a bit flat, I'm afraid, but sure it will do." She sat and picked up her glass.

"Okay," said Sandra, waving her glass. "Now I'm prepared for anything. Go on!"

Cara did.

"Jesus!" Sandra whispered minutes later as she cradled her glass.

Silence hung in the air now as Cara watched her friend. Then Sandra let a slow tear trickle down her face before quickly wiping it away, not wanting Cara to know she felt sorry for her.

"Are you okay?" Cara asked.

Sandra snorted. "Am I okay? Yeah, I'm okay, but, Jesus, are you?"

Cara nodded and her pretty face lit up. "I am fine now, honestly. It was a complete nightmare, but you know what they say: what doesn't kill you makes you stronger. Life goes on. I'll never fall for piercing blue eyes again."

"*Girls!*" a male voice boomed through the open letterbox and Cara and Sandra screamed.

Sandra jumped on the couch, roaring at a frightening pitch.

"It's just us! Dermot and Jonathan! What's going on in there?"

Cara dropped her head in her hands and began to laugh. She looked at Sandra's white face and laughed even more.

"It is not funny! I nearly peed in my pants! But no wonder we're jumpy after your story, Holy Mother of God!" Sandra wiped her brow.

"Not a word, okay?" Cara hissed after her as she got down off the couch and went to let the lads in.

"What the heck is wrong with you, Sandy?" Dermot stared at her as she opened the door. "Is everything okay?"

"Sorry," she said, her eyes wide open as she stared hard back at him. "We just got a fright, that's all." Then she nearly fell backwards. "Wow, Dermot, your hair!"

Dermot stood there, sporting a very closely shaven head. It was fantastic on him. Took years off him and made his cheekbones stand out like two armed guards. "Ah, thanks!" He ran his massive hand over it. "Had to be done, bit chilly on the ole noggin though."

"You two are seriously weird together, girls," Jonathan said as he wiped his shoes on Cara's new Welcome mat.

"Well?" Cara jogged down the small hall as they entered and Sandra shut the door fast behind them. "What news from the bank?" She hopped up and down on each foot.

"Okay, first of all, we will both have some of what ye are having." Dermot pointed to the empty wine bottle and the half-empty vodka bottle.

"Let's sit at the kitchen table – more space," Cara said as she tried to pull her fluffy slipper-socks off and push them under the couch. She didn't quite know why.

They sat and drinks were poured.

Jonathan rubbed his hands together before loosening his tie and opening the top button of his shirt. "It's not good news. No, worse than that, it's shite news. They won't even consider the loan they swore was sitting in the vault for me. They won't budge. I tried everything. Sorry, guys!"

"That's crazy," Cara said. "Sure we have it half raised already! Is there no way we can find other investors? What about calling a meeting in Knocknoly church hall and seeing what the locals say? The hotel has been a massive part of Knocknoly for so many years and it's a huge source of local employment and tourism. The locals have a right at least to know what's going on, don't they? It will affect a lot of businesses."

"We can try all right," Jonathan said "but I think it's a lost cause. The wonderful thing though is how touched I was at all the staff pulling together like that. I'd give anything to save the Moritz but I'm all out of ideas. Unless a Knight in Shining Euros appears through that door, the hotel is gone, I'm afraid, and possibly all our jobs too." He peeled the paper label from the vodka bottle.

"Would a Knight in Shining Sterling do?" Sandra suddenly said. Why hadn't she thought of it before?

They all stared at her.

"Who?" Jonathan and Dermot asked in unison.

"Jamie Keenan, the tennis player!" Was it her imagination or did Dermot's face cloud over for a split second.

"Why would he want to help us?" he asked.

"Yeah, why?" Jonathan asked.

"Because this is what he wants to get into – well, the restaurant trade. I'm sure he would help. I'm sure he'd be interested – as a business venture, I mean." She blushed now as she caught Dermot staring at her. "Listen, there is absolutely nothing romantic between us. He'll never settle down romantically but I know he'd love to settle in Ireland. What have we got to lose by approaching him?" She knew she was slightly drunk but she was sure it was a great idea.

"Okay, so how, when?" Jonathan asked.

"Let me get his number – it's back at the hotel – we can call him first thing in the morning."

"Okay." Dermot looked at her and recognised she was well drunk. "It's late now, guys – why don't we call it a night and let's meet say around seven thirty at the hotel and make a plan. We need to have facts and figures in front of us before we just cold-call the guy, yeah?"

"Agreed, sir!" Jonathan necked his vodka and Coke and kissed Cara unexpectedly on the cheek.

"Oh thanks! I mean, thank you, Jonathan, that was nice."

Sandra started to giggle under her hand. Oh no, Cara thought, don't let me laugh. But then she did – very loudly – as Sandra snorted back her guffaws.

"Seriously, the pair of you are very strange at times," Jonathan said and pulled up his tie. He needed to get back to the hotel.

"Sorry!" Cara shook her head at Sandra. "We must be a bit drunk. Beddy-byes time, I think! I will let ye out." She hiccupped now as if by way of explanation and escorted them to the door.

When Cara shut the door behind them, she padded down to her bedroom, slightly wobbly, and passed out instantly on top of her bed.

* * *

"So do you think Cara will still stay in Knocknoly if the hotel goes?" Jonathan stuffed his hands deep down into his suit pockets as they walked.

Sandra peered at him through her drunken eyes as she linked Dermot's arm. The night was wild and the wind so cold it took her breath away. She was also knocked out by Cara's story.

"Why do you ask?" She tried to keep a straight face as she tucked her head down into her coat collar. She'd seen the way Jonathan had looked at Cara Byrne that very first morning, when the lift doors opened, and over the last few months had seen enough to know he fancied her. Sly glances at her constantly and his attitude around her was always of such a sunny disposition. In fact, Jonathan Redmond had been in positively super form since Cara had joined the Moritz.

"I think she will, you know. I genuinely think she loves it here. Why do you ask?"

"Just making conversation, is all." He dipped his head now to try and cut the wind.

"Do you, Dermot?" Sandra squeezed his big arm tighter.

"Do I what?" He was miles away.

"Cara? Do you think Cara will stay put?"

"What's with all the questions about Cara tonight? I had a bloke around the yard earlier asking after her too. Wanted to know where she lived – bit of an oddball – told him to take a hike!"

"She's very popular . . . it's the red hair, I guess . . ." Sandra said.

"You two really seem to be getting closer." Dermot glanced at her inquiringly.

"Yeah, we've both been through a lot . . . not since my Aer Lingus days have I felt I had a close female friend . . . even some of the pilots . . ."

She stopped suddenly and pulled him up in his tracks as she pinched his arm hard.

"Ouch!" Dermot winced in pain.

"Piercing blue eyes? Piercing blue eyes! A pilot? Alex? But his name must have been Alex Byrne! No, no – Cara may have gone back to her maiden name – she asked me if I was going back to mine . . ."

"Are you okay, Sandy?" Dermot tugged his arm free and, rubbing it, turned to face her.

"Fuck, Dermot, this is so important I cannot tell you. Please think really hard about the guy who was asking after Cara today. The oddball? Was there anything about him that stood out?" Sandra was on her knees now, throwing everything out of her bag to find her phone. Lipsticks and eye pencils were rolling down the path.

"What is it, Sandra?" Jonathan bent and picked up her keys and put his foot out to stop the rest from rolling.

"Dermot!" she shouted up at him now, the phone in her hand.

Dermot was running his hand over his newly shaven head. "Why did you say piercing blue eyes? Do you know him? That's what he had – he had mad blue eyes." He raised his hands and dropped them hard by his sides.

She nodded, her face now deathly pale, as though every drop

of blood had just been drained out of her body. She staggered to her feet. "Oh God, no, she could be in danger!"

"Danger!" Jonathan spun Sandra around.

"Yes, danger, Jonathan. It's a long story but we need to get back to Peter's cottage right now. I don't think I should call. There's no time to call. Let's go. Let's just run!" She flung the rest of her stuff into her bag. "I think I know the guy who was looking for her. I think it was Alex Charles you were talking about, a guy I worked with. I met him again recently – he's Cara's ex-husband. I told him where she lived!" She turned and started to run.

"She was married?" Jonathan pulled Sandra up.

"*Let's go, I said!*" She started to run again and the two men fell into step beside her.

"But, apart from the eyes, what made you think it was him?" Jonathan panted.

"Something just hit me – I have a weird feeling," Sandra panted back as Jonathan sped past her.

* * *

Cara could feel her body being rocked gently to wake up. It was actually a really nice sensation. She wasn't scared or nervous or sleeping like a one-eyed dog. She was so relaxed. She couldn't even open her eyes. Then she heard her name being called very quietly. She knew she was dreaming but she wasn't letting the dream in. The familiar haunting voice called her name over and over again. She knew it was Alex but she also knew it was a dream. It was time that she ignored these ridiculous nightmares.

"Cara, wake up!" It was loud now and no mistaking how close it was.

Cara slowly opened her eyes. Alex sat on the edge of her bed. Dressed in a black polo-neck jumper and black jeans.

"Don't scream!" He held his hand in the air. "I have come in peace, I swear to God. Cara, please don't be afraid. I knocked and knocked but there was no answer. I came around the back and saw you asleep on the bed, in all your clothes. I checked the back door and it was open."

She sat up. She looked at him. He looked different. Softer.

"I have come to give you this." He handed her a letter, a white small envelope with her name printed in green ink on the front. "It's some kind of apology, Cara. It's nothing to what I put you through but it's part of my healing, and yes," he clasped his hands, long fingers intertwined, "I know I've a bloody cheek to talk about my healing after the things I did to you, the dreadful, dreadful things, but I can't change the past, Cara, I can only move forward. I have to accept my past is part of me, acknowledge the damage I caused, try and apologise and move on."

She didn't move. But she was near enough to her pillow and she knew what she had hidden under there. A hunting knife she had bought after the attack. She had slept with it under her pillow every night since.

"I have been diagnosed with schizophrenia, undifferentiated schizophrenia to be exact. I'm on drugs referred to as antipsychotics since they help decrease the intensity of psychotic symptoms. I've also started on lithium which is really helping. Obviously I have no reason to tell you all this."

She nodded and pushed herself further up in the bed and rested her elbows on the pillow.

"The reason I came here was to give you this letter but then I saw you passed out on the bed and I honestly got a fright. If you can believe that? It's so unlike you to sleep in your clothes and on top of the bed."

"Thank you, Alex, but you can't break into my home," she said, feeling the bulk under her elbows.

"I went to the hotel but you weren't there and I didn't want to leave the letter in case it got lost and never got to you. I asked a man in the stables where you lived but he was really rude. Eventually a woman in the coffee shop told me. Jesus, Cara, I am so, so sorry."

He looked it. He looked as he had looked the first night they had drunk in O'Donoghue's.

"The illness seemed to just take over again when I met you –

all the classic signs now that I know what they are. The second anyone you care about comes along it feeds the paranoia. I knew I was way out of control but I thought if I just got you to marry me I would feel okay, safe in the knowledge that if you loved me enough to commit your entire life to me there was no way you were going to cheat on me. I told my psychologist about my dad but that's not the reason I am like this. It's chemical. I am sick that's all there is to it. I need meds to keep me stable. I'm sure the police told you I haven't flown in a long time. I will never come to you again after tonight, Cara. You have my absolute word on that but I just wanted to apologise to you."

She was starting to relax slightly – maybe it was the vodka.

"I will never forgive myself for how I treated you and I am so happy you stuck that knife in my back because it was the bravest thing you could have done and, as horrific as this is going to sound, I think you saved both of our lives. I don't want you to be frightened any more. I knew it was a risk coming here but I wanted you to see my face, to see my eyes, and know I mean I will never harm you ever again. I will be heading to Florida next week and I have bought a little place there by the beach. My mother is coming with me and we are going to start again over there. I'm getting a desk job with the airline. The weather's beautiful, as you know – oh, listen to me rambling – sorry, that's a side effect – I can go off on tangents."

"Alex, it's okay, I am okay." It just hit her. Alex was ill. Now she could see it so clearly. How on earth had she not before? Mental illness was so taboo. People suffered in silence, scared to talk about unusual feelings so they always buried them deep within and therefore they eventually exploded. It was a stigma. Something to be ashamed of, as though they had any choice in how they were feeling.

"I will go now." He stood up and wiped his palms on his black jeans.

She tried to gather her thoughts. She could just let him go and bolt the doors behind him and run to secure all the windows . . . or she could trust him. She could release all the fear inside her and let it go out the door with him. Wave a final goodbye to them both. They fed each other. Without one there couldn't be the other. She knew what she had to do.

"Sit down. I'll make you a cup of tea before you go. You've been shivering."

"I know. I left my jacket in the car. I was honestly just going to hand you the letter and go."

"It's okay. Please." She slowly eased her fearful body off the bed.

Cara was so utterly exhausted by this fear.

"Did you know I met a mutual friend of ours in London?" he said as he stood up. "No," she said and shook her head.

"Yeah, I did, and I went straight back and told Darby, my psychiatrist. He helped me write the letter to you – okay, so he doesn't know I was hand-delivering it but I felt I owed it to you. It would have been too cowardly of me to just post a letter. I have been a coward for years and I will not be one any more. I am facing my demons."

The front door was suddenly kicked in and Cara stood open-mouthed as Jonathan ran for Alex like a man possessed. He grabbed him by the throat and pushed him hard up against the wall.

"Jonathan!" she shouted.

Dermot ran in now and beckoned for Cara to get back.

"It's okay, it's okay!" she shouted as Alex tugged at Jonathan's hands, gagging loudly.

Sandra ran in, then, soaked to the skin as the two men were – the rain was now pelting down outside. "Cara, are you okay?" she panted and then screamed when she saw Jonathan and Alex struggling.

"It's okay, Jonathan, let him go! He's not threatening me!" Cara screamed.

"I'll fucking kill you if you frighten her!" Jonathan yelled. "I don't know what's going on here but I saw the look on Sandra's face when she knew you were looking for Cara! I will kill you!"

"And I second that, mate!" Dermot stood tall in front of Alex now as Jonathan dropped him and he fell to his knees.

"It's over!" Cara held out her hands to Jonathan and he

grabbed them and held tight. "He just came to apologise and he's leaving for Florida. It's good. I'm glad he came. I'm so tired of being frightened of him." She shook her head fiercely. "I won't be scared any more."

"You sure you're okay?" he hissed, out of breath, rubbing his thumbs across her hands.

"Yes, finally, I am okay – finally I feel free of him."

The little cottage fell quiet and the only sounds were the heavy rain and the heavy breathing of its occupants.

"God, sorry, I'm going to be sick!" Sandra put her hand over her mouth and ran for the bathroom.

Dermot pulled Alex up. "I guess I don't have to say this but I'm saying it anyway. Never come near Knocknoly again. Right?"

Alex nodded and Cara let go of Jonathan's hands and approached him. She pulled the letter from the back pocket of her tracksuit. "Here you go!" She handed it to him. "I forgive you."

He slowly raised his arm and took the letter from her. "Thank you," he whispered and held the letter in his hands before ripping it up into four pieces and stuffing them into his pocket. She watched him move towards the front door. She knew she would never see Alex Charles ever again.

Chapter 28

The morning of the auction arrived and with Jamie Keenan in tow they all headed up to Dublin in a hired minibus. Dermot was driving and had to shout at them all several times to keep the noise down.

Old Mrs Reilly was almost on top of Jamie. "And now tell me where do you buy those tiny shorts of yours?" she asked and he laughed. "You really are edible, young man, do you know that?" She held her hand up in the shape of a paw and licked it.

"Leave the kid alone, you madwoman! Can't you see you're old enough to be his granny?" Big Bob, sitting across from them, called over.

"He's jealous." She nodded in his direction. "Wants me all to himself that one, can't stand the thought of you and me together." She winked at Jamie and he laughed.

"You'll make the chap sick!" Big Bob roared now and turned his head sharply to look out the window.

* * *

Jamie had been so enthusiastic right from the very start. Sandra had called him the following morning on a conference call with everyone around the table and asked him out straight if he had any interest. He listened quietly and, after Jonathan had relayed the facts and figures of the hotel, he had made a noise. It sounded like a child making a car noise. It went on for quite a while. Turned out he had been doodling *Jamie Keenan's Restaurant* over and over again on a tennis tournament brochure.

"I think it's exactly what I have been looking for, guys," he said eventually.

Everyone whooped and Jonathan shushed them.

"Okay, well, I can bring all the paperwork to you," Jonathan said, "and we can meet your solicitor today if that suits?"

"Great. Well, I'm in London all week. I'm up to my eyes in TV interviews today – but can you come here tomorrow?"

"Yes, Jamie, and listen, thanks so much," Jonathan said.

"See you then."

Jonathan hung up and looked around at his team – or, rather, his fellow investors – as they sat around grinning at him.

"God, Sandra, how do we thank you?" he said.

Sandra shrugged. "I'm sure you'll think of something!" she laughed.

Jonathan then ushered everyone out back to work as he had the bank manager coming, the Moritz's accountants coming and his own solicitor coming. It was a massive undertaking.

Although Jamie would be the main shareholder everyone else was buying a share of the hotel too. Some very small, some not so small like Jonathan's own. They needed to draw up contracts today. They would bid at auction under Jamie's financial backing, open a company and then split the shares after.

* * *

Sandra moved up beside Jamie on the bus. "I'd say it's been a while since you were on a minibus?" she laughed.

"Yeah," he said, "and I'm enjoying it! In fact, I must get myself one of these bad boys to truck around Knocknoly in. Be a bit of a babe-magnet, don't you think?"

"Thanks, Jamie."

"Thanks for what? It's all about me to be honest. I'm not

doing this to help you or anyone else – it's exactly what I had been looking for. I'm just so excited about finishing out this year and then starting my course."

"What course?"

"Oh, I'm doing a full year's intensive cooking course at Le Cordon Bleu in Paris when the season ends!" He looked really excited as he turned to her now. "Imagine, Sandra, I will have this opportunity to learn from the very best. I can learn about regional products and flavours. For more than a century Le Cordon Bleu has enabled aspiring chefs like me to turn their ambitions into a reality. I can't wait. I will come back and start running my own kitchen in my shareholder hotel."

"And you will be amazing, of that I have no doubt, but isn't there something you aren't telling me?"

"Ah shucks, babe!" He batted his eyelashes at her. "Yeah, I've made my decision. I'm retiring at the end of this tour. I'm done, Sandra. I need a change. When I held that trophy up and winked at you in London it hit me. The victory never lasts long enough. It's over all too soon but the pain and heartache of losing stays with you for weeks and sometimes even months. The Moritz came to me at the perfect time. I see it as a sign actually."

He looked happy and relaxed for the first time and Sandra was so pleased for him. "What about Carolina?" she asked now.

"What about her? It's all over, I'm afraid. She is engaged to Mario Setaela. A quick but incredibly passionate romance, she told me. She's happy so I'm happy for her. They both want the same things. I'm where I want to be right now and I owe it to myself to take this journey. It's funny, you know, I think I want a family but I don't think I ever want to get married. The commitment is too much for me – pathetic, eh?"

Sandra thought about this comment and digested it like a warm sticky toffee pudding.

"We're here!" Jonathan shouted down the bus before she could respond to Jamie. Cara was beside Jonathan, fixing his tie, and Sandra could hear her telling him to take a deep breath and calm down a bit.

"Okay, now listen, all of you – especially you, Mrs Reilly – no shouting out during the auction, I know how you get. Jamie is in control of the bidding. We are up against stiff competition so please don't get too excited just yet. This stud farm is very keen – . . ."

"Hold that keen – Keenan's here!" Jamie stood now and hit his head. He hung onto the handle at the top of the case-rack, towering body almost bent in half. "'*He who dares wins, Rodney, he who dares wins.*' I am usually the one listening to the pep talks. It feels great to deliver one for a change so here it is. Positive thinking, like Sandra says her little book *The Secret* says, is the key. I believe in all this. I believe in the power of positive thinking. We need to send our message out there. We will own the Moritz!" He squeezed out past Sandra now and pulled his bag down. He opened it and pulled out blank pages and pens and handed a sheet and a pen to everyone on the bus. "Now, let's put the power of visualisation to the test. I want you each to draw a picture or write a paragraph about us winning this morning. When you do this you are all generating powerful thoughts and the feeling of already winning. The Law of Attraction then returns that reality to us just as you saw it in your mind. He who dares wins!"

Jonathan punched the air now. "You are right! Do it everyone. Focus! Let's get in there, Jamie. The rest of you follow as soon as you're done."

As they took their seats in the cold air-conditioned bare room Sandra was miles away. She was staring at Jamie who was shaking hands with some people. She'd just nip to the loo again before they started.

"Are you peeing again?" Cara whispered as she stood to let her out.

Sandra darted towards the neon ladies sign, her bag clutched tightly under her arm. She closed the toilet door and sat on the toilet. Slowly she opened her bag and removed the fifteenth pregnancy test stick of the last two days. She pushed it under and peed on it. This time she didn't put it down and the thick blue line popped up in seconds, still in her hand. Sandra Darragh was well and truly pregnant.

Sandra slipped back out just as the auction was beginning. More than two hundred people were crammed into the room for the auction of the Moritz and seventy-four other properties.

The Moritz was up first. They all shuffled in and took up an entire reserved bench. The organisers hushed the room now and a grey-haired woman dressed in a tailored red suit with huge shoulder-pads took to the podium.

"Good morning, everyone, and welcome. If everyone could push up on the benches we might create more seats for those of you standing at the back of the room." There was a shuffle of feet and bags and coats. Then she spoke again. "I would like to announce that more than one hundred and ten thousand people have read the catalogue online, from over ninety countries."

"What catalogue? It's in a catalogue? What, like *Family Album*?" old Mrs Reilly said out loud before Big Bob shushed her.

"Did you not hear what Jonathan said, woman? No talking!" He reached over and patted her knees gently.

The auctioneer continued. "We don't take questions at this point, if you don't mind."

Big Bob put a protective arm around old Mrs Reilly now and nodded at the woman. "We understand," he whispered.

"So before we begin in the room, I'd also like to add that we have more than fifty registered overseas bidders from places including Hong Kong, Australia, Italy, the Middle East and the UK. The reserve price this morning is two million euro. Shall we begin?"

It was a slow build-up to the off-the-ground starting price of one point five million. In the current climate they had to climb to the asking price. Jamie played a blinder and took his time and whispered occasionally to his two solicitors on either side. Phone bids were coming in and people with phones glued to their ears raised hands, left the room, ran back in. When they hit the two million mark Cara watched Jonathan leave the room, his face ashen.

The bids kept coming in. It was nerve-wracking. Eventually, at two million eight hundred thousand, Jamie Keenan won, the proverbial hammer bashing the Moritz into their lives forever.

Cara stood on Tiffney's toes as she tried to get out from her place in the row. She ran to Jonathan who was across the road, pacing up and down.

"We did it!" she shouted, stuck in the middle of the road as cars whizzed by.

"Be careful!" he shouted at her. "What did you say?"

She looked up and down for what seemed like an eternity before a gap came in the traffic and she ran to him, breathless now.

"We did it! We won!"

His eyes lit up and he scooped her up into the air and swung her around. "Oh God, I don't believe it! Thank you!" He raised his eyes to the sky. "It's a dream come true, Cara!" His eyes welled up. "I finally feel I have achieved something – my mother would be so proud. Yes, I know Jamie is the major shareholder but a piece of the Moritz in now mine. I can put in all the work I always did but I gain more. I can't explain how much this means to me!" He pulled her in close and she could smell his aftershave crisp and clean. He gazed at her with a little smile on his face. "You know when I told you the night of Jenny and Max's wedding that I don't date staff and you laughed in my face and told me you weren't asking me out?"

She laughed and nodded.

"Well, I guess you aren't staff any more . . . you are a shareholder too . . ." His words hung in the air and she couldn't find her voice. "Whenever, if ever, you feel you are ready to date again, Cara, I would dearly love to take you to dinner at our hotel sometime."

Cheers came now from across the road and the two looked between the traffic. Tiffney and Mike were hugging, old Mrs Reilly and Big Bob were grinning wildly, Sandra was looking pale, obviously with the shock, and Dermot had his arm draped around her shoulders. Jamie Keenan looked cool as a cucumber.

"Let's go!" Cara tugged his sleeve and they joined the others and then they all headed to the nearest pub.

"Well done, everyone!" Jonathan began the champagne toast

and this time Cara enjoyed it. "The Moritz hotel is secure and the village of Knocknoly can rest assured we will bring in even more tourists with this fantastic new chef when he returns next year!"

Jamie Keenan took a bow.

Jonathan continued. "Delphine is happy to take up a place in Venice she was offered last year so she unfortunately will go when Jamie returns. I can't wait to get back to our hotel now and build up its reputation even more and make it the best hotel in Ireland!"

A huge cheer erupted.

"We have an announcement to make also," Mike piped in. "Tiffney has agreed to be my wife and we would like to get married in the Moritz hotel next Christmas!"

The reaction was deafening and the little group stamped their feet and clinked their glasses noisily and hugged the young couple.

"It will be our first family wedding," Jonathan said as Cara came over and stood firmly by his side.

Chapter 29

The afternoon sun was beating down hard for a September afternoon and Cara pulled one-year-old Ava Keenan's pink buggy under the sun umbrella. Dermot was covered in BBQ smoke and waving his tea towel at it and Sandra was laughing at him, turning the steaks carefully. The back garden of Mr Peter's old house was in full bloom and the roses Cara had planted smelt divine. Well, it was in fact Cara and Esther's home now and the little hand-painted sign above the front door said just that. Esther had moved, Victoria in tow, and they had stayed in the hotel while successfully buying and renovating the property.

When Cara had tried to apologise again for all she had put her through, Esther had frowned deeply. "It's in the past," she had said. "We are in the future. Look at me! I have a whole new life at my age and it's bloody marvellous. I love being around the hotel and I love Louise in the Loft, and you're right, village life is wonderful. I can bring Victoria into the shops and no one tells me to tie her up outside. There is just one thing, though, love . . ."

"Go on!" Cara had pushed her.

"When I die I still want to be buried with your dad in Dublin."

"Of course," Cara said.

As Sandra returned to the garden table and picked up her wineglass she also checked her sleeping baby, tilting the umbrella slightly to the left.

"Dermot has it all in hand, he says," she said, beaming at Cara.

"Does he now?" Cara gave her friend a big wide smile.

"It's like I said, Cara, he's so great, really great, but we are taking it so slowly. I don't want to ruin it, it's too good."

Sandra thought back now to Dermot's reaction when she told him she was pregnant with Jamie Keenan's baby. He was genuinely thrilled for her. Then she saw the look on his face change when she told him she had no intention of starting a relationship with Jamie but that she wanted him in the baby's life forever. He had bent his head and then looked up, his eyes dancing.

"Sandra Loughnane, I am truly mad about you, madly in love with you. I always have been and I always will be. I'm bloody ecstatic you are having a baby but I want to be with you too. I know this probably isn't the right time and I have no idea if you feel the same way about me but, as Jonathan says, if I keep these feelings for you bottled up any longer I will blow up!"

Sandra had moved in close to him and taken his face in her hands. "I thought you'd never ask, Dermot Murray," she'd whispered as she kissed him tenderly on the lips.

Sandra spoke to Cara again now. "You know, when I called Neil and told him that I was pregnant and that I would be living with Dermot, he burst out laughing and said it was hilarious that John Wayne got what he had always wanted in the end, just like in the movies. I asked him to explain this John Wayne thing and he said 'It's Dermot – he's John Wayne – he's like a cowboy. He's fancied you for years, Sandra.' I felt a little giddy when he told me that. He said that Dermot used to warn him not to hurt me. Imagine that! I feel so blessed right now, Cara. I have everything I want. I even met my parents for dinner last night. Since Ava has come along they want to spend more time with me. It's all good."

Cara knew exactly what Sandra meant. Cara wanted Jonathan so badly it hurt sometimes but she thought if she pushed for that last chapter of happiness it might be just too much. She knew the ball was in her court but, now that she had this house and her dream job and Esther living with her, she was afraid to ask for anything else. Jonathan wasn't pushing her. He hadn't asked her out again since that day after the auction but she just knew in her heart he was happily waiting for her.

"I am so happy for you and Esther," said Sandra. "She is so delighted to be here with you. I hope myself and Ava will always have the kind of relationship you guys have."

"Oh, you will – you are an incredible mother, Sandra. I love how I have Ava in my life now too. I adore that little girl and can't believe I am going to be her godmother – it really means so much to me."

"There is no one else in the world I'd rather have," Sandra answered simply.

"More steaks, Dermot!" Jonathan called as he appeared through the picket fence carrying two bottles of wine and a white parcel of fresh steaks. He was casually dressed in a navy T-shirt and jeans.

"Are they the ones I marinated this morning, J?" Jamie called out and Jonathan nodded as he took over at the barbecue.

Dermot handed him the tongs and wiped his hands clean. Then he went straight to Ava's buggy, leaned in and picked the tiny baby up. "Hello, my baby sweetness. I missed you today. Yes, I did! Oh yes I did! Kissies?" He smooched the baby's lips over and over again. "How are my other girls?" He exchanged smiles with Sandra and Cara before he took Ava into the shade to sit with Jamie and Esther.

"Dermot is incredibly sexy, though, isn't he?" Sandra asked Cara.

"Yeah, he is . . . but not as sexy as Jonathan," Cara returned distractedly.

Sandra stared at her friend, wondering if she realised what she had just said.

"What?" Cara made a face.

Sandra smiled. "It's about time you let yourself admit that one." She wouldn't push her friend. Baby steps.

"I'm really glad you're not sworn off men for life," Sandra admitted. "Not when you have someone as wonderful as Jonathan just waiting for you."

"I know," Cara answered her honestly. "Moving here, Sandra, has changed me so much. I just feel anything can happen. Life is so spontaneous. It's not planned any more – I mean nothing, absolutely nothing is predictable any more."

The wonderful smells from the barbeque rose into the warm summer breeze. Jamie Keenan had returned from Paris a magnificent chef. He just understood food.

Sandra had told him the night they had won the auction that she was pregnant with his child. He had nodded and asked her if she wanted to get married. She had laughed and said absolutely not and he had said "Thank God". He had been happy though and said he absolutely wanted to be a part of the baby's life.

"You know, I heard Jamie's seeing Tara from The Haven." Sandra leaned over and popped an olive in her mouth. "My God, I can't keep up with him."

"Listen, Sandra, why do you think the Moritz is packed out every single night. Apart from the reputation Jamie is gaining as a wonderfully talented chef, women want to gawp at him. He is gorgeous and single. They should put his picture on the Bord Fáilte billboards. And good on him, I say. He's doing what he always wanted to do and not hurting anyone." Cara flicked her red hair over her shoulder.

"You know, when I was wracked with guilt over being drunk that night here when I was unknowingly pregnant with Ava, Jamie sat me in front of the computer and showed me testimonials from alcoholics who drank serious amounts of alcohol through their pregnancy and had perfectly healthy babies. As distressing as it was to read, it helped me relax when I realised I hadn't harmed Ava. He's kind like that."

Cara laughed now.

"What?" Sandra said.

"I'm just remembering that night – as though the drama wasn't enough with Alex turning up here and Jonathan and Dermot ready to kill him, you shout out in the middle of it all 'I'm going to be sick!'"

They both laughed now like two schoolgirls. "When you told

me you were expecting a few days later after the auction it was the first thing that popped into my head. But I was so happy for you. I wish I could have taken a photo of your face. You were glowing. It was wonderful to be a part of that. To hear those words coming out of your mouth at last."

Sandra stared over at Dermot who was now walking around the garden with Ava tight in his arms, showing her the flowers along the back fence.

"It's still so unreal, Cara. I still can't believe I have her. I am just so in love with her. Motherhood is everything I thought it would be. It was so unexpected when it happened, I honestly think it took that first scan for me to believe it. She is truly my little miracle."

"We are both perfectly content. I know people think it's really odd that I want to live my life with Esther. I just don't care any more and in fact I'm proud of me and of the values I hold dear in my life. I know what I want now. I know what makes me happy."

They fell silent as they watched the activities of each person in this garden, all of whom they both now considered family. It was a tranquil moment.

"Like I said, it's so wonderful that nothing, absolutely nothing is predictable any more. Cara refilled their wineglasses and replaced the bottle in the icy cooler.

Both women shut their eyes and breathed easy in the soft comfy deckchairs. Suddenly there was a loud rustling noise and they sat up and opened their eyes in unison. Esther stood in front of them, bag of sweets in hand.

"Anyone fancy an éclair?"

THE END

If you enjoyed
The Other Side of Wonderful
by Caroline Grace-Cassidy
why not try
When Love Takes Over also published
by Poolbeg?
Here's a sneak preview of Chapter One

When Love Takes Over

Chapter 1

Dublin, October 2010

I'd known that the supermarket wine had been open in the fridge for over a week, that it was dirt-cheap and didn't smell great, but I sank it anyhow. Now my head was splitting in two. It felt like a woodpecker was drilling and scraping his claws on the inside of my brain to get out. I tried to lift my head off the pillow but the pain pierced me between my heavy sticky eyes and I flopped back down. I reached for the comfort of my much-loved Debenham's goose-feathered duvet but instead found a rather smelly hairy brown throw. Where the hell was I? I tried to move again and now realised I was naked. Stark naked. White breasts flopping from side to side as I tried in vain to catch them. Turning as fast as was humanly possible with the head I was nursing, I saw the bed was empty apart from my awful nakedness. The room was still out of focus as I squinted against the alcoholic poison swirling through my brain. Then I spotted my Trinny & Susannah wonder knickers, my Olympic champion of hold-in knickers, the one and only no-flesh-is-escaping-from-these-babies – on the floor. In all their shabbiness – once jet-black, now after a million washes merely dirty-carpet grey. Oh, the humiliation I felt that I'd actually worn them! What was wrong with me? Think, woman, think! No need – the lucky man was entering the bedroom. The light flicked on and hurt my eyes.

The shock was audible, I'm afraid, as I said rather too loudly: "Oh fuck! Christ! What?"

Paul smiled at me, though if it had been the other way round I'd have been mortally offended. "So was it as good for you as it was for me then, Mia?" asked the builder who had been putting an extension on Carla's house for the last two weeks.

Carla. I knew there was something else nagging me – we were going breast-shopping today! I was due to meet her in town at ten o'clock to help her try on the new boobs.

"Shit!" I sat up, my old boobs fell out, not the best look with the rolls of flesh on my white stomach clambering up to meet them. I threw myself back down. "PP Paul – I mean Paul –" (we called him PP Paul as he was never out of the bloody toilet) "please can I have a moment to get myself together?"

"Sure, Mee-Mee Mia!" He grabbed his white T-shirt off the edge of the chair and left the room.

I noticed he had a small tattoo on his left shoulder that looked like Gargamel from The Smurfs, but surely not? He was in good enough shape, if fairly hairy all over. Oh man, I sighed again, why do I do these things? I couldn't remember a damn thing but I knew as the day progressed every last little embarrassing detail would come flooding into my mind. Playing on widescreen HD. Voice-over by that man who voices all the big cinema movies, with the too-slow, booming voice. I found my bra and jeans under the bed but where was my top? Just as I was about to wear a Liverpool jersey I spotted in his very messy, overcrowded wardrobe, he knocked gently on the door and then called, "Just found this in the van, Mia!" I opened the door a smidgen and slid my hand out as he dropped my priceless, loved-and-treated-with-kid-gloves, black silk Karen Millen hides-a-multitude top.

In his van. It was in his van. Oh, Mia.

I looked at myself in the mirror. I was a fright. An absolute fright. I mean, I wouldn't answer the door to a blind postman looking like this. I was so pale, yet had red blotches all over my face. Brown hair like an eagle's nest. Bloodshot panda eyes. Beard-rash. Chapped lips – the severe dehydration I was suffering from certainly didn't help. I bashed down my hair with the back of my hand. Licked my fingers to try and rub away most of the black eyeliner and mascara from under my glazed green eyes. I pulled myself up straight, my five-foot-eight-inches straight. Apparently I carried my weight well (I often got told this like it was a great compliment). The silk top slid over my bulging stomach. I was in need of a trip to the gym, if only I had a membership somewhere. No skinny jeans for me, I'm afraid – my Next 'boyfriend' jeans were my 'It' jeans. Okay, okay, so they were from the men's department, but who could tell? And they fitted so much better. I rummaged around again for my high-heel Office FMB's. Under the bed I found a dog-eared copy of Catcher in the Rye and an old shoebox, but no boots. A yellow Doc Martens shoebox. I slowly pulled it out and my boots were revealed behind it.

"Cuppa?" He was holding out a chipped, yellow, stained Liverpool FC mug as I shoved the box back under.

"Emm, no thanks, I actually have to run – I have to meet Carla in town."

I stood up slowly and finished dressing as he stood there slurping his tea and staring at me. Perfect, white, straight teeth – funny I'd never noticed him this way before.

Should I thank him? Apologise? Shake his hand? It was embarrassing as we said our goodbyes and I breathed a sigh of relief as I made my way out onto the busy streets of Rathmines.

My whole being told everyone who passed me: 'I didn't go home last night – I'm a dirty stop-out whore!' (Well, maybe the whore bit was a bit strong but you know the feeling?) I felt dirty, not because I'd had sex with a stranger (well, he wasn't exactly a stranger) – oh no, I'd done that plenty of times before – but dirty and hung-over and slightly used. Call me a snob but the filthy student-type flat didn't help matters. It made me itchy. I stopped at Insomnia and ordered a latte and a double-choc-chip muffin and took my mobile from my bag as I wriggled onto a ridiculously high stool.

"Carla," I muttered through a mouthful of cake, some falling out of my mouth as I tried to stuff in as much as was humanly possible at once. I am on my way."

Two Skinnies, obviously just finished their morning Pilates, stood sipping their green teas and staring at me. Why didn't they sit? Did you burn more calories by standing? I made eye contact with one of them and they both looked away.

"Where the hell were you last night? I left the plastic on the latch all night!" Carla's breath was raspy as she walked briskly, no doubt holding her mobile well away from her precious ear. Carla was a walker. Yes, you know the type before I even tell you. She actually liked to walk. Preferred it to a car or bus, she said. She was a stunner too, of course (goes with the actually-enjoying-walking bit, I think).

Carla O'Leary had joined our small auctioneer's office, Clovers Auctioneers, two years ago, and had become the top seller straight away. Boy, could she sell a house! She was all blonde hair, black Armani suits with blinding white shirts. Owned a red Mini Cooper that never left the driveway. I couldn't have met her at a better time. Things in Number 31, Coolpak Park had been getting very tetchy between my mam and Samantha and me. Samantha was my much prettier, much thinner, much more successful, mother's Number One, younger sister – yeah, blah, blah, blah! She always was and always would be the smarter and the prettier one. She worked in IT (whatever that meant – I had no idea and, to be brutally honest, little or no interest to ask) but it seemed to earn plenty of money so I couldn't understand why she still lived at home. Dad left home years ago. In fact, I couldn't remember him ever living with us really. He shacked up with an Aer Lingus air stewardess in Dun

Laoghaire – Angela. She was once the Face of Dublin Airport – I think that bothered Mam more than her stealing her husband and our father. Dad met her at a funeral and that was that. He was gone the next week. So, to get back to Carla, when I heard she was looking for a flatmate for her newly owned first home – a massive renovation project in Ranelagh – I jumped at the chance and moved in.

"So meet me in the Collins Banks Clinic as soon as you get into town." Carla rang off.

Oh, did I mention she was also the nicest, kindest, most generous person I had ever met? I'd been waiting for a friend like her literally all my life.

I polished off the muffin and drained the latte, and was still wiping the froth from my mouth as I hailed a cab. These FMB's were not walking boots by any means and I wished I was as organised as Carla and had a squashed-up pair of flats in my bag – the type of shoes I saw on Off the Rails, a 'must have' item for every woman's bag, except I didn't have any. I didn't really have any 'must have' items to be honest. I wasn't a 'must have' kind of girl. I gave the taximan my destination and sat back and closed my eyes.

I remembered drinking wine in the house in Ranelagh (I couldn't call Ranelagh home, as home was still Coolpak Park – except that it wasn't home either), watching MTV, singing aloud to Girls Aloud live at Wembley. This involved screeching into the mirror above the TV, pouting and pointing my finger seductively. With Carla at an engagement dinner at the Unicorn Restaurant, I was all alone. There was something about a Girls Aloud concert on the telly with a few drinks on me that made me feel sexy. As though I was Cheryl Cole (she really should have gone back to Tweedy, though), up there grinding my perfect body to my perfect pop song. I ground my hips and swigged from my wine bottle as I roared the cheesy lyrics. Oh, I loved the clothes and the body – and the hair-envy I felt with a few drinks on me was depressing.

I was thoroughly enjoying having the place to myself and then I heard the doorbell – well, the plastic sheet with a bell attached by a piece of string that covered a gaping hole where a back door should be. It was PP Paul. He looked good and smelled great.

"I left my mobile here today," he explained to me, hands thrust deep into the pockets of his blue jeans.

He was about six foot one, I supposed, and was wearing a brown sweater and brown boots. He had black sort of messy, spiky hair, and was good-looking in an if-you-like-that-kind-of-look way. I didn't. I went for guys who were not so attractive. Less competition out there.

"Yes, yes, a drink in town sounds great!" I enthused when he suggested it.

Yes, it was all coming back now. Into his messy white van. Getting halfway up the road and then diving on him. Pulling my top over my head and him upping the never-used fifth gear to reach his flat in Rathmines in record time.

"Here ya are, love!" The taximan grinned cheekily at me in the rear-view mirror and pulled up outside the shiny medical centre.

I paid as he laughed quietly and hummed Dolly Parton's "Jolene" (smart arse) as I slowly counted out my change and got out – it was obviously a popular destination these days. I ran up the steps into the immaculate foyer and saw Carla at the reception.

Oh, what I wouldn't have given for two soluble Solpadeine at that point!

Big smile. "Hi there!" I managed brightly.

She was perched on the edge of a chaise longue. Wearing white jeans, black belt and a black shirt, with black wedges. Her sunglasses perched on top of her voluminous blonde hair. So much hair, all smooth and shaped and bouncy. She didn't have Girls Aloud envy, that was for sure. I caught sight of my reflection – well, it was hard not to in a small area covered in head-to-toe mirrors. Pasty, blotchy skin from sleeping in last night's make-up and stubble-rash.

The glowing, big-busted, luminous-toothed receptionist fussed around Carla. Just as well, as the look Carla was giving me was just about to become fifty questions.

"So, Carla, what size are you thinking of going?" the tiny brunette asked with her beautiful gold notebook and matching gold pen in her hands. Her perfectly manicured long red talons glinted in the light thrown from the chandelier overhead.

"That's exactly why I needed to bring my friend along, you see – I just can't decide. Yours look great, what size are yours?" Carla wasn't one for wasting time – she was direct and straight to the point. So was James for that matter, her well-to-do gentleman of a boyfriend. Old money, he called it. Old money bought him a huge house, The Tindles, on Killiney Hill, with tennis courts and apparently no need for a day job. Well, that wasn't altogether fair – he was a writer – although what he wrote was beyond me. No one had ever seen his work. As far as I was concerned, he was a lazy, spoiled, ill-mannered brat who didn't deserve Carla. Whereas Carla's straight-to-the-point was honesty, his was rudeness.

"Thanks so much, I'm a generous 36C," she beamed back and her teeth blinded me.

"Would you mind," asked Carla, "if I took a closer look?"

The receptionist duly obliged and obediently stuck out her chest in her pale-pink cardigan for Carla to gaze at.

"Miss O'Leary?" the doctor said, breaking up this very weird scenario.

We followed him down the corridor and into his disinfectant-smelling, yet weirdly trendy office.

I was well and truly bored. I know that's a bit selfish but, as far as I'm concerned, if you've seen one pair of jelly sticky-out boobies you've seen them all. I found a paper cup and drank lots from the water cooler as I oohhed and aahhed at Carla. I had told her a million times that I thought she was crazy to do this. She had beautiful small breasts but she was insistent. She'd be the first one to say that my opinion really mattered to her, but her heart was set on this so there was no more I could say.

She was naked now from the waist up and the doctor was doodling on her chest with a big smelly marker. Drawing arrows this way and that, and dots around her breasts, and I found this was mildly erotic. Suddenly I got a flashback of PP Paul bearing down on top of me, his hot mouth wrapped around mine as he explored my body with his tongue.

"Okay, I think we are happy with this then?" He reached into his desk drawer and pulled another lumpy plastic wobbly silicone booby-implant out.

Carla stood up and said quietly, "Excellent – a generous 36C it is then, and sure if I change my mind I can always come back." She smiled at the doctor.

"Don't forget to hold onto your receipt. This does not affect your statutory rights," I said in a low man's voice with my chin stuck into my neck, and as I laughed out loud they both gave me an uncomfortable look.

"And for you? You are considering . . ." He paused, looking down at a clipboard, then back up at me. I shook my head and he looked back down at his clipboard. "Liposuction then?" He tried to find his notes on me, flipping furiously through the pages on his clipboard, and then went crimson from the neck up when he realised his error.

I pulled myself up and stood tall. "Not today, doctor. I am perfect just the way I am, thank you!" I flicked my hair, turned and walked straight into his glass door.

"Are you on that computer again!" my mother screeched at me from the kitchen.

"It's an iPhone, Mam!" I shouted back. Hangover progressively getting worse and only shower and sleep would save me now.

Saturday-evening dinners were compulsory in 31 Coolpak Park and I was fed up with having my Saturdays taken up. I just couldn't seem to ever get out of the rut.

"It's from my boss Dominic so I have to reply, okay?"

Dominic was my boss and owner of Clovers Auctioneers, 26A South Frederick Street, Dublin 2. He owned the entire old building and he rented the other office spaces in there. He drove a brand-new BMW convertible (so ridiculous with teenage twin boys to ferry around to tennis, Gaelic football, rugby, soccer, wrestling). Dominic was what you would call . . . let me see . . . a nice way of putting this . . . a bit of a prat. He always wore black trousers, always – as a tribute to his idol Johnny Cash. He had a balding head but took great care of the five strands of hair that remained at the front (we suspected he wrapped them in tin foil getting into bed every night) – he wore bright, colourful shirts and stupid cartoon ties and crazy outdoor shoes (wacky, he called them – in fact, he called himself wacky). I know what I always want to do to wacky people – whack them! Hard! Snap them out of it. He would try and make us laugh all day every day and it was completely and utterly draining. How he ran such a successful business we couldn't work out. There were four of us in the office: himself, myself, Carla and his long-suffering wife Debbie who came in three days a week to take care of all the accounts. Debbie kept to herself really and didn't leave Dominic's small back office to come out into our main one very often.

He was emailing me now to remind me to be at Foxrock at ten o'clock in the morning for a private viewing of Number 34, Torquay Road. He often did this on a Sunday. It drove me insane. I asked on Friday evening before we went to the Palace if I was needed over the weekend and he said, "No . . . unless you want to work? Ha, ha . . . sure I know you – you'll be falling down drunk somewhere – like myself I might add!" Then he proceeded to lie on the floor World-Cup-celebrations-Gazza-style and mimic himself lowering pints (you get the picture). I especially hated the way he used the word remind as if he were doing me a favour. Then the iPhone email updated the page and it read, 'PS: Mia, please come and see me early on Monday morning before Carla and Debbie get in. I have something urgent I need to discuss with you. Did you hear me? Ha! I bet you said yeah. Dominic.' I pushed the stupid cursed iPhone (Dominic had bought Carla and myself one each) deep into my fake red Chloé handbag and made my way into the kitchen for the dreaded corned beef and cabbage. Oh, even the smell!

My world felt odd today. I certainly didn't adore my job but I adored not living at home and I was the wrong side of thirty and had never done anything else. The Irish economy had never been so bad and, while the entire country talked politics, I didn't. I didn't want to know. I wasn't stupid by any means but I couldn't get as heated about it all as some people. I had enough gloom in my life without all that. We all knew the recession was hitting Clovers – sure it was hitting every business but especially the property market. However, Dominic kept saying we were doing okay. Holding our own. Our jobs were safe. People were still buying houses, people still had to live. Yes, at much lower prices, but the market was still moving. Clovers also had properties on the books that we rented and renting was on the up and up. I had worked for Clovers since I left college. As sad as that may sound to others I actually felt a tinge of pride about it, don't ask me why. I know I wasn't exactly Employee of the Year, what with my favourite websites eBay and Perez Hilton and TMZ.com and all those distractions and the odd (well, not that odd) early exit to the Palace when Dominic was away from the office – but I was doing okay. I was interested in property – genuinely, really interested – and I wanted to own my own home someday. A sprawling old mansion somewhere in Roundwood in Wicklow near Daniel Day Lewis would be nice. We could sit by the open fire in the local Roundwood Hotel, sipping pints of Guinness and reading poetry. I could get some of those early days NHS John-Lennon-type glasses and sit at his knee. He could stroke my hair. Traditional Irish music piping away in the background . . .

Anyway I wasn't interested in working anywhere else, put it that way. Well, unless Daniel needed a PA, in which case I could dress in a skintight chequered pencil skirt (à la Joan in *Mad Men*) and a skintight low-cut white blouse, and walk elegantly and pain-free on six-inch stilettos (my body can be any size in Dreamland – no point in trying to seduce Daniel Day Lewis otherwise, the state my real body is in). He would gaze at me over our matching round-rimmed as I took notes, until one day it would be all too much for him and he'd drop his well-chewed pencil onto the old oak desk, stand up and take me into his strong method arms and say, "I can't contain myself any longer, Mia! It's you, it's been you for so long my body aches!" – all this is in the voice of Bill the Butcher for some reason. Scary to most women but sexy as hell to me. Ah, that would be nice. But hey, if that job wasn't on offer, as far as I was concerned work was there to pay the bills and not to be enjoyed. Although I did really enjoy it most of the time. Carla said she loved the job, that she couldn't wait to get into work every day and see what deals she could close. She would own her own business one day, I was sure of it.

I took my seat at the dinner table and picked at what I could. Samantha was in flowing form with IT this and promotion that and Niall this and Niall that (he was a long-term man on the scene). I didn't pay any attention but I nodded. Her voice droned. Two women could not be further apart in their lives than we were and I was slightly sad about this. But again only slightly. I did not lose any sleep over it, I assure you, didn't even feel guilty that I didn't lose sleep (if that makes sense?). We were terribly civil to each other. An outsider wouldn't even notice.

My mind was on PP Paul and the night was fast-forwarding in my memory. He was full-on passion. He had me naked in a matter of minutes – well, he would have done, except my jeans got tangled up in my boots and I had to reef the lot off with superhuman power myself. He explored my body with all his might. The wine had shed me of any inhibitions about my body and I duly gave as good as I got. I remembered his arms so tight around my neck it started to hurt but in a sexy way. A small shiver went down my spine.

"Did you fart again?" my mother barked at me.

"No, Mam," I muttered.

"Well, stop moving your arse around on that chair like you are trying to let a fart and pass me the butter."